Praise for *The Things That Keep Us Here*

'A masterly novel o̶f̶ ▮▮▮▮▮▮▮▮▮▮▮▮ l of dystopian nightmare that non̶e̶ ▮▮▮▮▮▮▮▮▮▮ t, made worse by the fact it may onl̶y̶ ▮▮▮▮▮▮▮▮▮▮▮ e face a similar scenario ourselves'

Daily Mail

'An amazing achievement. What makes it work is that Buckley explores a global catastrophe with such a narrow focus, and with complex characters that we come to care deeply about'

Linwood Barclay

'With crisp writing and taut pacing . . . this vivid depiction of suburban America gone bad is riveting'

Library Journal

'Carla Buckley's debut *The Things That Keep Us Here* stunned me. Here is an apocalyptic novel as topical as today's headlines, yet as intimate as a lover's touch. A brilliant debut that deserves to be read by everyone'

James Rollins

'A knockout debut of the decade'

LA Times

'Utterly engrossing. *The Things That Keep Us Here* is the book guaranteed to keep you up all night, as you follow one family's pulse-pounding journey through the worst that can happen and beyond'

Lisa Gardner

WITHDRAWN

KT 2116059 7

Also by Carla Buckley

The Things That Keep Us Here

INVISIBLE

CARLA BUCKLEY

First published in Great Britain in 2012 by Orion Books,
an imprint of The Orion Publishing Group Ltd
Orion House, 5 Upper Saint Martin's Lane
London WC2H 9EA

An Hachette UK Company

1 3 5 7 9 10 8 6 4 2

Copyright © Carla Buckley 2012
Reading group guide copyright © 2012 Random House, Inc.
Excerpt from *The Things That Keep Us Here* copyright
© 2010 Carla Buckley

The moral right of Carla Buckley to be identified as the author
of this work has been asserted in accordance with
the Copyright, Designs and Patents Act of 1988.

All rights reserved. No part of this publication may be
reproduced, stored in a retrieval system, or transmitted
in any form or by any means, electronic, mechanical,
photocopying, recording, or otherwise, without the
prior permission of both the copyright owner and the
above publisher of this book.

All the characters in this book are fictitious,
and any resemblance to actual persons
living or dead is purely coincidental.

A CIP catalogue record for this book is
available from the British Library.

ISBN (Hardback) 978 1 4091 1310 2
ISBN (Trade Paperback) 978 1 4091 1311 9
ISBN (Ebook) 978 1 4091 1312 6

Printed and bound by CPI Group
(UK) Ltd, Croydon, CR0 4YY

The Orion Publishing Group's policy is to use papers
that are natural, renewable and recyclable products and
made from wood grown in sustainable forests. The logging
and manufacturing processes are expected to conform to
the environmental regulations of the country of origin.

Kingston upon Thames Libraries	
KT 2116059 7	
Askews & Holts	28-Nov-2012
AF	£12.99
NM	30016765

For my husband, Tim, with all my love

INVISIBLE

PROLOGUE

I HAD BEEN TRAPPED IN THIS MISERABLY HOT SPACE for nine weeks, six days, and fourteen hours, with all the windows and doors locked and the shades drawn. Everyone I knew was out swimming or boating or just having fun, but not me. I was pacing from one room to the other, picking up magazines and tossing them down, turning on the television only to switch it off again. It had seemed like such a good idea back in March: sell the house and move to where we knew no one and no one knew us. But now I realized I'd only traded in one prison for another.

When the key finally rasped in the lock, I was kneeling by the narrow window, my face lifted to capture any stray breeze that decided to drift across the sill. I pushed myself up as the door swung open, and there was my sister.

"Finally," I said.

"Hey, you." Julie locked the door behind her. "So, what have you been up to all day?" Her eyes were clear, but that didn't mean she hadn't still been crying. Julie was a master at protecting me.

"Your dryer was making weird noises, so I unplugged it. And your mailman has the hairiest legs I've ever seen."

Your. Not *our.* The accusation lingered in the air. So many balls I'd tossed her way. Which one would she bounce back? But she surprised me. "I got you something." Reaching into her backpack, she handed me a book.

A thin, spiral-bound book with a flexible cover. I glanced at the title. *Knitting for Beginners.* "Give me a break."

"Dana, we talked about this."

"No, *you* talked about this."

She sighed, dropped her backpack on the floor. "I just hate that you're just sitting here, watching TV all day."

"I don't watch TV all day. Sometimes, I stare at the ceiling." *And count the hours until this will all be over.*

"My point exactly." She dangled a plastic bag by one finger. "I got you some yarn, too."

"Just . . . stop. I don't want to learn to knit. It's the stupidest thing I ever heard of."

She put her arm around my shoulders and gave a gentle squeeze. "Okay," she said, after a moment. "You hungry?"

Why did I feel a prick of loss when she turned away to make supper?

The plastic bag sat untouched beside the book all night and into the next day. I fashioned a clothesline by tying string from doorknob to doorknob, which worked fine until I tried to hang up a pair of jeans. The closet door flew open; the brass knob smacked the wall and clattered to the floor. One more thing for Frank to deal with when he got back from Afghanistan. He'd be thrilled.

Mid-afternoon, the next-door neighbor came home, her pickup rattling up the driveway. The truck door slammed, then all was quiet. She'd gone inside her house. In a few minutes, she'd reappear to stretch out on a bright orange towel in her backyard to sun her legs, a beer bottle balanced on the grass beside her. Her phone would ring and her giggling would skip across the yard.

Later, her boyfriend would visit and the two of them would go somewhere in the pickup, maybe one of the few local bars, maybe the lake. Or maybe they'd fire up her small Weber and the spicy aroma of roasting bratwursts would seep into Julie's small, steamy kitchen and make my mouth water.

What was our old next-door neighbor doing now? Not yet five o'clock, so Martin would still be at work. But his arrival home would be noisy and full of purpose. The slam of the car door, followed by the rumble of the garage door along its tracks. The growl of the lawnmower as he fired it up to cut first his grass, then ours, topped off by the chatter of the trashcans as he dragged them from the curb back into place behind our houses. He'd be humming as he wound up the garden hose, then stop and smile when I appeared with lemonade. The tang of cut grass would rise around us and the mosquitoes would swarm. He'd swipe his face with a handkerchief and take the glass, ask if I was doing my homework, or whether I was planning to tackle the weeds any time soon.

I'd left without even telling him goodbye.

I'd told Mrs. Gerkey goodbye, though. She'd blinked in surprise, clutching my last paycheck as though by not handing it over she'd keep me tethered there. I'd shrugged away the questions in her pale blue eyes. It wasn't as though I'd ever promised her anything, not in so many words.

Julie had picked out sunshine yellow yarn, a big fluffy cloud of it, impossibly soft. The book had drawings, each step diagrammed and numbered. How hard could it be?

By the time the key scraped the lock, my palms were sweaty and I'd gnawed my lower lip raw. As Julie stepped into the front hall, I hurled the knotted mess aside, the needles clattering to the floor, humiliated that she'd caught me trying—and failing miserably—at something so absurdly simple. Or maybe something else was weighing on me. "Why don't you get me a book on how to fix dryers?" I snapped at her. "You know. Something *easy*?"

After retrieving the needles as they rolled across the floor, Julie sank beside me on the lumpy couch. Her eyes looked tired but she patted my knee and smiled. Then she took up the jumbled mass of yarn. "You know, Mom always wanted to teach you to knit."

At the mention of our mother, something shifted inside me. I'd been thinking about her a lot lately. "I didn't know she could knit."

Julie nodded. She began pulling apart the tangles, winding the bright yarn around her finger. "And crochet. She made those potholders, you know."

Right. The white ones with red flowers, made of string, deceptively delicate. You could pick up a flaming skillet with one, which I had done once while burning French toast, and not even feel the heat.

Julie had wound the yarn into a ball and now held the knitting needles loosely in one hand. "Okay," she said, her gaze meeting mine steadily. "What does the first page say?"

Grudgingly, I opened the book. "You're supposed to cast on. Like fishing, but not." Fishing would have been a lot easier. Drop the line into the water and just wait. Fishing made me think of Joe, but I shook that memory away and focused on what Julie was doing. Her fingers were slim and long, capable of almost anything. She'd gotten our mom's hands, whereas I must've inherited our father's, stubby and square. I hated to think of anything else I might have gotten from him.

"See?" She drew the length of yarn around the tip of the needle and back down. Her shoulder pressed against mine, her voice assured and soothing. She smelled of soap and sun, a hint of lemon. "You hold the yarn like this. And when you bring it around, it makes a little loop."

"I tried that." And succeeded only in having the yarn snarl itself into a knot.

"Maybe you were winding it around from in front instead of

behind." Julie looped the yarn around in careful knots, every one exactly the same shape and size, lined up like little blossoms on the metal knitting needle. She twisted her wrist and the yarn flew free and the needle was once again bare. "Here," she told me. "You try it."

She cupped my hand around the needle, curving my fingers around it, then draped the yarn around my left forefinger. "Not too tight," she warned, guiding my reluctant finger. "That's it."

She was frowning down at the sun-colored yarn. Her lashes were long and dark, the small bump at the bridge of her nose just like mine. Her blonde hair waved back from her forehead, held by the brass butterfly clip I'd given her for her birthday, all I could afford. I dropped the needles into my lap and sagged against her. "I'm scared," I whispered.

"I won't let anything happen to you," she promised.

"I know." She never had. For five years, she'd been sister, mother, and father to me. She'd been everything and she'd asked for nothing in return. I pressed my cheek against the soft cotton of her sleeve. I had to tell her, but I couldn't. The words just wouldn't crawl past the stone lodged in my throat.

"After supper," she said, "we can try purling."

"Sounds like a disease."

She laughed, a tinkle of pure happiness, and the stone tumbled down my throat and nestled securely in my heart.

There are different kinds of prisons, some with walls and floors and doors, and others built even more sturdily out of things you can't see—love and hope and fear.

A week later, I went into labor.

ONE

———

[DANA]

I T'S A GREAT LINE TO STOP GUYS FROM COMING ON
to you in a bar. They ask, *So what do you do for a living?* They
expect to hear, *I'm in sales* or *I'm a paralegal.* If I'm wearing my
black boots with the stacked heels and maybe some lipstick, they
might push me into the lawyer category, or the owner of a little
boutique. They never expect to hear the truth. *I blow up buildings,* I say, and sip my wine. After hearing that, they usually back
away a little. Which is good. I don't like to be crowded.

The crowd that morning was staying far away, lined up all
along the twelve-foot chain-link fence encircling the lot, their
faces curious and belligerent, the police forming an uneasy bar-
ricade between them and me and the building I was going to de-
stroy. A hand-printed banner danced above their heads. You
might not think it, but bringing down a building can be a contro-
versial thing. People don't like change. It makes them worry about
what's headed their way next, and whether it'll be any worse than
what was there before.

Dingy clouds were doing a slow roll along the horizon. Chicago in mid-May could be unpredictable. "How far away does that look?" I asked my foreman.

Ahmed squinted. "I'd say we got a couple hours, maybe three." His broad face was washed in early morning light.

The guy was a wizard when it came to reading the weather. If he said two, maybe three, we'd be standing in a downpour come four. Two hours was good, three better. "We might just make it, then."

He nodded. "Have you heard from Halim?"

Another worry. "Halim will be here." Of course he would, but he hadn't answered any of the six calls I'd placed to him that morning. As decorous as my partner was, he could also be a player. He loved blondes, and Chicago was full of them. But he'd never crossed that line with me. I wouldn't have stuck around if he had.

A shout. Something sailed through the air and clattered onto the cement near my feet. A beer can. A policeman moved forward and the onlookers jostled.

Ahmed curled his lip in disgust and kicked it with his boot.

"Least it wasn't a bomb," I told him.

"Don't say these things." Ahmed looked stricken.

Implosions are wrapped tight in superstition: wind the detonation wire clockwise; rap the front doorjamb before entering; wear the same pair of boots from the beginning of a job until its completion, and if a lace breaks, replace it with a borrowed set. Most of all, don't ever joke about explosives, especially when hundreds of pounds of the stuff lie only fifteen feet away.

My cellphone vibrated. Halim? But no, the caller ID read PRIVATE CALLER. The caller had tried earlier, around six-thirty, and I was tempted to flip it open and let off a little steam at some telemarketer no doubt waiting to chirp good morning on the other end. But chances were it would just be a recorded call and it would take ten seconds for me to disconnect. Seconds I couldn't afford to waste, not with that storm roiling toward us. Fitting the hardhat onto my head, I told Ahmed, "I'm starting the walk-through."

A troubled look. "Without Halim?"

He didn't think I could do it. Didn't matter. I was still the boss, even if it sometimes felt in name only. "Start clearing the site."

The broad marble steps of the gracious old building seemed to sag beneath my boots. The old girl was ready to come down. She'd been up for a long time and weathered more than her share of storms. She was ready to go.

Shoving aside the heavy wing of fabric draped around the lower floors, I stepped over the threshold into pungent darkness. The interior sprang into view beneath the beam of my Maglite. Hard to believe hundreds of families once lived here, walked these floors. Everything that could have made the place a home had been yanked down and hauled away: walls, ceilings, floors, and window glass. All that remained was bare concrete, rafters, and the skeletal outlines of two staircases. The air hung heavy and blue, dust spiraling lazily down from the open ceiling in ghostly strands like Mardi Gras beads. I spun on one heel, seeing past the empty windows and crumbling columns, hearing the mumbles of long-ago residents, the babies' cries, and the laughter. The old girl held her breath, waiting. *I'm coming*, I told her. *Hold on.*

The clop of boots. Halim emerged from the shadows, his slim frame tidy in navy chinos and a crisp white workshirt. "Sorry I'm late," he told me. "I got an overseas call from my brother."

I looked at him with both relief and annoyance. So not a pretty girl he'd met at a bar, but something far, far worse. "How much this time?" I asked him.

He pursed his lips. He wanted to tell me it was none of my business how much money he lent his loser brother, but in point of fact, it was my business. Very much so, ever since we pooled our resources and started Down to Earth three years before.

"Don't worry." He glanced around. "We should get started, eh? What with the storm moving in."

"A thousand? Two thousand?" The business account only had three and change, but the frown on his face told me plainly that it now held nothing. "Halim." I felt a pinch of fear. "Tell me."

"A temporary setback," he said. "We finish this job and all will be fine."

It was the last time. Tomorrow morning, I'd be meeting with the bank manager to make sure any checks drawn on our business account in the future required both our signatures. But there was nothing I could do about it now. "I'll take the eastern half."

No railing along the staircase, the bottom riser chewed to rubble to discourage trespassers, the support walls smashed to pieces. Testing my weight with each step, I climbed to the twenty-sixth floor, winding past the narrow Chicago streets, to the furled tops of the trees, until finally the sleepy skyline spread before me. A month ago, I would have been gasping. Today, I made it in one long trek, with only my thigh muscles protesting the effort.

Streamers of sunlight spooled through the empty windows. Amid the drab grays and browns were daubs of neon yellow paint marking the load-bearing columns, and dense cobwebs of yellow, pink, and orange tubing. Colorful and deadly. I traced the lines up to the crevices we'd chipped into the columns and then packed with dynamite. The connections looked good. Untouched.

Halim walked toward me from the other direction, and we exchanged places silently, our worlds shrunk to fluorescent strands, electrical tape, and metal clips. We descended two floors to the next dynamited level.

The buzz of a jet overhead, the shrill blast of a policeman's whistle below. The protestors were growing more belligerent. *Great.* As if we didn't have enough to deal with, outracing the storm. Shouts sailed up.

Again, Halim and I crisscrossed paths; again, we retraced each other's steps.

Outside, a Bobcat started with a rumble.

Halim waited on the ground floor. "We're behind schedule."

And whose fault was that? I glanced at my phone and saw I'd missed another call from PRIVATE CALLER. We'd used up one of Ahmed's hours.

"You finish here," Halim told me, "and I'll check the basement level." He descended the crumbling stairs.

Stepping over a latticework of detonation cord, I ran my flashlight beam over the connections. A water leak had sprung up from somewhere—a pipe only recently turned off—and a shallow pool had collected in one corner, scummy with dust.

The Bobcat's roar stopped. In the sudden silence, I heard the slow *plink* of water splashing metal, and something else.

The noise didn't repeat itself. Rats usually flee buildings about to be demolished, driven by some fierce primordial instinct that tells them D-day is at hand, but maybe one had just gotten the message. I turned, sweeping my flashlight beam across the uneven floor.

A crumpled Styrofoam cup, boot prints stamped in the dust, a balled-up lump of rust-colored cotton splotched with paint. Light sparkled across a smooth surface. Glass. I frowned. All the glass had already been removed.

My walkie-talkie buzzed.

"Ready?" Halim's voice.

I depressed the Talk button. "Just about." I held up my flashlight, squinting into the shadows.

An empty bottle of Budweiser glinted back from the gloom beside a wall brace. Dust-free, it couldn't have been there long. How had we missed the bottle last night? The broken brick lying beside it must have been the source of the noise I'd heard.

Footsteps echoed. Halim strode toward me. "Showtime."

. . .

The crew gathered as Halim issued final instructions. There was confidence in his every gesture; his stance was easy yet authoritative. "Countdown in fifteen minutes." He broke up the group with a clap of his hands.

A plastic bag skittered across the pavement. A uniformed police officer stood beside a small makeshift enclosure composed of sandbags. He nodded. "All yours."

I dialed the prearranged number. "Stop the El," I told the operator.

"I'll tell them," she answered.

Overhead, a police helicopter swept by, searching rooftops for hidden onlookers. Television crews clustered a safe distance away. A covey of birches stood on the northwest corner, swaddled in geotextile fabric and shivering in the gusting wind. The dust and debris could be carried for miles; all of Chicago could be affected. "Think we should hold off?" I asked Halim, uneasy.

"Just run the monitor afterward and make sure to download the readings."

It had been my idea, a way to issue a preemptive strike against possible lawsuits. Running the air-sampling monitor wouldn't stop the dust from spreading, but I didn't argue. I was as eager as Halim to finish the job.

He picked up the blasting machine, a steel box with two buttons connected to the lead line, and held it out. Did he want me to hold it for him? He smiled, seeing my confusion. "This one's yours," he said. "You've earned it."

I'd never initiated the blast. Never. Halim was the expert; I was the trainee. But there it was, the small box that signaled I had finally broken through the final barrier. Automatically, I folded my fingers around the machine and held it tight. Halim couldn't pry it away from me now, even if he wanted to.

He held up his walkie-talkie. "All clear."

A round of "Clear"s sounded from the crew bosses.

"Ten, nine, eight, seven."

The police helicopter tipped and sailed away.

"Four, three."

A flock of swallows shot up.

"Two, one. Fire! *Fire!*" I sucked in a breath, then punched the small red button.

Silence.

A thunderous blast shook the ground. I grabbed the sandbag wall for support. Halim pulled me toward him. Another explosion, another earthquake tremor, three swift eruptions, a firecracker flare near the foundation. The building held itself for an agonizing two seconds, then it swiveled and slammed south.

Tsunamis of dust boiled up, obliterating the sky. A seismic wave rushed toward me, an enormous riptide, a roller coaster without rails. I spun and ducked. Fine spray pelted my head and shoulders.

Crooking my elbow over my mouth and nose, I cracked my eyes open.

Two stories of rubble. *Check*. Adjacent buildings standing. *Check*. Trees erect, leaves attached. *Check*. Street cleaners starting their engines, push brooms and water hoses already beginning to clear away the sidewalks and walls. *Check*. Earth still rotating. *Check*. The jostling crowd, compelled despite themselves to cheer and whoop. *Check*.

The roller coaster rolled to a stop.

"Not bad, huh?" Halim said.

We stared at each other, the steel box cradled between us, then grinned. The shoot had gone off perfectly.

Trucks rumbled around the dusty lot. Lightning forked in the distance as men shouted and shovels scraped. Halim had already conducted two on-air interviews. Down to Earth Implosion would be splashed all over the news tonight; our phone would be ringing off the hook the next morning. We might even have to turn away work. So what if Halim had cleaned out our bank account? By tomorrow, it would be fat again.

Halim stood in the middle of the debris field, Ahmed beside him. They were discussing something that had them both gesturing wildly. Ahmed was shaking his head.

One of the dump truck drivers strode across the lot toward me. I accepted the clipboard he extended and signed the form. "You know where to take it?" I asked him.

"Yes, ma'am."

A loud volley of shouting, the backhoe driver leaning out his window and waving. Ahmed started jogging across the site. He'd better watch his step. That was where the elevator shaft had been located.

I handed back the clipboard. The man jerked his chin. "Looks like something's up."

The trucks sat frozen, their engines switched off. Their drivers were sliding down out of the cabs and trotting toward where Ahmed now stood. Halim was running among them, heedless of where he placed his feet, sidestepping boulders and heaps of bricks.

It couldn't be asbestos. I'd supervised its removal personally, so what on earth could the driver have seen that was making everyone run toward him like that? A long-buried pipe, maybe. Something hidden in the walls, exposed now that they'd broken apart.

My phone jittered against my hip. I answered without thinking, walking toward Halim. "Yes?"

"Is this Dana Carlson?" A girl's voice.

"Speaking."

"You don't know me, but I'm your niece. I'm Peyton. Peyton Kelleher."

The world slowly canted sideways. I stopped walking.

"I'm sorry to call you like this. It's about my mom."

"Julie?" The name hiccupped out of me. It had been so long since I'd last spoken it.

"My mom's sick." The young voice was relentless. Ahmed gestured toward Halim. "She's got kidney disease. My dad's not a match. She's on the waiting list, but I was wondering . . ." The girl's voice wobbled, then trailed off.

What was I to do with this? None of it made any sense. Distracted, I asked, "Are you calling from Black Bear?"

"Yes."

As if to keep himself from falling, Halim grasped Ahmed's sleeve, his face twisted with horror. My stomach contracted. What was he looking at? "Let me call you back."

A few steps and I was there, too. Ahmed stretched out a hand to stop me, but I jerked away, staring at the ground.

There, among the shattered slabs of stone, lay a soft grubby hand, its fingers curled hopefully toward the sky, fingernails rimed with dirt. Not just a hand, but an arm dressed in thick red cotton. Farther down, a worn canvas sneaker protruded, the white ankle bare and vulnerable above the rubble.

Trembling, I bent. I pressed my fingertips to feel between bone and sinew, searching for the pulse of life but finding only cold unyielding flesh. My heart hammered hard for both of us, for this stranger lying beneath the building, and for me, the one who brought the building down.

Raindrops splattered the dust. Halim was watching, his eyes narrowed in thought. Already, he was trying to figure out how to let me take the blame.

TWO

A SINGLE OCEAN FLOWS AROUND THE EARTH, DI-
vided into five bodies of water, each subject to currents and
the pull of the moon. Everything is constantly changing. The Pa-
cific Ocean is shrinking, while the Atlantic Ocean is young and
growing. In a hundred million years, it will all look completely
different.

The ocean accounts for seventy-one percent of the earth's surface, and represents ninety-seven percent of the world's living
space. Man has explored less than five percent of it. Scientists estimate that only one percent of all marine life has been identified.
Millions of species remain undiscovered. The tiniest creatures on
earth live in the ocean, as do the largest. Creatures within the same
species look different. They have different behaviors, depending
on which region in the ocean they inhabit.

No one really knows how or why life began in the ocean. They
only know that it did.

. . .

First thing in the morning, the sidewalks cool and misty, the pale sun fingering through the trees. Peyton had no right making phone calls to strangers. Her mom would freak. But her mom was in the hospital, wasn't she, which was the whole point of making the phone calls to begin with. Now that Peyton had dared to dial her aunt's number, she couldn't stop. By seven-thirty, she'd tried four times, growing bolder each time, letting the phone ring and the message play out all the way, even waiting for the little beep at the end, before disconnecting without saying a word. The first time she heard her aunt's voice recite the message, her heart gave a funny leap. Her mother's voice. Her aunt sounded just like her mother.

The light at the intersection glowed red. A car buzzed by. Peyton stopped and set down her bookbag, reaching for her phone. She'd try one more time before school began. If she still had no luck, she'd try between classes. She'd just keep calling until her aunt finally answered. Maybe she'd borrow Eric's phone and unblock the number. Maybe her aunt was the kind who'd be tempted to answer a mysterious call from Minnesota. But if that were true, then wouldn't she have phoned or stopped by before? Wouldn't she be curious about her only family?

"Hey, PEYTON!"

Guiltily, she whirled around. LT Stahlberg puffed toward her on his bike, his doughy body sagging from side to side as he pumped his fat knees. "HI, PEYTON!" He let go of the handlebars to wave, which was stupid. He could see she was looking right at him.

Just what she needed today. Her heart sank. Her mom had told her a million times that LT wasn't dangerous; he was just confused. But her mom still thought of LT as the neighbor kid she used to hang out with. He wasn't like that around Peyton. Around her, LT always let his weirdo out. *Don't walk on the sidewalk when the streetlights are on. Don't use the microwave. It'll get inside your head.* LT was a kid trapped in a big guy's body, a kid who had thought it would be cool to set the hardware store on fire, with Mr. Stem's poodle trapped inside. Peyton's dad had had to run inside and rescue her, while the rest of them stood on the sidewalk like idiots. Peyton's mom had been really pissed about that. *You could've gotten hurt,* she'd said, furiously grabbing his arm and not letting go. But Peyton had seen the way she'd pressed her face against his shoulder, had watched her father's hand come up and cup her mother's head.

LT rolled to a stop and grinned at her. "I'm glad I found you."

Like they were playing hide-and-seek? "What is it?" she asked impatiently. "I don't have time for games today, LT. I have to get to school."

His eyes were so pale, as if all the blue had leached away, leaving behind only the memory of color. He licked his red lips and she winced. "I just wanted to know how your mom's doing."

How do you think she is, moron? Peyton bit down hard and shoved the words deep inside. Her mom would be disappointed if she was mean to LT. Her mom would want Peyton to be kind. "She's still in the hospital. The doctor thinks she'll be getting out soon."

His fat face collapsed with relief. "Okay. That's good. That's GOOD."

Not that good. "It'll be a while before she goes back to work, you know. You better find another nurse." She'd heard her parents talking. She'd heard them say how specific the judge had been about that. It wouldn't be at all cool if LT wasn't staying on top of his medication, just because her mom wasn't there to make sure he did.

He hunched a shoulder. "Amy's mean." He stuck his lower lip out in a pout. "Amy's not like your mom."

Like he'd know the least thing about her mom. Only Peyton did, and her dad. Her mom belonged to them, not this weird boy-man. The light flared green and Peyton hoisted her bookbag into her arms. She was done taking care of him. "See you," she said.

"BYE, Peyton!"

When she reached the other side of the street, she couldn't help it. She had to glance back.

Sure enough, LT was still standing there, holding on to his bike, looking up and down the street, as if bewildered about which way to go. Reluctant sympathy washed over her. She knew exactly how that felt.

The other students swarmed past Peyton in the corridor, their arms filled with books, talking and texting, rushing to get to class before the next bell sounded. Peyton leaned against the wall, pushing the phone closer to her ear, keeping an eye out in case she got caught using her cell. She couldn't afford to be kept after school.

The hall was emptying, the last locker slamming shut, the last door wheezing closed. Three rings, four. Any minute now, voice-mail would pick up. Peyton decided she wouldn't leave a message; she couldn't take the chance it wouldn't get returned.

Overhead, the bell blared, making her jump. She started to slide her cellphone closed when she heard the distant, tinny *Yes?*

She pressed the phone to her mouth. "Is this Dana Carlson?" Her heart was thudding. She hated the way her voice sounded, plaintive, almost pleading.

"Speaking."

Peyton cleared her throat. "You don't know me, but I'm your niece." That was lame. Why hadn't she rehearsed this? "I'm Peyton," she bullied on. "Peyton Kelleher."

"Peyton?"

Yeah. That's right. The niece you've never bothered to meet. "I'm sorry to call you like this." Again, that pleading tone. What was her problem? "It's about my mom . . ."

"Julie?"

There was the slightest tendril of interest in Dana's voice. Relief washed through Peyton. "My mom's sick. She's got kidney disease. My dad's not a match. She's on the waiting list, but I was wondering . . ." She paused to let Dana rush in with questions and reassurances, saving Peyton from having to say it out loud, but the other end of the line was heavy with silence. "She needs you," she said, simply.

They all needed her. And if Dana didn't get it—well, then there'd been no hope to begin with.

"Are you calling from Black Bear?"

Where else would she be? She felt the squeeze of panic. If her aunt didn't even know something so basic as where they were living, how hopeless was it? "Yes."

"Let me call you back."

Cold and sharp. Then Dana hung up.

Everyone looked over as Peyton pushed open the classroom door. Mr. Connolly did, too, but he didn't say anything, letting her slip herself off the hook once again. She hated that he did that just as much as she was grateful for it. His gaze lingered on her a moment, appraising. When she didn't burst into tears or walk into a wall, he turned back to the board.

"RNA polymerase helps drag free-floating nucleotides to the DNA template to build the complementary mRNA strands."

As Peyton slid into her seat, Brenna narrowed her eyes. Brenna wore cutoffs way higher than the regulation five inches. But no one would say anything. She wore a skinny black shirt that said *You Know You Want To*. No one would say anything to her about that, either. Bending over her paper and pretending to take notes, she whispered, "Did you finish the DNA extraction lab?"

Peyton dug out her notebook from the bottom of her bookbag. "Sort of." As in, she hadn't picked up a single colored pencil, written a single answer.

"It's due Friday." Brenna shook her hair out of her eyes, glancing over at Mr. Connolly to see if maybe he noticed how cute she looked doing that. "We'd better get together after school. I have practice until five-thirty. We'll meet after that."

"Sorry. Can't make it." Like Peyton didn't have plans of her own. She was heading straight to the hospital the minute the dismissal bell rang. Besides, it wasn't as if Brenna would actually *do* anything. She'd just sit there and text while Peyton calculated and drew organelles and wrote up the discussion on how to extract DNA from a strawberry.

"The mRNA then leaves the nucleus through the nucleic pores and floats through the cytoplasm until a ribosome clasps onto it."

Brenna frowned. "When, then?"

"I'll look at it tonight." Maybe, while she was at the hospital with her mom, she could get some homework done. She didn't even know why she was here in this classroom while her mom lay alone in that horrible room filled with machines and fake cheerfulness.

Nothing's going to happen, her dad had said, handing her the box of Pop-Tarts for breakfast that morning. *Your mom will worry if you don't go to school.*

They couldn't pile any additional worry onto her mom. She had to concentrate on getting better. Peyton worked hard to keep everything normal and happy for her. That was why she kept going to school, why she hadn't even mentioned the D she was getting in social studies. Nothing about Eric. Not a word about Googling Dana and discovering that her aunt wasn't a doctor the way her mom always said she was, but worked for some demo company. Everything had to be normal. Peyton could do it. It was just a matter of deciding.

"What is the stop codon that tells the ribosome to release the protein? Does anyone know why it does this?"

Six more hours until school let out. Nothing would happen in six hours. Peyton tugged her phone from her jeans pocket. Holding the phone under the table, she glanced at the display. No missed calls.

"What is the most vulnerable process that can breed mutation?" Mr. Connolly looked at her, then away. "Adrian?"

Dana would call back. She had to.

Eric sat in the courtyard full of kids eating lunch. When he saw her, his face transformed, like he'd been lit up inside, just because he was looking at her. When had she gotten this power? What was she supposed to do with it?

"Hey," he called. "I got you the last Gatorade."

Peyton dumped her bag on the picnic bench and took the plastic bottle he held out. "Thanks."

His hair was fresh-from-the-shower damp at the back of his neck, and he smelled of Axe. He'd just come from PE. She didn't know why she was noticing these things. It wasn't like she'd ever thought about what he smelled like before, or the way the muscles in his forearms bunched beneath his rolled-up cuffs.

"So?" he said. "Did you talk to your aunt?"

"Sort of."

"That's great. What did she say?"

"We talked for like two seconds. Then she hung up."

He considered that. "But you asked her, right?"

"I practically begged her." Twisting off the Gatorade cap, she took a long lemony drink. "She said she'd call back, but she hasn't."

"She will."

Peyton didn't say anything to that. Lately, everyone made empty promises. She was sick of them.

"She might not be a match anyway. Twenty-five percent of a chance isn't much. It's only one in four."

"I know." He was the one who didn't know. Life was perfect for Eric. He was safe with his healthy mom and dad and sister and brother. Twenty-five percent might not seem like much to Eric, but to Peyton it was everything. It was way more than the thousandths of one percent that a stranger would be a match.

"Your folks know you called her?"

"No." Peyton pulled her sandwich from the bag and took a bite. Her favorite, peanut butter, pickles, and mayo, but today, it tasted like sand. "I'll tell my mom when I go over this afternoon." Maybe. It depended on whether Dana called back. It depended on whether her mom was having a good or bad day.

He was silent for a moment. Then he asked, "How's she doing?"

"Okay, I guess." It was just another infection. There was no need to panic, but who went to the hospital if they didn't have to? Peyton tore at the crusts. She hated this helpless feeling. She hated soggy pickles, too.

He crumpled up the chips bag. "You want to get together this weekend? We could go to the movies, maybe hang out with Adam and Brenna."

"I thought they broke up." She felt hot, and looked down at her hands, the short fingernails painted different colors, the silver ring her mom gave her for Easter last year, the Band-Aid wrapped around one knuckle frayed along the edges.

"They're back together again." Eric put his hand on hers and rubbed his thumb across the back of her hand. His skin was warm and rough in places from where he gripped the tools when he worked on his car. He didn't really know what he was doing, and sometimes she worried that the car would suddenly accelerate or burst into flames, but there was something deliciously reckless about going for drives with him anyway. Just being with Eric felt like that. Her heart gave a funny little flutter.

Picking up his tray, he stood. "I'll see you later. Hang in there, okay?"

He walked away, sunlight swallowing him up until he was just a mirage. Her best friend. Things had been so much easier when that was all he was.

Peyton shoved the remains of her sandwich back into the paper bag, feeling tears sting her eyes. When had she become such a *baby*?

"Peyton?"

Mrs. Stahlberg hurried toward her across the noisy court-yard, her skinny arms working, her ugly face flushed. She was only the principal's secretary, but she always acted like she ran the place. Lots of kids made fun of her, but Peyton wasn't allowed to. Her mom was always telling her to be charitable because Mrs. Stahlberg carried a heavy burden being LT's mom. Not that being nice to her made much difference. She was always cracking down on Peyton about one thing or another. As if Peyton was the one with mental problems, not her stupid son.

She must've heard about Peyton using her cell at school and was racing out here to confiscate it, which was just great. What happened if Dana did call back? No one would be there to answer.

Peyton balled up her lunch bag and stood to face the conse-quences. It did no good to plead or sweet-talk. Mrs. Stahlberg was such a witch. "I'm sorry—" she began.

But Mrs. Stahlberg shook her head and put a hand on Pey-ton's arm, her fingers firm and unexpectedly moist. "Come along, honey. We need to get to the hospital right away."

THREE

[DANA]

MALE, FEMALE. I DIDN'T KNOW WHO LAY BENEATH the rubble. I told myself I didn't care, that agonizing over it wouldn't change the facts, but as I drove north, I felt as though I were the one lying pressed against the ground, the breath being squeezed out of my chest. Finally, I pulled over at a gas station in Wisconsin and huddled in the cramped bathroom lit by one narrow window, splashing cold water onto my face until the shaking finally subsided.

The police had separated me and Halim as though we were criminals united in an unspeakable scheme, questioning us in their cars, the rain sluicing the glass. Again and again, I answered their questions. Someone was dead because of me. It had been my hand pushing the button. The wipers swept across the windshield; the close interior gently steamed, smelling of stale coffee and pungent aftershave, and finally I said to the cop, "Look. I have a family emergency." *Family.* I could barely get the word out.

He gave me a skeptical look but let me go. He had my phone number, he reminded me.

. . .

The rolling Wisconsin hills peeled away as I entered Minnesota, and now farmland sprawled all around me. Towns popped up one after another like dusty beads on a string, so small and insignificant I was almost out of them before I realized I was in them. Leaving behind the lashing rains of Chicago, I had the dizzying sense I was headed into a worse storm. Not one that boomed and soaked the pavement, but a dark and spreading one of my own making.

When I told Julie I was pregnant, she stared at me for a long time. I'd expected anger, or worse, disappointment, but all I saw on her face was shock. *How far along are you?* she finally asked. I put my hand protectively on my belly, where I imagined the baby curled up, sleeping. *I think . . . four months.* Too late to do anything, and maybe I'd planned it that way. *You can't tell anyone,* I insisted. She'd tilted her head, with a worried frown. *Not even Joe?* I shook my head. *Especially not Joe.* I rubbed at my eyes, furious at my sudden tears. She didn't ask why; she simply stepped forward and took me into her arms, enveloping me in a fierce embrace. *Do you want to keep the baby?*

Yes, I said, with a desperation that surprised me.

We'll move to Hawley when school lets out, Julie said. *We can start over there.*

Not a word about Frank, or how disappointed he'd be in me, his young, foolish sister-in-law. Not a word about college, or how we'd afford the baby. Her voice was calm and certain, and I believed her. But no one could have predicted how things would turn out.

Stopping for a snack, I tried calling Peyton back to let her know I was on my way, but her voicemail picked up. *Hi! This is Peyton! Leave a message!* I dialed Julie's number, too, waiting for the clear sound of her voice and wanting very much to hear it, but her cellphone rang on and on. I paid for the bottled water and got back behind the wheel.

The sun was setting when Black Lake finally came into view. Hotels perched on the shore, their parking lots studded with cars. The water sparkled in the last rays of sun, looking deceptively inviting. But I knew it was heart-stopping cold. Growing up, I thought all water was freezing. The first time I stuck a tentative toe into the Atlantic and found the water as warm as bathwater, I'd laughed.

Dark woods frilled the far shore. Above the Norway spruce and tamaracks heaved the curving metal loop of a roller coaster. An amusement park? A Ferris wheel rotated beside it, surreal lights flashing in the twilight. I almost missed the exit for Black Bear, Home of the Golden Vikings, veering off the highway just in time.

The green plaster dinosaur with its scabbed knees and snout should have been stretching its long neck on the corner as I rounded the curve, as if protecting the town's only two gas pumps, which sometimes ran out of gas before the end of the month. Beside them should have been Miss Lainie's dank little Stop 'n Shop with its shelves of dusty cans and withered produce, and then a few hundred yards beyond that should have been that creepy trailer park. I'd dreaded biking past there at night. Half the time someone was screaming or moaning; whether from pleasure or pain, I'd never stopped to find out.

They were all gone—the dinosaur, Miss Lainie's store, even the trailer park. A ruthless hand had swept them away, plunking down instead a gas station with tidy rows of pumps and a convenience store with signs in the windows offering lottery tickets, homemade *lefse*, a sale on bait.

A car horn blared. I raised my hand in apology and accelerated through the intersection, too fast.

The boarded-up storefronts downtown were gone, too, replaced by eateries with awnings. Pedestrians lingered on the side-walks, swinging shopping bags or sipping from takeout cups, acting for all the world like they wanted to be there in the cheerful spill of lights.

It looked like the spook house had been renovated. A perky bay window smiled over the fresh green lawn, and the crumbling stone wall had been rebuilt. There wasn't a single car on blocks to be seen anywhere. I rolled to a stop in front of a modest house tucked beneath the spreading branches of a honey locust. Curtains fluttered in the opened windows. Lamps were on inside. Someone was home. I wondered if they were happy, if they'd been more successful in making this place a home than my family had. The sage green paint Julie and I had slapped across the boards was now cream, the shutters we'd painted black were now an earthy brown. *Our new start,* Julie had said as I held the ladder for her. *I think Mom would have liked this color, don't you, Dana?*

A few years later, up on the second floor, beneath the sloping bathroom roof, I'd held the pregnancy test in my hand and stared disbelieving at the solid pink line.

An American flag jutted from beneath the eaves of the brick house next door. Perhaps Martin still lived there. But I wasn't ready to see Martin just yet.

I drove on.

Julie's house was small and yellow, with a front porch that tilted toward the gravel driveway as if whispering a secret. I switched off the engine. Silence filled the car, a profound quiet that sounded like a thousand tiny insects buzzing in my ears. The air was cooler up here, fresher, scented with pine.

No one answered the doorbell.

Maybe Google had given me the wrong address. But no, the label on the rolled-up newspaper lying on the mat read *Frank & Julie Kelleher.* Strange no one was home. With a teenager in the house, didn't they have to do things like prepare dinner and supervise homework? Unless Julie was sicker than I'd realized. Maybe that was the reason she'd allowed Peyton to make the call. Maybe that was why I hadn't heard from her, or Frank. No, I decided. If Julie were really in trouble, Doc Lindstrom would have let me know. Or Martin. It wasn't as though I was that hard to find. After all, a teenager had located me without any difficulty at all.

Sitting on the front step, I checked my phone messages: a neighbor in Baltimore wondering when I was getting back to town so we could get together, a friend I'd made in the Chicago planning office calling to express sympathy, and Ahmed.

He answered on the second ring. "How was your trip?"

"Fine." I waved away the mosquito hovering by my cheek. "How is everything there?"

"The police left a few hours ago. We got permission to finish clearing the site. But now we are looking at paying the crew overtime."

A worry. "Have the police learned anything?"

"It was a woman."

That made everything seem much more personal, and doubly strange. How had a woman found herself in the lonely, predawn hours inside an abandoned building about to be demolished? "Who?"

"We don't know."

Across the street, porches were bathed in warm yellow light. Windows glowed, and shadows moved within, people gathering for supper. "Ahmed, please have Halim call me as soon as possible."

"Of course." His reply was smooth, and not the least bit reassuring.

Julie's house crouched dark and silent behind me. I eyed the split-level next door, the ragged line of houses across the street. I didn't want to ask a stranger where my sister might be. Far worse would be to talk to someone I did know. Maybe Peyton played a sport, and Julie and Frank and Peyton were all at a game. What sport? I wondered. Was Peyton tall and lean like Julie, a sharp point guard? It wasn't basketball season. Maybe she was a swimmer. Or ran track. Afterward, the three of them might have gone out to eat; with so many new restaurants in town, they'd have lots of choices.

After all, no one knew I was coming. No one would have hurried home to greet me. But I couldn't tamp down the uneasiness. Where was everyone?

Music wailed from the jukebox, someone else's heartbreak flayed through tinny speakers. People sat at booths along the wall, and a couple rotated on the small dance floor, the woman taller than the man and tenderly draped around his shoulders. True love.

I sometimes wondered about true love, what it looked like, whether it pounded toward you or sneaked up alongside and just astonished you one day. Did it wait behind a door I had yet to open? Or had it already walked past, in the guise of a stranger who'd glanced at me and moved on? My mother had given up on true love, and Julie thought she had found it in Frank: she'd desperately wanted it to be so with him. But wanting didn't make something come true. My brother-in-law was taciturn and stubborn, not someone I could ever envision embodying true love for anyone, let alone someone like Julie.

Though what did I know? Men had ventured in and out of my life, some of them staying long enough to make me wonder whether they were the one. But in the end, we'd drifted apart and there hadn't been a single true love among any of them. Well, maybe there had been one, but that had been long ago.

And there I was again, for the second time that day, peering down the path I hadn't taken. It was being back in Black Bear that was dredging up all this old history, memories that needed to remain buried. If I could, I would obliterate my past completely. It didn't do any good to look back over one's shoulder. The only thing to do was to keep moving forward.

"Leinie's, please," I told the bartender, taking a seat at the long curved bar. "On tap."

Someone had done a pretty good job of sprucing up the old Lakeside Bar and Grill. The battered linoleum had been pried up and replaced with light oak flooring; the bare plaster walls had been painted a deep red and hung with boating gear and old-fashioned road signs. A definite improvement, but the bar itself was still sticky with wax and the air rich with the same yeasty smell of beer laced with grease.

Years ago, Sheri and I had thought this was the big time. We spent hours giggling before our bedroom mirrors and gluing on false eyelashes, tugging on tight jeans and strutting around that pool table as if we had a clue. Did Peyton try the same thing? Did she doll herself up and borrow Julie's heels to sail in here on her boyfriend's arm? I tried to imagine it, but couldn't.

She'd had that high-pitched voice of youth, that breathless way of making everything into a question. *You don't know me? It's about my mom? She's sick?* There had been nothing there I could pin an impression on, no matter how hard I tried, nothing to indicate if she was scholarly, athletic, spirited, or contemplative. There had just been that soft voice lengthened by Midwestern vowels.

Why hadn't Julie let me know she was sick? Pride, or was Peyton overreacting? I'd finish my drink and head back to Julie's place. If no one was home, I'd just have to start knocking on neighbors' doors.

A jar with a photograph taped to its side sat on the bar, half-filled with coins and rumpled bills. Rotating it, I was surprised to see the fierce scowl of Miss Lainie glaring back at me. *What the hell you want?* the old woman seemed to snarl.

The bartender placed a mug in front of me, a perfect half inch of foam.

"Thanks." I reached for my wallet.

"It's on the house, Dana. Welcome home."

I took a closer look. Right, that overbite. He had to be one of the Petersons. "Fred," I guessed.

"I own the place now." He sounded pleased I'd recognized him. "Me and my brother. Going on two years." He nodded at the collection jar. "I saw you looking. We're collecting for her burial. You remember Lainie?"

Of course. How could I forget Miss Lainie? She was the most taciturn person I'd ever known, and given some of the work crews I'd dealt with, that was saying something. Miss Lainie chased people out of her store with a broom if they tracked in a flake of snow; she hovered behind them as they decided between Reese's Cups and Three Musketeers. She snatched coins from shoppers' palms, leaving behind painful red marks. One day Miss Lainie shortchanged me, and Julie marched right into the store and demanded the quarter back. Julie hated confrontation but she hated unfairness worse. "She owned the Stop 'n Shop," I told Fred Peterson. How old had Lainie been? Ancient, I decided. She certainly seemed ancient to Julie and me.

"Until she sold it and went to work at Gerkey's. In the gift shop, if you can believe it." He chuckled.

"Since when does Gerkey's have a gift shop?"

"Since Brian took it over five years back."

"Brian *Gerkey*?" How had that happened? Brian used to be so high on weed he couldn't turn himself around, let alone a family business.

My surprise made Fred chuckle again. "He's one of our most upstanding citizens now. He's married, got two little girls."

That lost, sad look in Mrs. Gerkey's eyes as I'd plucked my paycheck from her grasp. Everything had worked out in the end. "His mom must be thrilled."

"Old Alice? You betcha."

The waitress waved from the end of the bar, and Fred said, "Excuse me."

I studied Miss Lainie's picture. Hard to imagine her working behind the counter of a gift shop. She probably snapped at the customers to hurry up and decide, made a big production out of having to give them a bag to carry their purchases in. But it didn't mean she didn't deserve a decent burial. I tugged a bill from my wallet, folded it into a neat rectangle, and tapped it through the slot cut in the jar lid. What happened to people like Lainie, alone and poor at the end? I fingered the few remaining bills in my wallet, then pushed a second one through the slot. In another day or so, Halim would deposit the money from the Burnside job into our account and I could use my ATM card.

I picked up the mug. Good old Leinenkugel, Minnesota's unofficial state beer. The honeyed malt taste blew me right back to the blanket spread beneath the football bleachers, the backseat of Joe's car. I'd forgotten how cloying the brew was. So much for nostalgia. Next round I'd return to good old Sam Adams. No memories there.

I scratched the mosquito bite on my shoulder. In town less than an hour, and already the insects were feasting on me. It was like they sent up signal flares. *Over here, juicy one right here.* They never bothered Julie, though. Martin used to say it was because she was too sweet. Which meant, of course, that I was too sour. Martin always winked at me when I grumbled at the unspoken comparison. He never tired of teasing me.

Was I reading too much into one phone call, made by a girl I didn't even know? After all, people could live a long time with kidney disease. I could have gone to a doctor back in Baltimore to see if I was a match. Instead, I'd dropped everything and raced up here. Maybe I'd been waiting for an excuse to return. It was just curiosity, I told myself. Nothing more.

A man slid onto the barstool beside mine. "Hey."

Round-faced, droopy brown eyes, blond hair, potbelly straining at the front of his polo shirt. No one I knew. "Hi."

"Am I glad I found this place. Nothing worse than checking in to a hotel and finding out it doesn't have a bar."

"At least Black Bear *has* a hotel. Try the next town over and you'd have to pitch a tent." I should know. I'd spent an entire summer there once.

He laughed. "I'm pretty sure I don't want to be camping in a place called Black Bear."

"Don't worry. There aren't any bears around here. Head north toward the reservation, though, and you'll find plenty."

"I'll stay south, then. Martini," he told Fred. "And one for my friend here."

Fred looked over; I shook my head.

"I just flew into Fargo to meet with a client. I'm in specialty chemicals." He paid for his drink. "You ever see that movie, *Fargo*?"

A talker. Full of pent-up energy from being trapped in a plane and then driving across the endless flat countryside between here and Fargo. "Sure."

"Until I heard the girl at the car rental place, I didn't know people really talked that way."

Oh, yah. Sure they do, now. You betcha.

"No offense," he said, hastily. "You don't sound like you're from around here."

"I'm not." Not anymore.

The door opened to admit two newcomers, men who didn't glance over, but instead went straight to the pool table, lifting cue sticks from the wall rack. Mike Cavanaugh? Yes, though his face looked weathered, like the winters since I'd last seen him had been harsh on him. The other guy looked familiar, too. Wasn't he the band director's son? His hair had thinned to a fluffy circle around his head, and now he really looked like his dad. I'd better prepare myself, practice my happy face. No doubt I'd see a hundred more people I knew before I finally left town. An unwelcome thought. Just how long could I keep the mask in place before it slipped? I told myself I'd better finish up my beer and head back to Julie's house. The sooner I found out what I needed to do to be tested for a match, the sooner I could leave.

"So what's there to do in a place called Black Bear, if it's not camping?" Mr. Specialty Chemicals wanted to know.

"Fishing's big. And hunting."

Someone new had joined the pool players. A man, six feet tall, dark-haired. He had his back to me, but I recognized him instantly. The way he stood there with his head cocked to one side was unmistakable. My body registered it first, a familiar tug deep inside, then my brain caught up. Joe Connolly. My heart had conjured him up out of thin air. But of course he'd be here. This was his town, his hangout. Did I want him to turn and see me? Yes. No. Maybe.

"That lets me out, then. I'm more into golf, watching football, that sort of thing. Hey, what's that you're drinking? Is it any good? You sure I can't buy you a drink?"

"I'm sure."

Joe took the pool cue Mike held out and moved around the pool table. He was saying something that had Mike frowning and the band director's son standing motionless. Now they were all shaking their heads.

Joe was wearing his hair shorter now; I suddenly imagined the tickle of those hairs along my fingertips. His blue shirt was open at the neck, the cuffs folded to reveal tanned forearms, his jeans well worn, the hypnotic pull of wide shoulders leading down to trim hips.

"Specialty chemicals are the future, I tell you. They're gonna rule the world."

Joe leaned over the pool table. The hanging light cast his face in shadow, revealed the planes of his cheeks, his lips. I realized he was staring at me.

Slowly, he straightened.

I flushed and lowered my beer. Should I smile, or be cool? How ridiculous. I was acting like a kid.

"You don't really care, do you? You're not even listening. Lemme ask you something. You ever heard of nanotechnology?" Mr. Specialty Chemicals loosened his tie. "Seriously. Do you even know what that means? I don't know what the average person on the street knows."

Joe said something to Mike, and now he glanced over, too. "I'm not average and I'm not on the street."

"Right, right." He patted the air. "It's just an expression. So, do you?"

The band director's son was looking over at me, too. Not one bit of welcome or surprise on any of their faces.

"It's gonna change the world, believe you me. Insider tip, I don't mind sharing. You got any spare cash, that's where you should be putting it. Nanotech's gonna cure cancer, solve the energy crisis, stop world hunger." He burped softly. "You name it."

Joe was coming over, threading his way around the tables, his gaze intent on mine. Did we have anything to say to each other after all these years? Damn, he looked good, his dark hair still in compelling contrast to the bright blue of his eyes.

"Hey." I smiled, but Joe didn't smile back. So he didn't have the same fond memories I did. Fair enough.

"Dana."

When had I last heard him say my name?

"What are you doing here?"

Caution in his voice, and something else. Concern? "I was just passing by," I joked.

He shook his head, still not smiling. His fingers touched my arm, the warmth of his grasp singing through the thin cotton to my skin. "Excuse us," he said to the salesman.

"Sure, sure."

I slid off my barstool and followed Joe to an empty table. He pulled out my chair and sat down, looking at me with such compassion that I felt the faint prickle of alarm. "What is it, Joe? You're scaring me."

"Dana, I'm sorry." He shook his head.

The jukebox silenced, and in the small cupful of quiet, I said, "Sorry about what?"

He took my hand in both of his, dragged his chair closer. "You don't know?" he asked. "No one called you?"

"Peyton called me this morning. She said Julie was sick."

He nodded, looked away, then back to me. "Let's go outside," he said.

"No." I clutched at his hand. "She said Julie needed a transplant. That's why I'm here. I'll go now. I'm her sister. Maybe they don't even have to test me."

"Oh, Dana." Joe looked miserable. I wanted to place my palm against his cheek and comfort him.

"Stop." I pushed back my chair but Joe kept a tight hold on my hand.

"It's too late," he said.

"It's not too late."

"I ran into Martin. He'd just come from the hospital."

My teeth chattered. *No.*

All around us, people moved and talked, leaned back to pour a beer, laughed and waved a friend over. It wasn't too late. It couldn't be.

"Come on," I heard Joe say. "I'll drive you to the hospital. Frank and Peyton are there." He pulled me to my feet and slid his arm around my waist. Leaning into him, I stumbled to the door that swung open into the dark and unforgiving night.

FOUR

THE TOP LAYER OF THE OCEAN IS CALLED THE SUN-
lit zone. Ninety percent of all marine life lives there. This is
the only place where plants can grow and phytoplankton survive.
They're the bottom of the food chain and need sunlight to thrive.
Other fish thrive on them.

Animals that live here are transparent, like jellies, or camou-
flaged to mimic the play of light and shadow, like dolphins and
sharks. Coral reefs flourish along the coastline, and many fish
that live below swim up to feed among these densely populated
waters.

Out in the open ocean, away from swirling silt and sand, the
sunlit zone stays a constant clear blue. Divers have to be careful.
There are no landmarks and a person can get turned around.
They can think they're swimming up to where their boat waits,
but they might be swimming in the opposite direction, away from
the sun and down into the darkness. By the time they realize their
mistake, it's too late.

. . .

Mrs. Stahlberg drove Peyton straight to the hospital. No one bothered to sign Peyton out, or told her to get her books from her locker. So she knew before Mrs. Stahlberg swept her crappy car up to the hospital entrance, her ancient freckled hands white-knuckled and her old-lady lips pressed tightly together, that it was already too late.

Her dad insisted on seeing her mom. Peyton couldn't think about whether or not she wanted to, but he was gripping her hand so tightly, she thought her bones would crack. They stood there by her mom's bed and looked down. The white hospital sheet was icy smooth and pulled taut to her chin; her body barely lifted it, she was so thin. Her face was waxy. Someone had combed her hair but it still looked terrible, fine and sparse and lying in pale wisps. This wasn't her mom. Her mom had thick shiny hair that curled to her shoulders. Her mom had bright eyes. She sang in the shower and ate chocolate chip cookie dough right out of the bowl. She did crossword puzzles in red ink, and always, no matter what she was doing, stopped to smile whenever Peyton walked into the room. This wasn't her mom. This was a *thing*.

Now they stood in the hall listening to people try to console them, her dad standing close, Peyton with her arms wrapped tightly around herself. She was freezing. She had to get out of this place with its hushed voices, antiseptic smell, and surfaces that were shiny and dingy at the same time. Words skidded around her.

"*. . . just stopped working . . . I'm sorry, we tried . . . sometimes these things happen.*"

The ping of the elevator and tapping shoes, almost running. Her father's hand tightened on Peyton's shoulder. When Peyton looked up, she saw a woman striding toward her, a sweater pulled around her shoulders, her blonde hair mussed. For one heart-stopping moment, Peyton thought it was her mom alive and whole again, and coming to take her home.

But of course it wasn't. This must be her aunt, looking exactly like Peyton's mom and arriving too late to do anything for anybody.

Despair swamped over her, a black tidal wave of sludge. Peyton couldn't breathe. She didn't want to talk to this person. She didn't want to listen to someone explain the situation to Dana, didn't want to see the horror register on this stranger's face, didn't want someone to put their hand on her shoulder and introduce her and have Dana look at her and say something polite. The scream built up inside her, clawing at the sides of her throat.

"I'll be outside," she told her dad, just managing to get the words out. He simply nodded, staring at Dana.

Outside, the cool spring evening washed over her. Shivering, she looked up at the sky and the stars twinkling there, desperate to see her mother's face among them, smiling down and letting Peyton know she would be all right. Peyton looked and looked, saw only endless black and glittering pinpricks. She listened, heard only the far-off shriek of a train and knew she was well and truly alone.

Her dad didn't talk on the way home. He veered the truck from lane to lane, leaving a trail of car honks in their wake. Peyton should have reached out and grabbed the wheel, but she decided she didn't care. If they ended up smashed against a tree, well then, maybe that was the easier way.

Too soon, he bumped the truck up onto the driveway. A black SUV stood at the curb. Dana waited on the porch, her elbows cupped in her hands.

Her dad unlocked the front door. "I didn't know. . . . We don't have a spare room."

He sounded uncertain, not at all like the father Peyton knew.

"I can get a hotel room," Dana told him.

"We've got a pullout on the back porch," Peyton said.

Her dad shot her a look, frowning. Peyton got it. What had

she been thinking, blurting out a stupid offer like that? She hadn't been thinking. She'd just said the first thing that popped into her head, the thing her mom would have wanted her to say. Her mom was gone, but she was right there, too, opening Peyton's mouth and putting in the words.

"That all right with you, Frank?" Dana asked.

He didn't want her there. Peyton could see it in the way he squared his shoulders, could hear it in the long silence before he answered. "Sure," he said at last.

He held open the door and Peyton pushed past him into the lingering aroma of burned toast from that morning, and over-cooked coffee. She switched on the lamp, throwing shadows around the room. Dana walked straight over to the wall of Peyton's school pictures. What did she expect to find there? Peyton's mom wasn't in any of them.

Her dad rubbed his face. He put his arm around Peyton and held her close. He smelled of motor oil and lavender, the comforting blend after he'd been at work all day. She pressed her cheek against the rough fabric of his shirt. Had she been the one to wash it, or had her mom? She had to remember. Her mom's fingerprints were all over this house, tiny pieces of her that Peyton needed to collect and keep, all that was left.

"I could make some dinner if anyone's hungry. How does spaghetti sound?" Dana asked.

Her dad's arm tightened around Peyton. They hadn't eaten spaghetti in two years. It had been one of the first things to go when her mom had gotten sick.

No one answered Dana. Peyton knew her mom wouldn't have liked that. Her mom would have wanted Peyton to be polite. Despite everything, she would have wanted Peyton to welcome this stranger to their house.

"We don't have spaghetti," she said. "Mom couldn't eat tomatoes." If Dana had ever bothered to visit, she would have known that. There were lots of things they didn't keep around anymore.

Peyton's dad had insisted that if her mom couldn't eat it, then neither could they. Peyton always felt guilty at school when she poured ketchup onto a plate of french fries. Ketchup. Why was she thinking of ketchup? It was all Dana's fault, yanking Peyton's mind from its regular tracks and steering it onto this random, alien terrain.

"I'm not hungry," she said.

"Oh." Dana paused in the doorway. "Then I'll put on some coffee."

Her dad looked down at himself, as if surprised to find himself still in his work clothes. "Guess I'll wash up." He walked unsteadily away, brushing the doorway with his shoulder.

Peyton slumped into her dad's favorite chair and wished she had a puppy, something soft and cuddly and always happy to see her that would curl up in her lap. Pulling out her phone, she studied the screen. Eric had texted her a million times. So had Brenna, and a bunch of other kids. Everyone knew. Everyone was talking and buzzing and wondering. Tonight, right now, all these kids would do their homework, watch TV, and go out for DQ or down to the lake, everything safe and normal for them. Everything just as it had been the night before and the night before that.

Dana came into the room. "I brought you some. I didn't know if you liked coffee."

Peyton didn't. Like she could be won over with coffee, but she found herself reaching for the cup. It smelled good, like it always did first thing in the morning. She took a sip. Dana had stirred in milk and sugar, and it was delicious going down, warming and rushing right to her head.

The bathroom pipes clanged as her dad started the water.

Dana turned on the floor lamp and sat down on the sofa opposite. "Our shower did the same thing when I was growing up. That's how my mom used to wake me up for school, by turning on the water. It was almost as bad as when she came into my room, switching on the lights and belting out that awful tune." She scrunched her face up in thought. "I can't for the life of me re-member what it was."

Peyton examined the woman sitting there; the stranger who looked so much like her mom, and sounded so much like her, but wasn't. Peyton set her stupid cup of coffee down, directly on the wood where it was sure to leave a circle. "'Lazy Mary, Will You Get Up,'" she said coldly.

The corners of Dana's mouth curved up. "Don't tell me that's how your mom wakes you up."

"She did," Peyton said, clearly. She marked this moment. She claimed this memory for her own. "She doesn't anymore." Peyton stood. "And that's *her* cup."

Dana glanced down at the white porcelain cup she was hold-ing, the pink tulip painted on the side just visible between her fingers. "Right." Slowly, she leaned forward and set it down on the table.

Peyton left her there, walked down the hallway and into her room. From behind the closed bathroom door came the groaning of the pipes and the tapping of the water, and the raw sound of sobbing. She'd never heard her father cry. The noise was wretched, animal in its confusion. She wanted it to stop. She wanted to pound on the door and yell at her dad that he was only making everything worse, but of course she didn't. Instead, she turned on her bedroom light and stared unseeing at the walls, a kaleido-scope of color and alien images. This strange new world spread out in all directions. She couldn't tell if she was swimming up or down or even sideways.

People came by all the next morning, drinking gallons of coffee and talking in hushed tones. Everyone hugged her, studied her, said lots of sad things. Pretending she was okay made her bone-freaking-tired. Around noon, the house grew quiet. Dana disappeared somewhere, the grumble of her car moving away from the curb and fading into silence.

A little while later, her father appeared in her bedroom doorway.

"Hey, I have to go to the funeral home." His voice was gravelly, like a stranger's. He cleared his throat like he, too, knew it sounded weird. "Would you like to come?"

"Do I have to?" Her jeans were ripped at the knee, the threads unraveling. She picked at them, rolled the softness between her fingers. She couldn't bear to be around Mr. Ewing, the smarmy funeral director. She couldn't bear to pretend to be interested in something she wasn't.

"Of course not. If you want, you could stay here and pick out something for your mom to wear."

Like *funeral* clothes? She clutched her iPod. She wanted to blast the music, drown all this out. But her dad looked so lost. "No problem."

"I won't be long. Then we'd better go see Grandma."

She waited until he was gone.

Her mom liked sweaters. She had one she always wore when it was just the two of them lounging around, watching TV and gossiping, while her dad worked late or went out with his buddies. The blue color exactly matched her eyes. So what if the cuffs were a little frayed and there was a bleach splotch on the side? It was a tiny stain. No one would notice.

Peyton pulled open the middle drawer in her parents' bureau and stared down at the neat stack of cottons and wools. Outside, up close by the eave, a bird cooed. The back door banged open and the cooing stopped. "Hello?"

Peyton lifted up things, moved them aside. She ignored the rustling from down the hall. The Christmas sweatshirt, the red one with the lace across the collar. The black velvet one with rhinestone buttons. The lime green cardigan she always wore on

St. Patrick's Day, the one she swore gave her good luck. Peyton ran her hand across its softness, fingering the pearl buttons. No blue sweater with the white mark shaped like Alaska.

Cabinet doors opened and closed. Curiously comforting sounds that took her a moment to place: not her mom, but Dana, putting away groceries.

Maybe her mom had been wearing the sweater the day they took her to the hospital. Maybe that's where it was right now, pushed into some plastic bag and waiting for them to come retrieve it.

"There you are." Dana stood in the doorway. Tall and slim in her gray slacks, the waistband gaping a little at her waist where her blue blouse was tucked neatly in. "How do grilled cheese sandwiches sound for lunch?"

Peyton's mom made the best grilled cheese sandwiches. She buttered each slice of bread and used real cheddar. She kept the heat low and put a saucepan lid over the pan to make the cheese melt and keep the bread from burning. "Fine."

Dana crossed her arms. She wore her hair in a loose ponytail low in the back, an effortless way that was very pretty. "Will your dad be home?"

"Probably." She wished Dana would stop watching her the way she was, in that searching way, like Peyton knew all the answers.

"Where did he go?"

"The funeral home."

"Oh." She sounded disapproving. Maybe she'd wanted to go with him. "Mind if I come in?"

Peyton did mind, but Dana was already wandering around, looking at the decorative screen Peyton's dad had made that stood in the corner, the glass bluebird of happiness on her mom's nightstand, the framed wedding picture beside it. She picked it up. "She was so happy that day. She giggled through the whole ceremony. The minister had to keep stopping to let her compose herself."

Peyton's dad said it made him laugh, too, every time he looked down at her mom, with her lips pressed tightly together but her merry eyes giving her away. Peyton closed the drawer and opened the next one. Sometimes her dad put the laundry away, and he was always mixing things up. But no, there were her mom's turtle-necks that she'd still been wearing even though it was warm out-side, all perfectly folded in rectangles. She imagined her mother's hands neatly squaring them and pressing them flat.

Dana put down the framed picture, knocking it against the bowl Peyton had made in third-grade art class that held the spare change from her dad's pockets. "You need some help?"

How could she help? She didn't know where anything was. "I'm okay." Peyton lifted up the soft clothes, searching for a glimpse of cornflower blue.

"Are you looking for something for your mom?"

Obviously.

"How about a dress?" Dana turned and opened the closet door.

"Is that what I'm supposed to be looking for?"

"I don't really know. I guess you'd want something nice. Was there a dress she wore for special occasions?"

Does attending your own funeral count as a special occasion?

Her aunt sorted through the hangers, pulling out things and holding them up. "What about this? This is pretty."

Her mom's church dress, deep purple, long and slim and belted. Peyton found herself nodding. That was it exactly. That was what her mom would want to wear. The look on her face must have told Dana that, because she said, "Let's look for shoes."

They picked out a pair of black pumps, the heels still sharp, the leather uncracked. Peyton remembered when they bought them at the consignment shop. Her mom had been so tickled. *Five dollars!* she'd said. *And they fit perfectly!*

"We'll need some underthings," Dana said.

Peyton looked at her blankly. *Right.*

She pulled out a drawer and poked through the pink and white and black slithery things. She felt her cheeks grow hot. Seeing everything jumbled in a drawer, the very same place her mother went through every day, considering and deciding, just felt wrong. She pulled out something, anything, and dropped it on the bed.

"Why don't you let me go through that while you look for jewelry?"

Peyton turned away to her mother's jewelry box and sat down on the bed with it in her lap. She raised the lid and the tiny ballerina sprang up. It no longer rotated, though, and the music only played if she shook it.

"So, what does your dad do?"

A dull, adult question. *Do you like school? What grade are you in? Do you play any sports?* All the blah-blah-blah, getting-to-know-you questions that shouldn't be here in this room. Dana should have known the answers to all of them long ago. Peyton gritted her teeth. "He's a maintenance foreman."

"That's right. That's what he did overseas."

Overseas. A neutral term for the word they were never allowed to mention at home: *Afghanistan.* Peyton had made the mistake once of asking her dad how he'd felt being there; he'd gotten up from the table without saying a word and left.

Sorry, her mom had said. *He can't talk about it to me either, honey.*

Dana folded the dress, tucking in the underwear she'd chosen. Setting it aside, she sat beside Peyton. "I can't believe it." She gestured at the jewelry box. "Your mom still has that? I gave that to her for her thirteenth birthday."

Big deal. Like that was supposed to mean something? "She got me one when I turned thirteen, only mine has a yellow tutu." There. Let her hear that. Let it make her sad. How much her mom must have loved Dana, and Dana had never even sent her a postcard.

But Dana just said, "You're sixteen now, right? That makes you . . . what . . . a sophomore?"

"I'm a junior. I have a late birthday." She held out a gold bracelet. "Mom wore this sometimes."

Dana took it from her, holding it up so the little heart charm dangled. A frown puckered between her eyes. Was there something wrong with it? But Dana said, "It's perfect," dropping it into Peyton's palm and closing her fingers over it. Her knuckles were rough. Peyton's mom had the softest hands. She always said it came from having to wear surgical gloves all the time. "It'll look beautiful with the dress you picked."

Peyton hadn't picked the dress, but whatever. She closed the lid and set the box on her mom's nightstand, beside the magazine her mom had been reading, rolled open to the page she'd stopped at. The library book. A box of tissues. The spiral notebook she'd been carrying around for the past weeks.

Her mom never let Peyton read over her shoulder as she wrote in it; she closed the cover whenever Peyton entered the room, so Peyton figured it must be some sort of diary. She'd thought it was weird that her mom would start a diary now, after years of writing nothing but grocery lists. Maybe she used to keep one as a kid; after all, she had given Peyton a million journals over the years, pretty books that sat bare-paged on a shelf in Peyton's room.

She placed her palm against the cardboard cover. Her mother had been in such a hurry to leave for the hospital on Friday that she'd left this behind. Peyton shouldn't be reading her mother's private thoughts. A corner of paper peeked out from between the pages. Peyton opened the notebook to slide the loose paper back in and found herself staring at the first page.

Her mom's handwriting, all generous loops and swirls, filled the lined page, but there was no date printed at the top, no entry that started *Dear Diary*. It was just an orderly list of names and addresses. "Oh." She felt curiously deflated.

Dana leaned close to Peyton. She smelled good, like shampoo and soap, the way her mom used to smell, before she started washing her hands with that harsh lime-scented hand sanitizer every five minutes. "What's that?"

"These people." She frowned at the list. "I don't know who they are."

"Well, your mom was a nurse. Could these have been her patients?"

"She only worked in Black Bear. Some of these addresses are over in Hawley." She turned the page. There were dates and abbreviations, phone numbers, things crossed out and added in later, in a different-colored ink. "Here's Martin's name."

"Martin Cruikshank." Dana's voice warmed. "How's he doing?"

"Okay, I guess." Peyton liked the old guy. He told her stories about her dead grandma and made her mom laugh. "He works with my dad at the plant."

"Maybe I'll stop by. Does he still live beside your mom's and my old house?"

Every so often, her mom would slow the car as they passed the house down on Vintage Street, and remark, *Oh, look, Peyton, they took down the tire swing* or *they planted azaleas*. Her whole life, Peyton had thought of the little white house as her mom's childhood home; now here was Dana, crowding in. "Yes," she said, curtly. "But he's probably at dialysis." They didn't stop dialysis for anything, not even holidays, and today was Martin's dialysis day. Same as it had been her mom's day. She scowled and flipped the page.

"Dialysis?" Dana said.

Peyton studied her mom's handwriting. The words swam before her. Yes, Martin was on dialysis. He was way older than her mom, but that's where he was, at dialysis, while her mom was at the stupid funeral home.

"Would you like to come with me?" Dana asked. "The clinic's downtown, right? We could walk, maybe have lunch somewhere."

Like Peyton would ever want to spend another second in that horrible place. As if she wanted to spend another second yakking with Dana about who lived where and what her favorite subjects were at school. Like she could even possibly eat. "I can't." She said it with a vicious satisfaction. "My dad wants to take me to the nursing home to see my grandma."

First time she'd ever been glad about going to that creepy old place. Dana nodded, her cheeks pink. So she'd gotten the message she wasn't wanted.

"But not your grandfather?" Dana asked.

"He died a long time ago." But not so long ago that Peyton couldn't remember the way his laughter had rumbled out of him from deep inside, or how he had always sneaked her sticks of gum when no one was looking, even though her mom didn't like her eating candy. And of course Peyton had no memory at all of her other grandpa, the one who'd left long before Peyton was born.

"I'm sorry to hear that. He was a nice guy."

So Dana had known her grandpa. Maybe the only person she hadn't gotten to know was Peyton herself. Whatever. She spotted another name she recognized toward the bottom of the page. "That's Logan," she said, forgetting herself, forgetting how she didn't want to be talking to this person.

"Who's he?"

"Sheri and Mike Cavanaugh's little boy."

"Sheri has a son?"

"Two of them. Mikey and Logan."

"Really? Sheri was my best friend, growing up."

Peyton knew that. Sheri had said something to her mom once, or maybe it had been the other way around. Either way, since practically no one ever talked about Dana, it had caught Peyton's attention.

"Sheri Cavanaugh. I guess she and Mike got married after all."

They'd been married as long as Peyton could remember. She couldn't think of them as anything *but* married.

Dana reached over and tapped the page. "There's Miss Lainie."

That mean old lady. Oh, now she got it. "This is a list of all the people who have kidney disease." Her mom must have been keeping track of everything in this notebook. She'd talked about almost nothing else these past few months. Her parents had argued, her dad saying he didn't want her wasting her time, her mom insisting it was her time to waste.

Dana frowned and took the notebook. She flipped through some pages, stopped at a chart, then turned to where a map of the county had been taped across the pages, dotted with hand-drawn stars. She turned back to the front again. "Are you telling me Sheri's little boy has kidney disease, too?"

"Uh-huh." Logan was only four. They'd had to order special-sized equipment for him. Her mom had spent hours on the phone talking to Sheri, her voice low and soothing.

"And Martin?"

"He found out last Christmas."

An envelope had been tucked among the notebook's back pages. Dana removed it and scanned the return address. "It's from the Minnesota Department of Health. Mind if I read this?"

Peyton shrugged. She already knew what it said.

Dana shook open the letter. "Looks like your mom wrote them. . . . She was worried about the rate of idiopathic kidney disease in Black Bear." She glanced at Peyton. "Do you know what that means?"

Of course she did. When Peyton overheard her parents talking, she figured at first they were saying *idiot disease*. Turns out it wasn't that far off: *idiopathic* meant you didn't know the origin. You were clueless, like an idiot. "Yes."

"They wrote back to tell her that although the rate is high, it's within normal parameters."

"I know what that means, too," Peyton said, irritably. She'd taken a million math classes.

Dana folded the paper and stuck it back between the pages of the notebook. "Did your mom know why *she* got kidney disease?"

"No." Peyton's mom could have had the kind caused by diabetes or some weird cystic disease. She could have inherited it, but no, she got the totally random kind that showed up one day without warning. How did a person protect themselves from something they couldn't even see coming? The answer was, they couldn't.

"What about Martin, and Sheri's little boy? Is that the kind they have, too?"

"Yes." *Yes, yes, yes!* They were all part of the same special sick club. Did Dana think they sat around and chatted about this stuff? *So, how's the old dialysis working? Pull off enough weight today? Your fistula still bothering you?*

No one wanted to talk about it. Her mom went in for dialysis three days a week, and when she came home, she either looked better or she didn't. It wasn't like she came home and told them all sorts of stories over supper.

Dana handed back the notebook. "Oh well, honey. At least she tried."

Beneath the sympathy in her voice ran a strong current of dismissal. It was clear Dana thought Peyton's mom was nuts. Well, screw her. Dana may have been her sister, but she didn't know the least thing about Peyton's mom.

Peyton slapped the notebook shut and dropped it with a clang into the trashcan beside the bed. She hated to admit it, but Dana *was* right about one thing. What did any of it matter now?

FIVE

[DANA]

THE WINTER I WAS FOURTEEN, I SPENT MONTHS coughing, throwing up, or shivering from fever. As soon as I got over one thing, I came down with another. I missed the ninth-grade dance, the field trip to the pumpkin patch, and Sheri's first coed party. Throughout it all, Julie remained healthy, untouched by the diseases that laid siege to me. *It's not fair,* I wailed. *Why am I always getting sick and you're not?*

My turn will come, she'd said serenely. And I guess it had.

The dialysis center where Julie had committed three mornings a week of her life was a large, low-ceilinged space, shadowy and hushed, despite the rows of people in padded reclining chairs and the machines doing their relentless business. I wondered which chair had been hers, but didn't ask. Someone was surely sitting in it now, since all the chairs were filled. I glanced around and tried to figure it out. Had she been in the middle of a row, able to chat with people in the chairs all around her? Had she sat near the window and asked that the blinds be cracked open so she could see outside? Or had she claimed a corner where she could read in peace?

"Here we go." Martin leaned forward and, with his left hand, dropped two wooden tiles onto the Scrabble board. His right hand lay on the armrest. Two red-filled tubes snaked from the crook in his arm to the boxy machine beside him.

"*QIS?*" I said. "That's not a real word."

Martin raised his white eyebrows. "Sure it is." He held a tissue and from time to time dabbed his nose. He wouldn't let on how much he was grieving, and neither would I. We'd always understood that about each other. Deal, and move on.

"It's *chee*," he said. "Chinese for energy. And because it's a noun, I can put it with that *S*."

"You can't use foreign words."

"It's not foreign. It's the English word for the Chinese word."

"If you say so. I just never thought you'd stoop so low as to cheat."

He swept the tiles from the board. "Then I'll just come up with something else, missy."

I took a sip of tepid coffee poured from the nurses' pot. Two nurses were watching us from their station. I gave a little wave and they instantly got busy. "When did they build this place?"

"Opened six months ago, and not a moment too soon. The drive to Fargo in January was brutal."

His hair was so sparse, I could see right through the pale strands to the pink skin beneath. Age spots mottled his hands. Martin was sixty-six. He looked a hundred. He glanced up from the board and I raised my Styrofoam cup to hide the dismay I feared was written all over my face.

"So, you own your own demolition company."

"We specialize in implosions."

"Speak English, Miss No-Foreign-Words."

Good old Martin. "We collapse structures down on top of themselves, instead of exploding them outward."

"How does a little thing like you do something like that?"

"Doesn't take muscle to wire a building." The muscle came in dealing with the forceful personalities on a demolition site, and that sort of strength had no size limitation.

"You like it?"

"I do." There was a certain magic in the tidiness of it all, a way to restore a natural harmony to the world by clearing out the old to make room for the new. And how do you describe to someone who's never seen it the way the earth shakes when the building tumbles down, as if it were clapping its hands? "You should come to a shoot sometime. You'd love it."

He grunted, and we both knew he never would. "All this time, we thought you were a doctor."

I'd never even made it to college. I'd meant to, but it hadn't seemed important at the time, and now it was too late. But you didn't need a college degree to do implosions, just a steady hand. I nodded toward the board. "You could use that *I*."

"I see it, I see it." He fumbled with the tiles, then dropped a small handful on the board. One by one, he pushed them into place. "*Quit*," he pronounced. "Twenty-six points. Write that down."

"Two more than you would've gotten with that made-up word." Obediently, I jotted down the number. "You're ahead by fifty-two points."

"Yah, but it's not enough, not if you put that *Z* on a triple word score."

How on earth did he know I was holding the *Z*? He gave me a satisfied smirk. I shouldn't have been surprised. He'd always had a sixth sense about this game. How many times had he known exactly what I had and where I was going to place it, well before I'd even figured it out? "You still driving for Gerkey's, Martin?" I asked, though it was hard to believe he'd be on the road, making deliveries.

"Nah. I work security now. It's not so bad being inside all the time. The place is warm, and it always smells good. Even in the dead of winter when nothing's blooming, I'm breathing in laven-

der. Honeysuckle. Pear. I stop right there and suck in a deep lung-
ful of spring." He cleared his throat. "So how come you're spending
time with an old geezer like me, when you could be getting together with your old friends?"

"You *are* my old friend." Martin had been far more than that.
He was the one who'd escorted Julie so proudly down the aisle; he
was the one who'd instructed me on the finer points of driving
stick shift.

"Ha." But he looked pleased. "What do you think about Peyton? First time you've ever met her, right? Now, there's an interesting kid."

"Is she?" I asked. It was important to know. I couldn't figure
her out, this composed, dark-eyed creature who stood back and
just watched. Peyton was the only family I had left. No cousins,
aunts, or uncles, just a father who'd vanished one day, leaving behind a wife and two little daughters. If he'd gone on to start another family with someone else, it didn't matter. They could never
be family to me. There was Frank, of course, but he and I had
never really gotten along. We'd only just pretended to, for Julie's
sake. Now that she was gone, there was nothing holding us together. Nothing but Peyton, who visibly cringed whenever I entered the room. I realized I was clenching the pencil, the wood
biting into my fingers. I relaxed my grip.

"You bet. That kid can kick anyone's butt at Scrabble, including yours truly. You should hear her talk about marine animals.
Why, Brian Gerkey hires her to take care of his big, fancy aquarium when he's out of town. He could bring in someone from Fargo
to do it, a specialist, but he's happy with Peyton. That's how good
she is."

Was she content with that arrangement, taking care of someone else's fish, instead of going out into the world to see them for
herself? There had been no exotic trips in Peyton's world. That
much I knew from the worn rug in my sister's living room and the

chipped dishes in her kitchen cabinets. But surely there had been love.

"I can't believe Brian's taken over the plant," I said.

"He's been voted Businessman of the Year, two years running." He tugged at the sheet pulled to his waist. I'd been careful not to stare, but I hadn't been able to avoid seeing the fat mushy-looking vein swelling out of the crook of his scrawny arm. It looked swollen and tender where the two tubes were taped into place, one drawing the blood out, the other putting it back in. It made me cover my own arm protectively with my hand.

"Yeah? So who was his competition, Mel the Barber?"

He snorted with laughter. "I've missed you, Little Bear."

His old nickname for me. I'd missed him, too. But how could I explain that in turning my back on Black Bear, I had to walk away from him, too? "I'm sorry."

"I can't blame you. You had to get out, start your own life."

"Excuse me, you two." The nurse stood over us. Sue Delinski had been in Julie's high school class. The two of them had been on the basketball team together, Sue playing wing to Julie's point guard. She'd brought over a blender as a wedding gift, just showed up at the door one day with the wrapped and ribboned package, and I'd realized that Julie had had friendships that ran deeper than I knew. Had Julie been the inspiration for Sue going into nursing?

"Sorry to interrupt your game," Sue said, "but it's time to take your blood pressure, Martin."

"No problem," he mumbled.

Sue tapped the Start button and the blood pressure cuff around Martin's arm inflated. "We were all so sorry to hear the news, Dana. Julie was such a dear. How are poor Frank and Peyton holding up?"

"Hanging in there, I guess." Frank wasn't that young man I remembered, the one Julie loved so desperately, the stern, handsome fellow who'd seemed unfailingly solid and capable. Now he walked stiffly and his blond hair had dulled. It was obvious he didn't want me around. He'd said barely two words to me since I arrived. Grief, yes, but there was something else. Something simmering below the surface. With any luck, I'd be gone before it reared up and identified itself. I didn't want to hear what Frank thought of me.

"Such a terrible thing. We all loved Julie. We were praying a transplant would come through in time." Sue kept her gaze fixed on the glowing numbers on the machine, but her disapproval, oily and inevitable, slid toward me. *If only you had come through.*

But I hadn't known. In the end, Julie's life had spun out without me.

Sue scribbled on her clipboard. "It's funny. I'd forgotten how much Julie and you looked alike."

My sister lying so still, her porcelain skin drained of color, her hair chopped short. Her lips parted as though she'd been in midspeech. *I'll be right back,* she seemed to say. *Wait for me.* I'd pressed my cheek against hers, lifted her hand to my lips, but she didn't even smell like Julie. She was hollow, gone.

She must have aged since I'd last seen her, but I couldn't tell. I couldn't reconcile the sight of her in that hospital bed with the young and vibrant mother I'd left standing years before on the sidewalk.

A tear plopped onto my lap and I hastily scrubbed my eyes. But neither Sue nor Martin noticed; they had their gazes trained on the blinking numbers of the blood pressure machine. A beep, and the cuff audibly relaxed its grip around Martin's biceps.

"Your pressure's still too high." Sue frowned as she removed the cuff. "How are you feeling in general?"

"I got no complaints."

Sue shot me a quick glance. *You don't know?* I raised my chin defiantly, and she pressed her lips together.

"You never do." She sighed and patted Martin's shoulder. "It doesn't look like we're going to reach your dry weight today."

"Dr. Gunderson always sets it too high."

Julie had lived her whole life in this town. Had she been happy? "When was Julie diagnosed?" I asked.

"Two years ago, I'd say." Sue made another note on Martin's sheet, and he nodded.

"She didn't even feel that bad at first," he told me. "She was just a little tired. Me, I *itched*." He shrugged. "Nothing to race to the doctor about. That's the way it goes."

Only two years. I thought people could live for decades on dialysis, but what did I know? I'd never known anyone with kidney disease. Now, it seemed, I knew several. "A lot of people around here have kidney disease."

Sue gave me a look that said, *Hello, you're in a dialysis center.* Martin looked interested. "Julie said the same thing."

"I found her notebook." Strange how people could be summoned back to life merely by the sight of how they formed their *T*s.

"That's right," Martin said. "She was tracking the numbers. She thought the numbers were too high. She even wrote the Department of Health."

"Which I can't understand," Sue said. "Julie was a nurse. She knew these things come in cycles. Sometimes we see a rise in miscarriages. Sometimes, heart attacks. You can't blame her, I suppose. She was just trying to make sense of it."

Julie had gone to the trouble to pull medical records. She'd drawn maps, written letters, talked to people. As sick as she was, she'd made it a priority. But Sue had a point. It was probably just the musings of an extremely ill person struggling to make sense of the insensible.

"You really don't think she was onto something?" Martin asked Sue.

"How is that possible? The Department of Health looked into it. If there was something wrong, they'd have found it." She jotted something down on her clipboard. "Half an hour more, and then

I'll unhook you, Martin. Nice to see you again, Dana. I just wish it weren't under these circumstances." She hung up the clipboard and strode over to the next chair in line. "Ready for some ice chips, Beverly?"

I moved the tiles around on the wooden stand. I had some nice letters. The trick was maximizing their point value.

"Stop dillydallying," Martin scolded. "You gonna take your turn or not, 'cause I have a good word waiting."

I had the tiles. I'd been staring at them all along.

"Come on, come on. You don't think I can take it? Bring it on."

I removed five tiles from the wooden stand and arranged them on the board.

POISON

"Huh. Thirty-three points." He pulled over the pad to jot down the number. "Not bad. Never even saw it coming."

SIX

—

[PEYTON]

BELOW THE SUNLIT LAYER LIES THE TWILIGHT ZONE, so deep that only blue light can penetrate. It's really dark there. You'd think the animals that live there would learn to cope without the light, but instead, they rely on it for everything: scaring away predators, luring prey, looking for love, disguising retreat. In some species, it's language. Since there's no light source, the animals make it themselves, and it can be pretty spectacular. Picture a velvety darkness filled with delicate glowing necklaces, blobs of brightness that dart here and there, tiny cascading sparks.

The only people who've ever witnessed this light display are the scientists in submersible boats. As they descend, they watch through their portholes as animals emerge from out of the murk all around them, amid a steady fall of white particles. This is called marine snow and it's the remains of plants and animals from above. It makes the twilight zone look like a night sky sprinkled with stars. Maybe the creatures there look around and, amazed, wonder if they've reached heaven.

. . .

Arnie's Fresh Corn stand was open for business. Too early for corn, but there were fluffy green heaps of lettuces and boxes of bright red strawberries on the wooden table. Her mom would have squealed with delight and braked to a stop. But her dad drove past without even noticing.

"I decided on cherry," he said, "with a blue satin lining. Your mom's favorite color. She'd have liked blue, don't you think?"

It sounded expensive. Her mom would have *hated* it.

"Tomorrow we should go to the florist and pick out flowers. We need something to put on the casket." He swung the steering wheel and drove through the entrance to the nursing home.

"Okay."

"Roses, do you think?"

"Not red ones, Dad."

"I know. Your mom always said they reminded her of craft projects gone bad." When she didn't smile, he probed, awkwardly, "You okay?"

"I guess." Someone had planted yellow petunias by the front door, glowing mounds of color that seemed wrong somehow against the faded brick. A man with a walker stood by the door looking as if he was gathering his energy to burst into a trot.

Silence stretched out, and then her dad said, "Your mom was so proud of you, honey."

She winced at the nakedness of his grief. He never talked to her about feelings. Why couldn't he just go back to talking about that stupid casket?

"She's still here with us, you know. We just can't see her."

Whatever. Peyton hadn't decided about that.

"It'll be all right, honey." Was he talking to himself or to her?

He put a hand on her shoulder and steered her up the wide flat path to the nursing home doors. The place smelled wrong. Bleach, ammonia, cooked food, and old people.

The carpet was the worst of all, a trampled brown stained by things you just knew you didn't want to know about. Whoever had tried to scrub it clean had done a crappy job. Whatever these liquids and solids were had soaked in permanently, as though the residents were trying to stamp their mark on something, anything, before they died.

Her grandma shared a room at the end of the hall with Mrs. Gerkey. The two old ladies got along pretty well, which always surprised Peyton. With everyone else, they were cranky, angry at losing their memories and always complaining that no one wanted them. Today, her grandma sat alone, reading in her chair, Mrs. Gerkey off playing cards or doing chair yoga, probably.

"Mom," her dad began, and Peyton's grandma looked up, her eyes watery behind the thick lenses of her glasses. She held a child's paintbrush, rolling it between her fingers as if wondering what to do with it. They'd taken away her sable brushes after they found her snipping the bristles into stubs. A button pinned to her sweater had a long wire trailing across the room to the bed. That way, if she got up, the nurses would come running. "Karen?" She blinked at Peyton.

Peyton sighed. She was always confusing Peyton with her dad's sister. "Hi, Grandma."

Her grandma lifted her powdery cheek to be kissed. She never used to be touchy-feely. Now she always wanted to be kissed hello and goodbye; she was always snatching at Peyton's arm with greedy soft hands as if searching for something. Peyton stepped over the long cord, kissed her grandmother's cheek, then sat on the folding chair in the corner.

"How are you feeling today, Mom?" Her dad perched on the bed.

"Have you come to take me to supper?"

She thought he was the orderly. "It's a little early for that, Mom."

"It's pot roast today, isn't it?"

"Sounds right," he agreed in a fake cheerful voice.

Actually, it was chicken potpie. The menu was prominently written out in bold black marker on poster board and propped on an easel in the lobby, as if to encourage family members to stay and share. Her dad had never once eaten here. Only Peyton and her mom had, and afterward they'd stay and play pinochle, and her mom would pretend not to notice Peyton's grandma sneaking peeks at the cards.

"Listen, Mom, I have some bad news."

She peered up at him. "No pot roast?"

"It's about Julie, Mom. You remember Julie. My wife."

Her cheeks reddened the way they always did when her memory was challenged and she felt lost. Peyton crossed her arms. Why were they even here?

"She's gone," he said. "Julie's gone, Mom."

All the terms people used. *Gone, passed on, no longer with us.* Why pretend? Her mom was dead. She was turning back to carbon molecules. Period.

Her grandma gripped the arms of her chair. "I *told* her I would never tell." She looked to Peyton. "And I never have, Karen."

God. "That's good, Grandma."

"You tell Julie that. I love that girl."

"She loved you, too, Mom." Her dad straightened. "I guess we'll be pushing off. I'll be by Friday morning to take you to the funeral."

"Not *mine*," she said with alarm.

"No," he said. "Julie's."

"Julie's gone?"

"I told you, Mom. Remember?"

Why did he even bother? It wasn't like she'd get it the fifth or tenth time he said it.

Outside in the hall, Mr. G was pushing his mother in her wheelchair toward them. He saw them, and his face saddened. "Frank. Peyton."

"Hello!" Mrs. Gerkey was wearing a pantsuit so pink it made Peyton's head hurt.

"I was going to stop by later," Mr. G told her dad. "See if you needed anything."

Like what? What could he possibly give them that would help? All these meaningless offers, when all the while, people really just wanted to get away. Look at the nurses at the hospital last night, the way they'd fluttered around, then disappeared. But Mr. G didn't mean it like that. He was a pretty nice guy, and she had a hard time believing all the rumors of him being such a major druggie in high school were true.

"What's the matter?" Mrs. Gerkey demanded in her quavering voice. "What's going on?"

Mr. G told her, "Julie passed away yesterday," and she frowned, slumped in her wheelchair, probably puzzling through who Julie was and whether or not this affected her. "Oh. Julie. Miriam's daughter-in-law. Have you told Miriam?"

Yes, they'd told Miriam, and probably would have to keep telling her until her hearing conked out entirely, and then they'd have to start writing it.

"Don't worry about missing work, Frank," Mr. G said. "Take off as long as you want."

"I'll be in Saturday. We got to get that third line up and running."

He'd been excited, washing his hands at the sink after work and telling them all about the catalogue descriptions, the choices between this system and that. Her mom had laughed and teased him about being a kid with a fancy new toy.

"Me, too," Peyton said. "I'll be there Saturday."

The two men looked surprised. "You sure, honey?" her dad asked, and she shrugged.

She hadn't known until that very moment, and once the words spilled out, they made perfect sense. What else was she going to do? She'd be going back to school on Monday, too. The sooner she got back to her pretend life, the sooner she could pretend she had one.

They didn't go straight home. Her dad switched off the ignition and cleared his throat. "I'll be right back."

She refused to look at him, and after a moment, he sighed and climbed out of the truck.

The engine ticked. The neon sign glowed, red and inviting. *Lakeside Liquors*, OPEN. She sank in her seat, chewing her thumbnail. Someone walked by; cigarette smoke drifted in. Country music played from a car radio. What if she slid out of her seat and over behind the steering wheel, turned the key, pressed the accelerator, and caught the highway as it soared out of town, following it all the way to the end? Isn't that what Dana had done? She'd hated Black Bear, too.

The truck door opened, and her dad got in, leaning around Peyton to set a bulky paper bag behind her seat. "Want to stop for takeout?"

They never did takeout. Her mom worried about the money, and her dad worried there wouldn't be anything her mom could eat. "Maybe later."

"Yeah. You're right." He put the truck in gear. "Why don't we go home and regroup? Plenty of time to figure out supper later."

She hadn't eaten breakfast or lunch and it was going on five o'clock. Her stomach traitorously rumbled and her head throbbed. Though it was only a few minutes, it seemed like hours before her dad slowed to take the turn into their driveway. Her aunt's black SUV sat snug along the curb. Peyton bet it was clean inside, the dashboard polished and gleaming, the interior smelling richly of leather the way Mr. Gerkey's car did.

A hulking figure paced the porch. LT Stahlberg. *God*. Why

wouldn't he leave her alone? He came to the railing to peer at them as they turned in to the driveway. "Why doesn't he go creep on his own mom?"

Her dad grunted. "I'll deal with LT. Go around through the back door."

Dana was in the kitchen, wedging something into the refrigerator. Covered dishes sat all around her, taking up all the space on the counters and the kitchen table. She straightened as Peyton came in. "Hey."

"Hey." Peyton opened the cabinet and took out a glass.

"How was the nursing home?" Dana pushed the refrigerator door closed and it instantly sprang back open.

What was she supposed to say to that? *Horrible, as usual?* "Fine."

"The phone's been ringing." Dana crouched and reached into the refrigerator to move around a few things. "I let the answering machine pick up."

"Okay." It didn't matter to Peyton. Anyone who wanted to reach her would call her on her cell.

"I hope you like Tater Tot hotdish, because we've got three of them. I'd forgotten it was the signature casserole of the North Woods."

Peyton held her glass under the faucet. Her mom could never drink water whenever she wanted to. Peyton would sneak into the kitchen when her mom wasn't around and drink glass after glass, as if she were quenching the thirst for two people.

Her dad was taking a long time. Maybe LT wouldn't leave. Maybe he thought he could camp out on their front porch all night, until Peyton's mom reappeared or the aliens beamed him away. They should just call Mrs. Stahlberg and make her deal with him, but that usually made things worse. LT refused to talk to his mom. He said she was possessed.

"It's a lot of food." Dana put her hands on her hips. "I don't know what we're going to do with all of it."

"Mrs. Stahlberg could take some. She's got a freezer." Peyton refilled the glass.

"Oh. Good idea. How is Irene these days?"

Her mom never called her Irene in front of Peyton. She was always careful to say "Mrs. Stahlberg." Peyton shrugged. Mrs. Stahlberg was Mrs. Stahlberg.

Dana sighed with just a hint of annoyance.

Good.

"Where's your dad? I thought he was coming in."

"He's talking to LT." Someone had brought pie. Peyton lifted up the foil and saw dark juice staining the crimped pastry. Blueberry. Her favorite.

"LT Stahlberg? Wow. I haven't thought of him in ages. Anyone ever figure out what was wrong with him?"

"He's schizophrenic." LT was confusing. Sometimes he acted so dumb, like he was retarded or something. But other times, he totally got things. Look how he'd managed to set the hardware store on fire, right in the middle of the day, without anyone seeing him. Peyton's mom was always telling her not to underestimate LT. She said that his medications made him seem slower than he really was.

"Oh. I guess that explains a few things. How sad."

What was sad about it? It was just the way LT was. It wasn't like LT knew any different. It wasn't like he *cared.*

The screen door banged, and her dad came in, gripping the paper bag.

"Want some pie, Dad?" Peyton held a knife poised over the pie plate.

"Sure."

"Aunt Dana?"

"Maybe later, thank you. And call me Dana."

Yeah, that sounded better. She couldn't think of her as an aunt. "What did LT want, Dad?"

"Oh, he just needed to talk. Don't worry. He won't be back."

He was lying, telling her the safe thing, the reassuring thing. They both knew LT had a way of doing the unexpected.

The doorbell rang. LT again? But he didn't use doorbells. He said the electricity messed him up. When he came by to see her mom, he always banged on the door with both fists, not stopping until someone finally answered.

"I'll get it," her dad said. But when he returned, he had Mr. Connolly with him.

It was weird seeing her teacher in her house. He held a manila folder and some books.

"Joe," Dana said, her voice warm.

So she knew Mr. Connolly. From the way she was looking at him, Peyton guessed she'd once known him very well. And Mr. Connolly was looking back at Dana in the same way.

"How you holding up?" he said.

Peyton couldn't tell if he was asking her dad or Dana. Neither answered.

"Beer?" Her dad sounded terse, which surprised her. Peyton thought he liked Mr. Connolly.

"Sounds good," Mr. Connolly replied. "Thanks."

Her dad held out a can. "Dana?" he said, and she shook her head.

Mr. Connolly took the beer. "I'm sorry about your mom, Peyton."

"Thanks," she mumbled. Which was stupid. Thanks for being sorry, thanks for saying so? She handed her dad his piece of pie, licking the blueberry juice that had oozed out onto her finger.

"Thanks, princess." He balanced the plate in one hand and gripped a beer can in the other. He looked from one to the other. Then he set down the pie and lifted the can to his lips.

Peyton frowned hard at her own plate.

"I brought over your homework assignments for the week, Peyton, but of course you don't need to worry about them right now. Mrs. Milchman sent home a copy of *To Kill a Mockingbird.*"

"Great," Peyton said. She'd get right on reading that. He didn't catch her tone. He may have been talking to her, but he was watching Dana. It was as though a bubble encased the two of them, leaving Peyton and her dad on the outside. Peyton yanked out a chair with a loud, forceful clatter, and both Dana and Mr. Connolly glanced over.

He cleared his throat. "So the service is Friday?"

"One o'clock," her dad said.

"I'll make sure the principal knows. He's planning an early dismissal so everyone can attend."

"Appreciate that."

How dumb was that, everyone making such a big deal? The kids would all be excited about missing school, but they'd try to hide it. Peyton was glad she wouldn't be around to see any of their fake sadness in the days leading up to the funeral. By Friday, though, chances were good that everyone would have moved on to the next exciting topic. *Were Brenna and Adam doing it? Was that gross thing on Mrs. Olafson's nose cancer, or just a disgusting wart?*

"I'd better head out. I just wanted to come by and pay my respects." Mr. Connolly shook her dad's hand, nodded at her and Dana, and left, quietly closing the door behind him.

Her dad took a long swallow. "Couldn't wait, could you?"

Dana was folding up the paper bag. She turned. "Wait for what?"

"Back in town one day."

"Oh, come off it, Frank. He came by to bring Peyton her homework."

"Yeah. That's pretty convenient." He reached around to pull another can out of the cardboard case. Her mom wouldn't have liked that, her dad drinking two beers in a row, but she was gone. The rules didn't apply anymore.

"Dad, he's my teacher," Peyton protested.

But he didn't even look at her. "We don't hear from you for

years. Then, bam! You're back. Who called you? What the hell do you want?"

"To bury my sister."

The words were flat and ugly. Peyton set down her fork and swallowed hard. She *hated* Dana.

"That's it?" her dad jeered. "You don't want a nice keepsake?" His gaze roved the room and came to rest on the hutch. "How about her plates?"

Her mom's pretty blue wooden plates, lined up behind the glass. Every Christmas, her dad got her mom another one.

"Stop it, Frank—"

"How about this?" He grabbed the old pottery pitcher from the shelf, with its cream-colored finish and handle that curved like an ocean wave, the crack running up one side. "It's damaged, though. Probably couldn't get much for it."

Her dad was using his sarcastic voice, the one that could melt metal. Peyton hadn't heard it since she was little, but now it came rushing back. Her dad snapping at her for dawdling as she fumbled with her shoelaces. Her dad telling her mom the chicken was dry. Or even worse, her dad going silent and freezing out her and her mother as if they didn't even exist.

"What is your problem?" Dana asked.

He smacked the pitcher onto the counter and the crack raced up to the lip. Peyton flinched. Her mom had *loved* that thing. They'd found it together at the flea market.

"*You're* the problem. Julie took care of you. She did everything for you."

"You can't blame me for this." Dana's voice trembled.

"If you'd been here—"

"I *would* have been here. I'm here now, aren't I? But you didn't call me!"

"Julie wouldn't let me. She didn't want anything to do with you."

"I don't believe you."

"Believe what you want. Whatever it was that you did—"

"I didn't do anything! I loved her! She was my *sister*."

He snorted. "You have a funny way of showing sisterly love."

"You don't know anything. We got along great until you came along. Julie—"

"Sure. Julie was real happy, working all day, going to school at night, and trying to keep you out of trouble. Did you really think she was going to spend her life taking care of you?"

"And what life did *you* give her? She never saw anything of this world. You kept her trapped in this dead-end town!"

Dana didn't know anything. Her mom had *loved* Black Bear. She said she never wanted to live anywhere else.

"Julie was happy here."

"Julie was *loyal*."

"What does that mean?"

"She would have done anything to make you happy. She would have done anything to make you think she was happy, too."

Her mom *had* been happy. She said that having Peyton filled her life with joy. Peyton wanted to clap her hands across her aunt's mouth, and make her *shut up*.

"It kills you to know that Julie was okay without you."

"Sure," Dana shot back, mocking. "She did just *great* without me. How many experts did you consult, Frank? Did you even think about taking her down to the Mayo?"

Her father went still, all the air sucked out of the room. Dana wasn't saying this was her dad's fault, was she?

When her father spoke at last, it was in a low, quiet voice that sent a shiver down Peyton's spine. "We haven't seen or heard from you in years. You never even came home when your niece was born. But here you are, acting the devoted sister. You can try and fool the rest of the town, but you can't fool me."

"You're the fool, Frank. You don't know me, and you didn't know everything about Julie, either." Dana's face was white.

What did *that* mean? Peyton shoved back her chair. "Stop it! It was *me*, all right? *I* called Dana."

They stared at her.

"I thought she could help," she persisted, hating them both. "How screwed up was *that*?"

"Peyton, I just—" Her dad reached out.

"Don't touch me!"

Peyton whirled and ran down the hall. Slamming her door, she threw herself onto her bed and grabbed her iPod. Nothing was what it seemed. People could be related to you and be nothing like family. People could die and leave huge gaping holes. What rushed in to fill them was scary and wrong. She squeezed her eyes shut to let the music sweep her away.

. . . you didn't know everything about Julie.

Dana was the one who didn't know everything about Peyton's mom. She hadn't been around for Peyton's whole life, so why would she even say something like that?

Did you even think about taking her down to the Mayo?

Peyton couldn't remember if her parents had ever discussed going to the Mayo Clinic. Would it have made a difference? They had lots of doctors in Black Bear, a whole clinic full of them, and Peyton's mom went to them all the time. But still a tiny worm of doubt wriggled in, flaring briefly in the blackness before disappearing from view.

Maybe it *was* her dad's fault.

SEVEN

[DANA]

STREETLIGHTS THREW JULIE'S FACE INTO SHARP RE-lief as our small car hurtled through the night. She gave me a worried glance. *I should've known something was wrong. I'm in nursing school, damn it.*

That scared me. Julie never swore. *Is it because it's too early?* I grabbed the armrest as another wave of pain swept up my legs to my belly.

It'll be okay.

She was just saying that. She didn't know.

We sailed over the train tracks, and I gasped. *Julie, slow down!*

Sorry.

The emergency room doors swept open.

"Name, honey?" the admitting nurse said, peering over the half-moons of her glasses. The creases on her face showed what she was thinking: *Aren't you too young to be having a baby?* Of course I was.

"Julie Kelleher," I lied.

Julie fished in her purse and pulled out the ID and insurance card. The nurse examined the tiny photo, looked at both of us, then pushed back her chair. "Let me make a copy of this. I'll be right back."

Julie and I looked at each other, stunned. It had worked.

The urgent cooing of a dove woke me. Rolling over, I picked up my cellphone and glanced at the display. Seven. Halim would have been on the jobsite for over an hour by now, so why hadn't he called with an update? He knew I'd be worried. Was he simply busy with the usual post-blast cleanup, or had he gotten into worse trouble? Had I? I wanted to trust him, this smart, older man who'd become my mentor, despite our many differences. I wanted to feel that we were in this terrible situation together, standing on the same side of the fence. But I couldn't push away the memory of the calculation in his eyes as he stood over the dead woman. After all, a man who'd clean out a business account without his partner's knowing was not someone to count on.

The house was gentle with pearly dawn light as I made my way down the hall. My favorite time of day, everything peaceful and new, with just the soft gurgle of the coffeemaker to keep me company. A fresh start, all the previous day's mistakes erased. Beer cans rattled as I pulled the bin from beneath the kitchen sink. Six, seven empties? Frank would need more than a new morning to erase last night's mistakes. I dropped the old, used coffee filter into the bin and shoved it back into place. Who was I kidding? I'd made my own share of mistakes, too, letting Frank goad me into a fight right in front of Peyton. But emotion had swelled up from nowhere, and in an instant, I'd blazed up into that bitter, angry girl I'd once been, and had almost undone everything I had struggled so hard to make.

Then Peyton had run out of the room, leaving us standing there glaring at each other, before Frank finally wheeled around to watch TV in the living room, and I pulled out a bucket and tin of cleanser to scrub the kitchen like some madwoman. What he had insinuated about Joe was ridiculous. Insulting. If I was so intent upon rekindling a high school romance, I wouldn't have waited until now to do so.

I filled a cup before the coffee finished brewing, and stepped outside into the morning's dewy embrace.

Someone had built a rock garden. Our mother had had one, and Julie had always wanted one, so I supposed it was hers. Back home in Baltimore, spring was in full bloom, the rich vibrant colors of azaleas, lilies, marigolds, and peonies bursting across lawn after lawn. Here, the season was just getting under way. Smooth gray stones peeked out beneath a mat of leggy clover and dandelions. Furled violets waited for the sun to rise so they could turn and open their faces. A cement fountain, green with moss. Along the back fence, daffodils bloomed, cheek to cheek with straggly weeds that would send Martin into fits if he saw them. Near them stood a plastic playhouse, faded pink and blue. Peyton would surely have crawled inside it to have tea parties with her teddy bear. No, scratch that. Peyton didn't seem the sort to wear dresses and talk in baby lisps to a stuffed animal. More likely, she'd made it into a fort and plotted war games.

"Good morning, Dana." A short, square woman stood on the stoop next door.

I stared in disbelief. Irene Stahlberg lived next door?

Red-cheeked, black hair scraped tightly back from her plain features, Irene looked exactly as she had when Julie and I were growing up, even down to the floral housedress and the gold-wire eyeglasses perched on her pointy nose. She marched across the grass between the two houses, a bundle of flowers in one hand. "I have to say I'm surprised to see you, even given the circumstances. We all figured you were gone for good."

Irene had always been the sort to cut right to it. She didn't throw her arms open for a hug. No false show of affection for her. In that one way, at least, we could agree.

"Figured you had enough food." Irene thrust the flowers at me. Old-fashioned pink roses. "Julie's favorite," she said, gruffly. "First of the season."

The Julie I had known had loved tulips with their jewel tones and curved shapes, but I could understand the appeal of these flowers with their tightly clustered petals and heavenly aroma. "They're beautiful, Irene. Thank you. Would you like some coffee? Everyone's still asleep, but . . ."

"Maybe just half a cup. Before I head in to work."

Reluctantly, I held open the screen door. Couldn't she tell my offer had been purely polite, without a tinge of genuine welcome? I'd been enjoying the solitude, the first few moments of peace I'd had in weeks. But this was Julie's house; my sister would have wanted me to invite her neighbor in for coffee. "Are you still at the high school?" I asked, quietly shutting the door behind us.

"You betcha." Irene pulled out the coffeepot. "Administrative assistant to the principal."

Her pride was unmistakable, her voice loud and carrying. I wished she'd lower it. I'd only had half a cup of coffee, nowhere near the amount I needed to withstand the day. And I certainly wasn't ready to withstand another confrontation with Frank. "Congratulations."

Irene ignored me. She was staring into the refrigerator. "My heavens."

"Take some of it. Please. Everyone's been so generous—"

"Better not. You'll need it for the funeral. Though I imagine people will be bringing more by for that."

I'd forgotten that after our mother died, Julie and I had been deluged with wild rice soup and macaroni and ham hotdishes. I hadn't eaten ham since.

She withdrew the creamer and added a dollop to her cup. "Is it true what I hear? That you're not a medical doctor?"

She had me trapped in amber, the girl she'd once known, with a girl's impossible dreams. "Guess I'm too squeamish."

Irene eyed me. "Too restless, I'd say." She settled herself at the kitchen table. "The vases are beneath the sink."

Sure enough, there they were, pushed alongside the box of dishwasher soap and spray bottles of cleaners.

"I'm glad to have a moment alone with you, Dana. I wanted to see how Peyton is doing."

I thought back to the night before, and the shuddering slam of the bedroom door that had silenced and shamed both Frank and me. "I think she's all right."

"I'm worried about her. The shock of it all. We really expected Julie to pull through this infection. There was just no warning. One day she was making plans to come home and the next day, I get a call from the hospital." Irene pressed her lips together and stared into her cup.

I was moved. She had *loved* my sister. I'd been overly harsh, overly judgmental.

Irene cleared her throat. "Peyton's such a quiet girl. Is she talking to you? Has she said anything?"

I shook my head.

"Ah, that's just too darned bad. I was hoping. . . . After all, she's not the most popular girl. She doesn't cheerlead and she's not on any teams."

"Cheerleading's not the only way to make friends."

Irene hiked an eyebrow. Perhaps I *had* sounded defensive.

"She seems perfectly normal to me," I said, amending.

"She's a very serious girl. And she's got peculiar interests. The coral reefs, global warming, the energy crisis. The only thing she wanted for Christmas was a subscription to *Science* magazine."

"Being serious isn't such a terrible thing. At least she's involved in the world around her." At Peyton's age, I'd been interested in one thing, and one thing only. *Joe.* I set the vase on the kitchen table.

"Yes, well, you're not a teenager."

I looked up. "She's not being bullied, is she?"

"No, not that I know of. She does spend time with Eric Hofseth."

"Hofseth. That name sounds familiar."

"Sure. You remember them. They moved to town back when you were in high school. Nice family. Mitch works at the plant. Anna runs the church daycare. Eric's their middle child."

And he was Peyton's friend. Her only friend, or her boyfriend? I decided I wanted to meet him. "How's Walter?" An affable old guy who let his wife do all the talking and socializing. He'd had a thing for fixing bikes. There was always one in disrepair leaning against their porch or lying on their driveway, even in the winter with the snow heaped all around it.

She flapped a hand. "Driving me crazy, as usual. He retired a couple years back, decided to take up golf, a fool sport if you ask me. Ronni and Sam got married. Maybe you remember him. Any day now we're hoping to hear she's expecting."

"That's nice. I know she always wanted to have a family." Every time I babysat, Ronni insisted we play house. I'd be the dad; she'd be the mom, and her Barbie dolls would form a weird ring of children that constantly clamored for her attention by sprawling their long legs or bashing at one another with their stiff arms. The only way I could get any peace was to bribe her with *Saturday Night Live* and popcorn.

"I imagine you've heard about LT's troubles?"

I had to give Irene credit. She was as direct talking about her own problems as she was delving into other people's. "A little."

"I keep waiting and hoping for him to get better, but of course that's not going to happen. You don't see it when they're growing up. You think everything's going to be fine." She shook her head and held her cup to her lips, stained with a pale pink lipstick too youthful for her weary face. "He lives in a group home now, with a supervisor, but I still worry."

"I'm so sorry, Irene."

"It is what it is. So tell me: How long can you stay?"

"I'm leaving right after the funeral."

"But you'll be back."

Her expectation was plain: now that I had come back, I should come back regularly. "Sure." Even I heard the insincerity in my voice.

"Dana. That little girl needs you."

How could Peyton need someone she didn't even know? And since when did Irene think I was someone worth needing? "She has Frank."

Irene leaned forward, lowered her voice conspiratorially. "Maybe you haven't heard, you've been gone so long, but Frank has had a few *problems*." She jerked her chin toward the counter where the cardboard case out on its side. "Tell me that isn't his."

"What are you saying?"

"He swore off the stuff, you know. Promised Julie he'd stay sober. Went to AA for years. But just the other night, Walter saw him in a bar, and he wasn't drinking pop."

"How long has this been a problem?" Why had Julie put up with it for even one minute? But even as I asked myself that, I knew the answer. Julie would have put up with anything to keep Frank from leaving. Damn our father.

"Since he came back from the Middle East. A friend died in his arms. He doesn't talk about it."

How horrible. I'd had no idea. But now he was drinking again. I felt the first stirring of doubt.

"I hope you'll change your mind about staying." Irene levered herself up. "Someone needs to keep an eye on things here. And who knows? You might find that Black Bear isn't such a terrible place to live after all."

Ha. The chances of that were the same as a snowflake in a furnace. I watched Irene make her way across the thin grass, certainty in her gait. She'd delivered her message and expected it to be heeded. But I'd had good reason to leave town, and that reason hadn't changed.

. . .

A man strode into the hospital room. Tired green scrubs, receding hairline, tanned features. *Hello there,* he said. *I'm Dr. Swenson.*

I'd never seen him before in my life.

The nurse moved aside. *I'm concerned about the baby's heartbeat.*

What did that mean? I tried to push myself up onto my elbows, but another wave rolled up my body and pressed me against the pillow. Julie wasn't looking at me. She was frowning at the monitor.

The doctor seated himself behind my bent knees and disappeared from view. *How far along are you?*

She's thirty-seven weeks, Julie told him.

Hmm, he said.

What did that mean? That didn't mean *anything.*

Julie was there, her hand on my shoulder. *It's okay.*

But it wasn't okay. I could see it on her face. *I want Mom,* I whimpered.

I know, sweetie.

The labor nurse stood. *Time to push.*

Pain squeezed, left me floppy. *I can't.*

Honey, the nurse scolded, *the only way this baby's coming out is if you push.*

Julie gripped my hand. *We'll count.*

Counting didn't work. The ceiling tiles swam above me. I rose toward them.

Dana? Julie's voice came from far away.

I looked for her, found her watching me.

One, two, three—

The number climbed. I grunted and bore down.

That's it, the doctor said.

The nurse whisked a paper sheet over my chest as the doctor lifted the baby out and up. *Congratulations,* I heard him say. *You have a daughter.*

A daughter who was now sleeping in her bedroom down the hall, thirty feet away.

For sixteen years, I'd dreamed about her, wondered. I'd moved as far away from her as I could to keep myself from rushing to take her back. How many times had I picked up the phone to call Julie, only to set it back down? Now, of course, it was too late. Julie was dead. Peyton had grown up as someone else's daughter.

Turning, I found Frank standing behind me.

EIGHT

[PEYTON]

THE ABYSS LIES MILES BELOW THE OCEAN SURFACE.
No sunlight penetrates. Temperatures hover just above freezing. The pressure's profound. A person would be crushed to death long before they even reached this hidden zone.

Interesting things happen to creatures that live here. They either go miniature or they get gigantic. No one's sure why. Shrimp can be a quarter inch or a foot long; a squid that's an inch in the upper part of the ocean will be forty feet long in the abyss. They have flexible skeletons or jelly bodies, reproduce at a slow rate, and may or may not have eyes. But the most intriguing quality of all is how they can go long periods of time without food or company.

It's got to be lonely down there in the deepest part of the world, but they don't mind. They don't know any different.

Voices dragged her up through the layers of sleep, punched through the thin walls of her bedroom to where Peyton lay with her covers mounded around her. Sharp and angry, her dad and Dana going at it again in the kitchen.

". . . drinking again," Dana was saying.

"None of your business."

Peyton halted in the hallway, her sweater half pulled on. Chances were, her dad would think it wasn't her business, either.

"Irene said you'd been in AA. Maybe you should go to a meeting today."

Was the whole town talking about her dad's drinking? Peyton stalked into the kitchen. Her dad stood by the coffeemaker, Dana by the window. It was as though they hadn't moved from the night before, as if they'd battled all night long. The room felt stale from their fighting.

"Don't you guys ever give it a rest?" Stomping over to the refrigerator, she pulled it open and pretended to be interested in its contents. Her stomach flipped at the sight of milk, cheese, bottles of ketchup and salad dressing, endless containers of crazy sorry-your-mom-is-dead food. She waited for her dad to say something, but it was Dana who spoke.

"I'm going for a walk."

The room felt better after she left, familiar again. Peyton let the refrigerator door wheeze closed. Her dad hadn't shaved. His face was puffy and his shoulders slumped. "She's right, Dad. You used to go to meetings all the time." He'd always come back quiet and withdrawn.

"I will." He sounded like he was trying to convince himself.

He certainly didn't convince her. "It's been months, Dad."

"I *said* I would." The newspaper snapped open.

Fine. She grabbed a box of crackers from the pantry. Cheddar goldfish, the kind her mom used to get when Peyton was a kid. Dana must've picked it up. She'd probably scanned the grocery store shelves and thought they looked like something Peyton would eat. She tore open the package, aware of her dad rustling the paper behind her.

"Two days," she said.

"What's that?"

She nodded at the half-empty case of beer cans beside the sink. It would never have dared make an appearance while her mom was alive, and Peyton had even gone with her dad to get it. It felt like the unraveling of something, and both she and her dad were taking turns picking it apart. "We can't even get through two days without Mom."

Carrying a handful of crackers, she went to her room, sat cross-legged on her unmade bed, and reached for her cellphone.

Fingernails scratched against the mesh screen. Peyton rolled over on her bed and peeped through the blinds. Eric stood on the other side of the window.

She met him at the back door. "It's okay. No one's home." Dana was still on her walk, and her dad was out buying the wrong flowers for the funeral. She knew better than to hope he'd found an AA meeting. Not that her dad would care that Eric was over. In his present state of mind, he wouldn't notice that Eric was playing hooky. "Let's sit out here."

She pulled over one of the plastic lawn chairs and propped her bare feet up on the railing.

"Sorry I took so long. I would've got here sooner, but Connolly caught me."

"Ugh. Don't talk about him." The sun warmed her legs and the top of her head, fell along her arms like a golden cloak, wreathing her in light, and keeping the darkness climbing the walls of her house inside, where it belonged.

"I thought you liked Connolly."

His arm rested on the armrest beside hers, the muscles in his forearm thick, leading to the tender curve of the inside of his elbow, up to the point where the biceps bunched. She could remember when his arm was thin and hairless and looked exactly like her arm. Now it was like they were two different species. "He and Dana were drooling all over each other last night."

"Yeah?"

"My dad was so pissed off."

"How come?"

"I don't know. They got into a huge fight. It was crazy."

A little brown bird hopped hopefully along the rim of the old birdbath. He shook himself, then flew away.

"What's she like?"

"Dana? It's weird. She's always staring at me. And she stays up all night. Her light's always on." She didn't know why that bothered her so much.

The corner of his mouth crooked. She knew what he was thinking: that in order for her to have known that, she had to have been up, too. Whatever. "My aunt Karen's coming for the funeral."

"The one in California?"

Like she had a million aunts. Until Dana arrived, Peyton had just had the one. Her aunt Karen was sweet and nice and uncomplicated. She spoke softly and always made Peyton's mom laugh and Peyton's dad relax. Even so, it was going to be awful having her there. She'd only make Peyton realize just how small her family had become. "She's bringing my little cousins." Two boys who yelled and fought over everything, two people Peyton couldn't believe were actually related to her. Her uncle wasn't coming; he was too busy doing lawyer stuff. So this was it, a couple of people, gathering around for the tragedy.

When Eric's family got together, there were so many people, they spilled out of the house and onto the driveway and yard, laughing and bragging about the huge muskies they'd caught.

"What about your grandpa?"

She gave him a sidelong look. Eric wasn't talking about the dead one; he was talking about the one who'd left when her mom was just a kid. When Eric and she were little, they used to pretend that this grandpa she'd never known would reappear with pirate treasure or secret potions; they used to pretend he'd bring Dana along, too, a sort of princess who needed their help to save her.

Now that Peyton had actually met Dana, she knew with a certainty her grandpa would be a big disappointment, too. "Right."

She wriggled her toes and studied the play of nail polish colors. Just a few days ago, she had daubed on one of each shade she had, pink and red and blue and orange. "My dad's drinking again."

Eric didn't even look at her, which was right, which was good, but his fingers curled along the plastic arm of the chair. "Sucks."

"He started a few weeks ago. Right before Mom went back into the hospital."

Mom. Say it once, say it twice, maybe make her come alive even for the space of a moment.

"How bad is it?"

Wasn't even one drink bad news for a drinker? If he had two beers, did that make it twice as bad? If he had three, three times? Where was the line that separated okay from not okay? Her dad was climbing up a steep rocky slope, and once he reached the top, no one could stop him from falling down the other side. Which would leave Peyton even more alone. "He had a couple of beers last night." A lie. He'd had at least a six-pack. She'd known kids to get trashed on less.

"Just beer?"

Eric knew it had once been whiskey, too. He even knew when Peyton's dad moved out for a little while. "I ever tell you I found one of his empties hidden in my playhouse? I told my mom and that's when she kicked him out. I guess I figured that made it my fault."

He ran a finger along her arm. "Just because he drinks doesn't mean you will."

She got her gold hair from her mom, her height from her dad. Who was to say she hadn't inherited his trouble with booze and would die just like her mom did, way too young in a hospital room?

He fit his fingers between hers. "I don't have to go back to class."

"Aren't you supposed to be doing a presentation?"

"Whatever."

She closed her eyes and put her head back. The wind rustled the spring leaves. Bees buzzed. Her mom's funeral was tomorrow. Miss Lainie's had only been last week. A dark and terrible thought pushed in, something her mom always said, and it wouldn't go away.

Things come in threes.

NINE

———

[DANA]

J ULIE'S WEDDING WAS SIMPLE, JUST THE TWO OF
them, Frank's parents, his sister, Karen, and her new husband, and me. Julie stood at the altar in our mom's white dress,
nipped in at the waist to fit, her borrowed veil lacy about her
shoulders, and beamed up at Frank. The minister had to repeat
himself, she was so lost in joy. It made us laugh, even me, standing there in my ugly bridesmaid's dress. Frank's mother had insisted I wear one and had sewn it for me herself. *No reason to take
shortcuts*, she'd said, presenting me with the stiff taffeta thing.
Yellow. The one color in the entire rainbow guaranteed to make
me look like a plague victim.

I spent the weekend at my best friend Sheri's house so that
Julie and Frank could have the house to themselves. The minute
Sheri's parents went to bed, we sneaked off to Gerkey's, where the
usual Saturday party was in full swing. I had kicked off my shoes
and sunk onto the sofa in the employee break room, the skirt of
that hideous dress billowing up all around me.

Nice dress, Joe had said, putting his arm around me. And

Brian had leaned over with a can of beer. *Wanna celebrate?* I don't know who was more surprised, Brian or me, when I accepted.

So Frank had a problem with alcohol. Well, I couldn't fix it, no matter how emphatically Irene played the guilt card. I was the last person Frank would listen to, and I didn't even want to try. But I knew what Julie would have wanted. Julie would have been certain. *Help Peyton.*

Yes, my sister would have put that right into my hands and closed my fingers tightly around it. But just because I gave birth didn't make me a mother. It didn't make me magical or knowing or somehow specially connected to the baby I'd given up back when I was still a girl. I'd missed out on all those things that shaped a person into a mother. I didn't know when Peyton started to walk or lost her first tooth or had her first crush. I didn't know if she had allergies. I only knew that she came out squalling and silenced the moment the nurse set her in my arms. I only knew that she had soft downy hair and a way of turning down her tiny mouth as she slept, as though she was seeing something terrible coming her way.

The lake shimmered in the distance, bright with early morning sunshine, hopeful. A school bus lumbered across an intersection. Peyton's bus, or did she walk to school? People headed into the Catholic church for mass, and an orange tabby slunk past on the opposite sidewalk before disappearing into some bushes.

Someone stood in my old front yard, a man reaching up to unhook the bird feeder dangling from the lowest branch of the big locust tree. The memory whooshed back with force. My father had stood by that very same tree to tap a bag of birdseed into a glass tube. The image changed. Not my father in his brown suit, but a stranger in baggy jeans and a T-shirt. He was waving at me in a friendly way. How had that memory surfaced? I thought I'd buried them all long ago.

People sprawled on beach towels scattered across the sand. A mother and her child hesitated at the water's edge, holding hands. The lifeguard stand was empty; boats tied to the dock bobbed in the wake of a passing motorboat.

The sun was beating down and already I could feel the skin on my cheeks tighten, signaling the beginning of a sunburn. I pulled out a tube of sunscreen from my purse and squeezed some across my fingertips.

I'd returned to Black Bear ten years before, a sudden impulse to reunite with Julie and my daughter. I'd had a job interview in the Twin Cities—something that hadn't panned out—and I had found myself driving the rental car north instead of heading east to the airport. As I drove, I thought of all the times I'd dialed Julie's phone number, only to disconnect before the call went through. Six years had passed by then; I was a brash twenty-three, and I thought I could face my past and the choices I had made.

As I neared town, I pictured knocking on Julie's door and hearing her footsteps approach from the other side. She'd swing open the door and be astonished to see me. My small daughter would appear behind her and shyly ask who I was. I imagined the girl, the shape of her face and the color of her hair, the smell of supper cooking on the stove, Frank's voice as he called from another room, asking who was at the door, and I found my palms sweating on the steering wheel. My heart pounded so hard I couldn't hear the car radio. The blaring of a car horn made me realize I'd veered into oncoming traffic and I swerved back into my lane as the other car shot past, the driver looking over with wide-eyed fear. I pulled onto the verge and sat there, trying to push away the rising panic.

Maybe motherhood had changed Julie, turning her into someone I wouldn't know. Maybe she was glad I was gone, and that the very last person she wanted to see standing on her doorstep was me. Maybe the reason I hadn't heard from her was because she was terrified that any contact between us would shake down the house of cards we'd so carefully constructed.

I should call. I'd know just by hearing her voice whether or not she wanted me back in her life. But I found myself crying, sitting in that small car on the side of the road, my cheeks slick with hot tears. I couldn't bear to find out that Julie didn't love me anymore. I couldn't. So I turned my car around and drove back to the airport to reschedule the flight I had missed.

I told myself I would try again after I'd gotten a good job and had settled myself, when I was strong enough to withstand the possibility that Julie wouldn't want me back in her life. I kept telling myself that, but I should have known that that time would never come.

My cellphone bleated. I glanced at the display. *Finally.* "Halim!"

"Dana." His voice was liquid with concern. "How is your sister?"

Across the lake, the Ferris wheel rotated lazily. The buzz of the motorboat faded into the distance. "I was too late."

"Ah." A pause, and then he said, "I'm sorry."

"The funeral's tomorrow. I'll head back to Chicago Saturday."

"Yes, of course. I'll still be here."

Not a good sign. We should have both been long gone and on to our next job by then. "Ahmed said it was a woman."

"Yes, but they don't know her identity yet. They've released an artist's sketch to the media in hopes someone recognizes her."

Not a photograph, which meant she'd been badly disfigured. I shivered. I didn't know what happened to a human body after a many-ton building fell down on it. "I don't understand how we could have missed her—"

"There were countless places she could have crawled into. Don't punish yourself over this."

"You make it sound like she was there intentionally."

"Perhaps she was."

Who would choose to die that way? The woman must have been out of her mind. "What does the guard say?"

"Actually, that is one reason I'm calling. We're having a difficult time locating him. Would you happen to have his contact information?"

"He's gone?" Oh, God. That couldn't be good. "He's not illegal, is he?" At the very least, we'd be fined. At worst, we would lose our license, and with it, our livelihood.

"No, no. Of course not. The poor fellow is just nervous. We are all on edge, Dana."

"The poor fellow *should* be nervous," I retorted sarcastically. "Where the hell was he when she was breaking in?"

"We can't blame him. The building was completely stripped. We weren't expecting junkers. We hired him to guard the explosives and he did that."

That woman couldn't have been a junker. There wasn't anything left in that building for her to steal and sell on the black market, except for the explosives themselves, and I had seen for myself everything had been present and accounted for. "The entire lot was fenced. There was only the one gate. How on earth could he have missed her? He must have been drinking. Or maybe he was asleep." I looked unseeing at the woman and the boy, now wandering the shoreline. "That's what we get for hiring amateurs, Halim."

"He came highly recommended."

"Then, damn it—ask whoever recommended him how we can locate him."

"I have. Those contact numbers are no good."

Meaning Halim hadn't been that diligent in following through when he'd hired the man. For all his cleverness, he could be lazy when it came to tying up loose ends. He preferred to go on his own instincts. Halim had liked the guard, so he'd seen no reason to make sure the man wasn't anything but what he said he was. People didn't ask too many questions when things were going their way. After all, had I ever once asked Halim why he had brought me, a complete novice, into his company? I hadn't wanted to know.

"Maybe Ahmed knows whether the guard was friendly with anyone." I was grasping at straws. The guard had worked when no one else had, but still, there could have been some crossover, people coming in early for their shift, or staying late, congregating in the temporary trailer. Ahmed was good at picking up on that sort of thing. How many times had he warned me about a guy showing a little too much interest in our security combinations, or mentioned a brewing discord between a couple of men on the crew that needed to be headed off before it escalated into rage?

"Good idea." Then, in a different tone, Halim added, "The police have begun asking some difficult questions."

A seagull screeched overhead. "How difficult?"

"Licensing questions. Procedural questions."

Alarm traced a cold finger down my spine. "Why would they do that?"

"I think they're just fishing. Try not to worry. I've got matters well in hand."

Right. "You don't even know where the guard is."

"If you're so concerned about how I'm handling things, Dana, then perhaps you should return and handle them yourself." An uneasy silence, into which he sighed. "I didn't mean that."

We were both on edge. There was no point in discussing it further. "Call me if anything changes."

"You'll be the first to hear."

I cradled the phone in my hand as if it could reassure me that, indeed, Halim would call. Halim was a practical man. He'd only keep in touch as long as it benefited him. That calculating look on his face as we'd both stood over the dead woman had revealed his true nature. Halim was loyal to one person: himself. I'd known that and I'd still signed the partnership papers.

I hadn't realized that at the beginning. Halim had offered me a chance to belong to the small select group of people who imploded structures for a living. It was a secretive business, almost entirely family-built. But Halim had seen something in me that made him reach past his own brother and hold out his hand to me. I'd jumped without thinking. I'd quit my boring office job, signed the partnership papers, and uncorked a bottle of champagne.

And for the first few years, despite financial hardships, things had progressed smoothly. Halim had brought me along and I had turned out to have a gift for eyeing a building and seeing its weak spots. It had thrilled me to discover this talent within myself. But then the economy had tightened even more, and I had started noticing things, like how Halim sometimes took on a job without consulting me, ordered supplies without letting me know, hired and fired people without so much as a passing word. Things that told me Halim still firmly considered himself in charge and I was nothing but an employee.

In which case, why even bother to bring me in? It was time I found out. When I got back to Chicago, we'd have that conversation. I was ready.

"Dana?"

The woman who'd been down playing at the lake's edge with her child stood before me.

There was no mistaking those eyes and that crooked smile.

"It *is* you!" Sheri threw her arms around me, rocked me from side to side. "Omigosh, I heard you were back! I'm so sorry about Julie. You didn't even get a chance to see her, did you?" Sheri had filled out some; the extra weight had softened her features. She wore her blonde hair pulled back in a black elastic headband, exposing her high round forehead. "They should have called you sooner. I almost did myself." She hugged me tighter. She smelled of sun and sunscreen. "I just can't believe it! You owe me, sister. All these years and not even a postcard."

"Mommy?"

"Oops." Sheri drew back and put her hand on the head of the

towheaded boy beside her. "Logan, this is Miss Julie's sister. Peyton's aunt."

He peered up through his glasses, crinkling his nose and drawing up his upper lip, badger-like.

I smiled down at him. This was the little guy Peyton mentioned had kidney disease. He looked so young. "Logan! You have got to be Mike Cavanaugh's big boy."

He leaned against his mom and stuck his thumb in his mouth.

Sheri pushed down his hand, gently. "We've been married twelve years, Mike and me, if you can believe it. Logan's four. Our other son, Mikey, is in second grade."

Twelve years, two boys. Sheri had dreamed of being a groupie for Nirvana. She'd written love letters to Kurt Cobain and had his initials tattooed onto her ankle. The night he killed himself, she locked herself into the old pavilion down by the lake. I'd climbed through the window to coax her out.

"I'm hungry, Mommy."

"How about some grapes?"

"I don't *want* grapes. I *want* a banana."

"You know the deal, buster. How about a hamburger?"

"With cheese?"

"Sorry, honey."

"No ketchup, either," he said sadly.

Sheri clasped his small hand in hers and smiled at me. "Want to walk to the snack shack with us?" she suggested.

We found a table beneath an umbrella, on a small skirt of concrete fronting a restaurant with its doors propped open. Another table was occupied, a young couple, sitting close together, their hands intertwined.

"What are you having?" Sheri asked me. "My treat."

I'd never had that second cup of coffee. "Coffee would be great." Coffee would be heaven.

"Let me guess. Just a little cream, right? You always were so disciplined. Be good, you two—I'll be right back."

Logan and I eyed each other. "So you're four, huh?" I ventured.

He put his thumb back into his mouth and turned to look at the lake. Yep, that about summed up my conversational skills with kids.

We watched a motorboat churn across the water, a waterskier bumping along behind it.

"Here you go." Sheri slid a paper plate in front of her son. "Cheers." She tapped the rim of her cup against mine, smiling.

Logan peeled back the top of his hamburger bun and scowled at the patty. "Where's the mustard?"

"I'm sorry, honey. I told them plain."

"Want me to get some?" I asked.

He ignored me, replaced the top of his bun, and took a big bite.

"That's a good boy." Sheri patted his shoulder. "Dana, you'll never guess what I was thinking of the other day. That time we went sledding down that pile of snow in the church parking lot and you ran into that parked car buried underneath—remember?"

The old Chevy had been buried beneath ten feet of hardpacked snow. I'd shot directly into the hidden rear bumper. I rubbed the scar on my chin and smiled ruefully. "I think of that now and then, too."

"Remember when we used to ride our hobbyhorses everywhere?"

Galloping around the neighborhood, jumping over bushes, neighing the whole time. "We were such dorks."

"And when we stuck a gallon of ice cream on the windowsill and it melted down the side of the house? Why did we do that, anyway?"

"Weren't we hiding it from your brother?"

"That's right." Sheri laughed. "He never found it, but the wasps did. My mom had to push it off the ledge with a broom handle. Remember how mad she was?"

"How are your folks?"

"Oh, they're hanging in there. They've still got their place out on the lake, but I don't know how much longer they can hold on to it. Dad sold his practice a couple years back. His arthritis got so bad he couldn't do adjustments anymore. Now he just mopes around and obsesses about his cable bill. Having him home has made Mom a little nuts. She stays up till all hours, falls asleep at the kitchen table. The other day she left the burner on and forgot about it. If I hadn't stopped by, the whole house might have gone up."

I didn't want to hear this. It only made me long even more for my own mother. She would have been active and engaged. She would have made me laugh even while we were sitting in some specialist's office, talking about a hip replacement.

"I love Grammy," Logan announced.

"Sure you do. I love her, too." She ruffled his hair, then smiled at me. "So, have you seen Joe since you've been back?"

"He stopped by the house last night."

"He's a teacher now, you know. I'm really hoping the boys get him when they're in high school. He's supposed to be phenomenal."

I could just picture it: Joe earnest and enthusiastic, getting kids to listen, opening their minds.

Sheri toyed with her stirrer. "Sparks still there?"

The moment Joe had appeared in the kitchen, everything had stopped for me. There'd been a buzzing in my ears, and I'd been suddenly and profoundly aware of the pounding of my heart. Different from when I'd first seen him, in that busy bar where my automatic reaction had been to think about my hair and whether I'd remembered to put on earrings. But last night, in my sister's home where everything was stripped by grief, there had been no artifice. It had felt intimate and personal, but I had no way of knowing if he'd felt the same way. "It's been a long time. We've both moved on."

She frowned. "Joe tell you that?"

"I guess I just assumed it."

"You ask me, he's still got a thing for you. You guys never did resolve things. Maybe that's fanning the flames. Mike and I have tried to set him up at least a million times."

This was embarrassing, and I didn't like the surge of hope I felt, hearing that. I had friends in Baltimore waiting for me to return so we could play tennis or catch the latest movie. I had a pretty little condo surrounded by boutiques and cafés, where jazz music floated late into the night, and where I could walk along the waterfront to watch the sailboats glide past. I didn't have anything in this little town, other than regret and loss.

"I'm not saying he hasn't gotten serious with anyone," she said. "Trust me. Half the women in town would snap Joe up if he gave them the chance. There's something to be said for a guy who's smart and kind and gentle. The way he looks doesn't hurt things, either."

I arched an eyebrow; she giggled.

"Mommy?" Logan tilted his head to squint up at her. "You talking about Daddy?"

"You bet!" she said brightly.

I had once loved Joe, deeply and truly, in that all-absorbing, first-love way. But I was older now, and far wiser. There was no room in my life for adventures that would only lead me back to doors I'd slammed shut long ago.

"What about you?" Sheri wanted to know. "What have you been up to?"

"A lot of different things. I worked in a lab for a little while collecting samples, then answering phones at a nonprofit until they lost their funding. I had a couple of government jobs shuffling paper that made me really understand why people go postal."

"I thought you went off to college?" A tiny frown puckered between her eyes. She was waiting for me to explain the long silence, the lover who demanded I remain by his side night and day, the important job that took me to foreign countries, anything that might have prevented me from writing back, or calling once in a while. After all, we'd once been close friends. But there was no challenge in her expression, no hidden animosity. I relaxed. I guessed she'd moved on, too.

Something had blown into my cup. I dipped in a fingertip and tried to capture it. A bit of leaf. Who knew what else was floating around in there? I set my cup aside. "No, now I'm a part owner of a demolition business."

"Is that a joke?"

"No joke. Friends introduced me to this man, Halim Rajad. He was looking to start up his own company. I was looking to do something different."

"Oh. And you're in love with him? This Halim?"

"We're just business partners."

She nodded, distracted. "Hey, tiger. Don't wipe your mouth on your sleeve." She plucked a paper napkin from the dispenser and handed it to her son. "Did you know we have a new water park, Dana? It's pretty awesome. We love it, don't we, Logan? On Fridays, they have line dancing at Lakeside. And Orenson's now rents out paddle boats and Jet Skis."

"I want a Jet Ski." Logan balled up his paper napkin between his palms.

"We'll see." Sheri tapped the paper plate. "Eat up, honey."

"I'm done." He'd taken two bites.

"Okay. Why don't you go see if you can find any shells?"

"I guess." He clambered down from his chair.

We watched him wander a few yards away and crouch to study the sand.

"He's really cute," I told Sheri. "How's he doing?"

"You heard, huh?" She shrugged. "Oh, I don't know, Dana. We have good days, I guess. We're still getting the hang of it." She pulled his paper plate toward her. "Julie was trying to talk me into doing his dialysis at home. She thought it would be easier on him, but I don't think I can handle it. I don't have any medical training. What if something went wrong?" She raised worried blue eyes to mine.

What did I know about dialysis and little boys, how much she could handle, whether doing it herself would help or worsen the situation? Uncomfortable, I said, "I'd bet you'd figure it out."

"I'd freak out about something, and then he'd freak, and it would be horrible. The poor kid—he picks up all his cues from me. I have to be relentlessly *cheerful*." She bit hard into the burger. "It'd be easier if we knew why he got sick. It's the not knowing that's so painful."

"Julie was trying to figure it out."

"Yeah, she was." We looked at each other for an uneasy moment.

"Excuse me." A woman paused by our table, her hands on the handles of a stroller. "Is that your little boy?"

Logan stood by the lifeguard's station, flinging shells at the ducks. The birds flapped their wings and lurched back and forth, honking.

Sheri shot to her feet. "Logan? You stop that right now!" She jabbed a finger in the air. "That's *one*!"

Logan tossed a shell to the ground.

Up went two furious fingers. "That's *two*!"

He stamped his foot and whirled around. Pushing his hands into his pockets, head hanging, he trudged toward us, the very picture of dejection. He was so small. The lake behind him seemed impossibly vast.

"He's been so angry." The breeze swept a tendril of hair against Sheri's mouth, and she tugged it free. "We have him in play therapy, but you can see how much good that's doing."

"I'm sorry." It was an inadequate thing to say, but Sheri had turned her attention to her son, who now stood before her, mouth turned down, his small shoulders sagging with defeat. She stooped to brush the sand from his pants and backside.

"That wasn't nice, Logan. Why would you hurt those poor ducks?"

"They were bothering me."

"Oh, honey. They were not." Sheri hoisted him up onto her hip and pressed her cheek against his head. "I don't know," she said to me. "Maybe Julie was right."

She walked away, her child in her arms, before I could ask her which thing she thought Julie had been right about.

TEN

―――

[PEYTON]

T HE DEEPEST PARTS OF THE OCEAN ARE THE TRENCHES *that plunge for miles into the core of the earth. This is the hadal zone, named after the Greek word for hell.*

Here live mud eaters: mollusks, worms, starfish, sea anemones, and sea cucumbers. These creatures creep along the flat and featureless ocean floor, feeding steadily on the detritus no one else wants.

Nothing changes in the hadal zone. There is no dawn or dusk, no seasons, weather, ice age. There's no reason to evolve, because there's nothing to adapt to. The creatures that live at the bottom of the world are exactly the same as they ever were. They're all that remains of our past, and they're our future, too. Long after we're gone, they'll still be there, and they won't have any idea that we once were, too.

Peyton sat in the front pew between her dad and Dana. Her grandma sat on the other side of her dad, gripping his hand and leaning against Aunt Karen. People packed the pews behind her, filled the vestibule, and overflowed onto the front lawn. From all the way inside where she sat, she could hear the far-off echo of the loudspeakers outside, repeating Father Tom's words.

Sunlight streamed in through the stained-glass windows and fell onto the gilded objects on the altar. It warmed Father Tom's white hair, danced across the robed knees of the seated deacon. Light was all free and happy out in the air. Not like in the ocean. Sunlight could shine down only so far before the water particles scattered and dispersed it. The ocean kept a tight hold on its secrets.

Two years ago, when her mom was first diagnosed, she and Peyton had had a long talk.

Why did this happen to you?

I don't know.

Does it hurt when they put the needles in?

Sometimes.

Why don't they give you a graft instead?

Because they're prone to infection.

An infection had crept in anyway.

Music started and she stood. When it stopped, she sat. Someone sniffled and then hiccupped behind her. She clenched her fists. Why were *they* crying? She wanted to turn around and glare, tell them to go somewhere else. More music, swelling loudly to a chorus of amens, and it was finally over.

Shuffling out of the pew and into the aisle, she walked beside her dad, feeling the pricking gazes of everyone upon her. She knew exactly what they were all thinking. *I'm glad it's her and not me.* She stood on the sidewalk and watched the pallbearers load the casket into the hearse. Her dad helped her grandma into the front seat of the truck, and Peyton climbed in after. Dana took her own car, and Aunt Karen got into her rental with her two sons.

The hearse rolled in front of them, leading them out of town to the cemetery. Peyton had never spent much time out here. It all looked strange to her, as if she'd landed in a foreign land. There was the blue water tower that loomed in the distance. There were the three silos, the railroad tracks. A flag flapped outside an electrical substation, its ends a little frayed. Someone should replace it.

Over time, more questions came up, and her mom had always answered them.

Are you going to die?

People can live for decades on dialysis. I'm strong and healthy. There's no reason to think I won't be one of them.

What if you aren't?

Oh, sweetheart. You'll always have me right here, in your heart. I'll never leave you.

"You didn't tell me Dana was back." Her grandma clutched her old black pocketbook in her lap, twisting and twisting the metal toggle. She sounded alert.

"She came for the funeral," her dad said.

That wasn't the exact truth. It was more that Dana stayed for the funeral, but her dad was just simplifying things. Peyton prepared herself for the endless questions about whose funeral it was, but her grandma surprised her.

"You better keep an eye on her," her grandma said.

"Sure, Mom."

"You mark my words. She's trouble, that one." She let go of her pocketbook and took Peyton's hand in hers, her grasp surprisingly strong.

Her mom had been strong, too. She loved to smile, and she sang in the shower, and planted hundreds and hundreds of flower bulbs. She never, ever let on that Peyton needed to stay vigilant. Peyton should have known better. The purple shadows under her mom's eyes, the way she paused to catch her breath, the looseness of clothes that once fit, all should have told Peyton not to let down her guard. Peyton had gotten lazy. She'd let things sweep her up and propel her along. So she hadn't even been there when her mom died. She'd been at school, doing stupid school things, and her dad had been at work. Which meant that, at the end, her mom had been alone.

Do you believe in God?

Yes. Having you made me believe.

She hoped her mom had been right. She was terrified, though, that she'd been wrong.

ELEVEN

[DANA]

MY MOM DIED WHEN I WAS THIRTEEN AND JULIE was nineteen. Mom had been on her way home from work, following the same route she took every night—the two-lane road that curved through the woods and around the dark lake and tiptoed into our sleeping town. Julie was the one to wake after midnight and realize the car wasn't in the driveway. Julie was the one to phone the police, to answer the door when they showed up to tell her they'd found our mother's car at the bottom of the slushy lake, our mother still trapped behind the steering wheel. Julie was the one to come to my bedroom in the icy predawn light and wrap her arms around me tightly to tell me our mother had drowned.

I hadn't believed her, at first. My mom would never have left without telling me goodbye.

I don't remember much about her funeral, just a few things: sitting in the pew beside Julie, breathing in the sickening green odor of lilies; looking down into the rectangular pit carved into the earth and realizing with absolute clarity that nothing was in my control. Years later, I sat in that same church, while roses stood at the altar, and the same minister talked about Julie. And then I stood by her open grave, with the marker of our mother's grave beside it, and felt the true weight of being completely alone in this world.

Julie had such promise. She was beautiful, funny, astonishingly kind. She could have married into wealth, sailed the ocean, flown the sky. I'd accused Frank of keeping her stuck here in this North Woods town, assuming no one could be satisfied staying in one spot their entire lives. But maybe I'd been wrong. The people Julie had spent her life with had overflowed the church, and now they stood in sober ceremony as her casket was lowered into the earth. They'd brought by food, sent flowers, dropped off cards and letters, phoned. Maybe, in the end, Julie had been happy. Maybe, even if it hadn't contained me, this had been the life she'd wanted.

I stood at the kitchen sink, washing dishes that could wait and taking my time about it, too. I was done making meaningless chitchat, agreeing that my sister had been a wonderful person who would be missed, answering the same questions over and over. Where had I been? How was I doing? Was I married? Children? Wasn't it nice to spend some time with my family?

At one point, Alice Gerkey had rolled up in her wheelchair, still commanding although she'd shrunken to a gnome, and thrust out a bony hand. *It's good to see you, Dana,* she whispered as I bent to kiss her cheek. *You should come by the plant sometime, and see all the changes.*

"There you are." Frank's sister, Karen, reached around me to drop a handful of silverware into the soapy water. She resembled him, with her strawberry blonde hair and narrow features. On Frank, they were a handsome combination; on Karen, they looked a little pinched and unforgiving. But the smile she gave me was generous. "Why don't you let me take over so you can greet people?"

"That's all right."

Karen gave me a thoughtful look. "Guess it's hard being back after so long."

Outside the window, people congregated on the lawn. Peyton sat up at the top of the sloped backyard, a solitary figure. I'd been watching as I soaped plates, hoping someone would walk up the hill and join her, but so far, no one had. "I didn't know Frank had a drinking problem."

Karen turned with a sharp intake of breath. "Oh no. Don't tell me he's started up again."

So Irene hadn't been exaggerating. There really was something to be concerned about. "He's going through a six-pack a night. What do you think? Is this a big deal?"

"I'm not sure. I wasn't around when it was happening. I only know what Julie told me. She said he got remote. She'd talk to him and he wouldn't answer. She said it was like living alone, sometimes. The worst part was how he neglected Peyton."

I frowned at her. "What do you mean, neglect?"

Karen flushed, got busy with a dishtowel. "Nothing terrible. Frank's a wonderful guy. You know that, Dana. It's just that he didn't interact with her. After a while, she stopped going to him, greeting him when he came home from work, that sort of thing. Small stuff."

That didn't sound small to me. "How long did this go on?"

A pause before she replied, letting me know her reluctance. "Peyton was in kindergarten when he started treatment."

So those early formative years where I'd imagined Peyton growing up surrounded by happiness and love had instead been filled with fear and insecurity. Where had I been then? Baltimore, wandering around Fell's Point or hitting the newest bar, completely oblivious. No wonder Peyton was that quiet, serious girl Irene Stahlberg worried about. Peyton seemed so alone. In the three days that I'd been there, not a single teenager had stopped by to visit her, and there she sat, on that hilltop, surrounded by nothing but grass. Julie had been so *weak*. She should have stood up for Peyton. "Five years." My voice trembled with rage. "Six?"

"No, no. It wasn't every day. He'd go for weeks and be perfectly fine."

"Until the times he wasn't."

"Well . . . Julie kept hoping he'd get hold of it."

I heard the darker history in Karen's voice. "And?"

"Julie was at work, and Peyton was at a friend's house. Peyton took it into her mind to walk home. When she got here, she found Frank. She talked him into driving her back to pick up a book she'd forgotten." She turned a plate around and around. "Peyton can be pretty persuasive."

"They had an accident." That explained Frank's limp. Not Afghanistan, then. Closer to home. Somehow that made it feel even more deadly.

"Peyton wasn't hurt, thank God. But that was it for Julie. She packed up Peyton and moved out."

Yes, that sounded like the sister I admired and loved. Karen's words sank in. "Wait a minute. You're not blaming *Peyton* for talking Frank into drinking and driving?"

"No! Of course not. I'm sorry if it sounded that way."

That's exactly how it had sounded. Karen's eyes were wide with pleading. Julie would have forgiven her on the spot and thrown her arms around her. But Julie had always been the nicer sister. I grabbed a handful of silverware and dropped it in a basket. "Frank better get things under control. He's responsible for Peyton now."

"I'll talk to him," she promised. "It's just a terrible time right now. He'll get it together. Don't worry."

Of course I was worried. "Peyton doesn't have five years for him to get around to doing that."

She flinched. "It won't be like that."

"You can't know that."

Karen put a hand on my arm. "It's too bad we both live so far away, Dana. We should take turns being here, alternate holidays or something."

"Babysitting Frank? That's no solution." Karen and I weren't together in this. We were just two women related by marriage. That didn't make us two halves of a whole. The shape we made when pushed together was lopsided and incomplete. "I have to take these dishes in." I moved away and Karen's hand fell to her side.

"Frank's going to need us," she reminded me, sounding a little shrill. "He can't raise Peyton on his own."

"Lots of people do." I pushed past her into the dining room.

The small space was hot and crowded with people. I didn't see Frank, but Joe was leaning against the doorframe in that easy way he had, talking with Doc Lindstrom. I had a sudden urge to cross over to him, slide under his arm the way I used to, his arm warm and heavy along my shoulders. He didn't look over, but I was certain he knew I was standing there. That was the way it had always been with us; we could sense each other even when our backs were turned.

"Hey, Dana."

I turned at the familiar voice. Tall and lanky, his eyes the color of water, and a craggy nose he'd broken in a right-of-way argument with a mailbox when it refused to move as he was backing his car out of the driveway. Brian Gerkey. "Wow," I said, stepping into his hug. "You cut off your ponytail." I pulled back and regarded him. "And I don't think I've ever seen you without a Grateful Dead T-shirt on."

"You know how it goes." He gave me a sleepy, sexy smile. "After a certain age, it stops looking good and starts looking sad."

"I hear you're a grown-up now, running the plant and everything."

"Yep. Only way I could keep myself in race cars. It's good to see you."

I had mixed feelings seeing him, though. We'd had a complicated relationship. I thought he was lazy and spoiled and could sometimes be a bully. He thought I was bossy and headstrong, though the terms he'd used back then hadn't been as polite. "You got married, right?" I asked.

"That's right. A girl from Detroit Lakes. We have two girls, seven and three. She's home now with them. It's naptime. But she sent flowers."

Joe had moved into the other room, and was talking now with a group of teenagers. Their smiling faces were tilted up to his.

"Hey, I'm sorry about Julie. She was the best." Brian poured a cup of fluorescent orange punch and handed it to me. "If it wasn't for her, I don't think I would've gotten the clinic up and running as quickly as I did."

"What clinic?"

"The one at the plant."

"Julie worked for you? I thought she was freelance."

"She went freelance when she got sick."

I studied him, his face completely open and guileless. Brian wouldn't have fired Julie when she could no longer work full-time—would he? "So Gerkey's has a clinic *and* a gift shop now?" I asked, keeping my voice neutral. "I remember when there was just the one washroom, and we all had to share."

"Dude, I loved that washroom. It was the only place my mom never went."

And, because of that, it had been his favorite place to get high. "Seems like you're getting along okay with her now."

"Yeah, well. I grew up some." His gaze moved restlessly around the crowd. That was Brian, always angling, always searching for the next encounter. I wondered if he'd been as unfaithful to his wife as he was to his friends. "Mike!" he called. "Join us."

Sheri's husband and Joe's best friend. I hadn't greeted him when I spotted him in the bar that first night. Now I gave him a warm hug hello. He'd thickened around the middle and his shoulders had rounded a little, but he wore his dark hair clipped short and parted the same way he had in high school.

"Sad about Julie." His eyes were red-rimmed and he cleared his throat. "Real shame."

He was holding back tears. I hadn't realized he'd grown close to Julie.

"She was a saint with Logan, a real saint," he said. "She talked him through all sorts of hideous procedures. I don't know what Sheri and I are going to do without her."

Of course. Sheri had told me Julie had been helping them. "I'm glad you got to know her," I said.

Mike nodded and cleared his throat again. "So Sheri tells me you're in demolition."

"No kidding." Brian looked at me with interest. "Doing what?"

"She blows up buildings," Mike told him. "You know, like that high-rise they just brought down in Chicago."

"Oh yeah. Someone died in that one, didn't they?"

Now they were both looking at me with interest.

I flushed. It wasn't that I was keeping Chicago a secret. Not exactly. But I certainly didn't want to talk about it now, among all these people, in my sister's house on the day of her funeral.

"Dana! Dana Carlson!" Someone jabbed me in the side with a pointed finger.

Wincing, I turned to see Miriam Kelleher, her eyes narrowed and her mouth twisted in disapproval. Throughout the church service, she'd kept leaning forward to glare at me, sitting back only when Karen gently put her arm around her mother's shoulders. Then Miriam had faced me down in the middle of the path at the cemetery, gripping her walker as though she wanted to hurl it at me and refusing to budge until Frank finally took hold of her elbow to lead her away.

At first, I hadn't been sure what had brought on this change. Frank's mother and I had always gotten along okay. But when I spotted her an hour or so before, uncapping the saltshaker on the dining room table to give it a dubious sniff, I realized Miriam Kelleher had simply gotten batty.

"You should be ashamed of yourself!" she now told me.

Brian winked at me. "I know," he said to her in a cajoling voice. "Dana staying away all these years."

"Don't talk to me like I'm an idiot," she snapped. "I know exactly why she ran off like she did." She pointed a gnarled forefinger at me. "You're not here to make trouble, are you? You know it's too late for all of that."

I stared at her with mounting unease. Her eyes weren't as cloudy as I would have expected, her gaze not as unfocused.

"She's here for Julie's funeral," Mike said helpfully.

She waved a hand at him, peering at me. Then she smirked. "*You* know what I'm talking about. Did you really think Julie wouldn't have told me?"

My throat went dry. Julie couldn't have told Miriam. She wouldn't have told anyone. She was the one who'd sworn me to secrecy. I wanted to ignore this crazy old woman, turn and walk away, but I remained rooted in place, my heart hammering loudly in my ears.

"Mike," Brian said evenly, and nodded across the room. "I think Sheri needs you."

Sheri was kneeling in front of her young son, her fingers pressed to his forehead. She looked over at Mike. Her eyes were wide with fear.

Without thinking, I started toward her. Something was terribly wrong with Sheri's little boy.

Mike pushed past me, and I hesitated. Sheri didn't need me. Her gaze was fixed on her husband as he strode toward her. She stood as he scooped up Logan and they headed to the front door. People parted to let them through. Voices grew hushed.

"Those poor things," Miriam said. "They've had a rough time of it."

I'd forgotten she was there.

Logan had seemed perfectly fine the day before, if only a little cranky. But tonight, he'd collapsed against his father and let his head loll against Mike's shoulder. The stricken look on Sheri's face was terrifying.

I glanced to the window and saw that the hilltop where Peyton had sat all afternoon was bare. Miriam patted my arm and moved off, leaning heavily on her walker as she went. So her brief moment of clarity had passed. Frowning, I looked all around the room. Joe and Brian stood together by the front door, and Frank stood in the living room, surrounded by a group of people. In the opposite corner, Irene Stahlberg sat in quiet conversation with Karen. A cluster of teenagers perched along the brick hearth, their arms around their bent knees. I turned and turned, but didn't see Peyton anywhere.

TWELVE

[PEYTON]

SEAHORSES ARE SHY FISH THAT DWELL AMONG THE sea grasses and coral reefs in the shallow waters around the earth's warm midsection. They're slow swimmers, easily picked off by predators, so instead of running for their lives, they prefer to hide in plain sight, wrapping their curly tails around a blade of grass or a piece of coral and changing color to blend in with their surroundings. They don't have teeth or stomachs, so they feed constantly, greedily slurping whatever can fit into the tube of their mouth. They eat so fast that a mist of animal parts hangs around their faces.

It's the male who carries the eggs, tucked into a pouch on his tummy. He's pretty committed to his role. As soon as one brood is hatched, he mates to carry another. It's the female who travels for food. But even so, she doesn't go far, maybe a few feet in either direction. Seahorses like to pick one tiny patch of the ocean and stay put.

The only time in their entire lives that they're free is when they're born and the ocean currents catch them and sweep them along, turning them this way and that to see the world, before re-

leasing them to settle to the bottom and make their home. It's got to be a fun ride, so long as they're not caught and eaten along the way. It's only by pure luck that a seahorse survives to adulthood.

But isn't that true of everything?

The branches of the apple tree chopped the sky into blue diamonds. If Peyton tilted her head, the leaves moved in front of the branches and scooped out different sections of sky. Hard little green apples grew among them. Sometimes her mom had made applesauce, adding lots of sugar and cinnamon to overcome the sour flavor. They'd tried a pie once, but that had been a disaster, the apples all crumbly and sour. They'd each taken a bite, then looked at each other's twisted expression and both of them had burst out laughing.

Down the hillside, people walked in and out of her house, carrying casserole dishes and plates of cookies. They gathered in the kitchen and drank coffee. They wandered out onto the deck and collected in the driveway. Every so often, one would glance up at her, but Peyton's keep-away signals were working: no one came up to bother her.

The bark of the old apple tree bit through her clothes to her skin.

She didn't know where her dad was. She should be visiting with her aunt Karen, but Peyton didn't feel like talking about how school was and whether she played any sports. For a while, Mr. G had stood on the back deck, wearing the dark suit he'd worn to the church. He looked like a store dummy, and he kept tugging at his necktie. He should just take it off. Other people were in jeans and sweaters. People kept coming up to him and talking, but nobody made him smile. He'd liked her mom. Everyone had.

Peyton closed her eyes. The afternoon sun turned the inside of her eyelids orange, like she'd trapped flames inside them. Maybe she'd paint her room that color. A mosquito whined past and she blindly waved her hand. The whining faded, but she knew it would return. Mosquitoes really loved her. She was always drenching herself in DEET, but it didn't matter. Her mother used to tease her that she was just a banquet for mosquitoes.

The warm light across her face darkened; she opened her eyes.

"Hey."

Eric looked like a giant, the long legs of his dark slacks going up to the white of his shirt, where a swath of blue silk cut it in half. "Nice tie," she said.

"Everyone's looking for you. Your cousins want to play. And Brenna's been asking if she can come up and sit with you."

"Can you believe she wore a leather miniskirt? To a funeral?"

"She's clueless. Don't let it get to you." He sat down beside her. It felt good to have him close, but if he moved any closer, say, put his arm around her, she'd smack him. Or push him down the hill. He seemed to sense it: he just leaned back on his elbows and squinted at the sky.

"Your aunt Dana seems nice."

Nice was not the word she would've used to describe Dana. "My grandma says she's trouble." Which sounded scary, even coming from a crazy old lady.

"Yeah, but your grandma's not really all there, right?"

"Sometimes she is."

"So what do you think?"

She plucked a stalk of grass and split it with her fingernail. "I *think* I should never have called her. It's awful, having her around." Dana was always there: cleaning, cooking, *watching*. Meals were agony. Every time Peyton raised her gaze, she found Dana casually looking away. And just that morning, Dana caught Peyton just as she was sneaking outside to smoke a cigarette to ask if she wanted help straightening her hair, which only made Peyton worry that her hair looked like crap or something. But that wasn't the worst thing. "She and my dad *hate* each other."

"Yeah. You said."

"Sorry I'm so boring."

"I didn't mean it like that."

Kids ran laughing around the corner of the house, and an adult shushed them. The branches waved, scrambling up the sky shapes, then stilled to make new ones. Was the normal world the right size, or had it gotten huge and swallowed her up? The right size, she guessed.

"Did you hear Logan got sick?"

She turned her head, stared at him. His face was bland, his gaze fixed on the people moving around below them. "Sick how?"

"I think he was running a fever or something. You know, kid stuff." He shrugged.

Red lights danced in front of her eyes like sparklers. She pushed herself up.

"You okay?" Eric said.

"It's not kid stuff." How dumb could he be? Hadn't he heard a word of what she'd said all these weeks? Hadn't he listened to anything? Fevers were serious for people on dialysis. Logan wasn't just a regular kid. He was *a kid on dialysis*. "That's how it started with my mom."

And look how that had turned out.

At the kitchen sink, Peyton filled a glass with water. The house was hot and noisy, and she suddenly realized she had a fierce headache. She pressed the glass to her forehead, but it wasn't cold enough to help.

"There you are." Dana stood in the doorway. "I've been looking for you. How are you doing?"

"Peachy." Peyton scratched at her elbow. The stupid mosquito had found her after all.

Her aunt bit her lip. "It's quiet in your room. I could fix you a plate of food . . ."

Peyton took a long sip of water, wincing at the metallic flavor. The Culligan man was overdue. "I'm not hungry."

"You haven't been eating, Peyton. I know it's hard, but you should try to—"

"Cut it out. Stop talking to me like that. You're not my mom. You can't tell me what to do. You don't even *know* me."

Dana flinched, but her voice stayed calm. "That's true."

How could she stand there so untouched while Peyton was flying apart into a million pieces? "You couldn't have known my mom that well, either. If you did, you would've known she wouldn't have wanted you to wear pants to her funeral. You couldn't even be bothered to find a dress."

"If I'd known it mattered to you—"

"That's just the thing. You don't have a clue what matters to me."

Dana was staring at her. "You're right, honey."

"Stop it!" Peyton scrubbed furiously at a bug bite on her neck. "Don't call me honey! How dare you pretend to be sad about someone you ignored for years and years? You're a total hypocrite."

But Dana suddenly reached out and snatched Peyton's hand. She studied the skin on Peyton's elbow, pulled down Peyton's collar.

What was she doing? "Stop!"

Dana grabbed her hand and tugged her into the living room, where her dad stood with Mr. Connolly and Doc Lindstrom. All three men stopped talking as they approached.

"Doc," Dana said. "Look at Peyton."

Doc Lindstrom set down his glass.

"Look." Dana jabbed a finger at the back of Peyton's neck. "Right here. And here."

Peyton *hated* her.

Doc Lindstrom adjusted his glasses and peered at her. Peyton squirmed, then held still, suddenly afraid that if she moved, a billion baby spiders would erupt from a bump on her back or her arm. Maybe it was cancer.

Doc Lindstrom frowned. "What is it that I'm supposed to be seeing?"

"She's been itching."

"Yes?"

"Just like Martin."

Doc Lindstrom sighed. "Dana—" he began.

"They're mosquito bites!" Peyton yanked her arm from Dana's grasp. "It's not contagious, you know. You can't *catch* kidney disease." Tears burned her eyes. "Jeez, Dana." She stomped away.

Hours later, her bedroom door cracked open. Dana stood there, her form outlined by the hall light behind her. Peyton refused to turn down her iPod. "What?" She heard the belligerence in her voice and didn't care.

"Can I come in?" Dana didn't wait for an answer, then closed the door so that the room was filled once again with the eerie blue light from Peyton's lava lamp. She stood at the foot of Peyton's bed. "Everyone's gone."

What did she want—congratulations? A gold star? Peyton pulled out her earphones and twined the thin wires around a forefinger.

"I wanted to tell you before I said anything to your father." The glow from Peyton's lava lamp carved hollows around Dana's eyes and below her cheekbones, smudged her lips. "I've decided to stay for a little while."

Alarming news, confusing. Round and round the white wires went, cocooning her finger. "How come?"

"I guess there are just some things I need to figure out."

Like that was an answer. "I don't care what you need."

"Fair enough."

Blue bubbles rose in the belly of the lamp, forming soft

rounded oblongs that broke apart at the top and slithered down the glass into new and interesting shapes. Her fish hung motionless in their darkened tank. In the morning, she'd press on the light switch and they'd know it was another day. Peyton would put on her Gerkey's uniform and go to work, and it would be like a switch had been flipped for her, too. Today was the end of something, tomorrow the beginning of something else.

Why was Dana there? Peyton couldn't stand it any longer. "What?" she demanded.

"I just . . . Peyton, I'm sorry."

Peyton stared at her in disbelief. "You're *sorry*? Which part are you the sorriest about? That my mom's *dead*? Or that you never cared while she was alive?" Dana flushed and opened her mouth to say something, but Peyton rushed on. "Well, I'm sorry, too. Sorry that you're here and she's not. I wish you were the one who died."

She stuck the earphones back into her ears and rolled onto her side. Holding up her iPod, she let Dana see her thumb swirl the volume button all the way up. After a minute, she felt the quality of the air in the room change and she knew Dana had gone.

THIRTEEN

[DANA]

JULIE HAD SMILED AT THE SIGHT OF ME ON THE couch, knitting needles in my hands and yarn spilling over my lap. *Wow,* she said, coming over and sitting beside me. *Look how much progress you've made.*

It's horrible, I muttered. *Like something a dog barfed up.*

She laughed.

The baby kicked, making me gasp. It had surprised me, where babies could reach. *The baby's saying, "I don't want that stupid thing."*

It's not a stupid thing, Julie said. *It's something you're making for your baby, and that makes it special. Don't you wish you had something of Mom's to remember her by, something that she made just for you?*

Despair surged through me. I was beginning to forget what our mom looked like, what her voice sounded like. I couldn't figure out if she'd still be taller than me, or if we'd be wearing the same shoe size, if she'd be ashamed of me.

Julie spread the knitting across her knee. *How clever of you to think of making a blanket. It's a perfect idea.*

I stared hopelessly at the mess of yarn. I'd been trying for a sweater, but Julie was right. It did resemble a blanket. If I couldn't manage something as simple as knitting, how could I possibly manage taking care of a baby? It was all I could think about as I paced these rooms. The night before, I'd dreamed I was having a little girl. I woke up feeling a tiny flicker of joy. *Do you think dreams come true?* I asked Julie.

A pause, and then Julie stooped and kissed me. *You can do this, you know. You're going to be a wonderful mother.*

Irene straightened, seeing me, and pressed the dishwasher closed. "How is she?"

Wretched. "She's fine." I shouldn't have gone in. I thought that my wanting to make her feel better would be enough. *I wish you were the one who'd died.* Poor Peyton. All I'd longed to do was to put my arms around her and let her cry. I poured myself a glass of wine, and held a mouthful of wine against my palate. "I told her I was thinking about staying longer."

"You did?" Irene's face shone with relief. "Well, that's fine, then. That's wonderful news. Have you told Frank?"

"Not yet."

She nodded toward the window. "This is a good time."

I glanced toward the glass, where it showed full dark outside. "What's he doing out there?"

"Mowing the lawn. You know Frank. You can't talk him out of things once he's decided. Besides, it's better if he stays busy."

I watched her, her stout back to me, her hands busily working. "Did you know that Julie believed something made her sick?"

A pause, then she said without turning, "Well, yes. I know she was keeping track of who was getting sick."

Her hesitation told me this was a touchy subject. "Did anyone do any environmental testing?"

"I don't think so. What for?"

"Lead. Asbestos. There are tons of old buildings in town. The church, the library. Have any of them been checked out?"

A nervous glance at me. What was she worried about?

"Lead and asbestos don't cause kidney disease," she said.

"What about pesticides? With all the farmland around—"

"Julie thought of that. She had her blood checked regularly. Mind if I throw away the fruit salad? It won't keep."

"That's fine, thank you." The counters had been cleared, the food put away. The dishwasher began to hum. "You've done more than enough. I'll finish up."

Irene shook her head. "Better if I stay busy, too."

The moon hadn't yet risen, leaving the business of lighting the night to the lamps posted up and down the road. The lawnmower buzzed irritably in a far corner as Frank worked it over a stubborn patch of grass. Dangerous to be mowing in the dark; he could run over his foot or throw up a sharp stick. I switched on the porch light, and after a moment, the lawnmower silenced. Coming down the steps, I stood on the uneven surface of the driveway, my arms crossed against the chill of the evening air.

Frank emerged from out of the darkness. He hadn't changed out of his funeral clothes; his tie hung loose around his collar, and he moved with purpose. "Want to tell me what that was all about?"

"Martin said itching was a symptom—"

"You just never think, do you?" he interrupted. "The day Peyton buries her mother, you go telling her she's next."

"What if she is?"

"What the hell does that mean?"

"I think something made Julie sick." There. I'd said it out loud. My heart thumped with my daring.

A car drove past, music streaming out its open windows, laughter. As it rounded the distant corner, the street fell silent again.

When Frank spoke, his voice was low with warning. "What

exactly are you saying? That someone at the hospital poisoned her?"

"Of course not. Not someone. Something. Something in this town is poisoning everyone. Including Peyton."

"You're crazy." Flat. But he didn't move away. Some truth in what I was saying held him there. "We talked to the specialists. We studied the numbers. We did everything and then some."

"You didn't do everything. You didn't do any testing."

"Julie had every test the doctors could give her."

"I'm not talking about those kinds of tests. I'm talking about environmental tests. Did you check the air, or the water?"

"The air and water around here are fine. Cleaner than anything you'll find in the big cities you're living in."

"But you can't know that."

"What the hell are you doing, Dana? You really think this crazy talk is going to do any good? It's over. It's done. Julie's dead. Nothing you do can bring her back."

I *knew* that. I gritted my teeth. "It's *Peyton* I'm thinking about."

"Don't you worry about Peyton. You head on back home, wherever it is you're living now. I'm sure there are people there who care."

Meaning there weren't any here. "So, you're just going to let it go. The same way you did when Julie got sick."

All of a sudden, he was there, looming out of the darkness, his face white and hateful. "I was here," he hissed, his face inches from mine. "Not you."

"Yeah? Whose fault is that? Did Julie grab the phone out of your hand, Frank? Did she follow you around and keep you from calling me?" Let him hit me. I wanted him to. I'd claw him right back. I wasn't that insecure, lost teenager anymore. He couldn't hurt me. "*You* could've saved her, but you didn't."

He grabbed both of my arms as if he was going to slam me against the porch.

"Frank!" Irene slapped down the steps. "Let go of her. Dana, what's the matter with you? Both of you, *stop!*"

Frank squeezed, then flung away my arms.

Irene pushed her way between us and stood there, glaring at first me and then Frank. "Did Dana tell you the good news?" She hit the word *good* with emphasis, as if by saying it, she could make it true. "Dana's planning on staying for a while. It'll help Peyton to have her around, won't it?"

Frank's face darkened. Turning, he strode back to the lawnmower, and a second later, I heard it start up with a roar.

Later that night, while Frank slumped before the television, I walked quietly to his bedroom. Pausing in the doorway, I looked down the long empty hallway behind me, listening, then turned and tiptoed into the room. No one had tidied all week. The notebook sat in the wastepaper basket where Peyton had dropped it days before. I shook it loose from the tissues heaped around it. A creak made me whirl around, my heart giving a yelping thud. No one stood there. I was alone.

I made it to my room unnoticed, closing the door and reaching to turn on the small lamp. The room flared into light and shadow. I looked down at the notebook in my hand with its creased cardboard cover and its corners soft from handling. Maybe the answer was hidden somewhere within its pages.

When I finally fell asleep, it was to dream of billowing gray dust and sheets of paper fluttering down, filled with the answers to everything I'd ever wanted to know. But no matter how closely I peered, the writing remained inscrutable, the letters so tiny as to be invisible.

Early morning light shot through the screens, alive with dancing motes, claiming the small, close space. Patting around on the small table beside my makeshift bed, I located my cellphone, pushed myself up, and dialed.

A man's voice answered. "Down to Earth."

What was Ahmed doing back in Baltimore? "Hey." Someone was up, moving around in the kitchen. I lowered my voice. "It's Dana."

"Oh, Dana. I heard about your sister. Terrible thing."

"Thank you." I pinched the bridge of my nose, lack of sleep making my head throb and eyes feel gritty. "So you're all back in Baltimore?"

"No, no. Just me. Halim sent me to retrieve the New Orleans estimate."

Our next shoot. Good. The heady aroma of coffee drifted into the room, tantalizing. "They've nailed down the date, then?"

"Ah, no. They've decided to go with another firm."

I was stunned. Halim and I had worked for weeks putting together that plan. The owner himself had driven us to the airport and shaken both our hands. "He can't do that!" I fought to keep my voice controlled. "He signed a contract. Tell me he didn't ask for his deposit back."

"Not yet, but you know he will."

That money was long gone. We'd already spent it finalizing things for Chicago, paying for the airfare to New Orleans, the week at the hotel. Robbing Peter to pay Paul. It should have worked. It almost had. I stared at the ceiling, the wood darkened and streaked by time. "What about the crew? Have you paid them?"

A sigh. "How?"

"Use the money we got from the Chicago job. Make sure you draw your pay, too." Halim and I would have to live on credit for the time being. Damn the money he'd just loaned his brother.

"Mr. White has not paid the balance. He says he's waiting until the police inquiry is resolved."

No. That was impossible. He didn't have any legal right to do that. We'd completed the job and now he could go ahead and build his luxury high-rise. "Well, he can wait all he wants for that, but he can't get out of paying us. We'll take him to court."

Of course we wouldn't, but how else would we pry the money away from the man? I had no idea what the legalities were surrounding something like this. Could White claim the job hadn't been completed to his satisfaction? Was he entitled to hold back payment for liability purposes?

"Halim is hoping it won't come to that."

"Hope doesn't pay the bills. Tell Halim I'll give White a call." Clattering came from the kitchen. I lowered my voice again. "Have the police figured out who she was?"

"A homeless person. They think she was drunk and sleeping it off."

"Why there, though? Wouldn't it have been easier to find a park or a shelter? Why break into a guarded building?" Although we both knew just how well guarded the building had been.

"Maybe she'd been sneaking in every night, and unfortunately, this was one morning she didn't wake up in time."

We couldn't just keep calling her "she." "Do we know her name?"

"Jane Something. Washington, Hamilton. That is it. Jane Hamilton."

Jane. I'd pushed the button that had killed a woman named *Jane.* "Not the name of a woman who would break into an abandoned building. What had she been doing there? Does she have a family?"

"The father identified her body."

He'd been forced to look at what I couldn't bring myself to see. Had he held any hope for his homeless daughter, or had he been happy just letting her be? He certainly couldn't have foreseen the path she'd end up choosing. "That poor guy." What path would Peyton choose? Had watching her mother suffer, losing her at such a young age, been the kind of thing that could derail her? Look how my mother's death had derailed me. It was good I was staying longer. Maybe I'd been kidding myself thinking otherwise.

"That poor guy has been talking to reporters, Dana. CNN picked up the story. For the past few days, they've been showing a photograph of Jane, and the video of the building going down. When I came into the office this morning, I retrieved a number of phone messages, all of them threats. The last said he would report us to Homeland Security."

I sucked in a breath. Homeland Security terrified us all. Anybody working with dynamite had to watch their step and make sure they followed every obscure guideline and rule to the nth degree. One anonymous phone call could tie us up in knots for weeks, if not months. "That's ridiculous. Don't even go there."

"Forgive me, Dana, but we're Saudi. We have to go there."

And there it was. I could be worried about Homeland Security, but only as it affected my job. Ahmed and Halim were in a different situation entirely. I shivered again.

The wood veneer covering the walls of the small room looked orange in the light, the same whorls printed over and over across the cheap planks, no attempt to disguise them as anything but what they were: imposters.

"Ahmed, tell me something." *Be careful what you wish for,* my mother used to say. "Did Halim bring me into the company because I'm American?"

A dove cooed outside my window. The back door slammed and a car engine started up. A distant train's whistle. Ahmed's silence spoke the loudest.

So Halim hadn't seen anything special in me, nothing other than my eagerness to learn and my American citizenship. "The New Orleans contract's in the safe," I said. "You know the combination."

"Dana—"

"Tell Halim I'll be back in a few days."

"Halim said you were coming back today."

"Then I guess we're all full of surprises."

FOURTEEN

[PEYTON]

IT TAKES FIFTY YEARS FOR A SEA TURTLE TO DECIDE to have babies. When the time comes, the female drags herself out of the water and onto the shore and digs her nest. She lays about one hundred eggs, which takes an hour. Then she'll cover her nest with sand to conceal it before crawling back to the ocean. Every night for three weeks, she'll continue to do this. Sometimes, she'll dig a fake hole to throw off predators. When she's finally done, she abandons her babies. She goes back into the ocean and never once looks back. She'll spend the next two years swimming around, getting psyched up to do it all over again.

Meanwhile, the turtle eggs are baking under the sun, at the mercy of hungry crabs and birds and snakes. Maybe a hundred survive. When they finally emerge, they're teeny replicas of their moms and dads. They have the sense to know they're not free and clear, not yet. They'll wait until it's dark before scurrying as quick as they can to the water. If they're very lucky, they won't end up being someone's dinner on their way.

When they finally reach the water, they dive right in. And

then they disappear. No one knows where they go. It's years before they reappear as sturdy adolescents.

Scientists call these the lost years.

Peyton dropped the plastic bottles labeled with the Gerkey logo into the waiting carton. Pressing down the flaps, she pushed the box against the lip of the tape gun. The machine sucked the box from her grasp and spat it out on the other side. She carried the sealed carton over to the waiting dolly, placed it on top of the one she'd just completed, and returned to her spot by the conveyor belt. All around her, people worked doing the same thing. Drop. Push. Carry. Her shoulders ached and a paper cut throbbed across the web between thumb and finger, where the tape had caught hold of the latex glove and torn away a piece. The guy on the radio sang about hitting the highway his way. God, she hated country music.

On the other side of the spinning metal tray, Ronni hummed as she scooped up bottles. She loved working at Gerkey's. She liked the discounts. Half-price hand lotion. Seriously?

"So what's it like, having Dana around?" Ronni asked.

"Super." A big fat lie. But even though Ronni was ten years older than Peyton, she was too dense to see through the sarcasm.

"She used to be my babysitter, you know. She wasn't so bad. Sometimes she let me stay up and watch *Saturday Night Live.*"

It had been just Peyton and her dad in the kitchen that morning. Even so, she had felt Dana's presence everywhere, stretching out and touching them as they had breakfast.

Ronni pressed the tape flat. "I totally forgot how much Dana looks like your mom." She frowned, and Peyton could tell she'd just realized how lame *that* sounded.

Queen of the obvious, that was Ronni.

Ronni jerked her chin at the box Peyton had just taped shut. "Redo that one."

"Why? UPS doesn't care if the tape's crooked."

"It could get stuck in the automated machinery."

"Whatever." Peyton yanked off the tape. Ronni didn't used to be such a jerk. It had something to do with the hormones she was taking to get pregnant. Peyton had heard all about temperature charts and fluctuating levels and in general, way more than she'd ever wanted to know about the baby-making process.

The highway song ended and a new one began. Peyton groaned. "Not this one again."

"I love this song." Ronni clicked her pen and jotted something down on her clipboard.

"It's about *shoes*."

"It's about more than that," Ronni said, seriously. "The shoes are just a symbol. Besides, you used to like country."

Peyton had *never* liked country. "If you let me listen to my iPod, we'd both be happy."

"It's a safety rule and you know it. No earphones on the floor."

"There should be a safety rule about being forced to listen to lame music."

The whistle sounded. The assembly lines whined and the bottles trembled to a stop.

The floor was quieter now. She could hear the guys on the other line talking about their fishing trip last weekend. The country singer sang about an old sweater as they walked toward the time clock.

"What's next?" Peyton asked. "Her bathrobe?"

"I told you," Ronni replied. "They're symbols. Like, shoes mean freedom. Sweaters mean comfort."

Help me. "I know what symbols are."

The foreman nodded at them. "Hello, ladies." His gaze lingered on Peyton, full of sympathy. Peyton scowled and tugged off her gloves.

"Don't forget to put on a new pair when you clock back in, Peyton."

One time. She'd forgotten to put on a new pair of gloves one time, and after that, the guy lived to remind her. "It's lotion," she told him. "It's *supposed* to go on skin. It's not like we're making paint thinner."

He nodded at her, as if she hadn't said a thing, his gaze moving to the next person in line. Why did she even bother?

Ronni pulled out her ID card hanging on a lanyard around her neck and passed it beneath the scanner. "Coming?"

"Maybe I'll catch up with you later." The last thing Peyton wanted to do was sit around the break table with Ronni and her friends. One of them was pregnant, one was breast-feeding, which always made Peyton nervous about looking at her, and two had toddlers. All they did was talk about teething and diaper ointment and the sale at the mall on baby clothes.

Ronni shrugged. "Suit yourself."

Peyton pushed through the exit and let the door latch behind her. She'd need her ID to get back in, which was another dumb thing about the place. What was in the place worth stealing? Like someone from Banana Boat was going to pay Peyton a million dollars to tell them exactly what was in Gerkey's Baby Soft Lavender Hand Cream. Like there was anything in the whole freaking factory that was the least bit interesting at all.

Not that she'd ever tell Mr. G that. He took that stuff very seriously.

She'd discovered the large flat boulder her first day at Gerkey's. She still couldn't understand why no one else had found it and claimed it for themselves. It sat facing the lake, its basin gently scooped, and protected all around by pines. She wriggled into place, the cold stone stinging through the denim of her jeans. Later, the afternoon sun would glide across the rock and warm it. By summer, she'd be sweating.

She pulled out her cigarettes from her bag. Tapped one out, lit it, inhaled deeply. She tilted her head back and exhaled a stream of smoke.

By July, the lake would be warm enough to swim in. Though some people could tolerate the freezing temperatures earlier in the season. Eric, for example. Her mother, for another. She'd go running in, lifting her knees high and squealing, and then suddenly dive below the surface. She'd emerge, gasping, calling to Peyton to join her. But Peyton would refuse. She hadn't realized there would be a finite limit. She examined the cut on her hand. Just a little scrape, but it hurt every time she opened her hand.

She had to clean her aquarium when she got home. Maybe she'd pick up that plastic Keep Away sign she'd seen at the dollar store. But maybe not. It probably had lead in it or something. Her mom had gotten into that kind of thing, toward the end. Peyton knew all about how black mold could hide behind walls and how weed killer could seep into groundwater.

"Hi."

She squeaked and jumped. It was just LT Stahlberg standing beside a big tree and shuffling his feet. God. For some reason, he'd stuck aluminum foil under his hood. It poked out all about his round shiny face. No wonder his cheeks were so red.

"Jeez, LT." Her heart was racing a million miles a minute. "Are you creeping on me?"

"What? No!"

Sure he wasn't. "Well, cut it out."

He scowled. "You shouldn't be smoking. Your mom wouldn't like it."

Like he knew what her mom liked and didn't like. "What are you doing out here? Don't you have to get ready for work?"

He crossed his arms across his big gray sweatshirt. "I am ready."

Huh. So even Mr. G couldn't get LT to wear a uniform. Maybe he couldn't find one big enough. She eyed LT through the rise of smoke. "The loading dock's that way." She jerked her chin toward the building behind her, but he didn't move.

"I wanted to tell you. . . . I came by the other night. Did your dad say?"

She crushed her cigarette against the smooth surface of the rock and dropped it into the brush. Standing, she brushed off the seat of her pants. "I have to get back to work."

"Seriously, Peyton. You have to be careful."

Her mom had been careful, washing her hands every five seconds, measuring every ounce she drank, soaking the potatoes for hours and hours. Peyton knew exactly what being careful got a person. Nothing.

"You're always wearing those earphones," LT insisted. "That's how they get you. They talk right into your ears and hypnotize you."

"That's only true for country music."

He frowned. "Are you making a joke?"

"Don't be so stupid. There's no such thing as aliens." What was it with crazy people, fixated on something that wasn't real? Didn't they know there was enough real stuff to be freaked out about, right here on earth?

"That's not true." He touched the tinfoil fringing his face.

"Have you ever seen one?" she challenged.

"Well, no. But your mom said there's stuff we can't see that can hurt us."

"She wasn't talking about aliens, moron. She was talking about germs."

He blinked rapidly. "I miss her." His big dumb face, his pale lashes spiked with moisture, his blubbery red lips sagging. "She was my friend."

Her mom said not to let LT get worked up, that that was how he ended up burning down the hardware store. She said he had to take his meds and keep to his schedule. His breath came in jagged gasps. He scrubbed at his face with both hands.

It's all right. Peyton heard her mom's voice. *Look at me, LT. It's all right.*

But Peyton wasn't her mom. "Shut up, LT," she said fiercely.

He stared at her, his face loose and confused.

"She wasn't your friend. She was your *nurse.*"

Anger darted across his eyes. She didn't care. Her own anger swelled up and overtook her.

"And you stay away from me. I'm not your friend, either." She wheeled around and stomped toward the plant. She was late for her shift. She dared Ronni to say a word about it. She hoped she would.

FIFTEEN

[DANA]

DOC LINDSTROM USED TO HAVE HIS OFFICE IN A whitewashed two-story building, along with a couple of dentists and an orthodontist. One of my least favorite places in town, the small structure had always been associated in my mind with fevers, vaccines, and dental drills. I wondered if Doc had changed locations, but as I drove down the street, I saw the same wooden sign in the parking lot. The building itself looked a little worse for wear, its paint dingier, front steps tilting at a steeper slope, the gray awning more faded and drooping. Something else about it had changed. It took a moment to place it: all the trees around it had been chopped down.

Viola Viersteck looked up from her seat behind the reception desk and instantly came to her feet, her face collapsing into an expression of sympathy. "Oh, Dana. How are you holding up?"

The two old guys in the corner halted their conversation and glanced over.

"I'm fine, thanks." I'd never really known Viola, who'd been several years ahead of Julie in school, and I'd been surprised to see her at the funeral yesterday, sitting between her husband, another fellow I hadn't really known, and a sulky teenager who had to be their daughter. She and Julie must have grown closer over the years.

Viola came around the desk with her arms outstretched. "I was so worried when you called this morning for an appointment."

That caught the attention of the old geezers, who sat back and stared.

"It's all right," I said, stiffly submitting to her hug, embarrassed by her effusiveness. "I just have a few questions for Doc."

She held me out and looked at me. Her lashes were heavily mascaraed, her hair elaborately frosted, and her lips slick with gloss. The neckline of her blue sweater plunged, revealing plump cleavage. Black Bear's version of a diva. "How's Peyton doing?"

"Hanging in there."

"It's such a terrible thing. She pretty much kept to herself all day yesterday, didn't she? I didn't even get a chance to give her a hug. Tell her Brenna's mom says hi, would you? Brenna's Peyton's best friend, you know."

That thin little thing in the tight miniskirt was Peyton's best friend? "Oh," I said, and tried to sound enthusiastic. "That's nice."

She nodded, sending her long gold earrings swinging. "Why don't you take a seat? I'll let you know when Doc can see you."

Conscious of the curious gazes of the men sitting in the corner, I selected a chair as far away from them as possible. Periodicals fanned across the small wooden table beside me. *Lutheran Today. Golf. Midwest Living.* A plastic stand affixed to the wall offered brochures on colonoscopies, bone scans, and the first warning signs of skin cancer. I crossed my legs and stared steadfastly at the wall, until the old guys finally realized the show was over.

Geezer One cleared his throat and said to Geezer Two, "How's your son-in-law doing?"

"Eh, not so good. His harvest is down six bushels per acre."

"Rust?"

"Nothing like that. The number of tillers is way low. He can't figure it out."

"Too much rain?"

Money was going to be a problem. I could only ride on credit for so long before my cards were maxed out. I needed to follow up with White myself and do what Halim had failed to: make the guy pay us what he owed. I had White's cell number, but would he answer if he saw who was calling? It would be better to have a lawyer contact him. My neighbor in Baltimore worked in a law office. Maybe she could recommend someone willing to make a targeted phone call without charging the earth. I chewed on my lip. Just how long would Frank allow me to stay, rent-free? Sheri might be willing to put me up, but her little boy was sick. Last thing she needed was a houseguest.

"Dana?" Viola stood by the door. "You want to come on back?"

Both geezers swung their heads with renewed interest as I stood.

Viola swished before me down the narrow hallway, teetering on her stacked heels, and stopped outside a door. "Go on in," she said. "I'll let Doc know you're here."

A dark green room, lined with books and hung with framed diplomas. A heavy desk sat beside the lone window, two chairs ranged in front of it. Julie must have sat in one of these chairs as Doc Lindstrom told her what the test results revealed. She'd been a nurse. She would have heard the clock start ticking.

A voice behind me said, "Dana."

I turned to see the man who'd brought me into this world. "Hi, Doc."

Doc Lindstrom had aged. His shoulders were drawn together in a stoop, hair now completely white, skin like crumpled parchment. He patted me on the shoulder. "Have a seat and tell me what's on your mind." Settling himself behind his desk, he regarded me with concern. "Is it about Peyton?"

I flushed. He was referring to the scene in Frank's living room last night, my tugging Peyton over to him and pointing to the raised red bumps on her neck that had turned out to be nothing more than mosquito bites. Something I certainly should have recognized, something that only emphasized how much of an outsider I'd become. Then I caught myself. When had I started thinking of it as *Frank's* living room? "I'm worried about what's going on."

"Well, sure. It must have been quite a shock, coming home to this. There's been a lot for you to absorb."

"You don't know why Julie got sick."

"You should really talk to her nephrologist, Dr. Gunderson. He came to the funeral yesterday. Did you have a chance to meet him?"

"No, but I called his office this morning. His nurse said she could fit me in sometime next month." Which was ridiculous. I only needed fifteen minutes, I'd told her, but she'd remained firm, the implication clear: the doctor was busy treating people who *really* needed him. I pulled out Julie's notebook, and Doc Lindstrom leaned forward as I placed it on the desk between us.

He looked up at me. "This is Julie's."

"So she talked to you."

"Yes."

"Ten percent of all kidney disease has no known cause." I tapped a number circled in red. "But Julie calculated that here in Black Bear, it's *twelve* percent."

"The higher incidence surprised me, too, so I consulted Dr. Gunderson. He said that although the rate is higher, it's not high enough to trigger alarm."

"Really?"

"What we're seeing seems to be an anomaly, Dana. In a few months, it could fall back to the expected rate, or even dip lower."

As more people sickened or died. "You said 'seems to be.' What if it isn't an anomaly?"

"You mean, what if there is a cause, and we just don't know it yet?"

"Exactly."

"There's always that possibility. But Dr. Gunderson and I looked at all the cases. We couldn't find any reason to think otherwise."

"That doesn't mean it isn't there."

"Dr. Gunderson thinks there's no reason for concern."

"Julie *died*."

"You know," he said gently, "there are lots of reasons people get sick with kidney disease. We're learning more about it every day. There's injury to the kidneys, workplace exposure, medications, cancer, high blood pressure, polycystic disease, chronic dehydration, but Julie ran none of those risks."

"Irene said she got tested."

"She had me run every test in the book. I did everything I could think of, even covered a few out of my own pocket."

He'd taken care of Julie since the day she was born. He wouldn't have faltered now. "What sort of workplace exposure?"

"It's an interesting study. Sand workers. Which doesn't mean anything. We don't have a sand factory in Black Bear."

"But we do have miles of new beach." Sheri's little boy crouching in the sand, his fingers working to free a shell.

"You're saying people got exposed in that way?"

"It could be."

"Hard to imagine, though. A manufacturing setting's different, a lot of dust being churned up within a closed environment and getting inhaled deep into the lungs, where it can do all sorts of organ damage. But out on a beach setting . . ." He shook his head. "I just can't see it."

"If the wind was blowing?"

"Maybe while the sand was being dumped, there could be some residual airborne dust. But that would affect the worker, not the beachgoer. Beaches have been around for a million years. People have been walking on them forever, and all the people who live in the desert. There's been nothing to show they've developed kidney disease at any greater rate than other populations."

"That's naturally occurring sand. Maybe processed sand is different."

"That sand's been settled for years now. How does that explain the new cases we're seeing?"

"Maybe it just takes longer to show up in certain people than in others."

"Doesn't explain the profile of the people I'm seeing. If your theory's correct, I would expect to see teenagers dominate the patient group, since they're the group that spends the most time down by the lake, but I don't have a single sick teenager."

The phone on his desk buzzed. He leaned forward to push a button. "Yes?"

"Mr. Harrigan's in room two."

"All right. I'll be right there."

He hung up, and I said, "What if the sand's contaminated?"

"It would have shown up in other ways, Dana. We would have seen all sorts of physical complaints. Hold on." He rolled open a drawer and pulled out a sheaf of papers. "Dr. Gunderson gave me a copy of the report we're talking about, and I wonder . . . ah." He juggled some stapled sheets free. "Here it is." He scanned it and handed it over.

I read the heading. "Mortality from Lung and Kidney Disease in North American Industrial Sand Workers." I looked at him.

"If sand *were* the cause," he told me, "we'd expect to see an increase in lung disease, as well."

"And you're not?" The expression on his face was my answer.

"Dana, sometimes, things just happen. We may never know why Julie got sick." His voice was gentle.

I'd taken enough of his time. "Thank you."

"Anytime. I know you need answers, Dana. I only wish I had them for you."

"Julie thought there was an answer out there."

"I know." We stopped by the waiting room door. His face was kindly, fatigue etched in the deep grooves along his forehead and mouth. "It's good in the end that she knew we hadn't missed something. I'm sure it gave her peace."

"I don't think she was at peace at all." Julie had left that notebook on her nightstand, out in plain view. She'd wanted someone to find it and pore over its contents; she wouldn't have guessed I would be the one to pick it up, but that's how things had turned out. In this small, hopeless way, Julie had reached out, was still reaching out, and I wasn't going to turn away. Not *this* time. "I think she got sick before she could do anything more."

Something flickered across his face. It was gone before I could pin it down, but maybe it had been irritation. Or guilt. "What would she have done?"

Julie's notebook was thin, flexible. It wasn't enough to wage a war with. "I guess we'll never know."

Halfway across the lot, I looked up and there was Joe, leaning against my car. How many times had he waited for me like that, lingering against a wall or on the sidewalk, straightening when he saw me, his face helplessly changing? How many times had I felt myself changing, too, just at the sight of him?

The sun warmed my shoulders and glinted off the sidewalk. A car horn honked in the distance.

Joe smiled. "Feel like taking a ride?"

SIXTEEN

[PEYTON]

JELLYFISH DON'T HAVE EYES OR BRAINS. THEY JUST have bowl-shaped bodies and gaping mouths ringed by arms that sweep food inside. Tentacles dangle all around, like fishing lines. Some jellies have a few tentacles; some have so many they look like a tangled cloud. One of the most poisonous creatures in the sea is a jellyfish, a tiny animal called the box jellyfish.

Jellyfish randomly drift along with the current, letting their tentacles sweep along beneath them. As a tentacle brushes up against prey, it automatically releases stinging cells that numb the creature. The jelly then sucks it into its stomach to disintegrate. Nice.

For dumb, blind animals, jellies are powerfully resilient. Their poison cells remain active even after they're dead. Water pollution doesn't bother them, and when their habitat gets crowded, they simply multiply faster. But they do have an enemy.

If they leave the water, even for a second—the tide washing them onto the sand before rolling them back into the ocean—they die. Something irreversible happens to them. No one knows what.

It's interesting, right? One of the earth's most basic creatures turns out to be way more complicated than you'd think.

Ronni was pulling on latex gloves when Peyton pushed through the door. She wrinkled her nose. Add fifty pounds and some wrinkles, and she *was* her mom. Gross. "Were you smoking?"

"So what?" Peyton said.

That caught Ronni up short. She stopped in mid-tug and appraised Peyton, who merely reached around her to the container of antibacterial gel on the wall. "You're way too young to smoke."

Peyton had just gone through this with LT. Screw it. She squirted a cool dollop of gel onto her palm. "And you were way too young to have sex beneath the football bleachers."

Ronni blinked. "Who told you that?"

"Please. Everyone knows." Their initials were carved in the soft wood, along with dozens of other couples'. It would have impressed Peyton, actually, that Ronni had done something unpredictable like lose her virginity that way, but she'd gone on to marry the dude, so it didn't count.

Ronni looked worried, so Peyton added, "Your mom doesn't know." Like that would matter anyway. She rubbed her hands together, working the gel between her fingers.

Ronni handed her a pair of gloves. "Did you hear we got that contract?"

So Ronni was going to drop it. Peyton had scored something. She wondered what. "The government one?"

"Yep. Can we say 'job security'?" Ronni swept her hair back into a tight ponytail and wrapped the elastic around it. Not the best look. It made Ronni's face look particularly square-jawed, but Ronni was always obsessed about keeping her hair back. Like she'd get fired over tape with a hair stuck to it. "They'll have to expand the lines. Maybe I can move up." Ronni's eyes shone. "Not that I wouldn't ask to take you with me."

Right. Ronni would never do something like that. She wouldn't want to make waves or cause any kind of disturbance. It didn't matter. A year from now, Peyton would be leaving this dead-end town and going to college. Then she frowned. Dead-end? How had *Dana's* words gotten stuck inside her head?

Ronni's gaze flicked to something behind Peyton and she switched on a bright grin. "Hey, Mr. G. Congrats on the contract."

"Thanks, Ronni. Hi, Peyton."

"Hi." It was weird to see him in the middle of a Saturday. He usually only came in first and last thing to feed his fish.

"Got a minute?" he asked Peyton.

How humiliating. He was checking on her to make sure she was okay. He knew her better than that, should have guessed she'd hate to be singled out.

"I'll have her right back," he told Ronni, who nodded.

Out in the empty hallway, he said, "I've been hearing good things about your work."

Who would have told him *that*? "Thanks."

"You show up on time. You're always willing to take on an extra shift. That kind of responsible attitude's impressive."

The only reason she showed up on time was because her dad dragged her with him to work. And as for taking on extra shifts, well, it wasn't as though she had any choice. Every dollar Peyton earned went straight into her college fund. Lately, that had been the only money going in.

"I'm looking for people to train on the third line. What do you think?"

"Me?" Only old-timers got to work the line. Peyton was just a kid.

He grinned. "I figured you were ready for a change."

Making the stuff had to be way more interesting than packing the bottles it came in. Plus the pay was higher. "Okay."

"Great. I'll let HR know. They'll want to start training you right away, probably sometime next week."

She had final projects, exams coming up. The horrible social studies grade that she had no chance of bringing up to a C. She used to be at the top of her class. Her mom used to stick Peyton's report cards on the refrigerator. It had been a long time since Peyton had eagerly brought home her grades.

Without waiting for her reply, he said, "That's not the only good news. I may have a lead on a clownfish."

"Really?" That *was* good news. Mr. G said his clownfish was okay without a mate, but Peyton worried about Charlie. Sometimes the little black-and-white fish didn't seem as active as he used to be, like he was missing his old sweetheart.

"I'll let you know," he said, and started to turn.

"What about Ronni?" she said.

He stopped, his eyebrows raised. "Ronni?"

"Will she be moving to the line, too?"

"Ah." His face took on that careful look grown-ups got when they were watching what they said. "That'll have to be between her and her supervisor."

Why didn't he just say it? Ronni wasn't going anywhere. She was staying stuck in Packing where she'd been for years, and only Peyton was moving on. So this *was* a pity offer.

He glanced at his watch. "I'd better get back. I've got a call coming in."

He patted her shoulder and was off, leaving Peyton with nothing to do but go back to work.

Ronni glanced up as Peyton took her position beside the conveyor belt. "What did Mr. G want?"

Ronni was bossy and annoying. She talked endlessly about the stupidest things, like curtains and mascara. Her taste in music was horrible. But Gerkey's was her life. She came to work with a big smile, clocked in and out right on time, arranged to meet friends during every break and meal. She'd been so proud when she'd gotten promoted to supervisor. Now she stood waiting for Peyton to answer, her hand hovering over the bottles jiggling together beneath the motion of the conveyor belt.

"To tell me about a new fish he'd ordered."

"Oh." Ronni rolled her eyes. "I guess that *would* be important."

Peyton scooped up a handful of bottles and dumped them into the waiting box. Who was the bigger jerk: Mr. G for extending the offer? Or her, for accepting it?

On their way home, the streets honeyed with late afternoon sunshine, her dad asked, "So how did it go?"

"Fine." It went. "I heard we got that big contract."

He glanced over. "Means I might be pulling extra-long hours. What do you think—would you be okay with that?"

"Like every weekend?" How empty would that make the house? Would she notice his absence? Yes, she would.

"Maybe some evenings, too."

Her mom's medical bills filled the desk drawer at home. What if they didn't pay them? It wasn't like all those doctors had done any good. It wasn't like all those hours going to dialysis had done her mom any good at all. Peyton and her dad should just keep their money.

"Peyton?"

What did he want her to say, that it sounded like a blast, being abandoned day after day, night after night? "It's fine, Dad," she said impatiently, and he sighed with relief.

A boy skateboarded down the sidewalk, bending his knees to swoop around the cracks and holes. A freshman. She'd seen him around. "Mr. G's promoting me to Manufacturing."

"Yeah?"

He sounded surprised. Which meant Mr. G hadn't checked with her dad first. Was that a good thing or bad? "I'm getting trained next week." Her cellphone buzzed to let her know she had a text, and she pulled it from her pocket. Eric. *U done?*

Yes, she typed back.

"You want to work on the line, honey?" her dad asked.

It wasn't like her dad to ask her what she wanted. What was he trying to do, channel her mom? She shrugged. "I guess."

"You can't operate the machinery. OSHA regulations."

She hadn't thought of that. "Mr. G would know that, though, right?"

"He must have something in mind, but it's strange he'd move you there. Did he say why?"

Was he being dense on purpose? It wasn't as though Mr. G would have spelled it out. "Just that I've been doing a good job."

"Oh." He sounded pleased, just hearing what he wanted to hear. She knew how that worked. If you looked at things the way you wanted them to be, then you didn't have to deal with the way they actually were.

Another text. *We still on for 2nite?*

Eric had asked her the other day, in that other lifetime. She sorted through her feelings. Did she want to go out, hang with him like she used to? "Can I go out with Eric?" she asked her dad.

"Shouldn't you be tackling some of that homework?"

There it was again. Her mom took care of the school stuff. Her dad put on the storm windows and mowed the grass. He couldn't do both. He should stop trying. "Eric can help me."

He gave her a sideways glance, but said nothing. So that was a yes. He liked Eric, and was friendly with Eric's folks. Still she hesitated. Was it fair to leave her dad alone? Was it even smart, with all the beer he'd been drinking? Her phone buzzed again, impatient against her palm.

She slid it open and pressed *K*, then turned it off. "I won't stay out too late," she promised, and he nodded.

It wasn't until they'd gotten home that she realized that maybe the thing she should have been worried about was not leaving her dad home alone with beer, but home alone with Dana.

SEVENTEEN

[DANA]

I'D BEEN GETTING READY FOR A DATE WITH JOE WHEN Julie came and stood in the bathroom doorway. *What?* I asked, twining the curling iron through my hair. *How serious are you two?* she asked, and I laughed. *Is this where you tell me about sex?* She didn't smile back. *I hope you're smarter than that.* I groaned. *Do you hear yourself?* I retorted. She came up behind me, her face reflected beside mine in the mirror, mine a little lower than hers, the same fair coloring, the same blue eyes, doubled. *I like Joe,* Julie said. *But you're too young to be so serious.* Without thinking, I said, *Cut it out. You're my sister, not my mom.* Which wasn't fair. Which was really cruel, that day of all days, and even now as I stood beside Joe on the tarmac, I remembered the pain that twisted her features as she turned away, and I felt the full weight of shame.

Maybe that was the moment that changed everything for me.

I walked around the small white plane. Nearby, a couple of over-alled mechanics worked on another plane, larger than this one.

Beyond them, Boy Scouts sat cross-legged on the grass, listening to a guy in khaki as he walked around and gestured. Rock music thumped from the open door of the hangar across the way.

"Nice," I told Joe. "I never knew you wanted to fly."

"Sure." Joe stood on a foothold built into the side of the plane, leaning across the wing to unscrew a cap and peer inside. "I built this, you know."

I glanced at him, astonished. How many other things didn't I know about Joe?

He smiled at my expression. "Took me two years."

I'd heard of planes being assembled from kits, but had never seen one up close. I ran my hand along the bolted sheets of metal. It all looked real enough. "Remind me, how did you do in tech ed?"

Now he laughed. "Don't worry. I've taken it up hundreds of times. Handles like a dream. Come on. Let me show you Black Bear from the air."

"A dream come true," I muttered.

Grinning, he handed me up the small folding steps, and we both settled ourselves into the cockpit. He gave me a pair of headphones. "Put these on and we can chat. It'll get pretty noisy once I start her up." He consulted the paper pinned to a small clipboard, then opened the glove box and slid the clipboard inside. Pushing open the small window beside him, he called, "Clear!" Then to me, "Strap yourself in."

Loud sputtering as the propeller on the front of the plane began rotating, and a minute later, we began bumping across the pavement. The noise grew louder and we moved faster. He spoke into the microphone. The ground fell away and the sky opened up before us, endlessly blue and reaching all the way up into heaven.

Over the background rumbling, Joe's voice came clearly. "Nice, isn't it?"

Off to the right sprawled the amusement park: turquoise, yellow, navy, and red tent tops, a huge devil's head with horns, the

Ferris wheel. The roller coaster snaked up and down along the curve of woods.

"You still crazy about coasters?" Joe asked.

"I haven't been on one in years." I couldn't remember the last time I'd even been to a park, but I remembered the first time. It had been a little county fair with rickety rides, and I'd been with Joe. A lot of my firsts had been with Joe. "So you're Peyton's teacher."

He nodded. "She reminds me of you, you know. Her mind works in the same way, hopping from point to point."

I stared steadfastly out the window. Had he ever looked at Peyton and wondered at the color of her eyes, the shape of her face? "Irene Stahlberg says she doesn't have any friends."

"Peyton's okay. She's an independent thinker. She'll find her own way."

It made me feel good to know that Joe was there, helping Peyton navigate the rocky road of adolescence. It meant even more now that Julie wasn't there.

The pines thinned to grass, then to fields of wheat, stippled pale green and yellow, stretching all the way to the horizon. Brown patches of earth showed here and there. I turned in my seat to look back. In the distance, along the horizon, the crops shone in the afternoon sun like emeralds. Was that what the two old farmers had been talking about? "The wheat doesn't look good," I said.

"Farmers are having a tough year."

"Anyone know why?"

"You know what it's like. Sometimes it happens."

Joe knew better than most. His father had been a farmer. "How's your dad? I didn't see him yesterday."

"He moved to St. Paul to be near my sister and her family."

"That's nice." Joe's younger sister had worshipped him, and he'd pretended to hate the attention. But he'd been the one to stand up for her at school, and he'd gone to every one of her high school softball games. "Do you like her husband?"

"Sure. He's a good guy. They have a little girl, another baby on the way."

There, for the briefest murmur of time, hung the way our lives could have spun out, if we'd let them. We could be married, settled, taking turns unloading the dishwasher, carrying out the trash. I leaned my forehead against the cold glass and looked down at the lake, broad and placid below. "You still ice fish?"

He nodded. "I've upgraded some. Got a heater, a TV."

All the times we'd lugged sleeping bags and lanterns out to his dad's ice house, that shack dragged out to the middle of the frozen lake, our breath frosting the air. We'd curl up together inside the cozy space, almost never getting around to dropping a line. I stared at the deep blue of the lake below and pictured it white and gray in a low winter sun. "Remember when I dropped my bracelet?" Though it hadn't been my bracelet. It had been Julie's. Joe and I had been playfully wrestling and it had fallen right off. I'd felt the tickle of the chain sliding down my thumb, then immediately pushed Joe away and plunged my hand through the fishing hole, into icy black water. Nothing.

"You kidding? I thought I was going to have to fish *you* out."

I'd been furious at him for holding me back. Those reckless emotions, over-the-top and played to their full limit. Nothing touched me that deeply anymore.

The water sparkled. Somewhere among its depths lay the gold bracelet with the dangling heart, the one Frank had given Julie for their first anniversary. I'd stolen it out of my sister's jewelry box. Julie had been in tears. *I'll get you another,* I had snapped, though I never did. *That's not the point,* Julie had said, and turned away.

Apparently, she'd ended up finding her own replacement. Just the other day, Peyton had lifted it from the jewelry box, and it looked almost exactly the same as the original, though the heart was a little smaller and the links a little bigger, and altogether not as pretty. I wondered if it had pained Julie, fastening it around her wrist, if it had reminded her of all the ways in which I'd ended up disappointing her. "The lake's so blue," I said.

He nodded. "You can swim in there now. The town installed a weed puller."

Those long, silky fronds would wrap themselves around my ankles and calves, and squish unpleasantly underfoot. "Should have done it long ago."

"We didn't have the money for it back then."

Black Bear had been a miserable town on the verge of extinction. But no longer. We banked over the treetops, and below me, as the trees parted to reveal a clearing dominated by a large beige building, I saw the reason why.

"Gerkey's." I'd never seen it from above, never realized how isolated it was amid the trees, perched on the shore. All those hours I'd spent in that building, dipping candles, coming home blistered and nauseated from the sickening fruity aromas.

"Brian threw some great parties there."

I remembered. But the corporate-looking complex below bore no resemblance to its first incarnation as the secret weekend meeting place for all the teens in town. Had Brian's parents ever once suspected anything when they came to work Monday mornings, opening the door to the lingering aroma of marijuana, or tripping over the forgotten sneakers in a hallway, or finding the empty beer can inexplicably in the supply closet? We could not possibly have been as tidy or careful as we had imagined ourselves. We would have left clues behind. But Brian never said anything to me about getting into trouble with his folks, and Alice Gerkey had never once looked at me with anything but trust and affection. "Do you know how Mike and Sheri's little boy is doing?"

"Turned out to be an ear infection. It's like that every time

Logan spikes a fever, or loses his appetite. They're raw. I worry about them both."

"He has the same disease Julie had." Neighborhoods spun out below, roofs rolling out in branching lines, looking all the same, one dark rectangle after another. Sheets hung from a clothesline. A car crawled beetle-like along a narrow street. A town full of people, going about their regular business. What if something else was going about its business, too, and infecting every one of them? "Seems like a lot of people around here do."

He gave me a glance. "That why you were at Doc Lindstrom's?"

I looked at him. I hadn't even said a word about my visit with Doc Lindstrom. He smiled back and I felt something flicker between us. Why had I been so surprised by his perceptiveness? Of course Joe would have guessed why I'd wanted to talk to Julie's doctor. Joe had always been able to follow the track of my thinking, keeping me going along a certain path or sometimes pulling ahead and stopping me before I did something rash or risky. I looked away. Joe hadn't *always* stopped me. "He said the rate's only slightly elevated. He thinks it's just a matter of time before it goes back down—"

"But you think it won't."

The doctors who had taken care of Julie thought so. "What do I know? I blow up buildings for a living."

"I don't know, Dana." Joe's voice was thoughtful. "Maybe you're right. First Julie, then Martin. Logan."

"Miss Lainie."

"Miss Lainie," he repeated. "Exactly. Maybe it just takes an outsider to see something the rest of us are too close to make out."

An *outsider*? Was that how Joe saw me? My cheeks grew hot and I turned back to watch the fields ripple gold and green, green and gold.

The airplane thrummed around us.

Joe's voice came through the headphones. "What happened to us, Dana?"

I stared down at the wheat, alive and dead, dead and alive. *Stupidity happened to us,* I wanted to say. My own stupid, foolish self. I wanted to confess everything, but doing so would have been the most selfish thing of all. I forced my voice to be even. "I guess we outgrew each other."

"You know that's not true. It sure wasn't like that the last time we were together."

His face hovering above mine, the moonlight slanting through the branches above us, trapping him in light and shadow. "Joe, we were kids. What did we know?"

"All I knew was I was crazy about you. Then one day, it was over. No phone calls, no explanation. You wouldn't even talk to me in the hall."

I remembered that day. I'd gone to school in a daze and wandered from class to class, unhearing and unseeing, trying to figure out if I could tell that I wasn't the same anymore. I couldn't talk to Joe, not until I knew how to tell him. By the time I had figured it out, it had been too late.

"I came by the place you and your sister rented over in Hawley." Joe's voice was low. "You were in there. I heard the TV. But you wouldn't answer the door."

He would've seen in an instant exactly why I was hiding. For five interminable minutes, I'd pressed myself against the wall, eyes clenched tight and holding my breath, until at last the terrible pounding stopped.

The plane droned on.

Then I nodded toward the dark clouds massing on the horizon. "Storm's coming. We'd better head back."

EIGHTEEN

[PEYTON]

ANGLERFISH ARE BONY, LANTERN-JAWED FISH THAT *live deep in the abyss. They come magically equipped with their own fishing rod, an antenna that curves from the top of their head and dangles a glowing light right in front of their mouth. Curious fish swim over to check it out, and snap! They don't live long enough to warn the others.*

These are the female anglerfish. The males are tiny lumps that burrow into the side of the female and fuse, flesh to flesh. They live off the female and give her what she needs to reproduce. The perfect relationship, as long as he doesn't mind giving up his freedom and she doesn't mind having something forever jammed into her side.

Brenna's house was so new it reeked of paint and carpet. It was worse in the basement, where the smells were trapped and made Peyton's eyes water.

"We've seen this movie," Eric complained.

"Like a thousand times," Peyton muttered. She tossed a piece of popcorn at the bowl, and it missed, landing on the floor instead. Quickly, she scooped it up before Brenna's mom could appear and stand there, frowning, her hands on her hips.

"Who's watching the movie?" Adam snickered. He and Brenna sat bundled in the armchair, her legs across his lap and his arm slung around her shoulders.

"Shut up." Brenna pointed the remote at the big screen. "This is the good part."

Her boyfriend growled and nuzzled her neck. "I like my women bossy."

Brenna giggled, and pretended to elbow him away while letting him slide his other arm across her belly.

Peyton looked pointedly at Eric. *You owe me.*

He made an apologetic face. *I know.*

She ate another handful of popcorn. Adam was disgusting and Brenna annoying, but at least they weren't paying any attention to her. They weren't looking at her with big sad eyes, or asking questions that were supposed to be sympathetic but were really just plain curiosity. Like Peyton would really tell anyone what it was like to be her. Like she even knew.

But being here was better than being at her own house, where her dad wandered around like a ghost, and Dana could at any moment walk in the front door and say or do something stupid that only made everything worse.

The squeak of the basement door, and here was Brenna's mom clopping down the stairs in her heels. "How are we all doing down here?"

Adam straightened and put an innocent look on his face.

"Fine, Mrs. Viersteck," Eric said.

She wore makeup that made her skin look orange, and her clothes were way tight and way short. None of the other moms looked anything like her. "Want some chips? I've got some baked Lay's upstairs."

"Mom, just go."

"Oh, Brenna. Please don't talk to me like that." But she didn't really sound that pissed, more like she knew it was the kind of thing a mom was supposed to say. "Peyton, how are you, sweetheart?"

Peyton's cheeks burned as the other kids eyed her. "Fine."

"How's your dad doing?"

"He's okay." Peyton turned the string bracelet around on her wrist. The brightly colored threads cycled around. Orange, yellow, red, green.

"It's nice your aunt is going to stay and help out for a little while."

Brenna groaned. "Mom."

"Oh, for heaven's sake, Brenna. Just pause the movie." She returned her attention to Peyton. "She came in to see Dr. Lindstrom today. I hope everything's okay."

Peyton was the daughter of a nurse. She knew that wasn't the sort of thing Mrs. Viersteck was supposed to tell people, and it certainly wasn't the sort of thing she should be asking about. "I guess."

"I was surprised when she called to set up an appointment. I thought Dr. Lindstrom had stopped being her doctor long ago." When Peyton didn't respond, she reached up to adjust an earring. "It's just that she was supposed to go to him for her college physical, but she never showed." She shook her bracelets around her wrist. "I have no idea how she got into college without one."

"Fascinating, Mom," Brenna said.

So what was she saying, that Dana had been up to something, that she wasn't what she appeared to be? Mrs. Viersteck had been a sometime friend of her mom's, but Peyton could always tell her mom didn't really like Mrs. Viersteck. Whenever Mrs. Viersteck called to say she was dropping by, Peyton's mom always put the phone down with a little sigh of resignation.

"Well, it is fascinating. I've always wondered." Mrs. Viersteck patted the front of her skirt, smoothing it over her hips. "I guess she and Joe Connolly are still an item, huh?"

"People don't talk like that anymore, Mom."

"I'm people, and I do." Her mascara was so thick it clumped. She smiled and Peyton was pretty sure she'd just reapplied her lipstick. Who did that, put on lipstick to check the kids in the basement? "I saw her get into Joe's car. It was sweet, actually, reminded me of the good old days."

"Sweet," Adam said.

She gave him a look as if trying to gauge whether he was sincere or mocking. "Make sure you use that coaster," she told him, and smiled at Peyton. "Let me know if you change your mind about those chips."

The moment her mother's trailing hand on the banister disappeared around the curve of the stairs, Brenna dipped under Adam's arm and snuggled against him. "Can we get back to the movie, guys, or what?"

"Or what," Adam said.

He thought he was so original. Peyton could have seen that line coming from a million miles away.

Eric held open the door, and Peyton pushed past him onto the front porch into the cool night air. Rocking chairs sat lined up along the railing as if something was about to happen out on the grass and they didn't want to miss the show. Clouds had rolled in to cover the face of the moon, and everything smelled damp.

"I know what we can do now," she said. "Stick needles under our fingernails."

"Come on. It wasn't so bad. I thought you liked Brenna."

She snorted. *Right*. Brenna was the kind of person who assumed friendship, who confided in Peyton and asked her to be lab partners, *blah blah blah*, but Brenna was like that with everyone. It didn't mean anything. "You can be so dumb sometimes."

Why was she so mad? Was it because of Brenna's stupidity, Mrs. Viersteck's insincerity, or the pressure of sitting beside Eric for two hours and knowing he wanted to kiss her like Adam was kissing Brenna. Or maybe it was that Brenna still had her mom around. Brenna was so secure that she could treat her mom like dirt, right in front of Peyton.

"I guess." His voice was mild.

She narrowed her eyes at him. She could call him a major dork, and he'd shrug. It just made her madder. "Whatever."

He unlocked the car and Peyton climbed into the passenger seat. Eric's car, technically one he shared with his older brother, was a total beater, with rusted doorframes and sagging seats, but it rode low to the ground, and she loved watching the way Eric drove with one arm on the windowsill and the other hand on the steering wheel. He'd hung the big green fuzzy dice she'd given him from the rearview mirror, and now she reached up and tapped them to send them swinging.

Thunder rumbled distantly as he backed his car out of the driveway. "Did you Google your aunt after you got her phone number?"

His voice sounded a little too casual. "Why would I?"

He shrugged. "It's just that they're saying she killed someone in that building implosion."

That was ridiculous. She frowned at him, but he wouldn't look at her. "Oh, come on."

"For real. There was someone in the building when she blew it up."

Peyton slumped in her seat and frowned at the dashboard. "I don't believe you. Dana hasn't said anything."

"Well, but would she? Come on. Think about it. Your dad would be *pissed*."

Eric was right. Dana was playing them.

"Sorry." Eric glanced over. "I just thought you should know."

"Great. It's just one more freaky thing about my family."

"Everyone's family is freaky."

"No, they aren't. Yours is really, really not freaky."

The light turned red and Eric braked to a stop. Lightning flared.

The whole world was outside, and it was just the two of them inside the small space of the car, the air tinged with the musty odor from the discarded fast-food wrappers on the floor, and the tang of Eric's cologne. "How come you hang around me?"

He laughed a little. "Seriously?"

"Seriously." The dice had stopped rocking and now hung straight. "Lots of girls like you." *Everyone* liked him. "You're a normal guy. I'm all . . . twisted." Saying it hurt, a stabbing pain that lingered.

"Peyton. You're not that way."

So much wonder in his voice. The red glow from the stoplight slanted into the car; his gaze was steady on hers.

"When I look at you, all I see is this halo around you, like you're glowing," he said.

"You telling me to get a tan?"

He shook his head, no amusement there. Was he *blushing*? "You're just . . . it."

A car behind them honked, telling them the light had changed. The rain started, a soft patter at first, then a steady rapping on the glass. Eric switched on the wipers. She watched the street blur and sharpen, blur and sharpen, all the quiet houses massed around them, the people inside them coming together and moving apart. Two letters that spelled the world. *It.*

NINETEEN

[DANA]

A RAINY NIGHT IN A SMALL TOWN WITH NOTHING TO do. No one to visit, and neither of the two movies playing downtown sounded appealing. Neither did hanging around a bar, watching other people connect. It used to be a game, to see if I could get the guy in the corner to come over, or the girl on the stool beside me to tell me her life story. Now I knew just how shallow those interactions really were.

Rain pattered against the windowpanes as Frank worked at the dining room table, sliding papers around with abrupt crispness, as though he were searching for something and not liking what he was finding. A glass of amber liquid sat by his elbow. So he'd moved on to the hard stuff. He didn't glance up when I came to stand in the doorway.

"Where's Peyton?" I had arrived to find supper dishes piled in the sink, and Peyton's bedroom door hanging ajar to an empty room.

"Why?" He looked over at me, reading glasses perched on the end of his nose.

For a moment, I saw him, the brother I could have had. "I'm going to go through my stuff in the basement, and I wanted to see if she wanted any of it."

"Doubtful." He went back to his papers.

And there he went, the brother I would never know.

The space was dark and cool, cluttered with old furniture and holiday decorations, and the storm seemed far away. Boxes were stacked in the far corner. I yanked the string dangling from the rafters, and yellow light spilled down in a cone.

I pulled a heavy box toward me, smeared with dust, the dry tape offering no resistance when I pulled apart the flaps. Papers, probably every note I ever took, every test. Why had Julie kept them? She couldn't have imagined that I would want to wade through my theories regarding Nazi-occupied France. I shoved the box aside.

The next box was light, and rattled as I took it down. Trophies. Not mine, but somehow, magically, Julie's.

A tarnished figurine of a girl holding a ball aloft, cobalt blue ribbon wrapped around the stand. I remembered Julie sinking the final basket, putting her team over in the last second of the game. I'd yelled so loud I was hoarse the whole next day. You'd think that a trophy figure would show some emotion. You'd think the chin would be raised and the mouth stretched wide in triumph.

The door at the top of the stairs creaked open, letting in a wedge of light shining around a pair of jean-clad legs. Peyton came down the stairs, arms filled with clothes, not seeing me until she was halfway to the washer. She looked away, but too late.

"Hi," I said.

"Hi," came the reluctant response.

Up went the lid of the washing machine, in went the clothes. She shook in detergent, lowered the lid, pressed a button. Water rushed into the tub.

"Look what I found," I said as she turned to the stairs. "Your mom's old trophies."

"Yeah?" Grudging.

"Here's the one she got senior year. Her team voted her Most Valuable Player."

"I didn't know that."

"She was the best point guard our high school ever had."

"They have a plaque in the hallway."

"Really." The thought warmed me. "Her coach said she could've gotten a college scholarship."

"She didn't want that. She wanted to be married. She wanted to have me."

Said challengingly. I wondered who had told her that. Julie or Frank? Julie's senior year, she and her coach had sat at the dining room table in our old house, debating all the options. In the end, Julie decided she couldn't leave me. She'd told her coach in a low voice that I wasn't supposed to hear from where I perched on the landing, *She thinks people always leave.*

In the end, I was the one who left Julie.

"Do you play basketball?" I asked.

"Yeah, in middle school." She sat cross legged beside me, her short blonde hair feathery, and one knee poking through the denim of her jeans. She smelled of popcorn and rain. "I didn't make the high school team."

I didn't move, not wanting her to bolt.

Peyton pulled a trophy from the box and sneezed. "Yuck. Why did she keep all this stuff?"

"For you, I bet."

"Me? What am I supposed to do with it?"

"You could pass it to your own children."

"You kidding? I'm never having kids." She dropped the trophy into the box and wiped her palms on her jeans.

Would Julie have protested, hearing that, insisted that Peyton was too young to make such a decision? No, she would have kept silent and given Peyton space, the way she had done with me.

The next box was filled with odds and ends. Would this mix of stuff hold Peyton's interest, keep her close for just a few more minutes? I reached for a short red plastic tube. "Bet you don't know what this is." I held it out, and after a moment, she took it.

Shaking it, she pried off the top and tipped the tube to let small cardboard disks slide into her palm. She frowned.

"Pogs," I said. "They were big when I was a kid."

She poked one with a finger. "What do they do?"

"Nothing. You collect them and have wars with your friends. Whoever wins gets to keep the other person's."

She rolled her eyes.

"Pretty cool, huh?" I said lightly. "Bet you're surprised we had such fun games back then."

She made no comment, merely dropped the disks back into the tube, but I thought I saw the ghost of a smile touch the corners of her mouth.

I took out a stuffed sock monkey, its wide red mouth looking slightly obscene. "Yikes. I forgot about this guy. Your mom always said it gave her nightmares. Why did she even bother to keep it?" Maybe she'd imagined the two of us going through all this stuff and laughing. Julie had always been such a hopeless optimist.

"My mom kept everything." Peyton pulled out a poster and unrolled it. "Who are New Kids on the Block?"

I groaned. "You're making me feel *ancient*." An easy exchange, the beginning of something?

The creak on the stair shattered it.

Frank, coming down the steps and walking across the cement floor. The smell of whiskey rolled off him, and by the way Peyton wrinkled her nose, I could tell she smelled it, too. "Take a look at this, Peyton, and tell me if you made this call last month."

She got up to look at the paper he extended. "Where?"

He tapped the sheet and she shrugged.

"The phone company made a mistake. I just called that number a few days ago." She handed the paper back to him. "That's Dana's."

Ah. The phone bill. I'd hoped neither of them would ever know. Reluctantly, I got to my feet. "It's not a mistake. That's when Julie called me."

They both stared at me.

"Julie called you?" Frank scanned the paper then frowned. "*Five* weeks ago?"

Confusion played across Peyton's face. "You didn't tell me that."

No, I hadn't.

"Hold on a minute," Frank said. "You *knew* about Julie?"

"No," I said. "She didn't tell me she was sick."

"Why did she call you, then?" Peyton asked.

I couldn't bear to see the accusation on her face. I turned to Frank, who stood there, arms crossed, waiting for my reply. "I don't know," I admitted.

"You're telling me you two were talking," Frank said, "and she never said anything about being sick?"

"We weren't *talking*. It was just the one phone call."

"This doesn't make any sense," Peyton said.

Frank had his gaze firmly on mine. "What *did* you two talk about?"

"Not much. I couldn't talk just then. I was busy, in the middle of setting up a shoot." It sounded horrible, put like that. It didn't say anything about how stunned I'd been to hear my sister's voice on the other end of the line, how haltingly the few words we'd exchanged had come. It didn't describe the awkward gaps where both of us paused to let the other speak, only to find silence standing where words should have rushed in.

"You were too *busy*," Frank repeated.

This was why I hadn't wanted to say anything. This was how I knew the conversation would unravel, in ugly hopeless circles.

"That's not how it went," I said, miserably. "She asked if I was a doctor. She sounded disappointed to hear I wasn't."

"Mom wouldn't have cared about something like that," Peyton said.

Peyton hadn't heard the flatness in my sister's voice. Julie had cared, all right. I'd been embarrassed. It had made me feel defensive. I'd cut the call short, promised to call her back. But I never did.

"What else?" Frank asked. "What are you hiding?"

"Nothing." It had been a private phone conversation. It had nothing to do with either of them, yet there they both stood, expecting explanations from me, wanting to understand why Julie had called and, most of all, why she hadn't told either of them about it.

"Yes, you are," Peyton said. Her cheeks were flushed and her eyes narrowed with anger. "Tell him what happened in Chicago."

How could she know about that? The triumph on her face told me she knew the whole story. Now Frank was looking at me. "Someone got hurt in the shoot . . . ," I began.

"Someone *died*," Peyton corrected.

"Yes," I said. "Someone was inside the building when we shot it." Calm and certain, betraying none of my fear and indecision. I had a steady hand in wiring a building with dynamite. I had a steady hand here. "We don't know how she got in there. We think she may have been sleeping it off."

"You *killed* someone?" Frank said.

"We didn't know she was there," I said.

"What do the police say?"

I hesitated. I'd been gone for almost a week and the police detective hadn't once phoned. Because I wasn't a suspect, or because I was? "The police are still investigating."

"Are they looking for you? Are you hiding out here?"

"Don't be ridiculous. They know I'm here. They have my cell number."

"Will you talk to them if *they* call?" Peyton demanded.

"Peyton," I said, "I didn't know she was sick. She didn't tell me."

"You *must* have known something was wrong. You just didn't care."

But I hadn't known anything was wrong. Julie had completely fooled me. I could never have imagined that my sister would have been able to keep something so urgent from me, but she had. She'd changed. "I did care. I do care."

"I wish I'd never called you. I wish you'd never come back." Peyton's face was my sister's, the same downward tilt to her eyes, the same arch to her eyebrows. It was mine, too, the same face that stared back at me from the mirror each morning.

Frank put his hand on her arm. "Come on, princess."

She allowed herself to be pulled away. Frank didn't even look at me as they went up the stairs.

How is she? I had asked Julie in that brief phone call.

Peyton's fine, she had replied, and that was when I had learned the name my sister had chosen.

TWENTY

[PEYTON]

THE MOST TIMID OCEAN CREATURES ARE THE FEATHER stars, delicate animals that look like ferns and tuck themselves into crevices to hide. At night, when everyone's asleep, they gingerly extend their arms and feed on drifting plankton. They swim slowly or creep along the ground, and prefer still water. They're not a main food source for any species, and humans don't collect them. If they were to die off, no one would notice or miss them. They lead quiet, unassuming lives, with one exception.

Once a year, the females briefly spawn, releasing millions of eggs in one big burst. The moms frantically churn the water with their arms to disperse their babies and send them floating away to make a home for themselves somewhere else. They're hoping with all their hearts that this next generation will find it easier or happier or better. But what they don't know is that their eggs eventually settle and hatch in another part of the ocean identical to the place they'd once called home. All that energy and hope for nothing; it's better they don't know the truth.

. . .

Peyton woke boiling mad, her cheek pressed hard against her pillow. *Why?* Then the night before swam back to her, and she flung off the covers and padded over to her aquarium.

Tiny fish fluttered up from the bottom, tails and fins rippling, happy to see her, happy to know they were going to be fed. Her peaceable kingdom, everyone getting along. *You first. No, please, after you.* She unscrewed the lid on the food, took a pinch and sprinkled it over the tank. They darted around greedily. She waited a minute. They still looked hungry, jabbing the water surface with their teeny snouts, so she added another pinch. "That's it," she told them.

Dana's bedroom door was closed. Light showed very faintly across the sill, seeping onto the floor of the darkened back hall.

Her dad manned the coffeemaker as if he could physically draw the coffee down into the pot.

"Why is she still here?" Peyton demanded. "Why are you letting her stay?"

"She's your mom's sister."

"Like that means anything!"

"It means something to me."

That surprised her. But then again, her dad was kind of tight with *his* sister. Maybe that was the way it was with sisters. Peyton would never know. "Are we going to church?"

"Your mom would want us to," he said, and that was that.

Spooning cold cereal into her mouth, she stared out the window. He'd been up paying bills again at the dining room table. She hadn't been there watching but she knew how it had gone, the endless shuffling of envelopes, the anxious gripping and re-gripping of the pen as though that would make dollar bills spring from the nib. She thought of the accusing way he'd looked at her, questioning the phone charge. Five bucks. When had five bucks gotten to be such a big deal? She knew the answer: back when her mother had a twelve-dollar aspirin in the hospital. "The bird feeder's empty," she said.

Her mom's job. The little wood-and-glass house had probably been empty for weeks and Peyton was only now realizing it.

"Which one?"

"The regular one." She leaned forward and looked down. "The hummingbird feeder fell." It lay in two pieces on the grass.

Her dad grunted.

"I'll take care of it." She could do the bird feeders and the laundry. He could do the bills and grocery shopping. Bit by bit, they'd close the gap her mom had left. They'd take care of all the outside stuff. It was the inside stuff that was the problem.

The diner was busy after church, all the done-praying people going after the Sunday Dinner $5.49 Special, but Leslie had saved them their usual table by the window. "Here you go," she sang out, dropping menus onto the table. Just three of them now, instead of four. "Miriam, you want coffee?"

Peyton's grandmother picked up the menu with her knobby hands. "That sounds fine."

Leslie splashed coffee into the thick white mug. "Frank?"

"Thanks."

"You want a Coke, Peyton?"

"Okay." Leslie was nice, not in that fake way some people had, but genuinely nice. She smiled like she meant it, and she always saved a piece of blueberry pie for Peyton. She'd sent a condolence card in the mail, signed by her and her little boy, his letters irregularly formed and sliding off the page. *Love, Benjamin William Jervis.* It looked as though it had taken him a whole day to write it all out.

Her grandmother studied the menu, the plastic-covered sheet curled and smeared with fingerprints, its offerings unchanged for as long as Peyton could remember. Soups. Sandwiches. Entrées. Desserts. Her grandmother would tap the picture of the baked chicken and ask her dad how salty he thought the sauce might be; she'd let her finger hover over the chef's salad and ask him whether the ham was real or pressed. And in the end, without fail, she'd triumphantly decide on the fish.

Peyton had a ton of homework, almost a week's worth of missed classes. Her teachers would give her a break, but the year was wrapping up and projects were due. Finals were looming. What if she just couldn't do it in two weeks? Would they give her the summer? What if the next year rolled around and Peyton was still reading *The Odyssey* and writing up that DNA lab? She could stay stuck in her junior year forever, while everyone else passed her and went on to college. Eric had big plans. He was counting on his saxophone playing to get him in somewhere great; his parents were already taking him on college tours. The subject hadn't really been discussed in Peyton's house. Now it probably never would be.

"The sermon was very nice, wasn't it, Peyton?" her grandma said.

"Uh-huh." At least she knew who Peyton was today.

Her grandma set down the menu and crossed her hands on top of it. "Very thought-provoking."

She said the same thing every Sunday, even if it was a recycled Easter or Christmas sermon that they'd all heard a billion times, or if she'd managed to snore through the whole thing. She always woke right up when it was time to go, blinking and sniffing, to gather her things and get going on to the diner. She never acted the least bit embarrassed. She probably thought the minister's words sailed right through her subconscious mind and fixed her right up with the good Lord's message.

Leslie returned with Peyton's Coke. "You folks ready to order?"

"Mom?" her dad said. "What looks good to you?"

As if he didn't know.

"Well, let's see. I'm trying to decide. Is the salad made fresh today, or is it left over from yesterday?"

"Which salad, Miriam?" Leslie asked. "The chef's or the Caesar?"

So she was going to play the game, too.

"I was looking at the chef's salad, but the chicken does sound . . ."

"How about the fish?" Peyton said.

All three adults looked at her.

"The fish?" Her grandmother tilted the menu. "Now, that's an idea. I didn't see that."

Her father shot Peyton a look. "That's what I'll have, too."

"All righty," Leslie said. "Two fish platters." She smiled down at Peyton. "You on for a burger?"

Peyton nodded, feeling a little abashed. Her dad had gotten her back, though, with the fish order. Now she'd be surrounded by the fishy odor and the knowledge that the deep-fried golden objects on the plates to her right and across from her were once swimming happily in the nearby lake. She handed Leslie her menu. Well, at least they didn't serve calamari or shrimp, things that were recognizable as what they'd once been.

"With cheddar, right? Extra pickles?"

"Please." Eric teased her all the time about eating cheeseburgers. *Moo,* he'd say. *Don't cows count, too?*

Leslie tucked her notepad in her apron pocket. "Be back in a jiffy."

Peyton played with her straw. Now was when her mother would start searching her purse for a quarter. She'd teasingly ask Grandma what she was in the mood for, hip-hop or heavy metal. Her grandma would laugh and laugh.

Her dad cleared his throat and slid out of his chair. "Why don't I go check out the jukebox selections?"

He'd felt it, too. In a way, that made her feel better.

"That would be nice, Frank," her grandma said.

Peyton waited until he was halfway across the crowded room before leaning over into the cloud of baby powder surrounding her grandmother. "Grandma, do you remember my aunt Dana?" She had clearly known who she was the day of the funeral, but today could be another story.

Her grandma looked at her with her watery blue eyes that suddenly seemed icy. "Julie's sister."

Peyton nodded.

"What's she up to now?"

Which implied that she'd been up to something *before*. "The same kind of thing," Peyton replied cagily.

Her grandma pursed her lips. The skin around her mouth drew tight into wrinkles. "I would certainly hope not. I'd like to think she learned her lesson."

"I guess she hasn't."

"Julie spoiled her. That's the problem. Julie let that girl get away with everything. But who could blame her? She wasn't that much older than Dana, and she was trying to live her own life, too. That's what she needed to focus on, her marriage and her child. You ask me, it was a good thing, Dana leaving town when she did. Julie never could say no to her."

Her mom had never been that pitiful. Her mom said no to Peyton all the time. *No,* you can't see an R-rated movie. *No,* you can't eat ice cream for dinner. It was horrible thinking of her mom being so nice to Dana, and Dana not even bothering to call her back the one time her mom reached out to her. A headache skewered itself into the center of her forehead.

Her grandma sipped her coffee, the cup tipping precariously in her grasp. Peyton watched to see if she'd need to grab it, but her grandmother managed to set it back onto the table without splashing a drop of the hot liquid. "And those parties at Gerkey's." She shook her head. "I told Alice those kids were up to no good, but she said it was better they drank there than wander all over the highways. Julie wouldn't listen, either. She insisted Dana would never touch a beer."

So what if she had? Everyone drank beer. Even Peyton had

had a couple before the shifting wooziness convinced her that maybe it wasn't her thing. But her grandma wouldn't understand. She had rules about the most stupid things. Peyton had to take off her shoes when she visited. She had to sit with her knees together instead of cross-legged; she couldn't have pop with her meals, and no cookies except on a plate. Finding out Peyton had had a Bud Light would have made her cry with fear.

"Did she and Julie have a fight?"

"No, not exactly." Her grandma drew down her spidery white eyebrows. "Poor Julie. It was very sad, altogether."

Now they were going somewhere. "Like what?"

"Well, I can't say now, can I? It's a secret." Her grandma mimed locking her lips with a gnarled finger and thumb and throwing away an imaginary key.

Wait just a minute. What was a secret, and why on earth would her mom have shared one with her grandma? Peyton moved her fork, her knife. If she came at her grandma directly, the old lady would back away. Peyton would have to go in side-ways. She kept her voice casual. "Julie wanted you to tell me. She said it was okay."

"No, she did not. You are telling a fib, aren't you?"

It had to be a pretty good secret to make her grandma suddenly make sense. "Does my dad know?"

"Where are all these questions coming from?" Her grandma fixed Peyton with a glare. "You're not doing drugs, are you, young lady?"

Ugh. "Grandma. Tell me."

"No, I promised Julie. Where is she, by the way?" Her grandma looked around with a frown. "I'm getting worried now. It's not like her to keep people waiting."

"What was so sad?"

"Pardon?"

Peyton wanted to shake her. "You said something sad happened. Was it about my mom? Was it about Julie?"

"Julie?" Her grandmother gave her a pleasant, puzzled smile. "Where did you say she was?"

It was no use. Her grandmother had been derailed. Nothing Peyton said would get her back on track. She pulled her hand from her grandma's grasp. The old woman didn't even seem to notice. "She called to say she'd be late."

Her grandma picked up her cup again. "Oh, did she? That's all right, then."

Peyton sighed.

Her dad scanned the jukebox selections, Leslie beside him. She pointed to something and he nodded, smiled. Not his real smile, more a softening of the corners of his mouth, but a smile nonetheless. Five days already and he was smiling. How did a person do that? Peyton was sure her own mouth had forgotten how.

TWENTY-ONE

[DANA]

OUR DAD LEFT WHEN I WAS FIVE YEARS OLD. HE must've run, actually, given how completely he vanished. One day he was there; the next he was gone. I've never known why, and Julie swore she didn't, either. I have a few memories of him sitting in a chair by the window, hanging up the bird feeder, mostly doing stuff. He mustn't have talked much to me. I don't recall who told me he was gone, but it was probably my mother. I imagine she would have been calm, despite her own sadness, and I would have been pragmatic. *We'll still live here?* I probably asked. *I'll still go to school?*

Eight years later, Julie had come into my early morning bedroom to tell me our mother had drowned. I remember that more clearly. The sash of my sister's pink bathrobe tightly knotted, her feet inexplicably bare though the wooden floor had to be freezing.

Those were the dark days, those days limned with black and pinned to the timeline of my life, the days that marked the ends of some things and the uncertain beginnings of others. My father's silent leaving, my mother's sudden death. My baby's birth, swathed tight in a pain so powerful that it carried me to another realm entirely to watch my daughter's arrival into the world. But I endured it. I gritted my teeth and focused, knowing it would all be worth it. And it had been, for one single, beautiful day.

I was many things: stubborn, impulsive, driven. But I'd never once thought of myself as cowardly. As I lay on the thin, bumpy mattress that smelled of must and insect repellant, listening for sounds of Frank's and Peyton's departure, I realized that was exactly what I had become. A coward. Or worse, maybe it's what I'd always been, all along.

The shallow puddles glinted in the morning sun. Last night's storm had scrubbed the streets clean. When I reached the lake, the water throbbed extra blue, and the sky was painfully bright. The sand was pocked by raindrops. I started toward a vendor, the umbrella over his cart green-striped and beckoning, the appetizing aroma of coffee drifting over, when someone called my name.

Fred stood on the back patio of Lakeside, broom in hand. "Word to the wise," he said. "Don't buy coffee from Hank. He recycles his grounds."

"Right now, even that sounds good."

"Hold on. I just put on a pot. Let me fetch you a cup." When he returned with a tall paper cup, he waved away my money. "You kidding? We're not even open yet."

"Thanks," I said, and took a sip. "This is great."

"French roast. You're welcome to sit out here. I can set up a table."

"Thanks, but I think I'll go down by the lake."

"Have at it. I might join you after I get things going."

"Sure." I started to turn away when he said, "I almost forgot—your friend was in the other night, looking for you."

It couldn't have been Joe. Fred would have said so. "Which friend is that?"

"Big dude with tiny teeth. You remember. Some sort of sales-man."

Right. Mr. Specialty Chemicals. I gave Fred a pointed look, like *ha-ha*. "Too bad I missed him."

He grinned. "Feel free to come back for a refill."

I found a bench in the sun and wiped the wood dry with a handful of paper napkins. Sitting down, cup balanced beside me, I studied Julie's notebook for whatever it was I had missed. The more the answer eluded me, the more certain I became that it was there, somewhere. The numbers, the names, the addresses. Maybe if I plotted everything on a map, something would jump out at me. Then I saw it: toward the last page, a word in the margin that had been heavily crossed out. I held it up to the sun and squinted. My name, DANA. What did it mean? I sipped my coffee and thought.

This time five days ago, Halim and I had been placing charges, rolling out det cord, studying the blueprints one final time. We'd been focused on the job at hand, but also thinking about the next one. Would there be a next one? I hadn't placed a single phone call on our behalf. I'd left it all in Halim's hands.

Ahmed might have misled me. He might have wanted me to feel doubt and worry about whether I deserved to be Halim's partner. After all, he'd been there before I joined the company, and all along the way he'd let me know I was the intruder. Making sure he was the one who signed the delivery sheets. Keeping phone numbers from me at critical times. He'd be talking to Halim, and when I entered the room, he'd stop and look busy. Why had I put up with it these past five years? Because it kept me moving, kept me from dwelling on the past, forced me to focus on the future. All the reasons I didn't want to be back here in my hometown; all the reasons I couldn't leave.

"J-Julie?"

LT Stahlberg stood behind me on the path that cut between

beach and grass. He'd gotten fat, his sweatshirt stretching across his solid chest and thick arms, his big cheeks squeezing his eyes into slits. Aluminum foil was wrapped around his head, and his face was alarmingly red. Was anyone monitoring his blood pressure? "Hi, LT," I said, hoping I hid the dismay I felt seeing him looking so unwell. "It's Dana."

"Dana." He seemed to think about that, then nodded. "Julie's sister."

"That's right."

"Julie's gone."

"Yes." The simplicity of that welled up in me, pushed aside the busyness I'd protected myself with. I cleared my throat. "How are you? It's been a long time."

"Don't come over here," he said. "You've got sand on your shoes."

So he really hadn't changed. He used to huddle on the playground, terrified to set foot on the grass because of the worms. "What's the matter with sand?"

"It's made from rocks, from all over. Trucks brought it here, with different license plates. You don't know where those rocks are from. They could be radioactive."

Was this how I'd sounded to Doc Lindstrom? "You know, I was worried about the sand, too."

"You were?"

"I talked to Doc Lindstrom about it. He said it's perfectly safe. You remember him, right?"

"He put a cast on my arm."

That had been a long time ago. It had been bright pink and Brian Gerkey had taunted him mercilessly. *You a girl? That what your problem is, LT?*

I'd swelled up with an emotion so powerful that it burst right out of me. I'd wheeled around and smacked Brian with my skateboard, and I bet he still had the scar on his arm to prove it. The sight of the blood had sent LT running. It took Irene Stahlberg all afternoon before she found him, huddled in the pavilion, sobbing.

The summer I was fourteen and applying for a job, Alice Gerkey hired me on the spot without so much as glancing at my application, not saying a word about how I'd once beaten up her only son. I always suspected she felt he had it coming to him.

LT shuffled his feet. "Going to the doctor's what made Julie sick. All those things plugged into the wall. She used that stuff all the time. I tried to tell her, but she wouldn't listen."

"You talking about blood pressure cuffs, stuff like that?"

He crossed his arms over the bulk of his belly, rocking back and forth on his heels. "Doc Lindstrom uses those things, too. So he wouldn't know about the sand. No way, José. He can't know for sure."

"If you're worried about the beach, then why are you down here?"

His eyes widened. "Dana," he said, reproving. "It's the *lake*. The water absorbs the rays. I just wish I could get closer."

"What if you wore boots or something? You could walk out to the pier and sit on the end."

"That won't work. Sand gets in everything. It's good today because it's heavy from the rain. It won't fly up or anything right now. So this is a good time."

"It is a good time," I agreed. "It's quiet out here."

"You can hear your thoughts. You can hear if anyone's listening to them."

I was wrong. He'd gotten worse since the last time I saw him. I felt a tug of sorrow. "I hear you're living on your own now."

"It's a pretty cool place. There are three other guys and they're okay. I have to check in and out whenever I go anywhere, like to the store or to work. But I don't mind. At least that way someone knows where I am, in case the aliens find me and take me away."

Aliens were new. "Has that happened before?"

He lowered his voice. "I hear them talking. Sometimes I wake up in the middle of the night and they're whispering in my ears."

Poor LT, living in a frightening world peopled by his own nightmares. "Is that what the foil's for?"

He patted the thin silver. "It keeps them from reading my mind."

It probably made things worse, the foil rustling against his ears and confounding noise. I held up my cup. "You want coffee or something?"

"No! Don't come any closer. The sand, remember?"

"Oh, right." The sand that was now clinging to the bottom of his sweatpants. I hoped it fell off before he realized it.

"Dana, does it happen to you, too? When you wake up, can you tell that things have changed while you were sleeping?"

Change. Maybe that was it. He was looking at me, waiting. "Well, sometimes my dreams can make me think about things in a different way."

He nodded, sending the foil pieces sliding down his cheeks. "That's why we have to be careful. That's why we always have to watch."

What were his touchstones, the things he used to keep himself balanced? Had one of them been Julie? "It's good you're doing that."

"Yeah?" His face relaxed, and I wondered what small comfort I'd given him.

A low rumble made him glance upward. "I got to go. Planes can kill you."

He lurched down the narrow path, his feet making odd steps as he tried to avoid swaths of sand washed across the cement, as the low grumble of the plane chased after him.

Shielding my eyes, I squinted up at the white machine with its wings outstretched and tried to make out whether it was Joe's, but in the end one small plane looks pretty much like another, and I watched it grow smaller and smaller until it was just a speck sailing into the sun.

Martin smiled, seeing me. His cheeks were puffy, the skin stretched taut across his face. His look of surprised joy took me aback, and I felt ashamed. I had had every intention of leaving town the day before without saying goodbye, of just packing up my suitcase and driving away.

Turning to the nurse walking alongside him into the dialysis clinic's waiting room, he said, "I'm good now. My daughter's here."

I didn't let my step falter. I didn't react at all.

The nurse glanced at me, confusion evident on her face. We didn't know each other. "That's nice," she said. "Why don't you sit out here for a little while and make sure you're ready to go?"

Two Native American children played on the floor, and as Martin lowered himself to an upholstered chair, a crayon rolled his way. Bending, he handed it to them. "If I'd known you were coming, I'd have brought my Scrabble board, but Milly Peterson's using it. She's got some championship going."

"That's okay," I said. "I just wanted to talk, anyway."

"Oh, sure, then."

The nurse lifted an afghan from the back of the couch, a dizzying swirl of dandelion yellow and purple, and folded it around Martin's knees. She gave me a meaningful look, and I nodded. I'd stay with him for a while.

"How are you two doing?" she asked the children.

"Fine," the older one said.

"Is our mommy done yet?" the younger girl asked.

"One more hour, honey." The nurse patted Martin's shoulder, and walked back through the sliding doors into the dialysis room.

"What's up?" Martin asked me.

"I've been thinking that Julie was right—something's making people sick."

"Even though the Department of Health said it's all clear?"

"Even though."

His gaze moved around the room and came to rest on the children playing nearby. "Go on," he said, at last.

"I thought you might be able to help me figure out what's changed in Black Bear over the past few years." *Change*, LT had said. What had changed overnight, literally and figuratively?

The clock on the wall above his head chirred, and the hour hand struck one.

He sat back. "Let's see. Were you here when they opened that new highway north of town?"

"Highway 10?"

"Yes, that's the one. Took half the traffic right out of town, and the stores really suffered."

"I was here." Ten had opened way back when I was a teenager, and we'd christened it with drag races until the highway patrol stopped us. It had curved around Black Bear now for almost twenty years and could have nothing to do with what I was searching for.

"A few years back, we got a girl on the high school football team," he mused. "That was big news around here."

"That's not the kind of changes I'm talking about."

"I know, I know. I'm just trying to jog things loose."

He was right. I needed to let him do this in his own way. "Okay. A girl joined the football team."

"We added two more handicapped spots in front of the library. The Main Street Café started serving breakfast on weekends."

The younger girl looked up, the light polishing the glossy lengths of her hair. "We got new swings at school."

"There you go. We got new swings."

Which neither he nor Julie had been anywhere near. Satisfied, the little girl returned to her coloring.

"Of course, there's been lots of new construction downtown,

and all around the lake. That amusement park, couple new hotels."

"My mom works at the Duck On Inn." The older girl frowned as she industriously worked her crayon across the page. "She says the tourists are going to kill her."

The younger girl looked up. "Our mom's in there. She has to get her blood cleaned."

"That's right," Martin told them. "You're both very good little girls to wait for her so patiently."

A serious nod. "We're going to get DQ."

"That sounds nice," I said. The girl regarded me with round dark eyes, then returned to her coloring.

"Duck On Inn's a popular place," Martin said. "They got a real good fish fry on Fridays."

"Local fish?"

"Oh, sure."

So wait. Maybe we were onto something. "Are there any manufacturing plants that drain into the lake?"

"Well, sure. There's Gerkey's."

"Can't be that," I said. "Gerkey's has been around forever. We need to focus on what's new, what's changed recently."

He nodded, looked down, and plucked at the blanket across his lap. "You know, Dana, you've been gone a long time." His voice was gentle. He looked up with kind eyes. "Do you really care about what's going on here?"

"Of course I do," I said, stung. "This is my hometown. I grew up here."

His expression told me he didn't believe me.

"Well, hey." Sheri was there, smiling down at me, her hand on the back of Martin's chair. "Didn't think I'd see you two here." She looked from me to Martin, to me again. "Am I interrupting anything?"

"Look, Miss Sheri." The older girl clambered to her feet. "I drew you a picture."

"You did? Let me see." Sheri examined the piece of paper. "Gorgeous."

"I drew one, too," her sister said.

"Hers isn't very good," the older one said apologetically.

The younger one elbowed her.

"Ow!"

"Wow, look at these." Sheri took the proffered sheet. "These are just beautiful. I'm going to hang them on my bulletin board when I get to work tomorrow."

"For real?"

"You bet." Sheri sat beside me on the couch. "How you doing, Martin?"

"Not one of my better days."

She nodded with a deeper understanding than I could ever have, and I realized how this disease had united them, broken down barriers and allowed them to speak in shorthand. "I decided to take Julie's advice," she said. "I'm going to learn to do home dialysis."

"Good for you," Martin said. "You can do it."

"I hope you're right." She gave us both a wan smile. "Hey, listen. Why don't you come by for supper tonight?"

"That's all right," Martin said. "You kids go on without me. *Wheel of Fortune*'s on and I don't want to miss it."

"Dana?"

I suddenly very much wanted to have dinner with Sheri and Mike, see their home and their two little boys. "I'd love to. What time?"

"How about seven o'clock? We'll feed the boys earlier, and tuck them in. We'll have a real grown-ups' night out." She stood and looked down at the girls. "You two want to come in with me and check on your mom?"

The little girls skipped alongside Sheri, the younger one reaching up for her hand as the doors opened to let them into the dialysis room.

We watched them go. The waiting room felt barren, an empty silence stretching from wall to wall. At last, Martin sighed. "You know you can't bring Julie back."

"I know that," I snapped. "She called me. Out of the blue a few weeks ago. I didn't even give her a chance to talk. But she should have told me she was sick. I could have saved her." Instead, she'd very decisively crossed out my name in the margin of her notebook.

He reached over and took my hand in his warm, callused hands. "Maybe she didn't think she was the one needed saving."

TWENTY-TWO

[PEYTON]

STARFISH WILL EAT ANYTHING: CORALS, SPONGES, *worms, crabs, mussels, oysters, clams, rotting fish, sea cucumbers, sea urchins, mud, and sometimes even one another. They're focused and determined, working for days to pry open a clam, willingly fracturing their bodies in the process. They march through coral reefs, sucking out the polyps helplessly trapped in their tiny shells; they slurp down sea anemones and jellies, despite how bitter their poisons must taste.*

Other animals, seeing them approach, run for cover—at least the ones that can. The other ones burrow and hold themselves very, very still.

People, on the other hand, think starfish are charming. They stop and pick them up from the sand. They bring them home as souvenirs, maybe even make jewelry out of them. Isn't it funny to think that starfish die, not because they're so evil, but because they're so pretty?

. . .

Her grandma loved car rides. Peyton couldn't understand why, but it always meant that after church and the diner, they'd drive around the lake, her grandma with her hand on the windowsill, watching the boats and people go by. She'd lived in Black Bear all her life. What on earth could be so new and marvelous that she'd want to see it again and again? Peyton slumped in the backseat and seethed.

At last, they dropped her grandma off at the nursing home, and Peyton resumed her front-row seat. "Why does Grandma hate Dana so much?"

He glanced at her. "That what Grandma said, that she hates Dana?"

"Not exactly, but you've heard her. I think Dana did something to make Grandma really mad, something that hurt Mom."

"Like what?"

"I don't know. Grandma wouldn't say. All she told me was that it was a secret."

"You know your grandma doesn't always get things straight."

Not this time. Grandma knew something and she knew enough not to tell. Peyton slouched in her seat and watched the houses roll past. She should have guessed her dad would be no help.

"Why are you so interested in this?" he asked.

She sighed, exasperated. "It's about *Mom.*"

"Well, if Dana did something bad, your mom would have mentioned it."

"She didn't tell us she called Dana, did she?" Peyton shot back.

He frowned and she knew she'd struck a nerve.

Slightly abashed, she said in a softer voice, "Why do you think she kept that a secret, Dad?"

His voice was level when he replied. "I wish I knew."

. . .

Peyton poked the plastic tube to the gravel bottom of her aquarium, and the fish scattered, wary. Water began dripping into the bucket at her feet. She moved the tube around, watching to make sure she didn't accidentally suck up a fish.

She didn't need to worry about the loach. Plump and sluglike, they were firmly attached to the glass with their suckers, industrious and purposeful. They always seemed so earnest to Peyton, as if they were constantly trying to prove their worth. But the dwarf rainbow fish with their tiny glowing eyes could be unpredictable. They were hiding near the thing that looked like melted wax but was supposed to be a volcano. Peyton had walked into the kitchen one morning to find it beside her bowl and her mother at the stove, casually stirring the oatmeal. The endlers preferred the little arched bridge and the lighthouse, both of which had been tucked into the toe of her Christmas stocking. The leader of the tank, her dwarf gourami, liked the plastic palm tree that Eric had given her because he said tropical fish needed to feel at home.

From outside her window came a steady banging as her dad worked on her mom's car. Something or other had fallen off the week before her mom went into the hospital for the last time, and her dad had promised her he'd fix it. Peyton had no idea why he was working on it now, but maybe it was like why she was cleaning her aquarium. Something to do. Something normal.

Footsteps tapped rapidly down the hall. Dana always walked fast, as if she was impatient to get to wherever she was going. Peyton's mom had had a more thoughtful stride, as if she'd been enjoying the trip and the destination could wait.

The footsteps halted and Peyton knew without looking that Dana stood in the doorway. Peyton felt Dana's indecision and uncertainty, but she didn't look over to rescue her. Instead, she focused on the tube, moving it around to suck up the debris mixed in with the gravel.

"Hi," Dana said at last. "How was church?"

"Fine." It was church. If it was so special, Dana would have gone.

"I'm heating up a hotdish for you and your dad."

"I can do it. I did it last night." Letting Dana know they didn't need her. They certainly didn't want her.

"Right." Dana's voice trailed off. Then she said, "Is that a dwarf gourami?"

How did she know *that*? It wasn't like the fish was all that big, or all that remarkable looking. But somehow Dana had recognized it from where she stood in the doorway. She glanced over. "Yes," she said grudgingly.

"I dated a guy who had a tank of them," Dana said.

Despite herself, Peyton was even more intrigued. Not so much about the idea of her aunt dating, which *was* pretty interesting, but by the fact that she'd known a guy with a tank full of aggressive fish. So now Peyton had to ask, "How did he keep them from killing each other?"

"I think he had only males."

That made sense. Peyton found herself saying, "You can come in if you want." Then she looked back to the tube in her hand. Where had *that* come from?

Behind her, she heard Dana come into the room. Her footsteps were soft on the carpet. Peyton moved the tube to the next inch of gravel, poking it up and down to loosen the gunk collected at the bottom of the tank. She should have cleaned the tank weeks ago.

"You've got some neat posters," Dana said. "What's that fish called?"

Peyton glanced over and saw her aunt standing by the foot of her bed, looking at the huge skeletal monster with its pointed teeth and tiny dead eyes. "An anglerfish."

"Why is the background black?"

"That photo was taken in the abyss. There's no light down

there." It was only recently that scientists had been able to travel so deep undersea. They were discovering new species every day. Peyton couldn't wait until it was her turn to go, to climb into the submersible and strap herself in.

"He's lucky, then," Dana said. "He'd never find a girlfriend if she could see how mean he looked."

Girlfriend was a baby term. Dana meant *mate*. Did she think Peyton wouldn't understand the concept? So it was with some satisfaction that Peyton corrected her. "Her."

"Excuse me?"

"That's a her. They're dominant."

"No kidding." Dana sounded amused. She moved to the next poster, pinned above Peyton's desk. "There's one I recognize."

Big deal. Everyone knew what that one was. "That's a clown-fish." Her mom had gotten her that poster, back before she finally caved and let Peyton get real fish. "You know, like in *Nemo*."

"Actually, I saw one off the coast of Australia."

Really. "Like, in the ocean?"

"A couple of times."

Peyton had never been anywhere near the ocean. The farthest distance she'd ever traveled had been sixty miles west to Fargo, which didn't even have an aquarium. Mr. G's three-hundred-gallon tank was the closest thing to a coral reef that she'd ever seen.

"I didn't think I'd like it, but it was amazing," Dana said. " So many different kinds of fish, all living together in harmony."

"That's not harmony. It's the will to survive. They all get something out of it. The poisonous fish harbor the fish that lure prey close enough for them to feed. The smaller fish eat the left-overs the bigger fish drop. The weaker fish hide among the corals and sponges, and bring the food to them."

Dana nodded. She understood; she got it. "We couldn't stay down long. We had to take all sorts of precautions. We weren't allowed to touch anything, and we couldn't even wear sunscreen.

I got a terrible sunburn." She laughed softly, probably at the memory of it.

"Coral looks hard as rock, but it's really fragile. It can only grow under very specific conditions. The salinity has to be just right, the amount of sunlight, the temperature, the water current. If even one thing is off, coral dies."

"Our guide told us that one-sixth of all animal species live in coral reefs."

One-sixth of the whole world packed together in two-thousandths of the ocean. "If people only knew how important coral reefs are. All sorts of new medicines come from coral reefs. Antihistamines, antibiotics, even cancer drugs."

"Really?" Dana had her head tilted, her eyes focused on Peyton as though her whole body were listening.

"NOAA says we've already lost nineteen percent of coral reefs, and they predict we'll lose another fifteen percent in the next ten years."

"Because of global warming?"

"And pollution. Lots of things."

"Maybe things will turn around."

"No, they won't." Wasn't she even listening? Peyton yanked out the drainage tube from the tank. Water dribbled onto her toes. "It's already too late." The world would be over before she even got a chance to be really and truly in it.

"I'm sure—" Dana began.

"Don't," Peyton snapped. She didn't want any lame reassurances that the whole world would suddenly come to its senses and everything would be all right. Every time she passed an SUV belching smoke or a crushed Styrofoam cup caught in someone's flower bed, she knew just exactly where the world's priorities lay. "Why are you here, anyway, Dana? What do you *want*?"

"Your mom wanted me here."

"Since when did you care what my mom wanted? You don't even *know* what my mom wanted."

Dana said, "She left me a note."

Peyton had just picked up the bucket so she could empty it, but that stopped her. "What note?"

"She wrote down my name in her notebook and then she crossed it out. I think that's why she called me. She thought I was a doctor and she thought I could help."

"Don't call that a note. That's nothing."

"She was wrong, Peyton. I *can* help."

Peyton laughed. "Wow. That is amazing. I didn't know I had an aunt who could raise people from the dead."

"Stop it, Peyton, and listen. Your mom wasn't worried about herself. She was worried about *you*."

"Don't you think I know that? My mom *loved* me." For some reason, Peyton was crying. "My mom did *everything* for me!" She didn't know how she was going to survive without her mom.

Dana was crying now, too. "I know, sweetheart."

That only made Peyton cry harder, great wrenching sobs that hiccupped out of her. "You don't know . . . anything! What's my middle . . . name? Do you know *that*?"

Dana could only shake her head, mute and miserable. Peyton pushed past her, glad she'd hurt her.

Alone in the bathroom, Peyton upended the bucket over the toilet and watched the dirty brown water swirl down the drain. Her mom had worried so much about Peyton that Peyton stopped telling her things, stuff she'd kept back to protect her, things she thought weren't important but now knew were the most important of all: lime Jell-O at lunch that no one ate. Parallel parking in three moves instead of eight. The way Eric looked at her when he didn't think she was watching.

Those were the things that connected her to her mom and her mom to her, and when you took them all away, all you had left were two cardboard figures propped up and apart, not even touching.

TWENTY-THREE

[DANA]

Six hours after they released me from the hospital, I carried my suitcase out to the car in the dark. *You shouldn't be doing this,* Julie whispered, though no one was around to hear her. *It's too soon.*

Everything's been set up, I lied. *I'll be fine.*

The sharp cry of a newborn sailed out the window, and my heart twisted. Julie glanced over her shoulder. *You'll be back for Thanksgiving?*

That was when I finally told her. *I'm never coming back.*

Julie's face went white; she stared at me. *Then . . . You can't mean that.*

It's the only way.

I'll come visit you.

Don't. It has to be a clean break for both of us. Thank you for everything. You've been a wonderful sister. You'll be a terrific mom.

Dana. Her voice soared high in anguish.

You can't call or write me.

I can't just let you go.

Julie. I threw my arms around her, the last time I would ever touch my sister, though I didn't know it, and hugged her hard. *We'll always be together.*

Sheri swung open her front door and smiled at me brightly. Something was up.

"Dana. Come on in."

I'd barely taken two steps when the doorbell chimed again. "I hope you don't mind," Sheri said, putting her hand on the doorknob.

Of course it would be Joe standing on the front stoop. He looked surprised but then he smiled. I smiled, too, but the word he'd called me curled between us: *outsider.*

"Just like old times," Sheri said happily.

We joined Mike in the family room. He lay on the green carpet, propped on an elbow, playing with his sons. "Hey, Dana. Joe."

Light oak furniture, brown drapes, and mismatched pillows. A television screen dominated one wall, and a trio of hammered-metal ducks in flight decorated another. Toys lay scattered everywhere: blocks and puzzles, toy cars and army men, crayons and books. A child-sized table was by the fireplace, a big red plastic slide stood wedged into a corner. So this was what Sheri lived like, grown up.

"Come on in and dig out a place to sit." She wasn't the least bit apologetic about the mess, and I liked her for that. That was the girl I remembered, who wasn't bothered by the surface stuff, who went right for what was important. "You guys want anything to drink? How about a beer? Mike?"

"Need any help?" I asked, and she answered, "I got it."

Logan kneeled by his father. Clad in pajamas, his cheeks bright red, he smacked at his older brother's hand reaching toward the top of the plastic chutes they were constructing. "Mine."

"Stop it, Logan," Mike said. "It's Mikey's turn."

"How's Peyton doing?" Joe asked me. "Is she still planning on going to school tomorrow?"

"So far as I know." I hadn't followed her into the bathroom. I hadn't reached out and taken her in my arms. Instead, I'd leaned against the thin wall separating my room from the room where she stood at the sink, and ached for all the things I'd lost, and all the things I'd never have again.

"She was back at work, too," Sheri said, walking in from the kitchen and depositing beer cans. She handed her boys sippy cups. "Logan, last one before bed."

It couldn't be easy, regulating the fluid intake of a four-year-old. But Logan showed no signs of irritation as he took the cup and put it to his mouth.

"Ronni said she did all right." Sheri sat beside me.

"Ronni Stahlberg?" I asked.

"Ronni Williams, now. She and Peyton work together."

"Not for long." Mike held a toy piece out to his older boy. "Peyton just got moved to Manufacturing."

Joe paused in mid-sip and lowered his beer. "She's still a minor."

"It's that big government contract they just got," Sheri said. "Brian's got to get the new line up and running quick. You better be careful, Dana, or he'll talk you into coming to work for him, too."

Mike snapped a piece onto the plastic tower, his two boys bracketing him, absorbed in his every move. "Remember when he persuaded Viola Viersteck to run for mayor?"

"Not his fault she took him seriously." Sheri was watching the three of them. What did it feel like, to have built a family like this? Then I realized she was focused on the cup in Logan's hand, her own drink held poised before her lips as though willing her child to do the same.

"How did it go with the nurse today?" I asked.

Sheri tore her gaze from Logan, turning to me with a smile. "Okay, I guess. Mike's going to get trained, too, so we can help each other out. It'll be good, won't it, Logan, to have dialysis at home?"

Logan had his head bent, his cap of blond hair falling forward and covering his features. He swiped a hand beneath his nose.

"Don't let him touch the marbles," Mikey warned, but Joe was already leaning forward with a tissue from the box on the table.

The box had been closer to me. I hadn't even thought of it.

"Do you think he'll be okay to go in with you tomorrow?" Mike was saying.

The small space was filled with worry and concern, all converging on one small child. "I think so," Sheri said. "What do you think, Logan? Do you want to go play with the other boys and girls after dialysis tomorrow?"

"Tell Mikey to give me that one," Logan said.

"I'll take that as a yes." Sheri smiled at me. "I've got lasagna in the oven. It should be ready soon."

"Sure. So you work in a preschool?"

She shook her head. "I'm in the daycare at Gerkey's. It's a sweet deal. Logan comes to work with me, and I can bring Mikey anytime I want, like when he has a break or school lets out early."

I started to take a sip of beer, then stopped. "When did Brian add on the daycare?"

"Three years ago."

"The clinic and gift shop, too?"

Joe hitched forward in his seat. "He remodeled the building all at the same time."

He knew what I was thinking. "I don't know," I said, more to myself than to him. "That can't be the reason."

"What?" Sheri asked, bewildered.

Joe had his gaze trained on me. "Dana's been thinking Julie was right."

Martin, Julie, Lainie, and now Logan. Every one of them

spent time in the plant. They lined up like tin soldiers, *tap tap tap*. "What if it's Gerkey's?" I said. I'd been too hasty dismissing it.

"Sure." Mike laughed. "Everyone knows how dangerous hand lotion is."

"No, no. It makes sense. Joe, we saw it from the air. The crops all around the plant are stunted."

"Julie already looked at Gerkey's," Sheri protested.

"She did?" Julie had made no mention of it in her notebook. But it made sense that she would have considered Gerkey's. After all, both Frank and Peyton worked there. She would have been frantic to cross it off the list.

"She talked to Brian and she showed the numbers to the Department of Health."

"No one did any testing, though, right?"

"Of course not." Mike got to his feet. "Come on, boys. Let's try this out."

"What would they have tested for?" Sheri asked.

"I don't know. I haven't figured that out yet. It might be something buried in the ground. Did anything get dug up when Brian remodeled the plant?"

"Come on, Dana. This isn't like that movie *Silkwood*." Mike handed a marble to Mikey, and the boy stood on his tiptoes to drop the marble into the topmost chute.

It was true. That was the mental picture I had: the truck crunching onto the deserted gravel parking lot late at night, the men acting suspiciously about the big barrels of industrial waste loaded into the back of the pickup.

Logan crouched by the toy, clapping his hands and waiting for the marble to finish its circuit.

"Brian had regular contractors do the job," Sheri said.

"Maybe it's the new building materials. They can make a person sick. If the place isn't properly vented . . ."

"Of course it is," Mike said. "Your turn, Logan."

"How can you know if it's vented?" I turned to Joe. "What if he used some of that drywall from overseas that contains formaldehyde?"

Joe rubbed the back of his neck. "I never heard of drywall giving people renal failure."

"Could it be something in the lotion?" I pressed.

"Check it out." Mike snatched a bottle of lotion from the coffee table and tossed it at me. I caught it in midair. "See for yourself. There's nothing toxic in there."

I scanned the label. Water, glycerin, stearates, parabens. "The first ingredient is water. Is it from Black Lake? If that's contaminated . . ."

"We use purified water." He patted Logan on the shoulder. "Try again."

"No, not again." Sheri got up. "He's got to go to bed."

"Has Brian changed the formulations, gone with a new vendor?"

Sheri wouldn't even look at me. She bent and scooped Logan into her arms. "Mike, do you have Mikey?"

"That's got to be it," I said with growing conviction. "It's got to be the lotion. Everyone who's gotten sick—"

"That's enough," Sheri hissed.

I looked at her, stunned by her tone.

Sheri held Logan on her hip, her hand to his face, pressing his ear against her shoulder. "They can understand what you're saying, you know. They're not dolls."

I looked from her face to Mike's angry eyes and put down my can.

"Hey," Joe interposed. "I think that little guy's planning to take a marble to bed with him."

"No way," Mike said. "Logan, you wouldn't do that, would you?"

Sheri was stiff as Logan lifted his head from her shoulder. "Maybe," he said slyly.

"He's a magician," Joe said. "He's hiding it somewhere. I might just have to tickle it out of him."

Logan squealed, and Mikey jumped up and down. "Let me do it! Let me do it!"

"All tickle monsters upstairs!" Mike commanded.

Mikey pounded up the stairs, Mike and Sheri following, Logan giggling and trying to twist out of her grasp. Joe stopped on the stairs and looked down at me. "Hey," he said.

"Joe! Joe!" Logan called.

I shrugged, letting him go. This was his life now, not mine. Not ours.

Joe turned and followed the laughter up the stairs.

TWENTY-FOUR

[PEYTON]

EVEN THOUGH THEY LIVE IN THE WATER, FISH STILL get dirty. Algae get trapped between their scales and teeth; parasites burrow into their flesh. It really bugs them, but what can they do? It's not like they have hands or fingers to clean themselves up. So they rely on other fish, called cleaner fish, to help them.

Cleaner fish are tiny shrimps and fish that specialize in eating debris from bigger fish. They're in high demand. They pick a rock or piece of coral and wait. Other fish spot them and form lines, patiently waiting their turn. Even the most vicious, pointy-toothed shark will open wide and let these tiny fish drift inside to nibble away all the gross stuff.

It's nice to think of fish behaving in such a civilized manner. It's like they've been to church and heard the sermon. But among the cleaner fish lurk imposters, other fish that look just like the good guys. The bigger fish can't tell them apart. They let these bad dudes snuggle right up close, and zap! The fake cleaner fish nips off a chunk of flesh and zips away, a sneaky little thief.

The world is full of deception and misunderstanding, even where you'd least expect it.

Peyton lay in bed and stared at her darkened aquarium. Well before dawn, but there was enough ambient light to reveal the shadows of her fish hanging motionless, waiting for their day to begin. The water bubbled through the filter in the corner, their whole world perfect, warm and clean.

If her mom were still around, she'd make Peyton a cup of tea, and they'd sit at the kitchen table and talk a little as the sun glided over the horizon and filled the kitchen with pink light. Peyton got up and put on her bathrobe, then padded quietly down the hall to the kitchen.

She was surprised to find Dana there, her face glowing in the light from her laptop. Peyton whirled around, then thought, *Wait. This is* my *house.*

"Want some tea?" Dana moved a finger and the laptop went dark, hiding her in shadow. "The water's still hot."

Mind reading. Peyton paused in mid-reach for the metal tin filled with teabags. Pouring the water, she sat across from Dana and spooned sugar into her cup. Her ugly words from the day before crowded between them, hustling about looking for a place to settle themselves, and then just . . . vanished.

Peyton held her cup between both hands, one thumb hooked through the handle, and breathed in warm citrus vapor.

Two more weeks of school, her mother would say. *And then I'll have you all to myself.*

Outside the kitchen window, the bushes along the sides of the yard emerged from the blackness. A tree took shape. A bird cooed. Dana cranked open the window beside her and the sound clarified, rolled around the room in little swirls. "She's telling her kids not to miss the bus."

It did sound like that, gentle scolding like she'd told them a million times to brush their beaks and shake out their feathers. The tea was delicious. The warmth of the cup felt good between her fingers. Her mother pushed her gently. *Tell her it's okay.*

"My mom was trying to get her to eat out of her hand." The words just flowed right out of Peyton into the sleepy early hours. She shifted in her seat and stared out at her old playhouse taking shape on the other side of the glass, the roof bashed in where she'd jumped on it from the tree branch above.

"She used to play with leeches when she was little. She'd catch them in buckets and pretend they were families." Dana mock-shuddered. "Maybe that's where you get it from."

Peyton had never once played with a stupid leech. Those squishy brown things, as big and fat as her hand, and just as dumb.

"Your grandma used to call your mom Snow White."

That was interesting. Her mom had never told her that. Snow White had black hair and was kind of dorky, not like her mom, but still Peyton could see it.

"You would have loved your grandma," Dana said. "She would have spoiled you rotten."

Peyton knew all about what had happened to her grandma, how her car had slid into the half-frozen lake and sunk, trapping her inside. The first time Peyton heard the story, she couldn't sleep for months, certain that her grandma, all wet and covered with reeds, would come banging on her bedroom window, and demand to be let in. Peyton's mom had talked about her mom all the time: how she always put out a placemat and napkin even for just a glass of milk, how she pressed all her clothes, even T-shirts, how she woke the girls up for the first snowfall. That wasn't what Peyton wanted to know about. "What about my grandpa?"

Dana set down her cup. "My father, you mean?"

"Where is he, do you know? Is he still alive?"

"I have no idea."

"I Googled him but there was nothing. Do you think he changed his name?"

"I think he'd do whatever he had to, to keep us from finding him."

Which sounded like she had tried to find him, too. Dana had her face turned toward the dawn, the pulse beating softly in her throat. "Why did he leave?" Peyton wanted to know.

Dana shrugged. "You'd have to ask him."

"Did they fight or something? Did he drink?"

Dana looked at her. Peyton flushed, wondering what she was seeing. "I don't remember them fighting, or drinking being an issue. Frankly, I don't really remember him at all."

Peyton couldn't imagine not remembering her dad. Her life was bursting with memories of him. "My mom said he was tall, and that he had binoculars that he let her use sometimes when they went looking for birds. She said he loved birds."

"Yep. He sure did. More than he loved us."

Peyton's mom hadn't thought that. She would have told Peyton if her dad was hateful. Or maybe she'd been waiting for Peyton to figure it out for herself. "You really think my mom called you because she thought you could help figure out what made her sick?"

"I do."

"And that's what you're staying to figure out?"

Dana nodded, watching her. "Okay," Peyton said, and stood to wash her cup.

Brenna was sitting at the back of the classroom, holding her black Sharpie poised over her hand splayed across the lab desk. She didn't look up as Peyton slid onto the stool beside her. "You missed the DNA lab last week," she said.

Peyton had been looking forward to that lab. It would have

been like playing, stringing together colored paper clips into order and then unknitting and reknitting them to make a whole new helix. She would have asked to do lionfish DNA, or maybe a sea urchin. It would have let her look at a fish in a brand-new way, from the inside out. "I was a little busy."

Brenna scrunched her nose, like *Sorry*. "You didn't miss anything. It was totally the worst lab of the year."

Only because she had to actually do something instead of texting in her pocket while Peyton did the work. "How come?"

Brenna lowered the nib of her Sharpie and inked little pointy teeth along the side of her thumb. "Connolly flunked me. Which sucks."

Connolly didn't just flunk people. "What did you do?"

"I thought it would be easier to unzip the helix and make both matching DNA strands at the same time. Way faster, you know." She flipped her hand over and began on her wrist. "Because you weren't there."

Peyton had gotten the part about her not being there. "Mr. Connolly told us not to take any shortcuts."

"He didn't say that doing something like that would be a shortcut."

Yes, he had. He'd specifically cited that as the example. Nice as he was, Mr. Connolly was uptight about procedure. But Brenna hadn't been paying attention. She didn't think she'd needed to. She thought she could sit there and draw ink tattoos on her hands because Peyton was paying attention and taking notes.

"Buh-bye, brand-new Mini Cooper with the sweet leather seats. Hello, Grandpa's ancient piece of crap."

"Don't worry. Your dad'll change his mind."

Brenna glanced at her with eyes heavily outlined in black. "You think?"

Mr. Connolly came in and shut the door. "Good afternoon, folks."

"Good afternoon," Hannah warbled from the front row.

"What a suck-up," Brenna muttered.

The guy on the other side of Peyton sniggered.

Mr. Connolly set his briefcase on the floor by his desk. "For those one or two among you who aren't counting the days, I want to remind you that we've only got two weeks left until finals."

A groan went up.

"Aha. So I take it you haven't started studying yet, Robbie." Mr. Connolly slid his hands into his pockets and tipped back on his heels, looking around the room. His gaze rested on Peyton and he gave her a little nod. "Anyone?"

Sure enough, Hannah raised her hand and waved.

Brenna leaned across Peyton and said to the guy beside her, "You want to drop her, or you want me to?"

He flashed her a grin. Peyton frowned and nudged him, and he sat back.

"All right, listen up. From now on, we're going to spend the first fifteen minutes of each class period reviewing. By finals, you'll know this material backward and forward. You'll be dreaming about it."

"I know what I'm going to be dreaming about, and it isn't going to be DNA replication." Brenna picked up her red Sharpie and drew drops of blood from the tips of the dragon's pointy teeth into her palm.

"You sure?" muttered the guy next to Peyton, and now it was Brenna's turn to grin.

Adam watched from across the classroom. Peyton almost felt sorry for him, but he should have seen it coming. After all, he'd already been dating Brenna for two months, a full month past the expiration date on most of Brenna's relationships.

"Why don't we start with an easy one?" Mr. Connolly suggested. "Graves' disease. Adrian, why don't you tell the class the physical characteristics of this particular disease?"

Peyton picked up her pen. It had something to do with the

thyroid. Or was it the adrenal glands? Maybe it was a skin disorder.

Brenna held out her palm. "Which one's the heart line?"

Peyton tapped the end of her pen on the line curving around the meat of Brenna's thumb.

Brenna bent over her hand. She'd moved on to green ink, and her hand was looking tattooed. Brenna had a real tattoo, high on her hip bone, of a horseshoe. If Peyton got a tattoo, it would be of an Irukandji jellyfish, which was half an inch long and deadly. Or maybe a manatee, ugly and ponderous, but utterly peaceful and wise.

"Thyroid. Thank you, Hannah."

Thyroid, Peyton wrote. She couldn't even remember what the thyroid *did*, let alone what diseases affected it. She'd better study all the thyroid diseases, because, sure enough, Mr. Connolly wouldn't test them on Graves' now that he'd mentioned it in class. That was how he separated the wolves from the sheep. The sheep would dutifully study Graves' while the wolves ignored it and leaped over to hyperthyroidism, or whatever it was called.

"Moving on to Mendel's laws. Which alleles does someone with blood type O have?"

Okay. This was blood typing. That was a big topic. They'd spent over a week on genotypes and Peyton had found it fascinating. She had planned to do something for the science fair on it, but then her mom had been hospitalized with her first infection. After that, Peyton had lost interest in the subject.

"So if both parents have blood type A, what blood type must their child be?"

"Which one's the life line?" Brenna hissed.

Peyton sighed. Seriously? "It's the other one."

"Oh. Right."

"Come on, people. You should know this."

It was no use. She could write down every word he said from

now until the end of school and she still wouldn't pass the final. There had to be another way.

"By the way." Brenna leaned over confidingly, her black-rimmed eyes wide-open with false sincerity. "That sweater just does not work."

Yeah, Peyton would give that fashion tip the weight it deserved, seeing how it was coming from a girl with a pierced belly button and raccoon eyes.

After the bell rang, Peyton went up to the front of the class, where Mr. Connolly sat filling in the attendance sheet. "I'll be with you in just a second, Peyton."

Mr. Connolly wasn't so bad-looking, for a teacher. Obviously, Dana thought he was still hot. Maybe if he were younger, not wearing a tie but regular clothes, his hair longer in the front so that it came down to his eyes . . .

He looked up and she blushed.

"So, what's on your mind, Peyton?"

"I need to talk to you about making up the work I missed."

"Yes, I've been thinking about that. You're behind on a few other projects, too."

She'd had the time. That wasn't the question. But she just couldn't get her head into the same room as her work. "I guess I can stay after school and make it up."

"You need an extension?" he asked gently. "It's not a problem."

"Like summer school?" She'd already stared at the pages in her textbook a million times. Staring at them in June wouldn't make any difference. "I can't. I'm working."

"Right." He tapped his fingers on his desk, thinking. "How about this? How about you pick a topic and write up a report? Fifteen sources, minimum, twenty pages double-spaced."

She felt a glimmer of interest. "On anything I want?"

"Anything that falls within the parameters of this class."

"How about blood type and how it's passed from parent to child? I'd start with my family." She had all her mom's medical data. All she'd have to do was find out hers and her dad's.

"I like it. You'd need to expand the scope, though."

"I'd have to ask a bunch of people for their blood types." People would do it. It wouldn't be like asking them how much they weighed or earned. Blood type was totally impersonal. No one would care.

TWENTY-FIVE

[DANA]

BRIAN MET ME AT THE GLEAMING GLASS DOORS OF his brand-new factory. I was surprised to see him there; I thought he'd have me directed to his back office.

"Hi," I said. "Thanks for fitting me in."

"Sure."

A uniformed guard sat behind the long reception desk. I eyed him and raised my eyebrows at Brian, who shrugged. "Sign of the times," he said. "You need to sign in, too."

I dutifully wrote my name on the line. The guard handed me an adhesive label that read VISITOR and I pressed it onto my shirt.

"Why don't you come on back," Brian suggested, "and we can discuss this."

Apparently this wasn't going to be as easy as I'd hoped. I picked up the gray suitcase and followed Brian across the spacious lobby and down a hallway.

"That the monitor?" Brian nodded to the case in my hand.

"Yes." It was a ten-thousand-dollar air sampler that I didn't normally keep in the trunk of my car, but I'd planned to use it in

Chicago and had neglected to remove it before heading north to Black Bear.

"Interesting. I thought you did demo."

"I do. This is part of the follow-up work we do after a building comes down. I use it to make sure we haven't released anything hazardous into the air."

He frowned. "You won't find anything hazardous here."

I didn't reply. Doc Lindstrom had said workers breathing in sand dust were susceptible to kidney disease. This wasn't a sand factory, but it *was* a factory. There had to be all sorts of things in the air. "This place is huge," I said as we crossed another hallway. "And I hear you're still expanding."

"Just got a military contract."

"Military?"

"Sunscreen, Dana. That's all."

We entered a suite of offices. A woman sat behind a desk and smiled up at us. "That salesman called again," she told Brian.

"Pass him on to Jim," he said.

"I tried that. He's persistent."

"Well, just keep telling him I'm busy, and sooner or later he'll get the point." He pushed open the door to his office.

A room filled with sunlight. A desk stood along one side, and on the other, covering the entire wall, stood the largest fish tank I'd ever seen, aside from the Baltimore Aquarium.

"Wow," I said, walking over. It was gorgeous, filled with brightly colored fish weaving through the corals and sea plants. Anemones waved and infinitesimally tiny starfish clung to the sides of the glass. "Are those live corals?"

"You bet," he said. "They were just fragments when I got them. Now look at them."

Dozens of them, orange and yellow and purple, from flat fungus-like ones along the bottom to branched ones growing along the back to rippling ones that waved their plump tentacles around. "Peyton takes care of *this*?"

"She's the only one I trust. She helped me pick out that lavender coral, and she's the one who convinced me not to try seahorses. I admit it. She may have been right about that."

"She has a tank, too."

"Sure. I helped her pick it out. She was just a little kid when she first saw my tank. From that day forward, she had her heart set on getting one of her own."

A framed photograph of a woman was on the wall, her arms around two pretty little girls in matching blue dresses. She had to be his wife.

"So, Dana," Brian said. "What exactly are you looking for?"

"I'm not sure," I admitted. "Something airborne. Maybe something got released when you built the new plant."

"Nothing that would make people sick. Besides, this is a green plant. Even the paint's nontoxic."

I hadn't known that, but I pushed on. "It has to be something new, something that's changed only within the last few years. How about a new candle scent?" Those cloying aromas used to make my eyes water.

He was shaking his head. "I discontinued the candle line five years ago. It wasn't a profitable segment for us. Now we focus on specialty creams and lotions." He held up a hand. "And I haven't reformulated any of them. We pride ourselves on using the old family formulas. The same ones we used back when you worked here."

So he remembered.

"Look," I said. "I know this makes you nervous, my coming in here and suggesting your plant's making people sick. I hope I'm wrong. But what if I'm right?"

"You can't be. We'd know."

Apparently not. "What are you afraid of?" I said, and that sleepy look vanished and became acute, the calculating businessman emerging behind the former doper, a Brian I'd never seen before. I felt a prickle of unease.

"Fine," he said. "You've got thirty minutes."

We started in the lobby.

"Looks like a Dustbuster," Brian said as I pulled the small white machine from its padded case.

"Same principle." I held the monitor horizontally so the rubbing alcohol wouldn't drain out, and switched it on. A double dash pulsed, then disappeared. A few seconds later, a number glowed in the small black window.

Brian leaned in. "What's that mean?"

The number was similar to the one I'd taken outside to establish an ambient baseline. "It looks like the air's fine here. Let's check the clinic." Where Julie had worked.

No one was there but the nurse, a young woman wearing regular clothes and an ID hanging from a lanyard around her neck.

"Hi," she said, smiling with uncertainty.

"Don't mind us," Brian told her carefully. "We won't get in your way."

"No problem."

I walked over to the desk where Julie had once sat. There was nothing out of the ordinary here, just a telephone, a computer, glass jars of cotton balls and Q-tips. I pressed the button on the monitor, and was both relieved and disappointed when the number came up showing there was nothing in here, nothing at all.

The daycare was a riot of primary colors, noise, and motion. One woman tended the small children, while another rocked a baby in a rocking chair, neither of them Sheri.

"Is Sheri working today?" I asked.

Brian looked to one of the women, who answered, "She called in sick this morning."

Logan must have taken another turn. I wished I hadn't said anything the night before. I wished I'd waited until Joe and I were alone.

"Still nothing, right?" Brian said.

I glanced at the monitor. "Right." Which was great. Which

was fantastic. Little kids were everywhere, coloring, playing, laughing, climbing a little plastic slide. A spike in here would be devastating. "Let's try the gift shop."

Rows of bottles and jars lined the glass shelf. Fragrance wafted through the air. Brian said, "Lemon verbena," and I nodded. The clerk watched curiously as I walked around, pressing the button and reading the display. Nothing.

Brian checked his watch. "I've got a conference call," he said.

"You said I had thirty minutes," I reminded him, and he set his jaw but allowed me to push past him. I did the women's locker room by myself. It was painted industrial gray and had a row of showers, mirrors, and even a scale. What, did Brian think after a day of work, all a woman wanted to do was see how much she weighed? It told me something about his wife. She'd had that careful look about her in that photograph on his desk.

"Anything?" he asked when I emerged.

"No. See if there's anybody in the men's locker room, would you?"

The men's locker room showed nothing, and neither did the cafeteria, filled with the aromas of tomato and beef, and people who stopped their conversation to stare at me.

The storeroom was impressive, lined with long metal shelves filled with huge containers. Fat canvas sacks lay on the floor. I stopped and read one label. "Stearic acid?"

"It's a vegetable fat. It's used as a thickener."

I went on to the next one. "Zinc oxide?"

"Reflects sunlight. Are we going to go through these one by one?"

"Just tell me. Are any of these new?" Padimate O. Glycerin. Lecithin. Dimethicone. Methylparaben.

"I told you. Everything's the same. Everything we use is FDA-approved. No weirdo additives, nothing bought under the counter." He had his arms crossed and was leaning against the wall. "We're a family-owned business, Dana. We don't screw around."

I took readings, at the front, back, and center of the room. Still, the monitor kept saying, *Nope. Nothing here.* "Let's check Manufacturing."

"Julie didn't go into the manufacturing area."

"It's the most obvious place. We have to check."

"Look, Dana. It may just seem like hand lotion to you, but it's an incredibly competitive industry. You have no idea. We're just the little guy, trying to hold our own against the giants. You'd never even get this far in Procter and Gamble. You wouldn't even get in the door."

"I just want to run the machine. I won't even look at what they're doing."

"Three hundred people depend on me for their livelihoods."

"You want me to sign a confidentiality agreement?"

He hesitated. For one incredulous second, I thought he'd take me up on it. Then he turned on his heel and I followed him down the long white hallway to a double door without windows and a lockbox attached to the wall. I remembered when it was just a door, propped open with a shipping crate.

"Wow," I exclaimed. "You really are serious about security."

"I told you. It's a competitive business. There's a lot of money in skin care." He punched in a code and swung open the door. "You have to glove up."

This wasn't the small, low-ceilinged room I'd once worked in. This place was two stories of blazing white. Pipes ran along the ceiling and fed down in spirals to rows of industrial-sized bins and funnels, manned by lab-coated people wearing paper masks over their noses and mouths. Conveyor belts looped around the exterior. Electrical boxes were mounted at regular intervals.

Brian handed me a paper mask. "This, too."

People watched me as I walked around. Their gazes darted from me to Brian, and then to one another. Brian stopped to speak to one woman in a long white lab coat. I frowned down at the machine in my hand. Could it be malfunctioning? No, it would display a code if there were something wrong. It was working perfectly.

"What about runoff?" I asked.

"We stopped running waste into the lake when Brian took over."

Not Brian's voice, but Frank's. Surprised, I looked up. Frank stood there in his gray coveralls, wiping his hands on a dirty rag, and wearing a face mask. His eyes regarded me coldly. My heart suddenly thumped with guilt, as if I were a little kid caught with her hand in the cookie jar.

"What are you doing here?" he asked. "What is that thing?"

"I told you," I said. "I think something made Julie sick. I'm testing the air in here."

"It's all right, Frank," Brian said, turning back. "She's not finding anything."

"You don't have to put up with this on my account," Frank told him.

I bristled at that. "I want to check the lake."

The three of us stepped out into the warm spring afternoon and wended our way through the trees, the matted pine needles cushiony beneath our shoes. A bird cawed high above. A hawk, my father would have said. I gritted my teeth. It was being here that was summoning him back into memory. Peyton had brought him up, too, as we sat sipping tea in the predawn. Julie had apparently painted Peyton a nice portrait of a man who liked birds and carried around binoculars. I hadn't been as careful as my sister had been. I'd let my anger show.

The trees rose behind us as we stood on the shore, the lake peaceful and still in the clear sunshine. No ripples or gurgles of underground pipes pushing debris into the water, no muck limning the sand.

"What did I tell you?" Frank had pulled off his mask and now it dangled from a finger. "Sorry, Brian."

Talking through me as though I wasn't even standing there.

"No problem," Brian replied easily. "I think this was good. It calmed people down seeing Dana walk around with that thing. You know how riled up they got before."

"Before what?" I asked.

The two men exchanged a glance, but neither replied.

"You mean, before, when Julie was asking the same questions?" I said. "Were you humoring *her*, too?"

"Of course not," Brian said.

He was so calm, as though none of this involved him. "What if it was *your* wife, Brian? Wouldn't you want to know what had made her sick? What if it was one of *your* little girls hooked up to those machines?"

"Hey," Brian said sharply.

"That's enough," Frank warned.

I wheeled around. "That what you told her? That you'd had enough?"

"I never told Julie what to do."

"But you didn't help her, either, did you? You didn't support her, or try to get to the bottom of anything. You just let her feel that she was crazy, thinking what she was thinking."

"She was running around talking to people, exhausting herself. She'd drag herself home at all hours. It was pointless. She was sick and she needed to rest, and focus on getting better."

"What she needed was for you to believe in her."

"You don't know shit."

"I know my sister loved you." My sister, who'd believed in fairy-tale endings, had died knowing they were all a lie. No one lived happily ever after.

Frank's jaw tightened. "Meaning what? That I didn't deserve it?"

I'd never thought so, and he knew it.

"Look," Brian said to me. "You ran your samples. Take this

path around the building. It'll lead you to the parking lot." He turned to Frank, dismissing me. "Got a minute? I've got a call I'd like you to sit in on."

The two men walked back through the trees to the building. I watched them go, my gaze settling on the taller figure, and knew I'd been right. Brian wasn't to be trusted. But having that confirmed didn't make me feel better.

A motorboat buzzed in the distance. The water rolled to the shore; a breeze rustled the branches and stirred up the scent of pine. I looked down at the monitor in my hand and switched it off. I'd taken well over forty readings. Not a single one of them was positive.

If there was something out there, it was well-hidden.

TWENTY-SIX

[PEYTON]

T HE VIPERFISH HAS NEEDLE-SHARP TEETH THAT JUT
out of its distended lower jaw and curve all the way up to its
forehead. All he has to do is bite down and his prey is pierced
through and through, unable to wriggle away. The viperfish can't
really close its mouth but that's all right. He's willing to sacrifice
that convenience for the ability to easily snare a meal in the deep
cold water where food is hard to find.

But he has to be really careful when he bites down. If he mis-
judges, he can get stuck with jaws cranked wide open, with no way
to dislodge the fish and no way to consume it. Then, locked together, eye to eye, he and his captive wait for death to find them
both.

Who's the real winner then?

"Mr. G wants to get you started on the line." Fern glanced at her
watch and strode down the hallway, Peyton trailing in her wake.
"Though I don't know how much we can get done in an hour."

Not her fault, though Fern made it sound that way. Peyton

had come straight from school. Maybe Fern didn't approve of teenagers working in Manufacturing, either. Maybe Peyton had taken the job from one of Fern's friends.

She shuffled along in her bootie-covered shoes, hair encased in a net, lab coat flapping at the knees with the cuffs of the sleeves folded up to keep from drooping down to her fingertips. No fashion statement there.

Fern stopped by the door and punched in the code. "We change the code regularly."

Yeah, everyone knew you had to watch out for moms wanting to steal vats of baby lotion.

The big room hummed with movement and noise as people moved around making sure all the machines were doing their thing.

"Here's the rundown." Fern stopped by two small metal containers screwed to the wall and tugged a set of latex gloves from one and a paper face mask from another. She handed both to Peyton, then removed a set for herself. Sliding the mask over her mouth and nose, she pulled the elastic around the back of her head, and her voice grew muffled. "I don't expect you to memorize it, but it'll at least give you a general idea of how things work."

Peyton fitted the mask over her own face and tugged on her gloves.

Fern set off briskly down the center of the room. "Ingredients are stored in a large storeroom next door. We work with fifty-pound bags of materials, and you're not expected to cart those around. The guys in the storeroom do that, and they use dollies. I don't know where you'll be assigned yet . . ."

"Sunscreen."

"Oh?" Fern arched an eyebrow.

Peyton shrugged. "Mr. G told me he needed me working on the third line."

"Well then, let's head over there. That makes sense, I suppose. It's one of our least complicated formulations." Meaning a dumb kid like Peyton could be trusted not to screw it up. Fern stopped and fixed Peyton with a stern look. "You do understand our formulas are proprietary. That means you have to keep them secret."

Peyton knew what that meant. "I signed the form."

"Mr. G has lawyers. They'll sue."

"My dad works here. I'm not going to do anything stupid."

"Right." Her expression softened. It was that same sorrowful look Peyton had endured on the faces of her teachers all day. *That's right,* she was saying to herself, *poor little motherless girl.*

Peyton was glad the mask covered her face.

People stood at various stations along the catwalk, studying gauges, jotting notes on clipboards, watching as big paddles churned gray glop. Some of them looked familiar, but it was hard to tell with just their eyes peeping over the bridges of their masks. Three of them stood close together studying a caliper-looking instrument, murmuring and shaking their heads. Another passed by and stopped to contribute a comment that made them nod in agreement. She watched, transfixed. What was she doing up here, pretending she knew anything? Working in Shipping was a much better alternative. Nothing could go wrong there except for getting a paper cut or running out of packing tape.

Fern patted the funnel suspended above the first vat. "This is how we add ingredients. We do it sequentially, to ensure uniform mixing and consistent texture. Everything's on a timer. Larry, this is Peyton Kelleher. Frank's daughter."

"Hello, Peyton, Frank's daughter."

"Hello."

"I'm just about to add the Z4."

"If you've already got it measured, could Peyton do it?" Fern asked. "Mr. G wants her to get up to speed quickly."

"Well . . . it's his company. Go ahead. You got three minutes."

Three minutes wasn't much time. Her palms felt sweaty. "What do I do?"

"It's all been loaded into the system. All you have to do is push this button and guide the funnel."

Well, sure. She could do that.

Fern made a motion, and Larry stepped back behind Peyton.

"Did you hear what happened?" Fern whispered.

"Hear it? I saw it."

"Do you think he asked her?"

"The way I heard it, Dana asked him."

Peyton stilled, listening. Fern must have caught it, because now she turned away and dropped her voice to a murmur.

Big metal paddles churned white muck that very definitely already looked like lotion. What would adding Z4 do? Larry had said she had three minutes. Did that mean the timer had already gone off, or it was going to go off in three minutes? She didn't see a timer anywhere. She glanced behind her to ask and saw Fern and Larry with their heads close together, still gossiping about Dana. Well, what was three minutes? Might as well push it now. She turned back and her shoulder brushed the funnel, sending it swinging. A cascade of white powder spilled into the vat, then swung back to dump a stream onto her. She leaped back, smacking at herself.

Fern yelped. "What are you doing?"

"I got it, I got it." Larry shouldered Peyton aside and punched a series of buttons.

Peyton's cheeks flamed. *Stupid stupid.*

The assembly ground to a halt. People were looking over.

"It's my fault," Fern said. Larry nodded without looking up. He was levering up the paddles and examining the dripping liquid.

"Let's go," Fern said.

Feeling very much like a student being hauled to the principal's office, Peyton climbed down the stairs and followed Fern across the floor. She looked down at herself helplessly. She hoped it wasn't expensive powder.

. . .

"It was my fault." Peyton sat in the passenger seat of her dad's truck, lab coat bundled in her lap.

"Of course it wasn't," her dad answered. "Did someone tell you it was?"

"They didn't have to." She fingered a button on the lab coat, wiping the powder away from the slick surface with the side of her thumb.

"Fern should've known better than to let you run the machinery without any training."

"They just told me to push a button. I'm the one who screwed it up."

"What were they doing while you were pushing this button?"

"Talking."

"What about?"

For some reason, she didn't want to say. "Nothing."

He glanced at her. "Well, it had to be something for them to have left a kid alone with a million-dollar piece of equipment."

A million dollars? She sat back. Things could have been worse, *far* worse. What if she had broken the machine? The enormity of it made her physically sick. "I'm moving back to Shipping."

"Don't say that. Brian thinks you can handle this. I do, too."

She looked out the window. There was the sign for Black Bear. Her dad flipped on the turn signal and they swept onto the road leading to town. "They were talking about Dana."

"Fern and Larry were?"

She nodded.

They drove for a little while. At last, he spoke. "Dana thinks something made your mom sick."

"I know."

"You do?" He sounded surprised, and something else. Annoyed?

"She told me."

"Well, it's not true. You know that, right? We talked to the doctors. Doc Lindstrom ran every test he could think of. There was nothing we could have done."

She remembered. She and Eric had researched it themselves, hunched over his laptop and searching medical sites, scrolling through page after page after page. None of it had made any sense to Peyton. "So why was Dana at the plant?"

"She was testing the air."

"The *air*?" Like, the air they breathed all the time they were there? *Hours* and *hours* of breathing that air?

"Hey," he said, looking at her. "It's okay. She didn't find anything."

His voice was even and she believed him. So why was her stomach twisted into knots? "I'm going out with Eric tonight." Giving him fair warning. *You'll be alone.*

"Sure."

They were on their street. A group of kids were walking down the sidewalk, headed toward the lake. Their laughter came in through the opened truck windows.

Dana's car wasn't at the curb, which meant that maybe she wouldn't be home for supper. Again. Peyton could tell her dad had noticed. His face had relaxed a fraction. So he was relieved, too.

She gathered the dirty lab coat together; she'd have to wash it before she went back to work.

TWENTY-SEVEN

[DANA]

PUBERTY HAD NOT BEEN KIND TO ME. AT THIRTEEN, I grew six inches and curves, seemingly both at the same time. Julie hadn't known what to do with me. She'd slipped through her teen years like the swan she'd always been, but not me. I was ungainly and emotional. I was a giraffe and an elephant slapped together in disharmony, and miserable. At last Julie had said in despair, *Try running*.

The path around the lake used to end abruptly in gorse and dirt, as though whoever had installed it had given up. But now that old stopping point was gone, the new gray asphalt continuing on as though it had always been there, extending far into the distance and curving out of sight.

It had to be Gerkey's but it wasn't. Was Peyton at risk or not? My shoes thudded; my breath pounded in my throat. Had Julie been happy with Frank in the end or not?

My cellphone was ringing. I stopped and retrieved it from my pocket.

"Dana."

"Halim." Panting, I walked in circles, cooling down. "How nice of you to return my call."

"I'm sorry I've been difficult to reach." His voice was cool. He hated it when I was sarcastic. "But I understand you spoke with Ahmed."

"Oh yes. He gave me an earful."

A slight hesitation. *Good.* I'd caught him off guard.

"I was hoping to have something to tell you, Dana. I didn't want to trouble you, given your personal concerns. Nothing's official yet. We're still waiting for the autopsy report."

Not a word about my not returning when I'd said I would. Was he worried about my absence or relieved? "What's taking so long? It's been six days."

"They are doing a toxicology screen. Apparently, these results take time."

"I guess that's good," I said slowly.

"It's very good. If she was high on something, that would explain why she didn't know where she was."

It wouldn't explain how she'd sneaked past the guard. It wouldn't explain how we'd missed her. The breeze freshened, flattening the long grasses and sending a sandy spray across my ankles. "I've been calling White, but he's not picking up. You need to go over and talk to him. Don't let him weasel out of paying us." My mortgage was coming due, my cellphone bill. I'd been buying groceries and gas all week, and every time I swiped my credit card, I held my breath, waiting to see that it had been rejected.

"I haven't just been sitting here, Dana." His voice was sharp. "I've been working on it."

"Tell him we're going to start charging late fees. Contact the people in New Orleans and send them an invoice for our out-of-pocket expenses."

"That's not how we usually do it."

"We don't usually have clients cancel on us, either."

"It's insane. The woman had been living on the streets for years. Her family never saw her unless she needed money or a place to sleep. She was addicted to methamphetamine and she fished other people's food out of the garbage. For this, they've hired a lawyer."

I couldn't blame the Hamiltons; this was their daughter and sister. She'd mattered. "We need a lawyer."

"Lawyers are expensive."

He was going to quibble about money now? "Then tell your brother to repay those loans you've made him."

"He'll pay me as soon as he can." Halim's voice was smooth, coated with lies. That money was gone. His brother would never repay us, and we both knew it.

I'd made a mistake, one I kept repeating. I'd been so grateful that Halim had asked me to share his business dream that I'd given him free rein. I'd been so relieved to have Halim handle the police investigation that I'd willingly left town. I was still acting like the kid sister, the one who kept taking the easier path, no matter that it wandered around aimlessly. The sun beat down hard across my shoulders. I looked at my feet, the laces untied on one sneaker, the mosquito bites ringing my ankles.

"What about the guard?" I asked. "Have you found him?"

"No, and I doubt we will. Which is too bad. It would have been helpful to know if he saw anything Monday night."

"This is all my fault."

"Dana." His voice was low with warning.

"When we were doing our walk-through, I found a beer bottle. It was new, no dust on it. It wasn't there Monday night."

"You can't be certain of that. Besides, the bottle could have just as easily been left by the guard."

"If you hadn't been on the phone with your brother, we wouldn't have rushed the walk-through. We could have verified where that bottle came from. We could have found her."

"Are you saying this is my fault?"

Was I? "Even if the family doesn't sue—"

"We won't let that happen. You can't be talking that way. I know it is your way to take on everyone's burden, but this is not yours to bear."

"I don't take on people's burdens. That makes me sound pathetic."

"But you do. The crew, Ahmed's sister-in-law. You're always putting emotion over business."

"I can't believe you'd say that. I'm the one who gets people to pay up. I'm the one who negotiates hard."

"In this business, Dana, there are few people who listen to women."

Wait, wait. "What are you saying?"

A family was picnicking on the shore, the parents laughing as the kids splashed in the water. The children were tossing pieces of bread to the seagulls, shrieking as they swooped in.

"Nothing you don't already know yourself. You may do the talking, but I'm the one our clients listen to."

"That's insulting."

"It is the truth."

I'd been gone a week and no one had bothered to contact me: not suppliers, customers, even our own office staff. Did I really want to hear the truth? Yes, I decided. I did. "Tell me, Halim. Why did you bring me into your business?"

"You know why. I needed someone like you, someone smart and capable, someone to take over when I retired—"

"No. Let's stick with the truth. You never had any intention of my taking over the business. You only brought me in because I'm American, because that was the only way you could order explosives and get permits. What you needed was someone like me who would believe your lies."

A cold pause. When Halim spoke again, his voice was firm. "Let us allow this current business to settle itself."

"And then what?"

"And then we'll talk."

"I'm done talking." I closed my phone.

Try running, Julie had said, and in a way, I'd been doing that ever since.

TWENTY-EIGHT

[PEYTON]

CHIMAERAS ARE THE DARK SHEEP IN THE SHARKS *and rays family. They're weird: long-bodied, smooth-skinned, ribbon-tailed creatures that resemble land animals with their oddly shaped heads and faces. Rabbitfish, ratfish, elephant-fish, ghost shark. There are more than forty in all.*

They live mostly in the deep and we don't know much about them. They keep to themselves. They're the only fish in the entire ocean that breathe through their noses as well as through their gills; they have small mouths with stubby teeth that they use to grind their food. They wind through the water like dancers, moving their large fins up and down and all around. But their most distinguishing feature is their eyes, which are huge and emerald green, and infinitely sad, as though they know they don't belong anywhere.

The Dairy Queen was bright and noisy, voices clattering against the tiled floors and Formica-topped tables. The afternoon matinee had just ended and people jostled in line in front of the cash registers. Peyton scraped her spoon around the rim of her plastic cup. "I think my dad's going to give me my mom's old car."

"Tight."

She wasn't sure how she felt about it. Even if she Windexed it from top to bottom, it would be loaded with impressions of her mom, her perfume lingering in the seat cushions, the grooves where the heels of her shoes had dug into the floormat, the little silver charm dangling from the rearview mirror: *Life is a journey*. It might be comforting; it might be too painful to bear.

Eric stripped the wrapper from his straw. "Adam's freaked that Brenna's going to dump him."

"Adam's smarter than I thought."

"What, she say something to you?"

"No, but she was all over the guy who sits next to us in bio."

"That sucks."

"He should've seen it coming. Brenna never lasts longer than a month."

"I guess."

She licked fudge sauce off the sharp brittle edge of her spoon. "Can I borrow your SparkNotes for *Mockingbird*?"

"Sure." He rolled his shoulders, the cotton of his shirt stretched taut. "My dad says he can get me a job at the loading dock this summer."

"I thought you didn't want to work at Gerkey's."

"Either that or stay at the lube shop. Gerkey's pays better."

"Manufacturing pays better than the loading dock. If you wait a few days, I bet a job will open up there."

"Cut it out. I bet people spill stuff in there all the time."

"But Fern was so freaked out."

"Doesn't matter. Mr. G would never fire you. Who'd feed his fish?"

She made a face at him, but he had a point. "I guess."

It had grown dark outside. A bolt of lightning made her glance out the window. Another storm was rolling in. "My mom called Dana just before she died."

She'd never said it out loud, both words together: *mom, died.*

"Yeah?"

"Dana says it's because my mom wanted her to help figure it out."

No need to say what *it* was. Eric had heard all about it.

"Why would she call her?"

"Because she thought Dana was a doctor. Because Dana was her sister. She went to the plant today, to take readings with this instrument she had."

"No lie. What kind of instrument?"

"Who cares?" She pushed her cup away. The place was getting noisier, kids from school piling up in booths. "Let's go," she said, and Eric nodded.

Outside, the air was fresh with the smell of damp vegetation. Thunder rumbled overhead, and it started to rain, fat soft raindrops. Eric's car was parked at the back of the lot. They ran as the drops came faster, silvering their vision.

Eric fumbled for his keys, extended the fob and pressed a button. A siren sounded.

"Wrong button," he said.

She jumped from foot to foot. Another flicker of lightning.

He shook the keys and tried again. The siren silenced.

"Eric!"

"I know, I know." He leaned past her to reach the door and slide the key into the lock. "There," he said. "Princess."

He stood right beside her, warm, smelling of the rain. He looked down at her, his face cast in shadow, his eyes dark and unreadable.

"Peyton," he said. His voice sounded wondering.

Raindrops danced on her head and tapped on her shoulders. He bent toward her. She held her breath.

His lips were soft, barely touching hers. She moved closer. He tasted of ChapStick and peppermint ice cream. He made a sound deep in his throat. A thousand butterflies swooped in her belly. She could feel the dampness of his shirt against hers as he pressed her against the cold metal of the car, the roughness of his chin against hers.

"Get a room!" someone yelled across the lot.

Heart pounding, Peyton pulled away.

Eric's eyes were dark and intent, a stranger's eyes seeing things she didn't recognize, wanting things she was afraid to name. Overhead, thunder grumbled. He lowered his mouth again to hers but she leaned away and shook her head. "I have to get home."

He blinked and, just like that, he was Eric again. "Right."

The house was dark when she let herself in, just a single lamp burning in the living room. Dana's car was gone but her dad's car was in the driveway. She walked through the living room and found him standing by the kitchen window watching the rain dance down the glass.

"Hi," she said.

He glanced at her with a small smile. "Hi, honey. Got caught in the rain, huh?" He put his arm around her. He smelled the way he used to, not the sour yeastiness of beer but the clean honest scents of the factory and motor oil and very faintly of the cologne he put on first thing in the morning. She rested her cheek on his shoulder and he drew her closer. "Have a nice time with Eric?"

"Uh-huh." *I've had my first kiss,* she longed to say. She and Eric would never be the same again, even if they both wanted to. First kisses, she now knew, were permanent.

The rain pattered on the roof. Her mom used to love the rain; she'd sit on the back deck and watch the dark clouds roll in, the wind whip the trees into a frenzied dance. At the first booming crack of thunder, her dad would open the door and make her come back in. She'd do so reluctantly.

Her dad said, softly, "It's going to be all right, Peyton."

But she knew that wanting it to be so didn't make it true. It would just be different, that was all.

TWENTY-NINE

[DANA]

I SPLASHED THROUGH THE COLD RAIN, FOLLOWING the little lamps tilted along the path. Huddled beneath the overhang, I rang the doorbell, clutching the bottle of wine and shaking the drips off my arms. Busyness was behind the door the chatter of voices, someone calling, funny kaleidoscope music. And then the door swept open to reveal Sheri, a scene of light and motion playing behind her.

"Dana?" She looked surprised, but not annoyed.

I felt ridiculously grateful, but I couldn't help noticing the puffiness around her eyes that told me she'd been crying. I could see Logan playing in the living room behind her, laughing at something his brother was doing. He looked okay. Maybe she was just tired. "Sorry for stopping by like this." I held up the wine. "I thought . . ."

Cartoons played loudly on the TV. Mike was busy collecting books and stacking them into a basket. I guess I hadn't thought. I should have realized this time of night would be about the kids and their bedtimes.

"No problem. Come on in. Let me get you a towel so you can dry off. Mike, could you put the boys down tonight?"

The look he gave his wife was full of worry. "Sure."

We sat on the back porch, lights out, wind buffeting the screens, our feet tucked beneath us to escape the cool dampness. Another stormy night. Northern Minnesota could be like that in the spring.

"I heard you were at the plant today," Sheri said. "But you didn't find anything."

"You sound disappointed."

"I've been thinking about what you said last night. Maybe I was too quick to dismiss it. Maybe something is going on at the plant."

Is, she said. Not *was.* "What's the matter, Sheri? What happened?"

She paused, held her head at an angle, listening for something inside the house I couldn't hear. Then she relaxed, returned her attention to me. "So what are you going to do now?"

So she didn't want to talk about it. All right. I could understand that. "I don't know. I've run out of ideas. At some point, I have to get back to Chicago. Something went wrong on our last job."

"Like what?"

"Someone died in the blast." So simply said.

"Someone you know?"

"A homeless woman. She got inside the building somehow, and we didn't find her when we did our walk-through."

"You never said anything."

"It happened the same day Julie died."

"Oh, Dana. How terrible for you."

I squinted at my glass, but the liquid was clear as water in the dark. "I didn't see you at the plant today."

She put back her head to stare at the ceiling. Another crack of thunder that made me jump. Sheri was unmoved, as if she'd gone to a distant place in her head. "You ever get lonely?"

"Sometimes." Loneliness breathed on my neck in the middle of the night; it walked beside me as I grocery-shopped, drove to work, cleaned my apartment.

Sheri sighed. "It's funny. I'm always surrounded by people—friends, family, neighbors—but it doesn't matter. You ever think of all those goofy little things we did? We found them so hilarious at the time. After you left, something would happen and I'd say to myself, 'I can't wait to tell Dana,' and then I'd realize there was no Dana to tell."

The patter of small footsteps in the house behind us, the firm closing of a door.

She'd been a good friend. And I'd repaid her with deafening silence. "I didn't deserve you."

"That's the thing. You never felt you deserved anything."

"That's not true."

"Remember how upset I was about Kurt Cobain? You had finals the next day but you spent the whole evening with me, making me feel better. All those times I called you in the middle of the night, freaked out about something or another, and you always answered. You never once called me."

"Sure I did." I'd stared at that pregnancy test. My first thought had been to call Sheri. I'd had my hand on the receiver, but then had slowly withdrawn it.

"It wasn't just me," she said. "It was Joe, too. You pushed away everyone who loved you. Even Julie."

I hadn't come here for this. I didn't want to hear it. I'd stopped by because she hadn't been at the plant that afternoon, and I was worried. And maybe feeling guilty, too, for making her so upset the night before. "Sheri, what's the matter? You don't sound right."

"It's your dad, right? His leaving like that made you feel like you didn't deserve to be loved."

There he was again, that shadowy figure from my past, springing up two-dimensional and looming. "That's a cliché."

"Doesn't make it not true."

"Lots of people have dads who leave them. I'm not some pathetic case, Sheri."

"Of course you're not," she said. "You're one of the strongest people I know."

I sat back, surprised. Was that really how she thought of me?

"How are things going with you and Frank?" she asked.

She remembered how upset I'd been when Julie told me she was marrying Frank. I was sixteen. I was certain he'd make me move out, but he'd been the one to move in. I'd never given him a chance, but then again, he'd never given me one, either. "I've been avoiding him. Did you know he has a drinking problem?"

"Don't tell me he's started up again."

"It's not every night. I don't think he's drinking during the day. I saw him at the plant this afternoon and he seemed sober. I can't tell how bad it is. I can't tell how worried I should be." I wanted her to reassure me. I wanted her to tell me that she knew Frank and that he'd pull himself together, but she remained silent. "He was going to leave Julie," I said. "She was sick and he was going to leave her."

Lightning lit up her face, distant with thought. "Marriage is tough."

Where was she? Where had she gone inside her head? "Are you and Mike okay?"

At that she pushed back her chair and stood. "We're fine."

She went to the little bookshelf behind us. Reaching up into the basket on the top shelf, she pulled out a pack of cigarettes and a lighter. "Mike's secret stash. He doesn't know I know."

Sitting back down, she lit up with a trembling hand, the tiny flame shaking as she held it to the tip of her cigarette.

"Sheri," I said. "Tell me."

She exhaled. "I heard from the doctor today."

"Logan?"

"It doesn't look like dialysis is working."

"They have him on a transplant list?"

"They put him on it the minute he was first diagnosed. So we just have to hope something comes through. The doctor doesn't think we have a lot of time."

My throat closed.

"When he was born, I worried about all the regular things. Was he gaining enough weight, sleeping on his side, developing normally? But this was one thing I didn't think to look for, the one thing I didn't know to worry about." She reached over and tapped the cigarette against the railing, a damp sizzle. "It was just a little rash across his tummy. I thought it was because of the laundry detergent I was using. The doctor thought it was a food allergy. God, what I wouldn't give for something like that."

The storm lashed about us. Rain ran in a steady stream from the gutters, splashing so close I could almost reach my hand through the screen and touch it.

The tip of her cigarette flared in the darkness. "I was cleaning out the attic the other day and you know what I found? That old Ouija board. Remember how we used to try and channel John Lennon?"

"You thought he could help you with your songwriting career."

"All the things I was so desperate to find out. Did Mike like me? Would I get an A in history? Were my parents going to get a divorce? I had to know everything. I had to protect myself. But maybe I was wrong. Maybe it's better not to know the future. We might do stupid things if we did."

"Like what?" We were talking softly, the branches rustling and tapping the screen.

"If I had known how sick Logan would be, how he'd never have a childhood, would I have tried to have him in the first place?"

Julie had brought my baby to me that last day, wrapped loosely in the blanket I'd knitted, stitch by uneven stitch. My arms had curved instinctively to hold the trusting weight, and I'd pressed my cheek to the soft skin and inhaled. Closed my eyes to live a whole lifetime in that brief instant.

Sheri was looking at me. "Would you want to know?"

And be spared a life filled with regret? Yes. But no one could be happy knowing what was coming. That wouldn't be living, either.

"I don't know," I told her. "I wish I did."

THIRTY

[P E Y T O N]

*N*OT ALL SEA CREATURES LIVE IN THE SEA. SOME *float on top of it, clinging to enormous floating mats of sargassum seaweed. These animals eat, mate, and spend their entire lives drifting with the current, while keeping a tight hold on the tangled grapelike fronds. If they lose their grasp, they sink to the bottom of the ocean and die.*

Imagine always being on guard, knowing that all you'll ever see of the world is a few inches of seawater. Wouldn't the stress drive you crazy? Maybe one day you'd decide just to let go. As you fell through the water, you'd twist this way and that, trying to catch a glimpse of all that you'd missed. Maybe those few minutes would be worth it. You'd have to hope with all your heart it was. Because once you let go, there's no way you could change your mind and grab back on.

The endlers had done it again.

Peyton actually had her finger against the rigid disk of the light switch when she spotted the disruption a few inches below the water's surface, like a pearly splinter. A trick of the light? She crouched and looked through the glass. A cloud of tiny new babies, perfectly formed, utterly still, as if waiting for permission to move.

She had to hurry.

The grass was cold and damp on her bare feet, the driveway prickly with pebbles and sticks from last night's rain as she walked fast to the garage. Over in her yard, Mrs. Stahlberg was a lumpy shape bent over her rosebushes, probably salting slugs or, worse, shaking poison all over everything to kill the Japanese beetles. Peyton had told her not to use those chemicals. They only ended up in the groundwater, but Mrs. Stahlberg had thrown her hands up in the air. *Oh, Peyton. One little flower patch isn't going to matter.* Well, it wasn't one little rose garden. It was all of them, hundreds of thousands, every rose gardener saying the same thing.

Peyton hurled her garage door along its creaky tracks, and ten feet away, Mrs. Stahlberg straightened.

"Peyton? What on earth are you doing out here, dressed like that?"

Peyton was wearing an oversized T-shirt. Everything was covered.

But Mrs. Stahlberg clearly hadn't been expecting company. The bun on her head dangled just over one ear as though she'd slept on it wrong, and the hem of her housedress sagged. She tugged the sides of her sweater together. "Peyton. Is everything all right?"

Peyton yanked the string to the overhead light, flooding the gloomy space with a weak light that didn't reach the corners. "Just getting something."

"Like what?"

Peyton didn't have to explain everything, just because Mrs. Stahlberg wanted to know. *"Something."*

Why hadn't Peyton thought to store it under the kitchen sink, or even in the basement? It could be December with four-foot drifts of snow she'd be working through to retrieve it. But she hadn't been thinking. This whole past year, none of them had been thinking.

"Surely you could have put on a robe, honey."

Surely Mrs. Stahlberg could have put on a bra. "I won't be long."

"You never know who's looking."

The only one looking was Mrs. Stahlberg and maybe her creepy son. LT sometimes came around and stood in the bushes looking up at the house he had once lived in but didn't anymore. And LT didn't count. He was weird, but he wasn't a perv.

The tank stood on a back shelf, the glass grimy with old cobwebs. At least the filter and heater were sealed in a heavy plastic bag. Her mom's doing, no doubt. Another reminder of how large that space was that her mom had left behind. Peyton scowled, and walked quickly back to the house, through the kitchen, and down the hall.

She ran the water into the bathroom sink until it was warm enough, and filled the tank she'd just rubbed clean.

"Good morning, Peyton." Dana stood in the doorway, her hair mussed and her bathrobe loosely knotted. She'd come home late the night before. Peyton had awoken to the quiet click of the back door and the sudden flare of light as Dana turned on the overhead down the hall.

"Morning." Peyton slotted in the filter and the heater. The gravel would have to wait.

"Peyton—I need to talk to you about something."

Peyton hurried down the hall to her room. How long had she been gone? Ten minutes, probably. The rainbowfish were sluggish in the morning. They might not even be awake. She set the tank on her dresser, dropped in the Stress Coat to condition the water, and picked up her net.

"What's the matter?" Dana said. She'd followed her.

"My fish had babies."

She came right up beside Peyton, and they both looked through the glass. The tiny fish hadn't moved, though the adult endlers were beginning to stir. It was the sunlight starting to make its way into the room. She could have had all males, but she had felt sorry for them, living in that male-dominated world, showing off their stripes and flashy fins only for each other. She'd had to include two females.

Oops, over there, a rainbowfish darted through the doorway in the fake lighthouse. Peyton dipped in her net. She might be able to scoop them all up in one try.

There.

Carefully, catching the drips with her hand, Peyton carried the net over to the little tank and lowered it into the waiting water. The newborn fish were still for a moment, then suddenly zipped apart, like something had exploded in their midst. Peyton laughed. She couldn't help it.

Dana had her hands on her knees, peering into the little tank. "I thought fish produced eggs."

"Not these ones." They looked like guppies now, but when they grew up, the males would develop all sorts of coloring—orange bellies, black tails, blue backs. Peyton nudged the small tank to face the bigger tank so the mommies could watch their babies play.

"Were their parents going to eat them?"

"Their mothers might. The rainbowfish definitely would." They were normally mellow fish. It wouldn't be a problem once the fry got bigger. Peyton pressed the light switch on the bigger tank, and the fish there came alive. She picked up the container of fish food and dusted some flakes onto the water's surface.

"Will the babies eat the same thing?" Dana wanted to know.

"Just less of it. A fish's stomach is the same size as its eye."

"Cool."

It *was* cool, all the intricate ways in which nature played itself out. As Peyton set down the fish food, she saw Dana had picked up the container of Stress Coat. "That's not food," she said.

Dana raised her gaze to hers, then set down the bottle. "Right."

The bathroom door closed, and the water pipes shuddered themselves awake. Peyton's dad, starting his morning routine.

"Excuse me," she said, and Dana moved aside.

Peyton carried the paper towels she'd used to clean out the tank into the kitchen and pulled out the trash bin from under the sink. There, beneath the banana peels and damp coffee grounds, she spied the solid brown lip of a bottle. Beer? She poked away a plastic wrapper to reveal the sturdy shoulders of a whiskey bottle.

Her dad had tricked her, waiting until she'd gone to bed before pulling out the hard stuff. And here she'd been, all stupidly happy about her new fish. She'd let him trick her into thinking he was okay. Or maybe not. Maybe he hadn't been hiding this from her at all. Maybe the person he'd been trying to fool was Dana.

Did he think Dana could do something, keep him from drinking the way he had? If so, then Peyton should show Dana the bottle. It was scary, thinking about her dad slipping back to that distant place and leaving Peyton all alone. The last time, Peyton had had her mom. Who did she have now? Not Dana, that was for sure. Dana wasn't someone Peyton could ever trust.

Peyton dropped the paper towels on top of the bottle, making sure it was completely covered, then pushed the trash bin back into place. She had to accept the truth. With her mom gone, she had no one.

Except, maybe, Eric.

THIRTY-ONE

[DANA]

SURPRISE, I TOLD JULIE WHEN SHE GOT UP THAT
morning. I held up the knitting. She'd been right. It made a
much better blanket than sweater.

How come you're up so early? she said, yawning.

The baby had hiccups.

She sat beside me, fingered the rows. *Dana, this is great.*

I'm almost done. All I need to do is figure out how to end it.

Let's see, she said. *What were the directions again?*

A Closed sign hung in Lakeside's window. Still, someone might
have arrived early to start getting ready for the lunch crowd. I
rapped on the door and peered through the glass. A man emerged
from the gloom inside. Fred. He grinned when he saw me.

"Looking for coffee, huh? You can take the girl out of Minnesota, but you can't take the Minnesota out of the girl."

The interior was cool and dark, heavy with the compressed
odors of stale cooking oil and beer.

"Cream, right?" He brought two cups over and we sat at the

counter. "So what's up? I know you didn't come all the way down here for a cup of French roast."

I took a sip. Perfect. "I wanted to ask you about that salesman from the other night." Mr. Specialty Chemicals. I had scanned the description on the bottle in Peyton's room, and the word had leaped out at me. *Chemicals.*

He scratched his arm. "I wouldn't have guessed he was your type."

"Ha-ha. Would you happen to know if he's still in town?"

"Let's see. Probably. You couldn't shut the guy up about that big deal he was closing in on and how he was thinking about buying a lake house. Can you see him ice fishing?"

"You know where he's staying?"

"Don't have a clue. Try the Tremont, though. It's got the cheapest rates in town, and given how lousy a tipper the guy was, I'd say that would be the place for him."

It turned out to be the third place I tried. I was at the reception desk when I heard that East Coast twang behind me. There he was, ruddy-faced, sparse hair swept back over a square forehead, striding across the lobby to keep up with a man in jeans and a sports coat.

"Never mind," I told the front desk clerk. "I found him."

"Come on, man," he was saying. "Let me talk to my boss, see if I can rework the figures."

The other man looked familiar. Doug Miller? Couple of years older than me, he'd been at Julie's funeral, though he hadn't come to the house afterward.

"You know you can't beat our quality."

Doug mumbled something, too quietly for me to make out.

The salesman shook his head. "Why haul me all the way out here for nothing?"

Doug passed me on his way to the front door, gave me a quick nod. I nodded back as I walked over to where the salesman stood, stuffing papers into a soft-sided briefcase.

"Hey," I said.

He glanced up, his gaze blank, then he brought me into focus. "Hey." He rested his hand on his briefcase, giving me his full attention. "I've been looking for you. You never warned me about the mosquitoes." He snapped the flaps on his briefcase. "I thought Florida was bad. Heck, this town even makes New Orleans look like a paradise."

"It's one of our hidden treasures. So how did your meeting go?"

"Guess you heard. They totally played me on this one, brought me in to make the other guy blink. I'd told my boss the deal was in the bag." He picked up his case. "My wife already traded in her minivan."

"You're talking about Gerkey's?"

"Didn't have the decency to tell me this on the phone. They had to let me drag myself out here and wait around for a week before delivering the news. That's no way to treat a guy."

"No," I said. "It isn't." We began walking to the elevator. "You said you sell specialty chemicals?"

"That's right." He punched the elevator button. "The wave of the future."

"What's special about the chemicals in hand lotion? I've looked at the ingredients—"

"They're not there. You won't find them listed on the label."

"Why's that?"

"People are touchy about what goes on their skin." He snorted and watched the elevator door. "Like socks don't touch you."

I had no idea what he was talking about, but he'd said something the other night in the bar. What was it? "Are you talking about nanotechnology?"

His eyebrows pinched together. "How did you know that?"

"You told me. What's so special about nanotechnology?"

"It just means small."

The elevator door slid open. I moved to keep him focused on me, and put my hand on his forearm. "How small? As small as a grain of salt?"

"A grain of salt would be a *planet* to a nanoparticle."

There it was. My heart gave a funny little hiccup of recognition. I'd had my monitor set to pick up particles the size of asbestos fibers. Nano-sized particles would have slipped right by, undetected by the monitor's sensors. The answer had been there all along. "You know," I said, "I never got your name."

"Greg," he said.

"I don't know anything about nanotechnology, Greg. I'd love to hear more. Can I buy you a cup of coffee?"

"I've been inside this hotel for days now, waiting for a phone call. Get me out into the sun and you've got a deal."

See? Julie had said, her hands on mine, guiding and patient. *All you have to do is carry this loop over to the other needle, and draw it tight.*

THIRTY-TWO

[PEYTON]

SEA SPONGES LOOK LIKE PLANTS BUT THEY'RE ANI-
mals, the only ones of their kind. Eyeless, limbless, mouthless,
organless, bloodless, and nerveless, they're the most basic animals
in the ocean. They absorb nutrients from the water that flows
through their pores and up into their big central column. It's like
they're eating. Plants can't do that.

They're thickly laced with tiny bones that make them hard
and crunchy, and they're bitter with poisons. They can grow on
any rocky surface, and they grow quickly. If the water plops a
baby sponge onto a coral reef, the sponge can, and will, quickly
overtake the coral, so the coral's not happy to see one floating its
way.

For all their lack of personality and flavor, sea sponges are
still among the most popular creatures in the water. Their multi-
ple crevices and great wide-open bowls make fantastic hiding
places for other animals, who hunker down to escape predators.
They don't mean to be helpful, and they'd probably prefer to be
alone, but there you have it. It's the price they pay for staying
stuck in the same place and never going anywhere.

. . .

Hannah was at it again. Every time Mr. Connolly asked a review question, Hannah waved her hand to answer. Sometimes, she even stood. As if he couldn't see her, right there in the front row.

"Maybe she'll break an ankle," the kid beside Peyton hissed to Brenna, and Brenna grinned back.

Peyton wished they'd shut up. She was jotting things down as quickly as she could, her mind filling with questions every time Mr. Connolly said something, but emptying just as quickly when he moved on to the next topic. Cell mitosis. Cytokinesis. The list was endless.

Mr. Connolly wheeled around the front of the classroom, enjoying the repartee and lively discussion. He wouldn't flunk her, not when he knew it would go on her college transcript. She nibbled a hangnail. Would he?

After the bell rang, he waved to her as she was filing out the door. "Got a minute?"

"Sure." She held her books to her chest while he closed down the PowerPoint slide show and shut the lid on the computer.

"Have you made a decision yet about that project we discussed?"

His eyes weren't an ordinary blue. They were more like navy, and they looked right through a person. She dropped her gaze to her string bracelet and twisted it around her wrist. "I guess," she mumbled.

"That a yes?"

She shrugged, nodded.

"Okay. Well, what about volunteers?"

"I can ask the Hofseths and probably the Stahlbergs." It was the least they could do for constantly butting into her life. Maybe Ronni would ask her husband, too, so that would make five people. Too bad she was only doing blood type. It would be cool to track LT's schizophrenia through the family. Maybe next year she could do something like that.

"I can ask my folks and my sister if they'd be willing to participate."

That was totally weird, but she wasn't going to tell him that. Besides, that made four more people. "Okay."

The sunlight skimmed smoothly along his cheek then stopped at the tiny strip of dark bristles along one side of his jaw. He'd missed that area, shaving that morning.

"I hear you're moving into Manufacturing," he said. "That's a lot of responsibility."

"You don't think I can handle it?"

"You've got a lot going on."

What did she have going on? Nothing, and since when was it his business? "Can I go?"

"You've got a lot of schoolwork to get through this summer. Not just my class, but language arts. Math. You're slipping in Spanish, too. None of the teachers wants to give you an incomplete. Working full-time at the same time may be too much for you."

He'd talked to every one of her teachers? Who did he think he was, her guidance counselor? "I have to get to my next class."

"Peyton, I'm sorry, but I think it's time we had a talk with your father. If he knew—"

Her cheeks flamed. No way was he going to talk to her father about any of this! Her dad didn't need this. "I told you I can handle it."

He shook his head. "I care about you, Peyton. I think you could go far. I think you could be anything you wanted to be."

"Why do you care what I could be? That's not your job. Knowing my aunt doesn't make you part of my family."

He frowned and Peyton knew she'd crossed a line. But all he said was, "Let me know if you have any trouble getting volunteers."

And he was just a teacher again. Nothing more.

. . .

Lake Avenue was quiet. The oaks arched overhead, dappling the sidewalk with afternoon shadows. Peyton was tired. She felt like this had been the longest day ever. Eric waved at one of the volunteer firefighters out in front of the fire station, hosing down the engine. His uncle. Eric had another firefighter uncle, but he was nowhere in sight. Good thing, too. He was the joker who liked to squirt Eric with the hose whenever they walked by.

"Guess what?" Peyton said. "My endlers had babies."

"Those the ones that eat their babies?"

"I saved them this time." They stopped at the intersection. "In a couple of weeks they'll be big enough to go back into the tank with their mom and dad."

"Maybe you should just get rid of the mom."

Casually said, then Eric's cheeks flamed. He stared at the red light. "Sorry."

"Stop it," she said. "You can't do that, watch everything you say."

He nodded, but he still didn't look at her. The light changed and they began to cross the intersection. She could tell he was still feeling bad. "I saw Mrs. Stahlberg not wearing a bra this morning," she said, helping him.

"Gross," he said. But he gave her a smile, letting her know he appreciated the effort.

"I've got to do this stupid blood-type project. Do you think your mom would let me use your family?"

"Sure. You can ask her when you come over tonight."

"I'm coming over?"

"We got that Spanish vocab test, right?"

She'd forgotten. "Right." They used to study at Peyton's house, taking over the living room with their books and papers. Peyton liked hearing her parents in the kitchen, talking about their day. But that stopped when Peyton's mom started taking longer and longer naps. Now she and Eric didn't even consider going any-where but his house.

"Whoa," Eric said, and she followed his gaze to where a large, fat man crouched in the Stahlbergs' bushes. "Is LT vacuuming the *dirt*?"

LT had his back to them, his arm moving back and forth, the insect buzzing of a vacuum cleaner going. "He is *so* messed up." She raised her voice. "LT."

LT rocked around. A gray Dustbuster drooped in his hand. He smiled and fumbled with the switch. "Hi, Peyton. Hi, Eric." Straightening, he brushed off his gray sweatpants. He was wear-ing the same gray hoodie, too, and no doubt those were the same sheets of tinfoil smushed all around his head.

"You better get out of there," Peyton told him. "Your mom just sprayed poison."

"Yeah?" He hastily stepped out with big goose feet, and some-thing red fell out of his pocket and onto the ground. "Can you see the poison on me, Peyton? Is it on my clothes?"

"No. You're good." She had no idea. But it wouldn't help to tell him that. He'd only freak out more than he usually did.

"Why are you vacuuming out here?" Eric asked.

That was Eric, thinking you could get a straight answer out of a crazy person.

"Looking for particles."

Good luck with that one. The whole yard was filled with par-ticles, of dirt, plants, air. "Well, you'd better stop messing with your mom's rosebushes."

"I guess." He wiped the top of the Dustbuster with his sleeve. "I'll ask Dana. She can help me."

"Are you talking about her going to the plant yesterday?" Pey-ton asked.

"She had a machine that looked like this, and it could *see* the electricity."

"I don't think—" Eric began, and Peyton put a hand on his arm.

"You know she didn't find anything, right, LT?"

"Not *there*. But what about here?" He hunched his shoulders. "What if it's what made me this way?"

So he knew how he was. He understood he was different.

"You can't detect electricity with a Dustbuster," Eric said.

"Oh." LT frowned down at the machine in his hand.

Peyton was tired of this crazy conversation. She bent to pick up the red thing that had fallen out of his pocket. A small, thin book, fringed with yellow Post-it notes.

"Stop!" LT shrieked. "Don't touch that!"

But she'd already picked up the book. The cover was worn, the pages well thumbed.

"Don't, I said!" LT grabbed at her wrist.

Perversely, she kept hold. "What's your book about?"

"Don't!" He shook her arm. Post-it notes fell through the air.

"Dude." Eric grabbed LT's arm.

LT lunged. "Give it to me!" His hands were claws. They scratched at her skin, instantly raised long, furious welts.

Eric had him by the shoulders, pulling him back. "Leave her alone!"

"I just wanted my book! She wouldn't give me my book!"

Eric turned to her. "You okay?"

She nodded, cupping her arm to her stomach where Eric couldn't see it. No blood, but her arm *hurt*. LT was crab-walking, plucking the yellow pieces of paper from the grass and jamming them into his book. He made a sort of humming sound.

Eric gave her a slight shake of his head. *He's crazy.*

LT lumbered to his feet again, the book all sloppy with folded pages. He shook his head, refusing to look at her. A piece of foil drooped over one eye. It crinkled against his forehead and stayed there, stuck by sweat. "I told you, Peyton," he mumbled. "I said." He swiped his finger beneath his nose, just like a little kid.

"You did," she told him. "I should've listened."

THIRTY-THREE

[DANA]

PEOPLE STREAMED PAST ON THE SIDEWALK. I MOVED aside to let a woman pushing a stroller by, cellphone clenched between shoulder and ear, shopping bags bunched beneath the stroller handles.

Greg halted outside a shop window. "Oh, man. I forgot to pick up souvenirs. My kids are gonna kill me."

"Get something with a loon on it," I said impatiently. We weren't really going souvenir shopping, were we?

"Good idea." He turned away from the window. "So you want a lesson in nanotechnology."

"Yes," I said, relieved. We turned the corner onto a quieter street, lined with awnings and outdoor seating. "It's about small particles, you said."

"Really small particles. It's simple in theory. You take a regular substance like, say, silver, and mechanically reduce it to a very small particle size. And the reason you do that is because when things get that small, they change. Hocus-pocus." He waggled his thick fingers. "Silver becomes antimicrobial, which means it resists germs. That's why manufacturers are sticking nano silver in everything—baby strollers, toothpaste, pencils." He eyed me. "Probably in that shirt you're wearing. Your cellphone, your running shoes."

I resisted the urge to kick off my shoes. "Is that what you sell—nano silver?"

"I wish."

An older couple strolled past, their small gray dog sniffing the sidewalk in front of them.

"Lucky me, I got stuck with the cosmetics line. I couldn't do clothing, oh no. Not the easy stuff. I had to be assigned the super-secret, we'll-kill-you-if-you-tell-anyone stuff."

I stopped walking. "Like what?"

He stopped, too. "Nano zinc, nano titanium."

Where had I seen zinc and titanium recently? Of course. "You're talking about sunscreen." *It's only sunscreen,* Brian had said.

"You got it. At nano size, zinc and titanium not only refract sunlight better, they make the lotion go invisible when it's rubbed in. Remember that white glop we used to wear as kids?"

"But I've looked at the label. It just says zinc oxide."

"I told you. People are sensitive about what goes on their skin, so the manufacturers don't spell it out. Zinc is zinc, after all. Right? The government's okay with them not telling you what kind of zinc it is."

"And this is the kind Gerkey's uses?"

"Sure is. Of course they don't put it on their label. They know everyone's after organic, good-for-the-environment crap. Say the word *nanotechnology* and you've got the tree huggers banging down your door."

Zinc oxide, Brian had said. He hadn't specified that it was nano-sized. "But it's still zinc oxide, right?"

"Well . . . that's up for debate."

"But you just said zinc is zinc."

"That's what the *government* says. But the scientists are saying something else. I read the papers, you know. I go to the conferences. I got to know what I'm dealing with, even if my boss wants me to keep my head in the sand." He rubbed his forehead. "You heard about asbestosis?"

"It's a fatal lung disease caused by breathing in asbestos fibers." It's why I took readings after a shoot, to make sure we hadn't inadvertently released a cloud of the criminal stuff.

"Not just asbestos. They've found that certain kinds of nanoparticles do the same thing. Nanotubes, they're called, and you'd freak if you knew how much of it companies were pumping out every day, all over the world. It's a miracle we all don't have asbestosis."

I stared at him. "You're exaggerating."

"Wish I was."

"If that were true, it wouldn't still be on the market."

"Right, just like tobacco. Nano money makes tobacco money look like a joke."

"You're talking billions."

"*Trillions*. Trillions upon trillions. I told you. Nano's the wave of the future."

A little girl skipped past, followed by her parents holding hands and swinging their arms. Did I imagine the coconut scent of sunscreen trailing after them?

"Nano's completely unregulated. You could put radioactive waste in sunscreen and the FDA would look the other way. Same thing's true everywhere, not just here in America."

"The government monitors everything." Look at the hoops I had to jump through to order dynamite for a shoot.

"Ah, but that's the thing. That's the beautiful irony of it all. The government has taken a wait-and-see approach. Regulators don't have a clue whether or not nanoparticles are safe. They approved its use without checking first, but now the research is starting to come in. And you know what? I predict that even so, the government will find some way to justify its continued use."

"I don't believe in a government that's blind to the needs of its citizens."

He laughed. "Look it up. Scientists aren't keeping silent. They've written hundreds of research papers. More are coming out every day."

Here was the playground beside the Lutheran church, kids on swings, parents on benches. "I've never heard of any of this."

"You will. It just has to get to the sexy stage. This one might do it. These Chinese scientists showed that if you inject lab mice with nano zinc, they go into organ failure and die. Doesn't happen with regular zinc. Just nano."

"What kind of organ failure?"

"Kidneys, primarily. But like I said, the FDA says that since it's just zinc, same stuff they stick in vitamins, it's got to be harmless."

There was a buzzing in my ears. Children's laughter floated over. Traffic moved along the street. Sunlight dappled the pavement, fell across our bodies in long patterns.

Sunscreen. The Australian dive guide had warned me. I couldn't wear it diving the coral reefs. It killed the tiny polyps that lived inside the coral, turning the delicate rosy-hued coral to white skeletons.

"I don't believe it," I said slowly.

"Believe it."

"If it's so terrible, why do you sell it?"

"Someone's going to. Might as well be me."

He had his gaze set on the kids on the swings, their bodies leaning back, their feet tilted toward the sky. "It's too late, you know," he said. "We've already released nanoparticles. We can't get them back. They're too small. We don't know how."

A childhood memory surfaced: robins pecking at something in the middle of the street. I'd stopped on my bike, curious. A car approached, going fast. Some birds flew away, but some didn't. They were killed instantly. I went running into the street, waving my arms, but the next car forced me back to the safety of the side of the road. Some birds flew off; some stayed and were struck. Over and over, the scene was repeated until there were no more birds in the air or on the branches. They all lay on the road.

I told Julie when I got home, sobbing. *How could they be so greedy?*

It was their nature, Julie said. *They couldn't help themselves.*

"My sister used to work at Gerkey's." My voice sounded like a stranger's. "She just died of kidney disease."

He halted, took a long look at my face, then shook his head. "So it's already started."

Everyone used sunscreen. Those laughing children on the swings. The people eating lunch on the benches. That mother sitting on the blanket and holding her baby in her lap, a sunbonnet fitted over the small, round head. No doubt the baby's arms and legs were covered in it. No doubt that mother had taken care to rub it into her baby's skin. She thought she was keeping her child safe. "If this stuff is everywhere, and it's as dangerous as you say, then why is it only just now showing up here?"

He folded his arms and looked across the pretty little park studded with fruit trees.

"Well," he said at last, "I guess it's got to start someplace. Might as well be Black Bear, Minnesota."

THIRTY-FOUR

[PEYTON]

IN 1979, THE FIRST MANNED SUBMERSIBLE BOAT, *Alvin, was scooting along the barren ocean floor when its head-lights picked out something surprising in the vast blackness: eight-foot-tall creatures shaped like white straws. They clustered around the cracks in the bottom of the ocean, where the earth's molten interior sent out gasps of hot, poisonous air. Tubeworms. They'd been there for hundreds of thousands of years and no one ever knew. No one guessed that anything could possibly withstand such terrible conditions.*

The worms themselves are red, frilly headed, and shy, duck-ing back into their tubes the moment they feel threatened. When they're born, they suck up as much bacteria-rich water as they can. Then they seal themselves off, becoming creatures without legs, eyes, internal organs, or mouths. What they do have is an entire kitchen staff trapped inside their skin: the bacteria, once swimming around in the open ocean, now work inside the worms, converting the metals in the vent water into nutrients for their hosts.

Tubeworms grow fast and can live for hundreds of years. Not

much fazes them. But they're completely dependent on their envi-
ronment. If a vent closes up, the tubeworms die, simple as that.

Everything has a stopping point. By the time you see the signs,
it's too late to do anything about it.

Peyton examined the broken pieces of the hummingbird feeder. The plastic bowl had cracked apart before and her mom had painstakingly re-glued it, but this time, the edges were crumbly. Too many harsh winters when they'd left it hanging too long had compromised the plastic. She could squeeze out an entire tube of superglue and it wouldn't do any good. Pulling out the trashcan, she dropped the plastic pieces in. That made the first thing lost since her mom's death.

Her arm smarted where LT had scraped his fingernails across the skin. A car door slammed. She looked up to see Dana walking up the driveway, carrying a small gray suitcase.

"Hi," Dana said.

Peyton hadn't seen the suitcase before. "Hi."

In the kitchen, Dana set the case on the kitchen table and raised the lid to reveal a shiny white plastic machine.

LT was right. Dana's machine did look like a Dustbuster. "Is that what you used at the plant yesterday?"

Dana nodded. "But it turns out I had it set for the wrong thing."

"Oh." That didn't sound good. She felt her way forward. "And now you know what the right thing is?"

"I think so." Dana picked up the machine from its foam bed and pressed a switch. The thing started to hum. "I'm looking for nanoparticles."

"In my *house*?"

Dana glanced at her. "It's all right. I'm just checking."

But it wasn't all right. Dana's hands were shaking.

"I want to call my dad."

Dana nodded. "That might be a good idea."

Which only scared Peyton more.

Dana started in the kitchen. Holding the machine in one hand, she moved it around the room, stopping for a moment to press a button and watch the little window on top. Pantry, cabinets, stove, refrigerator. Peyton imagined her pacing through Gerkey's, doing the same thing. Her aunt's calm deliberateness was both reassuring and unnerving.

"Anything?" she said.

"Just normal ambient levels."

Peyton rubbed her upper arms and followed Dana as she walked through the dining room, stopping by the hutch holding their special glasses and Thanksgiving platter, the small desk where her mom sat to pay bills. Then they went into the living room with the fireplace where they hung Peyton's Christmas stocking, the front hall closet crammed with coats. Dana spent a long time in Peyton's parents' room, going over the bed, into the small closet, pulling out the bureau drawers, then checking the hall bathroom they all shared, opening up the medicine cabinet and uncapping the hand lotion her mom applied every night, the face cream she rubbed onto her cheeks.

They traipsed down to the basement and walked along the walls, crisscrossed the entire floor. Every few minutes, Dana stopped and took a reading, then glanced at Peyton to give her a reassuring smile. They went back upstairs. Dana stopped outside Peyton's bedroom. "Mind if I check in here?"

"Okay."

Dana pushed open the door and stepped inside. The water burbled in the aquarium. Light shined in through the half-closed slats of the blinds, falling across the mounds of clothes, the unmade bed, the books stacked every which way. Behind them, the back door banged open.

"Peyton?" her dad called.

"In here, Daddy."

He was there in an instant, his hand on Peyton's shoulder. "Dana, what are you doing?"

But Dana wasn't listening. She was staring at her machine. "I got something."

Her voice was unsteady. Dana looked all around, turned in a little circle, then stopped and stared at the ground, at the dirty laundry mounded there by her feet.

Her father's fingers dug into Peyton's shoulder. "What the hell does that mean?"

"The level just jumped." Crouching, Dana lowered the monitor and pressed the switch again.

"That's impossible. We don't have asbestos in here."

"I know." She raised her face to both of them. Her eyes were dark and hollow. "But you do have something else."

The lab coat lay on the deck, bundled in plastic bags. Peyton half expected the bags to untie themselves and spring open to puff the powder back up into their faces.

"I'm not sure that'll do any good," Dana said. "But they have to ship the stuff in some sort of container. Something that must be impenetrable." She yanked off the latex gloves she'd put on to dispose of the lab coat, turning them inside out as she did so. They went into another bag, and then another, all tied with quick vicious knots.

Peyton hadn't been wearing gloves when she unbuttoned the coat. She'd carried it into and out of the car with her bare hands. She'd dropped it on top of her clothes and forgotten all about it.

"You said this guy was a salesman," her dad said. "Not a scientist."

"Yeah, but he was right. I checked it out. Those websites he was talking about are real. I can show you. They're written by real professors at real universities."

Her dad rubbed his face. "You can't believe everything you read online. Even you should know that."

That was true. Peyton's teachers were always saying that.

"Look, the bottom line is I got a reading a hundred times above ambient level."

Peyton had seen the number herself, an endless course of digits that flickered across the small gray screen.

"Instruments don't lie. There's something really wrong here."

"So you got a high reading. I'm not debating that. What I'm saying is you don't have a clue what it means. Everyone puts nano zinc into sunscreen. They've been doing it for years. That's nothing new."

"What's new is that scientists in China found that it causes acute renal failure in mice."

"In *mice*. Inject mice with enough stuff and you can make them sick with anything."

"It can't be a coincidence, Frank."

"I agree. It's not a coincidence. You were looking for it."

"Fine." Dana crossed her arms. "Let the EPA decide. They'll know what to do. We need to notify them anyway."

"So they can what, tear my house apart?"

"I'm talking about Gerkey's. I got one high reading off a piece of clothing that's been lying on the floor for days. Can you imagine what the readings would be like in the middle of the factory?"

"I was wearing a mask," Peyton said suddenly. "When I was mixing it. So it's okay, right?"

Her dad slid his arm around her shoulders. "Absolutely."

"We don't know that," Dana corrected grimly.

Her father's hand squeezed, hard. "Of course we do. If OSHA says those masks protect us, then they do."

"Don't lie to her just because she's a child."

Her dad released her, gave her a little nudge. "Peyton, go inside, please."

"No way, Dad."

"Go."

His voice was flat, final. She let the screen door bang behind her to convey just how helpless and furious she felt, and stomped all the way to her room. Throwing herself on her bed, she stared at the ceiling. She wasn't three years old. She probably knew more about chemistry than they did, combined. Her mom wouldn't have shooed her away. She would have sat down and discussed all the angles. But she had kept that notebook and its contents from Peyton. So maybe she didn't know her mom as well as she thought.

Voices came through her opened bedroom window. She crawled to the side of her bed and peeped out through the slats. The two of them stood squared off, Dana with her back to Peyton, straight, her narrow shoulders thrown back, her hands clenched into fists.

". . . another word," her dad said.

"She deserves to know the truth."

"Yes, but not from you."

"At least take her to the doctor."

"She goes every year."

"It's a simple blood test!"

"I'm not scaring her over this."

"Julie died not knowing what killed her, Frank. She died not knowing if Peyton had been exposed, too."

Peyton rolled onto her back. Raising a hand, she rotated it in the slanted stripes of sunshine. The three red stripes LT had left looked like plain scratches. Nothing about her whole arm looked the least bit irregular. She touched her cheek, ran her fingertips along her jaw, but the skin felt completely normal. She took in a deep breath, held it, and exhaled, and there wasn't the tiniest twinge. But just because she couldn't see or feel the particles didn't mean they weren't there.

It was just like tubeworms. For hundreds of years, people didn't know they existed. But that didn't mean they hadn't been there all along.

THIRTY-FIVE

[DANA]

THE DAY I FOUND OUT I WAS PREGNANT WAS ONE OF those sunny, blustery March days that couldn't decide whether it belonged to spring or winter. I drove all the way to Fargo to buy the test, wandering the drugstore aisles, gathering shampoo, strawberry licorice, looseleaf notebook paper, watching the checkout counter and waiting for the old guy to go off duty. Finally, he was replaced by a teenage girl who ran my purchases across the scanner, her hand barely pausing at the small pink and white box. But when she raised her gaze to mine, I saw sympathy.

Despite the directions on the box, I didn't wait until the morning to take the pregnancy test. I was two months overdue, and every minute stretched out to an hour. Sure enough, the little line turned a solid blue. I pressed my hand to my belly and tried to imagine the unimaginable: a baby. I stared at my reflection in the mirror and started to smile.

A baby.

. . .

Supper was silent. Frank sat at the head of the table, working his way through the meal I'd heated up. I lifted my glass of water and wished it were something stronger. I wondered if Frank was thinking the same thing. That morning, there had been no empty cans on the counter, and none overflowing the trash bin. So maybe he was getting things under control.

Between us, Peyton kept her head down and nudged scalloped potatoes around her plate with her fork. She was thinking about that lab coat. So was I. That number had been huge. I'd stared at it for a full second before it registered, and then I'd looked at her. She'd spent so much time in her bedroom. How many times had she stepped on it? How many particles had she released into the air, and then breathed in?

Peyton glanced up at me and frowned.

"Good news," I told her. "This is the last of the hotdishes. I'll go grocery shopping tomorrow. Any requests?"

She shook her head, and Frank pushed his plate away. "So what's going on in Chicago?" he asked me.

Meaning, *When are you leaving?* He had to know I wasn't going anywhere, especially not now. He was trying to get a rise out of me, drawing the line firmly between us. "The police are waiting for the toxicology report," I said.

"Why?" Peyton said. "What difference will it make?"

"They're checking to see if she was on something when she broke in."

"And if she was, then they won't arrest you?"

"I'm sure they're not going to arrest me," I said, though I wasn't the least bit sure. If they went after Halim, he'd tell them I had helped lay the charges. He wouldn't even hesitate to share the blame. Did I know any lawyers? Maybe there was someone in Black Bear I could talk to. Glancing up, I found Frank watching me.

He turned to Peyton. "Let's go work on your mom's car while we still have some daylight."

"But Eric's coming by to pick me up. We have to study."

"Fifteen minutes. There's some stuff you need to know. Come on."

The back door banged behind them as I ran hot water into the kitchen sink. Julie had stood here countless times, soaking these dishes in this sink, scrubbing at them with this sponge.

Frank's voice came in through the opened window. "This is the dipstick. It sits in there and you should check the level fairly regularly."

"How regularly?" I heard Peyton ask. "Like even when it's freezing?"

"I'll help you stay on top of it then. Now, you don't want to run out of oil or the pistons will seize up."

"I guess that's important."

"Don't they teach you this stuff in driver's ed?"

"Dad, my teacher had really bad B.O. Who could ever listen to what he was saying?"

Frank grunted. "Pull this out and hold it up to check the level. You're looking to see if it reaches that line, and whether it's clear. If it gets dark and thick, it needs changing."

"Is that clear?"

"Hard to see in this light, but yeah. It should be. I just changed it recently."

"Okay."

"You'll want to make sure not to touch it with your bare hands if the engine's been running. It's metal, and it'll get burning hot. Use a rag or a paper towel."

"This seems awfully complicated."

"You need to know this. I won't always be able to bail you out."

"All right, all right." Then, "Dad, I've been thinking. I'm going to apply to the U."

"You sure? They don't have a marine biology program."

"It'll be closer to home."

"A little distance won't be a problem."

"I know, but . . ."

"But what?"

"You know."

A mosquito whined at the screen, insistent, determined to come in.

"Hey, no worries," Frank said. "I'll find the money."

"Right."

"I'm serious. Besides, I'm still buying those lottery tickets."

"Oh, Dad!"

Setting the last dish in the rack to dry, I wiped the counter and dried my hands. I checked the clock on the wall. Six-thirty. I might be in luck if I hurried.

The first time Brian Gerkey stopped by, Julie watched with a frown as he lounged on our sofa, eating Oreos and laughing about something that had happened at school that day. When he left, she leaned against the door with her arms crossed. *What was that about?*

No big deal. I shrugged. *We're just friends.* Secretly, I was delighted. Brian was a year older and infinitely cool. Everyone wanted to be his friend.

It is a big deal. I've heard about him. He's trouble.

I snapped back, *I'm not stupid.*

Just . . . be careful.

She held my gaze until I rolled my eyes and said, *Fine. I'll be careful.*

It was Julie who should have been careful around Brian Gerkey.

THIRTY-SIX

[PEYTON]

OCEAN WAVES ARE CONSTANTLY MOVING AND UNSET-
tling things. The fish themselves are always on the prowl.
But even the ones that swim great distances to mate or find food
know exactly which rock, which piece of coral is their home. It's
freaky, like they have an internal GPS. Salmon and box turtles
live their entire lives traveling the ocean, yet when it's time to
spawn, they return to the exact same spot where they were born.
How do they do that? Even-tempered fish will suddenly turn vicious and rip apart a fish they think is moving into their space. A
sea anemone will let one clownfish live among its poisonous spires,
but no more. When the clownfish takes a mate, it has to somehow
convince its home anemone to let its partner in. The anemone
knows who belongs and who doesn't.

The Hofseths' living room was warm and bright with lamplight. A
baseball game playing on the TV had all three Hofseth men riv-
eted, including Eric, who didn't even like sports that much.

"Esconder," Peyton said.

Eric's gaze drifted to where she sat cross-legged on the couch beside him. She waved the flash card at him, and his face twisted into a parody of concentration.

"Um," he said.

"To hide," she said.

A roar from the TV and his gaze shot back to the screen.

"Here we go!" Mr. Hofseth leaned forward in his chair, elbows on his knees.

"He's going to walk him." Eric's older brother, George, home from college, lounged sideways in the armchair, his long legs flung over the upholstered arm. *I'm back,* his posture said. *I was gone, but now I'm back. Make room.*

"He wouldn't do something that stupid," Eric said.

"Does it all the time."

Peyton nudged Eric and held up the flash card. *"Cocinar."*

"To make."

"To cook," she corrected.

He shrugged. "Close enough."

"Not even."

His younger sister, Mary, came in and did a little pirouette that made her short pleated skirt bell out over her gray leggings. "Does this work?"

"Move," George ordered. "Jeter's up."

Mary ignored him. "Peyton, what do you think?"

Mary was way cooler than Peyton had ever been. She straightened her hair to a glossy sheen; she wore just the right amount of lip gloss and eyeliner; she had that casual thing going that made people listen to what she said and care about what she did. The only thing Peyton had going for her was that she was a junior and Mary was only a freshman. Sooner or later, Mary would figure out that Peyton was the last person to ask about making a fashion statement, and things would change between them.

"Is she decent?" Mrs. Hofseth called from the dining room, where she sat piecing together a jigsaw puzzle. The upstairs hall-way was lined with shellacked Monets, Rembrandts, and van Goghs. Peyton couldn't imagine where she'd find room for her current challenge, a Renoir portrait of a serious red-haired girl who looked like she knew something she didn't dare talk about.

"Pretty much," Peyton called back. She held up a flash card. *"Viajar."*

Eric's gaze skittered to the card. "To fly."

"Try again."

"How short's the skirt?" his mom called.

Really short. Mary would never be allowed to wear it to school. "She's wearing leggings." Underneath a *really* short skirt. "Eric." She shook the card. *"Viajar."*

"To buy?"

"No, you dope. To travel."

He nodded, his gaze drifting back to the television.

"Cleavage?" Mrs. Hofseth again.

Mary groaned. "Mom. Ally's waiting."

"She's got on a hoodie." Peyton knew Mary would unzip it the minute she left the house to reveal a gossamer-thin tank top be-neath cut low enough to show the lace trim on her bra. All the girls in ninth grade dressed like that, or at least Mary and her crowd did.

"And what have you got on underneath, young lady?"

Peyton hid a smile. So Mrs. Hofseth had caught on to her daughter.

"A T-shirt."

"Show Peyton."

Mary groaned, widened her eyes theatrically, and unzipped her hoodie in a flash to bare a green shirt.

"It's a T-shirt," Peyton called back. She said nothing about how it rode up high on Mary's belly.

Mary grinned at her.

"All right, then you can go," Mrs. Hofseth said. "Make good choices."

"I will." Mary made a face that said the last thing she was going to do was make good choices. "Peyton, you still haven't said. Does this work?"

"It works," George said. "Now move."

"You look great," Peyton said.

Mary squealed and flung her arms around Peyton. She'd drenched herself in a floral body spray that made Peyton's eyes water. Eric pretended to gag, and pushed her away. She giggled. "Bye, Daddy."

Mr. Hofseth waved a hand. "Bye, honey. Have a good time."

"Home by nine," Mrs. Hofseth said. "It's a school night."

"Okay." The front door slammed, leaving the house much quieter and feeling a little emptier.

"You hungry?" Eric asked.

Code for *Let's go into the kitchen and get away from my family*. But Peyton didn't mind staying put. She loved Eric's family.

"You getting up, Eric?" Mrs. Hofseth called. "Mind making some popcorn?"

Now Eric groaned.

His mom was like that, zeroing in on her kids, aware of their every move, sometimes even before they'd twitched a muscle. Eric called it her Mom Antenna.

"Get me a beer, would you?" George asked.

"Get it yourself," Eric said.

He'd do it anyway. Just like he'd microwave popcorn for his mom. That was the way Eric's family was. They acted like they didn't care, but their love shined through.

Peyton pushed herself up. "You want anything, Mr. Hofseth?"

He didn't take his gaze off the screen. "I'm good."

In the kitchen, Eric tore the cellophane from a packet of microwave popcorn. "You want some Coke with this?"

"I'm good."

He gave her a look. "You okay?"

So much for acting normally. Eric had seen right through her. "You ever heard of nanotechnology?"

"Sure. It's amazing. It's wicked cool."

"Seriously?"

He nodded. "Seriously. It can do all sorts of stuff, like turn regular paper into batteries. Pretty soon, we won't even need silicon chips anymore to power our computers. And the health applications are ridiculous. They've got these sensors they can stick in people to track cancer cells and zap them before they even start growing, and they're showing it can disrupt viruses like HIV and influenza."

She'd never heard of any of that. He was just standing there, holding the popcorn package, like he'd been completely derailed from reality. "How come you've never talked about it before?"

He shrugged. "You're not interested in stuff like that."

"So we just talk about stuff you think I'm interested in?"

"Well, yeah."

"Since when?"

He looked uncomfortable. "I don't know."

But she did. Since they stopped being just friends and began being something else. "Well, cut it out."

"They already use nanoproducts in all sorts of things, you know." He pushed the microwave buttons. "Televisions, clothes—"

"Sunscreen?"

"Well, yeah."

"So what if *that's* the reason my mom got sick?"

He started to laugh, then stopped and looked at her face more closely. "Come on."

"Dana says this stuff is dangerous."

"Don't tell me she's one of those." He made his voice mocking. *"Technology's going to ruin our planet."*

"She says there's this study that showed nano zinc can cause kidney damage."

"Uh-huh."

"She didn't make it up."

"The government regulates that sort of thing, Pey. They'd never let anything out without testing it first."

Her father's words floated back to her. *You can't believe everything you read online.* "I guess." Eric looked so serious. She could trust him. She could tell him anything and he'd believe her completely. He never used to be like that. Used to be, he'd argue right back. Now it was like she knew something he didn't, that she was wiser. Better. She hated that. She reached up and swept off his baseball cap, turned it sideways.

"Dude." He came close and looked down. "Don't mess with the cap."

She pressed her palms against his chest. His lashes were pale from the sun, his eyebrows smooth and soft. She wanted to run her finger over them.

Something altered in his expression, and he bent his head toward hers. Suddenly, she was standing on a cliff looking down, dizzy from the height and the certain knowledge she was going to jump.

"What?" His voice was husky.

"Nothing."

"You're a million miles away."

"I'm right here."

He smiled a little sadly. "Sometimes I feel like I've lost you, which is dumb." He reached up and set his baseball cap facing forward again. "Because how can you lose something you never really had in the first place?"

THIRTY-SEVEN

[DANA]

THAT FIRST WEEK OF AUGUST, I WOKE UP FEELING queasy. Julie had already gone to work. The apartment had that stillness to it that told me I was alone. The day's heat had begun to build, and the shades hung limp in my bedroom windows. I pushed myself up against my pillow, the solid weight of my belly pinning me in place. I was supposed to check the weather reports. I was supposed to stay hydrated, but all I could do was stare up at the ceiling and think, *I cannot do this for one more day.*

Back then, time had crawled from moment to moment, but now it spilled through my fingers. I couldn't hold on to it. I shifted from foot to foot while Brian carefully spooned out fish food and dropped it in the tank filled with purple and pink corals. "Come on, Dana. You want me to change my formulation based on some reading you got?"

"An abnormally high reading."

He screwed the lid onto the food container with an efficient twist. "Look. We use nanoparticles. It's no surprise to me that you got a reading. That's like saying you found a banana in a grocery store, Dana."

"What if it's making people sick?"

"Right."

"What if it is?"

"Look. The minute the FDA gives the word, we'll reformulate. It might be moot by then, anyway. The industry's constantly changing. We might be onto a whole new technology by then."

"Why take the chance? Reformulate now."

"Impossible. Sales went through the roof when we switched."

"Other companies use regular zinc."

"Name one that's turning a profit, one that's broken into the top ten. Hell, the top fifty." He switched off the overhead light and held open his office door. The hallway was shushed with emptiness. "I've worked hard to turn this crappy little mom-and-pop business into a real success story, and I'm not messing with it just because you got a wild hair about nano zinc."

"It's not just me. There's tons of research beginning—"

"Research. Right."

"Check it out for yourself. It's all online."

"If you don't mind, I'll let the government tell me what's safe and what's not."

"You can be the forerunner . . ."

"I can make sure my employees get paid."

"You owe it to them to make sure their workplace is safe."

He gave me a sharp look. "I know what my obligation to my employees is."

"Just let me take a few readings," I begged. "I can come in after everyone's gone for the day. No one needs to know."

"You make it sound like I'm hiding something." He turned a corner and I lengthened my stride to keep up.

"You're not listening."

Flip, flip. He was switching off lights as we went, the king of his castle.

"You're the one who isn't listening, Dana. This stuff is all FDA-approved. Until they tell me I should stop using it, I'm going to keep on keeping on."

"Who knows how long it will take for the FDA to respond? Julie's dead. And Sheri's little boy may not make it."

He stopped, the sound of his footsteps falling into silence. We'd reached the lobby. The halls stretched out in all directions. The parking lot outside the front doors was bathed in the tangerine and rosy glow of a sunset. In here, everything was bleached bone.

"Don't you pin that on me." His face was stone, the face of a stranger, and I glimpsed the man who ran a small empire, the man who made a salesman wait for a week before dismissing him, the one who by sheer force of will had turned a small town around from the edge of despair.

I searched his features for the friend I'd once had. "Brian—I'm not pinning anything on you. But you can't just ignore what I'm telling you."

He sucked in a breath, released it. "Look," he said. "I know you're upset about that. Julie was great. I get it that you're having a hard time dealing with her death."

Julie was *great*? That was how you summed up a person? "That has nothing to do with anything."

"Tell me something, Dana. How come you're so cut up about a sister you haven't even bothered to visit since high school?"

"You can't win this, Brian."

"Look around you, Dana. I've already won."

Hawley Hospital was twenty-six miles southwest of Black Bear, thirty minutes by car, twenty-five if you gunned it and weren't held up at the train trestle. I sat in my car and studied the bland stucco building through the windshield. It looked exactly as I remembered; even the maples lining the front walk were the same height, but I had to be wrong about that. I hadn't exactly been paying attention to the landscaping.

A sedan drove by, slowed to take the curve into the visitors' lot. A young couple emerged, the woman leaning on the man's arm, their faces turned toward each other as they walked toward the entrance. I imagined them heading to that room on the second floor, the one facing south with the sink missing a chunk of porcelain along the back rim, with a window that didn't offer a sunrise or sunset, just middling sky that gradually darkened and lightened.

Julie had arrived home just after six that day. *Sorry I'm late,* she said.

It's got to be a million degrees in here, I complained.

She laid a cool hand on my forehead. *Are you sure it's just the heat?*

She worried about everything. Was I eating enough, sleeping enough? Was there enough gas in the car in case we made a midnight run? Julie grew very protective those last few months. And distant, as though she could see something coming from far away.

I wished she were here now, to tell me what to do.

I started up my car, drove slowly out of the parking lot and turned onto the highway leading back to Black Bear.

It was late by the time I got back. I let myself in with the key I'd found hanging on the brass hook. A brass *J* dangled from it. Julie's key. I held it loosely in my cupped hand, imagining it resting in my sister's palm, then turned to hang it back up.

A voice spoke out of the darkness. "So you're back."

Frank sat by the kitchen window, moonlight throwing his face into high relief. He'd meant to startle me.

"Brian called," he said. "He wants that lab coat back. I looked but I couldn't find it."

The lab coat was stowed in the trunk of my car, where I hoped it couldn't release any more particles. "I've got it," I said. He'd been drinking, I realized with dismay. The air stank of whiskey, and a bottle sat on the table before him. "And even if I returned it, he can't cover up what I found. I've already downloaded the readings onto my computer."

"No one's talking about covering anything up." He tipped the bottle to the glass by his hand. "That coat's his. Peyton shouldn't have taken it out of the building."

"I'll talk to him. I'll let him know Peyton has nothing to do with this."

"I don't want you talking to anyone. You've already done enough talking."

It was late and I was tired. Frank and I would never agree on anything, so why try? "You're drunk," I said with disgust. "Go to bed." I turned to go.

"My God," he said. "You sound just like Julie."

I whirled around. "Do I, Frank? I'm glad. Someone needs to talk to you. Someone needs to straighten you out."

"You're the last person to straighten anyone out. Last I heard, you killed someone."

I gritted my teeth. That had nothing to do with anything. "You're the one who has the problem. You need to get yourself under control."

"Or what?"

"Or I'll take Peyton." The words just slipped out. I hadn't even realized I'd been thinking them.

He snorted. "Peyton's not going anywhere."

"She's not safe here."

"You don't get to decide that. She's my daughter."

My heart pounded. *Tell him.* "You think she doesn't know you're in here, drinking? You think she doesn't smell it on you the next day?"

The scrape of a chair and he was there, looming out of the darkness. "You don't know anything."

"Julie should have never come back. She should have kept Peyton as far away from you as possible."

He grabbed my arms and shook me. "Shut up."

My heart pounded. I'd never seen this side to him, this violence. Afghanistan had changed this man in ways I'd never understand. What kind of life had Julie lived? What kind of house had Peyton grown up in? "Did you hit Julie?" I hissed. "Is that why she left you?"

"No!" He released me and I stumbled back. "Of course not! I loved her."

I rubbed my arms. He was telling the truth. "Maybe you never touched her," I said. "But you hurt her anyway."

"Don't you think I know that?" He fell into his chair and sat there, head bowed.

I left him there, lost among his own memories, his own regrets. I stayed up for hours, huddled on my makeshift bed, scrolling website after website. There were hundreds of products containing nanoparticles being manufactured and sold all over the world. Scientists were raising concerns, and consumer organizations were issuing warnings. So Greg had been right. There was something terrible going on.

Toward dawn, I picked up the phone and pressed the buttons. It was early and I was prepared to leave a message, when someone answered.

"My name is Dana Carlson," I said quietly. Was I doing the right thing? Was this what Julie would have wanted? "I believe the factory in my hometown is making people sick."

THIRTY-EIGHT

[PEYTON]

SEA ANEMONES ARE CANDY-COLORED SQUISHY ANI-mals so delicious looking, you'd want to pinch off a piece and pop it in your mouth. You wouldn't get that far, though. The instant you touched it, a coiled stinger buried beneath a trap cell door would lash out and punch a painful poison into your skin. It's the law of the ocean: the prettier something is, the more dangerous it is.

Anemone mouths are pursed tight in the middle of their juicy little bodies. On the opposite ends are pedal disks that glue them into place on a rock or piece of coral. They can creep along very slowly, and some can swim, but on the whole, they usually prefer to patiently wait for food to find them. Their cute little selves just sit there, arms waving delicately in the water, and an octopus or a starfish or a fish can't help it. They swim over to take a look and pow! The anemone grabs them, stuns them with poison, and leisurely nibbles away. That's another law of the ocean.

Curiosity will kill you.

. . .

The news crawled through school like a centipede, climbing up and down the walls and across all the floors, its little legs working busily. By second period, it was all people were talking about. Peyton sat there and wished someone, anyone, would just freaking change the subject.

"I heard it was a gas leak," Hannah said.

Gerkey's didn't operate on gas.

"They found drugs in the locker room."

Probably Ronni's prenatal vitamins, the ones she took *just in case*.

"I heard a boiler blew up and people got burned."

Yeah? What boiler would that have been, the one in the next county over?

Mrs. Milchman sat on her desk, swinging her legs like she was proud of them. She wasn't as bad as Peyton's Spanish teacher, who always wore low-cut shirts and tight skirts that made it particularly gross when she was acting out a scene for them. "I don't think so, guys," Mrs. Milchman said. "The front office would have gotten calls from your parents."

Hannah nodded. "This is a safety zone."

"You mean tornado zone," someone corrected.

"No, safety zone. Like if there was a terrorist act or something. This is where people would go."

"Like Black Bear's a training camp for terrorists."

"I'm just saying."

They were all just saying, but none of them knew. Peyton had passed Eric in the hall earlier, and even he'd looked a little worried.

"They don't put people in quarantine for an industrial accident." That was Hannah Know-It-All. "They just hose them down."

"You learn that from *Criminal Minds*?"

Laughter.

"Someone poisoned the lotion and *that's* why the EPA's there."

"Poisoned lotion. Ooh. Scary."

More laughter.

Peyton wondered if the EPA had badges and guns. Maybe they were corralling everyone outside on the parking lot.

"I'm just telling you what I heard."

Maybe nanoparticles sank to the bottom of a person and rose to fill every organ, until a person couldn't breathe or swallow. Or maybe they started on the outside and pressed their way in through a person's pores. Maybe it had all been there, right in front of them, and no one had been able to see any of it.

Everyone was staring at her.

Milchman said gently, "That's all right, Peyton. Never mind."

When the bell rang, Peyton was the first one out the door.

After gym, while everyone was getting changed, Peyton stood in the entryway, just around the bend in the wall that kept the boys from seeing in but far enough out of the tiled room so there'd be cellphone reception. A couple of other girls huddled nearby with their own phones pressed to their ears.

Her dad answered on the third ring. There was background noise and he spoke loudly. "Peyton? Is everything all right?"

"What's going on?"

"Hold on." The noise dissipated. He must have shut a door or something. "You heard the EPA's here?"

"Everyone's talking about it. They're saying there's poison in the sunscreen."

"Goddamn it."

Peyton was shocked. Her dad never swore.

"Well, you know better, right?"

"But Dana said—"

"I don't care what Dana said. She doesn't know what she's talking about."

"She found that stuff on my coat, Dad. And what about those Chinese scientists?"

"This is how rumors get started."

"Stop treating me like I'm stupid."

"I'm not doing that."

"You've been doing it since Mom got sick. *Everything's going to be okay. It's not a big deal. Lots of people get kidney disease.* Well, it wasn't okay, was it, Dad? You made me think it was! You made me think it was okay to go to school and forget about it."

The other girls were looking at her. She glared at them until they turned away. "Tell me the truth for once, Dad."

"The EPA showed up this morning. They talked to Brian. He's been showing them all over the plant, and they've been collecting samples."

"Like Dana did?"

"Pretty much."

"Are they closing down the plant?"

"Of course not."

She heard the truth in his voice. Okay. Things couldn't be that terrible, then. But still. "Have they found anything?"

"Not that I know of."

Maybe it took time to know. "What if they do find something?"

"Then it means we have to tighten up on our safety protocols."

That made sense. Maybe they had thicker masks that would work. She lowered her voice. "It was Dana who called them, wasn't it, Dad?"

"I don't know."

Yes, he did. He knew as well as she did. "The EPA wouldn't have shown up if she was wrong about this, Dad."

"I'm sure they have to investigate every complaint, even the ones that don't make sense."

Peyton hadn't known that. The other girls were straightening up and shoving their phones in their pockets. A teacher must be coming. "I have to go, Dad." She hung up before he could say another word.

. . .

Eric was waiting for her after school, leaning against her locker. "Hey," he said, pushing himself up.

"Hi." She worked the lock and swung the door open. "I missed you at lunch."

"Yeah, sorry about that. I stayed behind to do a chem lab."

They pushed through the school doors. The parking lot was emptying, cars screeching out, radios blasting. The track team ran laps around the football field. Balls thudded in tennis courts so new Peyton could still smell the paint.

"Crazy day, huh?" He took her hand, the callus on his thumb from the sax scratchy along her palm.

"Dana was the one who called them."

"I figured."

"My dad said the EPA had to come out, but I don't know. Maybe she's right. Maybe this nano stuff is dangerous."

Eric didn't say anything.

"Hello?" she said impatiently. "Did you hear what I said?"

"I heard." They stopped at the intersection to wait for the light to change.

"Doesn't that freak you out?"

He shrugged.

Why was he being like that? She persisted. "So what if it turns out she was right?"

"I told you. The government wouldn't let people use nanotech if it wasn't safe."

"You were the one who said it was a good thing that Dana was checking things out."

He frowned, staring at the light. It glowed, a long steady red. At last, he said, "My dad works there."

"So it's okay to talk about it when it's just about my mom, but when it's about your dad, we can't?"

He didn't answer.

So there it was, that thick solid line between them, the one that had always been there but that she hadn't seen until now. She stood on one side looking over with longing, and he stood on the other, looking away. She pulled her hand out of his and wrapped both her arms around her books.

"I'm sorry," Eric said at last.

He never said he was sorry. He meant it, though; she could tell. Was she ready to let it go? His profile was to her, his mouth turned down. He was her best friend. He knew her like no one else did. "Forget it," she said.

He didn't look at her, but his face firmed with relief. "Okay, then."

"Okay." She let him take back her hand. *Okay.*

THIRTY-NINE

[DANA]

N ICE AFTERNOON, ISN'T IT?" THE WAITRESS FLIPPED the thick white mug over and filled it with coffee. Her nametag read *Leslie*. "You ready to order?"

"I'll stick with coffee, thanks."

"Oh, sure, but if you want any chocolate silk, better let me know right away. We've only got a couple pieces left."

The plump pieces of pie were prominently displayed on the counter behind her. *Homemade,* the hand-lettered sign announced, and normally, I would have succumbed to temptation. But I couldn't bear the thought of eating anything, so I just said, "I'm fine. Thanks."

She moved to the booth behind me. "You hear about the trouble down at the plant?" she said to the people sitting there.

They grumbled a reply. I tuned them out. A tube of sunscreen poked out of my purse. I'd automatically started to apply it that morning and caught myself just in time. A new tube, an expensive brand filled with antioxidants. I couldn't bring myself to throw it out. Was the danger in the manufacturing process or in the product itself? Until I knew, I'd hold on to it, just in case. It would serve as a reminder of all the other things I'd have to be on the watch for. Athletic socks, glass cleaner, shampoo. Toothpaste.

Bells jangled. Two men stood in the doorway, one tall with a short brown beard, the other younger, wearing gold-rimmed glasses. It had to be them. They had the weary look of not belonging.

I raised my hand, and the older man nodded. The two of them threaded between the tables toward me. "Dana Carlson?"

I couldn't tell from their expressions whether or not they'd found anything. "Thanks for meeting me, Dr. Neuberger."

"Bill, please." He shook my hand, then indicated the shorter fellow beside him. "This is Dennis Hoffmeyer from Moorhead University. I called him after we spoke yesterday afternoon. This sort of thing is his field of expertise."

"Hey." Dennis slid into the booth after Bill, and the waitress came over.

"You didn't tell me you were waiting for someone." Leslie beamed at the two men. "Can I get you fellows anything? We've got the best pie in Black Bear, make it every day, seven, eight different kinds."

"Sure," Bill said. "Coffee, and whatever pie looks good."

"Make that two," Dennis said.

"All righty." She turned over two cups and filled them. "You change your mind about that chocolate silk, honey?"

"I'm good," I said. "Thank you."

"No problemo."

She moved off and I leaned forward. "Did you find anything?"

"It's still too early to say for sure. We did pick up some elevated readings throughout the plant. We took soil and water samples, too."

I let out my breath. "I forgot to mention that the wheat hasn't been growing all around town."

Dennis looked interested. "We didn't notice that on our way into town."

"I saw it from the air. It's gradual, something you wouldn't spot from the ground."

He turned to Bill. "We should check that on our way out of town."

Bill nodded. "Hard to imagine, though."

"But something could be seeping into the ground and preventing reproduction from occurring."

"You read anything about that in the literature?"

"Something's ringing a bell. I'll go back and look."

They were fired up about this. That was good.

Leslie returned carrying two plates of pie, lemon meringue jiggling with meringue. "The lemon's out of this world." She topped off my cup and winked at me. "I brought an extra fork in case you wanted to share. Let me know if I can get you anything else."

"Will do," Dennis said.

I waited until she'd walked over to greet two more customers. "Did you get that link I emailed you?"

Dennis nodded. "I read it on the way over. It's a preliminary finding. Its primary function is to suggest where research should be focused. I've emailed the research team to see if they've done any work in that area. We'll see what they say. There may be data they haven't released yet."

"Okay."

"Dennis is going to take the samples we collected back to his lab to conduct the chemical analysis," Bill told me. "The EPA's not funded to monitor nanotechnology."

"I can't believe I had an opportunity like this right in my own backyard," Dennis said. "Everyone's trying to get research going in this field. Sunscreen manufacturers are notoriously secretive."

I wasn't interested in the research potential. "How long will it take before you know something?"

"I've got a few grad students who can help. Say, a couple of days."

Bill turned to Dennis. "I'll be in your neck of the woods day after tomorrow. Why don't I drop in, see what you've got?"

Dennis forked off a bite of pie. "I should be in all afternoon."

Great. They were rushing the analysis, and following up quickly. I'd know something soon. Maybe within days. "My niece was wearing a mask when she spilled powder all over herself, just one of those disposable paper ones. Do you think she breathed in any of it?"

"It's possible," Bill answered. "Those masks don't filter out particles anywhere near that small. If the powder puffed up into her face, she might have taken some in."

"I'll have her tested." It didn't matter what Frank said. Peyton would understand. I'd make her see how important it was.

"Better hold off right now. We have to figure out what we're dealing with, first. No sense in alarming her."

"But if she's sick . . ."

"I understand. But there's no reason to believe a single exposure would have any ill health effect."

"Doubtful, really," Dennis told him. "My guess is it would be prolonged exposure."

"*If* there's a causal link," Bill said.

"Right." Dennis turned to me. "Like we say, it's too early to know what we're dealing with."

"But we know it's nano zinc," I insisted. "That's what Gerkey's uses in their sunscreen."

"Let's wait and see what our analysis reveals." Bill pushed his plate away. "Speaking of which, we'd better hit the road."

"You'll let me know what you find out?"

"You bet." Dennis fished a business card from his shirt pocket. Reaching across the table, he handed it to me. "Nice to meet you."

Bill set some money on the table. "Good call, by the way. Sunscreen. Who'd have thought it?"

FORTY

THE SPERM WHALE AND GIANT SQUID DESPISE EACH other. The giant squid wraps its powerful arms around the sperm whale in a choking hold, squeezes hard with its biting suckers. The sperm whale cranks open its enormous mouth and all its teeth to bite the squid in two.

No one's ever actually witnessed the battle. Scientists have only pieced it together from the aftermath: the gaping bloody wounds on the sperm whale's body, the undigested squid beaks lying in its belly. The sperm whale, upon catching sight of the giant squid, will leave its usual swimming zone and dive deep, deep, deep after the squid, chasing it all the way to the bottom of the ocean. The giant squid will race away from the sperm whale, its only enemy. Everyone else in the ocean is terrified of the giant squid.

At some point, the giant squid turns to face its opponent. What happens after that is anyone's guess. They're well matched in size and fierceness. It's hard to say who would win in a fair fight. But my bet's on the sperm whale. Anything with that much purpose and determination eventually has to succeed. It's just a matter of time.

. . .

Peyton spread the pages out on her bed, the tests, the doctor's reports, the pamphlet her mom brought home the first week that
showed what she could and couldn't eat, the map to the old dialysis center in Fargo, a ruffle of parking vouchers. She sorted carefully through them for the test results from when her mom had
been tested for a match. She pressed it flat and studied it. There.
Her mother's blood type was O.

She opened her notebook. She'd make it like a family tree.
She could glue little pictures of everyone on their specific branch,
and color-code the various alleles as they fell through the
branches. She'd need poster board and fake leaves from the craft
store. Her mom would have loved that. She would have said, *Peyton, you're so creative.*

She shook a box of colored pencils onto her bed. She wrote on
one branch, *Julie Carlson Kelleher,* followed by her blood type.
On the branch beside it, she wrote her dad's name but left the
blood type blank. She angled a little limb between her parents'
branches, connecting them. That's where she wrote her own
name. Now she needed her blood type.

The basement was cool and dark. The boxes where Dana had
gone through her things were still sitting on the floor where she'd
left them the other night. Peyton was surprised her dad hadn't
said anything to Dana about picking up after herself. He liked
things tidy.

The box of her baby things was on the top shelf where her
mom had put it, beside the one containing stuff from when her
mom and dad had dated. *It's just junk, Mom,* Peyton had protested, handing her mom the big black marker to write on the outside. *It's memories,* her mom had corrected. *Everyone needs those.*

She hadn't said it but Peyton knew she only meant happy
memories. Peyton's mom had been good about throwing away the
bad ones.

Peyton set the box on the floor. The first thing lying inside was her stuffed bunny. She lifted out his limp form, his ears and legs floppy, his threaded-on eyes pulled loose from the fabric so he looked cross-eyed. She pressed her nose against his belly, inhaling deeply, the way she used to. She sneezed. He was just dust now.

Here were some drawings she'd crayoned in elementary school. A self-portrait looking very serious, wearing a triangle dress. A poem to her mom for Mother's Day, a misspelled version of "Roses Are Red." A purple poster-paint handprint for Father's Day. A handful of greeting cards, a rattle shaped like a clown that must have been important to her, a fleecy blanket, a bib. She pulled out the blanket, yellow and soft. For some reason, she remembered it, remembered refusing to sleep without it clutched beneath her chin.

Back in her room, she studied the index card she'd unearthed. It still had tape on it from where it had been fastened to her hospital bassinet. *IT'S A GIRL!* Just below that was written in heavy black writing, *B+*. So that was her blood type. She sat on her bed, then frowned.

Something was wrong with the small tank on her dresser.

The baby fish were just hanging there in the water, not pulsing around the way they had that morning. Fish didn't just rest, not unless they thought it was nighttime. Peyton's bedroom, though, was flooded with daylight.

When Mr. G answered the phone, there was chatter in the background. Not work chatter, but home chatter, a child piping up in the background, saying "Daddy."

Mr. G said, "Hold on, sweetie," to his little girl, then to Peyton, "Hey, what's up?"

"I'm sorry." This was his cell number, the one he'd given her for when she was watching his fish while he was out of town. The one she was supposed to use if there was an emergency. She was pretty sure this qualified, even if it wasn't an emergency with *his* fish.

"It's okay."

"My endlers had babies this morning."

"Hey, that's awesome. How many in the drop?"

"Six."

"The mothers get any?"

"I don't think so. But by the time I found them, they'd already consumed their yolk sac." Which meant they'd been at least a couple of hours old. "So there might have been more."

"Still. Six live fry is great. Congratulations."

"I don't know. When I left for school, they were swimming all over the place. But now, they're barely moving." A tiny tail flickered and one drifted slowly to the bottom, nosing the glass.

"Huh. You check the water temp?"

"Seventy-eight."

"I know you conditioned the water and fed them, right? So what about the filter?"

"I'm using my old one."

"Well, maybe that's the problem."

She turned the tank to study the cylinder. "It looks okay."

"But you can't be sure. Tell you what. Stop by tomorrow after school. I'll give you the one I bought for Melinda that she hasn't used yet."

"Dad!" Melinda protested in the background, and Mr. G laughed. "It's for Peyton," he told her. "Her fish had babies."

"You think they'll be okay until then?" Peyton asked. It wasn't as though she had a choice. The pet store had already closed for the night.

"Absolutely."

She frowned at the little silver fish, wavering in the water, their double sword tails looking deflated, like they had nowhere to go and no reason to try. "Thanks."

"It'll be good timing, actually. I might have a lead on a clownfish."

He'd been looking for months, ever since last September when his female died. "That's great," she said.

"Dad!" Melinda called, and Mr. G laughed again. So much easy laughter. "I better go, Peyton. Looks like I have a tea party to attend."

Peyton waggled her fingers at the endler babies. None of them were floating. Even so, it might not be a good idea to have the tanks so close together. The mommies and daddies wouldn't want to watch. She propped up a notebook between the two tanks.

The back door slammed. Her dad? No, Dana, standing in front of the refrigerator with a bunch of grocery bags on the table behind her. She wore her hair loose today, though the smile on her face was tight. "Hi." She pulled out a container of leftovers, pried off the lid, and dumped its contents into the trash.

Peyton's family never threw away leftovers. Never. "Everyone's saying you called the EPA."

Dana paused in mid-reach. "I had to, Peyton. Brian wouldn't let me in to do the testing myself."

He'd let her in the first time. What had changed between then and now? "Did they find anything?"

Dana let the refrigerator door fall shut. "Yes."

"Oh." Peyton felt small and scared. "Can they fix it?"

Dana turned and looked at her. "They can't take back the particles that have already been released, but Brian can make sure the plant doesn't release any more."

"Is it too late?" *Is it too late for me?*

Dana hesitated. "It's a simple blood test. I can take you after school tomorrow."

Peyton couldn't go after school tomorrow. She had to get that fish filter. Even so, she didn't want Dana to be the one to deal with this. She wanted her dad to decide whether there was anything they needed to do. "It's okay." She looked around at the groceries sitting everywhere. There was a lot of it, enough for two families.

Dana was watching her. "It's all organic. I got a bunch of different things. I also bought bottled water. We have to stop drinking from the tap."

"You think the *whole town's* poisoned?"

The door banged and there was her dad, cellphone to his ear. "They're overnighting the replacement part." His gaze skimmed the kitchen and came to rest on Peyton. "I'll check it in the morning. Just leave it. You better hit the road. Gerkey's not paying overtime until we have all three lines up and running."

That sounded harsh. It was strange picturing Mr. G as a boss, making those kinds of decisions, ordering people around.

"Right. See you tomorrow." Her dad pushed his phone back into his pocket and turned to Dana. "You cost us a day's work."

Here they went again. Peyton picked up a box of macaroni and cheese. There was a cartoon drawing of a little girl with pigtails on it, who looked unreasonably, undeservedly giddy. She wanted to throw it through the window.

"Don't blame me. Blame Brian. This is his fault."

"Nothing's ever your fault, is it? What the hell is all this?"

"We need to switch to organic food, Frank. No more using water from the tap."

"What's this *we*? There's no *we*."

"Fine. Then you and Peyton."

"I think I can manage to take care of my own child."

"Like you did your wife?"

Jab, jab, jab. Peyton couldn't stand it anymore. She snatched up a jar and hurled it at the wall. Glass exploded against the wall, a spray of bright red liquid.

Dana gasped. Her dad reached out but Peyton pushed him away.

"Get out," she told Dana, standing there frozen. "Just get out."

Her dad was there, his hand on her shoulder. "Peyton," he said, and Peyton shook her head furiously.

Dana looked so slight, and the way she was standing there,

balanced on one foot, her arms crossed, reminded Peyton painfully of the way her mom used to stand when she was talking on the phone, completely absorbed in the conversation. Peyton blinked hard and looked away.

"I'll leave in the morning," Dana said.

Peyton should have felt powerful; she should have felt victorious. So why didn't she?

Her dad sat on the back deck long into the night, watching the moon as Peyton watched him through her window blinds, lifting the glass to his mouth over and over and over again.

FORTY-ONE

[DANA]

T HE PHONE CALLS STARTED THE NEXT MORNING. Still early, the pearly wash of sun slipping along the counters and pooling on the floor. I was the only one up, so I lifted the phone from its cradle. At my soft "Hello," there was only silence and then a click. A dial tone burred. Probably a teenager.

The rich smell of coffee hung in the air. Holding my cup close, I breathed deep. In an hour, I'd be packed and ready to go. I'd try one of the hotels along the lake. I hoped my credit card could withstand the charge. It wouldn't be for more than a night or two. Surely the EPA would have their results by tomorrow. They'd take action, and I could head back to Chicago and the trouble that awaited me there.

The wall was dented where Peyton had hurled the jar of spaghetti sauce. It would need patching, re-wallpapering.

The phone rang again, startling me. Hot coffee slopped down my fingers. I wiped my hand on a dishtowel and snatched up the receiver. "Yes?" Hissed, impatient. It had to be the same caller. Another pause during which I felt the presence of the person on the other end, then the click. Dial tone.

Uneasy now, I stood by the window. Golden light filled the flower beds along the garage, overgrown, more weed than flower, but still some pink blossoms peeped out. Peyton would be all right. The EPA was all over the plant. They'd keep her safe.

Still, I hadn't slept the night before.

The phone shrilled. I jumped.

"What the hell's going on?" Frank grabbed the receiver. "Who is this?" he demanded. A moment passed, then he raised his bloodshot gaze to mine. Pajama bottoms that tied at his waist, the buzz of whiskers along his cheeks, he looked old, worn down. Hanging up the phone, he said, "They hang up on you, too?"

"Just leave it off the hook." When the EPA got their results, Frank would take Peyton to the doctor. Surely he wouldn't deny the truth then.

The creak of the front screen door. Someone was on the porch.

"The newspaper?" I said, and he shook his head, already moving.

A fat white envelope sat wedged between the wooden frame of the screen door and the doorjamb. Something was scrawled across the front in large, bold black letters.

PEYTON.

Frank stooped to retrieve it as I stepped onto the porch and glanced up and down the quiet street. "See anyone?" he asked.

The sidewalk was empty; no cars moved in the distance. Whomever it was had left in a hurry. "No."

Frank grunted.

We'd gotten threats, Ahmed had said.

I whirled around. Too late—Frank was already sliding his finger beneath the flap. A shower of fine white powder drifted out.

"What the hell?" he snapped.

We stared in horror at the tiny mound of powder by his foot. Not anthrax, but something just as lethal. Nano zinc.

"Shit," he said.

How much had we just inhaled? The slightest breeze, and it would be off, cycling through the air to the kids on their way to school, the people walking to the lake or to town, mowing their yards, walking their dogs. "Don't move," I said, thinking desperately. We had to cover the powder that had already fallen out, and somehow contain what remained in the envelope. I'd grab the vacuum cleaner from the hall closet, but how much would escape? It wouldn't do any good. The stuff was too tiny to be caught by ordinary measures.

Frowning, he tilted the envelope toward him and gave it a little shake.

I grabbed his wrist. "Are you insane?"

He yanked away, and held the envelope to his face. He shot me a look of pure disgust. "Baby powder."

"You sure?"

"I know what baby powder smells like."

"What's with the phone, Dad?" Peyton's voice was sleepy, untroubled. She stood blinking and yawning, her arms wrapped around herself in the early morning chill.

Frank pushed the envelope into his pocket. "Nothing, honey."

"Can I take the first shower?"

"You bet," he said.

The door smacked shut behind her.

"What kind of sick person would do something like this?" I raged. "Soon as Peyton's off to school, I'm calling the police." She shouldn't know about this. But would she be safe at school?

He was shaking his head. "Won't do any good."

"Why not? They can't get away with this!"

"Did you see anything? Anyone?"

"You know I didn't. But maybe there are fingerprints on that paper."

"Doesn't matter. The sheriff's son-in-law works at Gerkey's." He was frowning, his mind elsewhere.

"What?" I demanded, impatient.

"Get your car keys."

My SUV sat parked at the curb. Frank unlocked the driver's door and popped the hood.

I teetered on the curb, wanting to see, wanting not to get too close. He stared down at the battery, the spark plugs and hoses. Reaching in, he parted wires, turned caps, lifted belts aside.

"Frank," I said, wanting him to be more careful.

"Just be quiet for once, will you, Dana?"

A door banged and Irene came out onto her front stoop. "Car trouble?"

"It's okay," I answered tersely. Then in a lower voice, "Frank, you don't know what you're doing. Get out of there."

"Stand back," he said, and strode up the driveway to the garage.

Irene was standing in the shadows of her porch. When she caught me watching her, she retreated hastily, letting the door bang behind her, but I knew she stood just inside, peering through the gauzy curtain.

Frank returned, carrying a flashlight. Crouching, he shined the narrow beam of light upward along the underneath of the engine. He went all around the car like that.

"Anything?"

He didn't answer.

"Frank. What's wrong?"

He stood and switched off the flashlight. Frowning down at my car, but not at me, he said, "There was some talk at the plant yesterday."

"Yeah?"

"I told you. People are upset." He released the hood and let it fall shut.

"Upset enough to put a *bomb* in my car?"

"You really have forgotten what it's like, haven't you?"

Had I?

One Halloween night when I was little, Mom had to work,

leaving Julie in charge. We were sitting cross-legged sorting our trick-or-treat candy when the pounding started. The front door, the back door, the windows along the side of the house. All were shaking and rattling at the same time. Whoops and calls sounded from outside, the throaty barks and howls of werewolves and witches eager to snack on little girls.

Julie grabbed my hand and hauled me up the narrow stairs to the bathtub. There we crouched, hushed and terrified, hidden behind the shower curtain. We couldn't see out, so surely they couldn't see in. Julie wrapped her arms tightly around me and held me close. *It's probably just those stupid kids from school,* she whispered. I pressed my head against my sister's chest and heard the reassuring thump of her heart.

Now my sister was dead, and it wasn't the monsters that rattled doorknobs and cracked eggs on the mailbox you had to fear. It was the monsters you couldn't see. The ones who kept their masks of friendship firmly in place and their true intentions disguised. Those were the ones you really had to worry about.

Peyton. The envelope had been addressed to Peyton.

FORTY-TWO

[PEYTON]

SEA SLUGS ARE CALLED THE BUTTERFLIES OF THE *ocean. They're not like they are on land, fat slimy lumps of tissue that wreck gardens and that no one likes. In the water, they're transformed. They come in an array of shockingly bright colors and are intricately put together. Some have spiny protuberances; some look like they're feathered. Others are furled like precious silk. They creep just as slowly along the ocean bed as their cousins do on land, so they're not aggressive hunters, though they are indiscriminate eaters. Whatever they catch is fair game.*

Because they can't run away and they have a difficult time hiding, you might think they're the most vulnerable creatures in the ocean, but you'd be wrong. Despite their pretty coloring and cute little bodies, they're desperately, fatally poisonous, and other creatures have learned to leave them alone. It's a good thing to know: looks can be deceiving.

Peyton studied the cereal box. Not her usual brand, something organic masquerading as regular. Like the cheerful little drawings on the front and the name, Happy Honey Ohs, would deceive her. She wanted to say something to Dana, let her know exactly how she felt being marooned with this healthful crap, but her aunt was on the phone in the living room. This was the last morning her aunt would be around, probably for forever. Well, that was just fine. They'd gotten along without her for Peyton's whole life.

"Do I have to eat this?"

Her dad tightened the cap on the thermos. "You should eat something."

She waggled the box at him. "It doesn't even have sugar in it."

"Then add some," her dad said, and Peyton knew he was done discussing breakfast. His hair was damp from the shower and his cheeks freshly shaved, but his eyes were bloodshot and his hand trembled as he set down the thermos. Probably from staying up and drinking all night. *Oh, Dad.*

She turned so she couldn't see him and pushed the cereal box back into the pantry. "What's your blood type?" she asked.

"Don't have a clue. Why?"

"It's a project I'm doing for Mr. Connolly. I'm making this family tree. I've got Mom's and mine, so all I need is yours."

"Ask Doc Lindstrom. He should know."

"Okay." She grabbed a banana from the bowl on the counter. She'd eat it on the way to school. How different could organic bananas be from regular? "Bye."

"Hold on."

She stopped, hand on the back doorknob. "What?"

"Who knew you spilled powder the other day?"

His voice was casual, but his gaze made her nervous. "But you said I wouldn't get in trouble. You said everyone made mistakes."

"That's right. You're fine. I just wondered."

People didn't just wonder stuff. There was something he wasn't telling her. "Everyone, Dad. *Everyone* knew I spilled that stuff and screwed everything up."

He reached out a hand but she was gone, whirling away and letting the back door slam shut behind her.

The classroom windows were cracked open, letting in the buzz of a lawnmower, the hoot of a distant train. It would be summer soon. After work, she and Eric could go down to the lake and swim, then go to the amusement park and ride the roller coaster over and over and over.

"Peyton?"

Her Spanish teacher was looking at her expectantly. Across the room, Brenna smirked.

"*Por favor,*" Peyton said.

When the bell rang, Brenna came over as Peyton shoved her books together. "My dad says your aunt is nuts."

"Whatever." No argument there. If she hurried, she could meet Eric between classes.

"My mom says Dana's always been a real troublemaker."

"Since when do you listen to what your mom says?"

"You want to hear what else my mom said?"

"Not really."

Brenna's face darkened.

"Ready?" Eric called.

Brenna stomped away.

"What's up with her?" Eric asked.

It wasn't worth talking about. "Can you give me a ride to the plant after school?"

"Sure. I can put in my application, too."

Good. She was glad that Eric would be working at Gerkey's. They could totally hang out together. "Want to do DQ after?"

"Can't. We got that thing at Brenna's, remember?"

"What thing?"

He stopped and looked at her.

"Oh," she said, getting it. "That thing she didn't invite me to."

"I don't have to go."

"No biggie. Pool party, right?"

"Sorry, Pey."

"Seriously," she said. "I don't care. Maybe we can do something tomorrow."

She smiled at him.

"Okay," he said, after a second.

They were at her classroom door. "Bye." She walked into the room and that's when she finally let the smile off her face.

"Here you go." Mr. G handed Peyton the filter he'd promised her, in its little box.

"Thanks," she said, and he smiled.

Mr. G had the most amazing aquarium, filled with stony corals. He had special blue and white lights set on a timer to mimic day and night, which he said soothed the fish and fooled them into thinking they were still in the ocean. Peyton thought that was impossible. Maybe the lights went on and off, but the water temperature didn't change, and there were no waves. Those fish might not know where they were, but they knew for a fact that they weren't in open water.

The refugium tank bubbled below. Peyton bent to make sure the Banggai cardinalfish inside was doing okay.

"Look how big he's grown," Mr. G said. "All that urchin and sea grass, just for him to hide in."

He knew she hated the Banggai being down there all alone, without any friends to pass the time with. She straightened to look into the big tank. Bright orange anthias darted everywhere, and an anemone opened and closed its pink arms. The fleshy meat coral looked plump, the encrusting corals a riot of branches and mushroom shapes. Teeny starfish dotted the sides of the tank, the passive reef variety that wouldn't harm corals. Coco worms, red frilled creatures, were tucked among the crevices of the live rock. A big clam with purple lips sat at the bottom, looking smug. Nearby, the white goby worked on his burrow in the bed of sand, diving in and backing out to spit out the sand he'd collected. The cleaner shrimp with its delicate spiky legs and antennae hovered nearby. They were a pair, the goby and the shrimp, despite their many differences. Probably the only real friends in the whole tank.

"Here's the new guy," Mr. G said.

The black-striped clownfish swam within the water-filled plastic bag floating in the corner of the big tank. Sure enough, he was an onyx percula, which was pretty rare. That's why it had taken Mr. G so long to find him. He was about half the size of Charlie, Mr. G's other clownfish, which was good. No fights over turf between them. She leaned in. The new fish flicked his eyes toward her. "He looks happy," she said, knowing that was what Mr. G was waiting to hear. But she didn't think he looked happy; she thought he looked wary, like he knew his world was going to be turned upside down, again.

"He's already had his first meal."

That was a good sign. Sometimes new fish went on hunger strikes.

"He and the Desjardini tang have been eyeing one another. I can't decide if that means they like each other or not."

The large brown-striped fish drifted to the far corner, as if she'd already forgotten all about the newcomer. She could be faking it, though. Tang were crafty that way. "She doesn't like him."

"Don't worry, Peyton. I'll stay on top of it."

But he wasn't here all the time. He went home at night, and he took business trips. There would be plenty of opportunities for the tang to take a vicious nip. Yes, Peyton decided, the new fish looked uncertain. Like he knew this wasn't going to be the best setup.

"Here we go." Mr. G undid the top of the plastic bag and up-ended it, letting the new clownfish slide into the tank.

Nothing at first. The new fish sat still, as though he wasn't sure where he was or what he was supposed to do. The purple tang swam over and past, then cycled back. The Desjardini zipped around the top layers. Charlie had his back to the new fish, playing hard to get, or genuinely not picking up on the changed dynamics of the tank. Then he swam to the top and down again, and came to an abrupt halt, like, *Whoa*.

"That was fast," Mr. G said.

Charlie swam closer. The new fish treaded water, his little gills opening and closing. Charlie circled and circled, drawing nearer and nearer.

"Little does he know he's going to be a Charlotte soon."

Clownfish were born male. Over time, the more dominant ones became female. The new fish flipped around to face him. They wavered in the tank, inches from each other. Would they fight or would they decide to get along? As a rule, clownfish were a docile species, but it could still take them a while to settle down. Charlie puffed up his fins, letting the newbie know he was in charge.

Mr. G's face was reflected in the glass. "Did Fern tell you I spilled powder the other day?" she asked him.

He watched the fish. "She had to fill out a report."

"If the EPA finds anything, is it because of me?"

Now he looked at her, appraising.

A knock. The secretary stood there. "Sorry to interrupt, but Martin called. It's LT."

Mr. G straightened. "I told him. He has to wear his uniform."

"It's not that. He's not even supposed to be working today. He got in somehow and he's going around looking for cameras."

"Like security cameras?"

She grimaced. "Like the miniature cameras that aliens put into people to monitor the human race."

"Martin can't handle this?"

Martin was half the size of LT and old.

"LT's trying to get into the daycare."

"For crying out loud."

No one said not to, so Peyton followed Mr. G and his secretary down the hall to the lobby. Voices grew louder as they got closer.

"There's no such thing, LT."

"That's what you say! But I saw them!"

Martin stood, arms crossed, between LT and the daycare door. Inside, Sheri Cavanaugh watched through the glass, a baby balanced on her hip. "Those weren't aliens," Martin said. "Those were people from the EPA."

LT rocked his enormous self from side to side. "EPA's the *government, isn't it?*"

"I can't let you in there, LT. You know that."

"LT!" Mr. G called.

LT whirled around, and his blubbery face crumpled with relief. "You'll let me in, won't you? I got to make sure the kids are okay!"

"Give it a rest, LT," Mr. G said. "Only parents are allowed in the daycare."

"But they won't look. You know they won't!"

Ronni trotted toward them, snapping off her gloves as she moved. "Stop it, LT. Look, you're scaring the kids."

"You're not the boss of me," LT said.

"I'll tell Mom. I'll tell your home supervisor."

"I don't care."

"Sure you do, LT," Martin soothed. "Come on. We can look for cameras outside."

"The cameras aren't *outside*. They're *inside*. Why can't you see that?" LT shoved Martin, and the old guy fell back against the wall.

"That's enough!" Mr. G grabbed LT's elbow.

Peyton hadn't known Mr. G could yell so loud.

Mr. G marched LT away, LT struggling and trying desperately

to shake him off, but Mr. G held tight, even though LT was so much bigger than he was.

"You okay, Martin?" Peyton asked, and he nodded at her, rolling his arm around as though checking his shoulder. She could tell he was embarrassed.

"I better go check the back doors," he mumbled, and walked away.

Sheri pushed open the door to the daycare. She'd set the baby down and she came over to Ronni. "Has LT been taking his meds?" she said in a low voice.

"I guess not."

"You better get on it. You know what'll happen."

Ronni pushed her hair back with both hands, turned and saw Peyton. "Don't look at me like that. This is all *your* fault. You and your stupid aunt."

If Peyton's mom were still alive, LT would be behaving. "Don't you mean it's my mom's fault?" Peyton shot back.

Ronni set her mouth in a hard line. "How long do you think people are going to be sad for you, Peyton? Trust me. It won't be forever."

She pushed past Peyton and stalked down the hall after her brother.

"She didn't mean it," Sheri assured Peyton. "You know she's just worried about LT."

"Whatever," she said, but she knew things would never again be the same between her and Ronni.

FORTY-THREE

[DANA]

JOE STOOD IN THE EMPTY CLASSROOM, STUFFING PA-
pers into a briefcase.

"Hey," I said. It was odd to see him in front of the whiteboard, instead of at one of the desks.

He glanced up. "Hey." His expression was perfectly neutral.

The way we'd parted the other night stood between us, making me feel awkward and shy. There was something else there, too, something strange and unwelcome, in the way he quickly turned away to retrieve something from the bookcase behind him. Maybe he wasn't as glad to see me as I'd hoped.

I wandered over to him, but he didn't look back up and flash his usual grin. What had happened? Was he just distracted with end-of-the-school-year stuff? Or was he worried about something else? "This town's crazy," I said.

"Yeah?" Now he was paging through the book.

It was a textbook. How fascinating could it possibly be? "Someone came by this morning and left an envelope addressed to Peyton filled with white powder."

Now I had his attention. He set down the book and looked at me. "She didn't mention that."

"She doesn't know. Frank and I got to it before she did. Turns out it was just baby powder."

He frowned. "Good."

"Frank said people have been talking. He checked my car for a bomb."

"I'm sure no one would do that." He pushed the book into his briefcase.

"That's it?" I said. "That's all you have to say?"

"What do you want me to say, Dana?"

"What is wrong with you?"

"Nothing's wrong with me."

"So there's something wrong with *me*?"

"I hear you've been busy."

So that's what he was upset about. "Look, someone had to call the EPA, Joe. You knew what was going on. You were just as worried as I was."

"Brian just got a huge government contract. He'll lose that if he has to reformulate. He's already put in the third line. He's extended his credit to the limit."

"Are you saying it's okay for him to keep using dangerous materials?" I was shocked.

"Of course not. But you could have given him a little notice before jumping to conclusions. He could've gotten his finances in order, cut back on his supplies, tried to keep his business from going under."

"I *did* give him notice."

"Did you talk to him, or did you tell him how it was going to be?"

He was closer to the truth than I wanted to admit. Still, that wasn't the point. "He wouldn't even listen."

"Dana, this isn't about you and Brian and your power struggles. Other people are involved. Hundreds of people."

Now I was mad, too. "I know other people are involved," I retorted. "Like Peyton."

"Like *my* niece."

"Your brother's kid? What does this have to do with her?"

"My brother works at Gerkey's. He's afraid he's going to lose his job."

"Oh," I said, abashed. "I didn't think—"

"Exactly." He snapped his briefcase closed. "That's the thing, Dana. You never stop and think about anyone else."

Where had *that* come from? "Just forget it. I don't know why I came here, anyway." I stalked toward the door.

"There you go, running away again." He flipped off the lights and pushed past me.

There was nowhere to go but to follow him down the empty corridor. He punched through the heavy doors to the parking lot, the heat shimmering up from the asphalt in waves.

This wasn't how I wanted it to be. This wasn't the way I wanted to leave things. I took a deep breath, hurrying to keep up with his long strides. "Joe, we need to talk about this."

"Talk about what?" He held up his remote and his car beeped. He reached inside and set his briefcase on the passenger seat. "About the note you stuck in my locker? About moving and never saying goodbye?"

"Joe—"

"I wish I could have been that person for you, Dana. The one you trusted. The one you loved. But I finally figured it out. I'm just the guy who once loved *you*."

"Wait," I said. I put my hand on his forearm.

He pulled away. "I waited for sixteen years. I'm done waiting."

He climbed into the front seat, and I moved back to let him slam the door. This was so unlike him. "Come on, Joe," I pleaded helplessly. "Don't leave."

"Funny." He turned the key and the engine started up. "I once asked you the same thing."

. . .

As those last few months went on, Julie tried to get me to tell her. *It's his responsibility, too, Dana.*

No, I said. *He can never find out. Never.*

But it's not fair to him.

Since when has anything been fair? I shot back.

Your baby's going to need to know his or her medical history.

Will you leave me alone? I opened my textbook. *I have to study.*

Why are you being so stubborn about this?

Why are you being so pushy?

I'm just trying to help.

I don't need your help.

You don't have to be alone.

I looked at her. *I am alone.*

Julie's face softened. She came over and stroked the hair back from my temple. *You'll never be alone, Dana. You'll always have me.*

FORTY-FOUR

[PEYTON]

THERE ARE OVER FOUR HUNDRED DIFFERENT KINDS of sharks, ranging in size from the puny eight-inch dwarf lantern shark to the fifty-foot whale shark. They've been around forever, since way back at the beginning of time, before landmasses even formed, and they haven't evolved that much since. Guess they figured they'd nailed it to begin with.

They have thousands of teeth, all specially shaped, each one backed by a row of baby teeth just like it. As a tooth falls out or is yanked out during a confrontation, the next tooth in line moves forward and takes its place. Their whole bodies are covered with flat, pointed teeth called denticles, each of which is anchored to the shark's body to form a rough mesh. Not only does this skin protect them from injury, it's also thought to help them speed through the water. Sharks are formidable hunters.

Though all sharks are carnivores, eighty percent of them don't mess with humans. Of the twenty percent that do, it's more of a reluctant engagement. People push it, though, descending in metal cages to get a close-up view. They throw chum in the water to lure them out. In a feeding frenzy, sharks have been known to attack the cages and *the people inside, pushing their huge snouts through the bars and showing their vicious teeth. Hard to feel sorry for those divers, though.*

After all, if you play with sharks, you're going to get bitten.

Peyton handed her dad the potholder. "Do you think Mr. G fired LT?"

"I wouldn't be surprised." Her dad peered into the pot and tapped the wooden spoon on the rim. Peyton would have just stuck the leftovers in the microwave, but her dad had wanted to give it that extra touch, take that extra step to show just how normal everything was. Supper wasn't something nuked on high for ten minutes. Supper was stirred, tasted, served.

"What will LT do now?"

"I guess he'll have to find another job."

"Like what? No one else will hire him."

"Someone will."

"Mom said if LT didn't have a job, he'd end up in jail or a mental institution."

"It'll work out."

Why was she so obsessed with LT's welfare? Who cared what happened to him? He was weird and creepy. But lately she'd realized he was just as lost as she was. Maybe they were more alike than she'd thought.

The phone rang. Her father frowned. "Let the answering machine get it."

It was the third time the phone had rung since they'd gotten home.

"What do you think?" he said. "Do you want to eat in here?"

They sat facing each other awkwardly across the small table beside the window. Their very first meal together, alone. So this is how it would be from now on.

He leaned over and set a keyring by her plate. "Your mom's car is good to go."

Yes! "You're giving it to me?"

"I'll transfer the title to you this weekend."

"Thanks, Dad." It wouldn't be so bad. It'd be great, actually. She'd get used to driving her mom's car. She could fix it up and make it her own. She dragged her fork through the mound of wrinkled green peas on her plate, stabbed at a limp curl of ham. "This doesn't look very good."

He chewed, swallowed, nodded. "I might have cooked it a little too long."

"Do I have to eat it?"

"No. Just finish your milk."

How had Dana's supper gone? Was it strange for her, too, to be alone? Ha. She'd probably loved it.

Her dad rinsed the dishes in the sink and Peyton loaded them in the dishwasher. "I called Doc Lindstrom's office. You know, for your blood type? But his nurse said you had to sign a release form or something."

"Sure. I'll try and stop by tomorrow."

"Don't forget," she warned. "I have to get this done by next week."

"I won't," he promised. He opened the cabinet and reached for the brown bottle tucked up high on the top shelf.

"Why are you doing that?"

He glanced at her. "Doing what?"

"That." She nodded to the bottle in his hand.

"Aw, princess." He twisted off the cap. "It's all right."

"That's exactly what you used to say. Don't you think I remember? You used to tell Mom that all the time. *It's all right, Jules. It's okay, Jules.*"

"Peyton—"

"Don't do this to me, Dad."

He set down the glass. "All right," he said.

Anyone could tell he didn't mean it. "I'm going out." She snatched up the keys he'd just given her. She thought maybe he'd tell her to hold on and he'd come with her. But he didn't.

. . .

Her mom's lucky charm swayed on its chain from the rearview mirror as Peyton took the corner, the little airplane twisting and untwisting. *Life's a journey.* The tissue box on the floor bumped her ankle; a receipt sailed out the window. The car smelled of the green tea lotion her mom applied to her hands at red lights.

Peyton turned the radio up loud. Classic rock, but at least it was better than country. She'd get one of those things that allowed her to plug her iPod into the cigarette lighter. Then she could listen to real music.

Eric's dad was out by the mailbox getting the mail. "Hi, Mr. Hofseth."

"Hi, Peyton."

"I just got my mom's car."

"I can see that."

He didn't smile at her like he always did. So maybe he'd gotten some bad news in the mail. Maybe an overdue bill. That was the kind of bad news that could upset her dad for days. "Well, say hi to Mrs. Hofseth," she said, and he nodded. She'd already texted Eric to call her later, so he could know she was okay about the party. So she could pretend.

The lake danced in front of her. People were everywhere, lying on towels, going in and out of the souvenir shops. Things were gearing up for Memorial Day. It'd be the first holiday they'd have to get through without her mom. A small holiday. They could practice on it, prepare themselves for the big ones.

The nursing home had the entrance doors propped open. The receptionist looked up with a smile. "Hey, you."

"Hi."

Mr. Macomber sat bent in his wheelchair, asleep, his hand lifted as if asking someone the time. Residents were being fed in the dining room by the aides, big cloth bibs spread beneath their chins and across their shoulders. Organ music played and wavery voices sang about happy days being here again.

Her grandma sat in her recliner, tethered to her bed by the long plastic lead. Mrs. Gerkey sat in her wheelchair, restlessly working the wheels back and forth. The two old ladies had been talking and now they stopped and looked up.

How sad was it that this was the only place she had to go.

"Have you come to take me to supper?" her grandma asked.

"I'm not the aide, Grandma. I'm Peyton."

Mrs. Gerkey reached up and took her hand in her cool, soft one, and gave it a squeeze.

Her grandma's watery eyes regarded her, the eyebrows thick and white and whiskery.

Mrs. Gerkey said, "Frank and Julie's daughter, Miriam. You remember Julie."

"Julie. Yes." Her grandma tightened her grip on the arms of her chair. "Has she come to take me shopping?"

"Maybe later." Peyton wandered around the room. She wanted to say, *I got a car today,* but her grandma wouldn't care. She wanted to say, *My aunt moved out this morning and my dad's drinking again,* but she might not care about that, either. Peyton didn't know why she'd come here, after all. But now she was here and the two old ladies were looking at her, so she was stuck. A vase of paper flowers sat on the dresser, with a mirror tilted to show Peyton her throat. She reached over and tipped it up to see her face. It looked steadily back at her. "I'm doing a project for school, Grandma."

"That's nice."

"It's like a family tree. I need to put you down, too." Peyton wouldn't ask her grandma for her blood type. She'd probably roll up her sleeve and extend her arm.

Mrs. Gerkey said, "That'd be very nice. Miriam, you'll need to find a photograph you can give Peyton."

"Yes, all right."

"Check that top drawer, Peyton," Mrs. Gerkey said.

The fat leather album sat there among folded cotton handkerchiefs and little cardboard boxes that sat in their lids, filled with brooches, knobby rings, heavy chains.

Peyton sat down on the bed and opened to the first page. She'd been through this album a million times and knew there was nothing she could take for her project. Everything in it was too old and there was only one copy. She'd take a photo of her grandma with her cellphone instead. She tapped a page. "Here you are with your mom." Peyton's great-grandma looked happy, the breeze lifting a raft of fluffy blonde hair off her forehead.

"Yes." Her grandma leaned forward. "That was when I was just a little girl."

"And there we are, Miriam." Mrs. Gerkey pointed to a picture of two women with smooth hair in dresses that reached below their knees. "Your grandmother had just had your father."

Her grandma nodded. "We both had our babies late in life."

"Brian was my lucky surprise," Mrs. Gerkey said.

It was crazy to think of Mr. G as a surprise, much less a baby. A turn of the page revealed him as a toddler holding on to the bar of a wooden pushcart. A teenaged Aunt Karen sat cross-legged, smiling demurely while the six-year-old version of Peyton's dad, instantly recognizable with his intent expression and high hairline, stood off to one side. They both looked like they'd been caught in the middle of something.

Here was her parents' wedding portrait. Her mom held kind of droopy tulips and her dad wore an ugly brown tux the color of a Hershey's bar.

"Julie was a beautiful bride," her grandma said.

Her mom's hair gleamed a soft gold, curving around her face. Her blue eyes were wide, her skin perfect. "How come there aren't any pictures of Dana?"

"Oh." Her grandma's hands trembled. She moved them back and forth as if wiping something off her lap.

Mrs. Gerkey leaned forward and patted Peyton's knee. "You stop bothering your grandma, honey."

A thought struck her. These old ladies had been friends for forever; they probably knew everything about each other. "Tell me, Mrs. Gerkey."

Mrs. Gerkey reached out for the album and placed it in her own lap. "It was a sad time, my dear. No need to relive it."

"But I should know if it's about my mom."

"People don't need to know everything."

"So you *do* know."

"It's none of my business, too."

She was so smug. "Did you hear about the EPA?" Peyton's heart pounded with her daring.

Mrs. Gerkey hiked a penciled eyebrow. "A lot of trouble and worry over nothing."

"The EPA wouldn't be there if it was nothing, Mrs. Gerkey."

"I've been around a long time, my dear. I remember all sorts of scares that turned out to be nothing."

"And plenty that turned out to be real," her grandma piped up.

"Miriam," Mrs. Gerkey said, chiding. "That's different."

"Maybe," her grandma said.

Aha. Peyton had accidentally poked something free, some secret these two old ladies were holding on to. "Like what?" she asked, with interest.

She was looking at her grandma, but it was Mrs. Gerkey who answered.

"Let's get a cookie," Mrs. Gerkey said. "They're making Snickerdoodles today."

"My favorite," her grandma said happily.

Peyton stayed for another hour, eating cookies with the old ladies in the small coffee shop down the hall and trying unsuccessfully to steer the conversation back to scares that turned out to be real. But, in the end, she left having eaten way too many cookies and with the certain knowledge that Mrs. Gerkey knew something very important that she had no intention of revealing.

FORTY-FIVE

[DANA]

THE TELEVISION DRONED FROM THE BREAKFAST
nook. The weather report. The farm report. Entertainment
news. I pulled the lever on the coffee urn, and out dribbled the
last inch of pale brown liquid. As soon as the front desk clerk returned, I'd let her know we had an emergency on our hands. I'd
eaten my share of hotel continental breakfasts, and they ran the
gamut from extravagant waffles made to order to sealed plastic
packages from the nearby gas station. This one teetered toward
the pitiful end of the spectrum, with green bananas and day-old
doughnuts. But until the coffee ran out, I'd been okay.

I stood by the window, sipping the weak brew, eyeing my car
parked as close to the entrance as I could manage. It had spent
the night bathed in bright yellow light. I'd fastened a small piece
of tape across the hood to warn me if anyone had popped it; I'd
make sure to check the underside before I got in. Paranoid, right?

*". . . no cause for concern. Russian officials say they're looking
into the unexplained deaths. In other news, last week's implosion
in Chicago that left one person dead has the victim's family talking."*

There it was, playing out in full color, my shoot from the week before. I hadn't actually seen it on film yet, and the beautiful crumpling of brick and cement to a tsunami of powder took my breath away, even though at the same instant, it made my skin pop out in goosebumps. As those stones were raining down, they were falling on Jane Hamilton.

"*. . . possible irregularities during the demolition. The owner, Dana Carlson, could not be reached for comment.*"

They hadn't even tried to reach me, and there had been no mention of the *other* owner. How had Halim managed *that*?

Halim answered on the second ring. "I heard," he said grimly. "There's been a leak."

"What does that mean? Who talked?" I paced the small space. A family came in, chattering, and I moved to the lobby.

"One of the crew, most likely. They haven't been paid."

"I told Ahmed to pay them out of the Burnside funds."

"That account was empty."

Because Halim had been only too eager to bail his brother out with money we didn't have. No wonder the crew was angry. I was angry, too. "So they went after me?"

"It's as much about me as it is about you, Dana. I was the one who let you wire without a permit. Look. We'll tell the authorities I was training you but that you didn't place any of the charges yourself."

A lie. Halim had been there, working alongside me, monitoring everything I did. But I had snipped the det cord. I had stuffed the charge in the crevice that I had drilled. I had placed the charges. And in the end, I was the one who set them on fire.

"Dana?"

"I'm thinking."

Did I trust him? Was this some ploy the machinations of which I couldn't understand, or was he genuinely trying to protect me?

"Well, think about this. You don't want to end up in jail, do you? That's where they'll send us if we don't agree that I was the one who handled everything."

"Maybe we shouldn't be talking on a cell line," I said tartly.

"You need to come back. I understand this is a difficult time for you personally, but you've been gone long enough." When I didn't say anything, he said, sharply, "Dana?"

"I heard you," I said.

But I didn't say I was going to listen.

Wheat fields ran alongside the highway, sprawling all the way to spiky pines in the distance. A semi roared around me, its cargo filled with chickens whose feathery little heads peeked out between the frets of their cages.

Moorhead sat on the Minnesota side of the Red River, crouched in the low shadow of its larger sister city, Fargo. The university dominated the northern part of town, a series of bland buildings following the curve of the river. The School of Public Health was one square structure among many. A student directed me to the top floor.

Fluorescent lighting turned the corridors white. A bitter metallic odor stung the air. Every door had an index card slotted into a metal frame beside it. I stopped in front of one and knocked.

"Come in."

The two scientists stood in front of a whiteboard scrawled with notations. Dennis Hoffmeyer smiled when he saw me. "Hey," he said. "Join us."

"I hope you don't mind my dropping by."

"Not at all."

Bill Neuberger pulled out a chair, a rickety thing on wheels. "Careful. Don't lean back."

"Coffee?" Dennis said.

"No, thanks." I couldn't sit. I didn't want coffee. "You said today you might have some answers."

The men glanced at each other. "We were just talking about that," Bill said. "You were right about it being nano zinc."

"We can't figure out how it's getting aerosolized," Dennis said. "It could be during the manufacturing process when the zinc's added to the sunscreen slurry, but that's just a guess. We don't know much about the behavior of nano-sized particles."

"I'd be surprised if it's a mechanical process," Bill told him, and Dennis shrugged. Evidently this was the debate I'd interrupted.

It didn't matter how the zinc had gotten there. It only mattered that it had. "What about the water samples you took?"

"Looks like it's in both the lake and groundwater."

"So the water's not safe." Everyone in town had been exposed—moms mixing baby formula, kids brushing their teeth, old folks washing their hands. Everyone in Black Bear needed to stop turning on their faucets and switch to bottled water. Forget about fishing, swimming, and watering their gardens. But how did you stop breathing the air? "What about the soil?"

"Yeah, it's there, too, but in much lower concentrations." Dennis glanced at Bill. "You know, it'd be interesting to chart the dispersion. I'll assign some grad students to this full-time."

Interesting? I stared at him. He couldn't be serious. This wasn't *interesting*. This was *terrifying*.

"We should coordinate our efforts," Bill told him. "I'd like to set up air-sampling monitors downwind of the plant. What's your timing look like?"

"The important thing," I interrupted, "is that you both know there's too much. You know it's dangerous."

"Well, that's the thing." Dennis looked at me earnestly, the light winking off his gold-rimmed glasses. "We don't really know. Nanotechnology's too new. We haven't established threshold parameters. We don't know what amount's safe."

"Nanotechnology's been around for *years*." I was confused. "How can you not know what's safe and what isn't?"

"It's only recently that it's been applied to consumer products on such a large scale. Science has had a hard time staying on top of it."

"But people in Black Bear are *sick*."

"I understand these are your friends and neighbors." Bill stood tall and authoritative in his button-down shirt with the cuffs rolled up, his beard neatly trimmed. He had the air of a man used to speaking in front of large groups, a little bit of a politician, and I instinctively mistrusted him. "But even though we've found a high incidence of nanoscale zinc, we can't be certain that it's causing any ill health effect. After all, the incident rate is still within accepted normal parameters."

"The good news is that nano zinc doesn't penetrate the skin," Dennis added, boyishly eager. "The Chinese study you found injected the mice with nanomaterials. You see the difference?"

I wasn't an idiot and I couldn't be charmed by his enthusiasm. "It can still enter the body through cuts and scratches. It's not as if people wash their hands after putting on sunscreen."

"We still don't know at what level, if any, it causes problems," Bill pointed out.

They both sounded so calm. "I don't get it! I thought you were worried about this. I thought that's why you dropped everything and rushed to Black Bear."

"You misunderstand," Bill said. "We *are* worried. After all, this is how health threats get discovered. A nurse in Texas was the one who sounded the alarm about the increased rate of anencephaly. And it was a mother in Massachusetts who found out the water supply in her town was giving people leukemia." He saw the horrified expression on my face, and hurriedly patted the air. "I'm not saying that's the level of crisis we have here. But we have to be methodical. We can't just draw hasty conclusions."

"You'll at least shut down the plant until you *do* know."

"No." He shook his head. "We can't."

He couldn't mean that. He *didn't* mean that. "I guess that's the FDA's job," I said slowly, feeling my way. But neither man nodded in affirmation. My heart started to pound, and I suddenly regretted my earlier decision not to sit. "But you can recall the sunscreen, right?"

"It's far too early to take those measures. Our findings aren't actionable."

"But you've found something that doesn't belong there! Why isn't that enough to stop production?"

"There's been no violation. The plant is operating within EPA protocols."

"Then change the protocols."

"That takes time. And studies like this one."

"We're at a very exciting point in time," Dennis told me. "We're mining new terrain. It's studies like this one that will reveal the true health risks inherent in nanotechnology."

"There's nothing the EPA can do as a regulatory agency," Bill said. "It's not like Homeland Security. We have no authority to act."

"So you're not going to do *anything*?" I said, incredulous.

"We are doing something," Bill replied stiffly. "We're going to go back and collect more samples."

I didn't want to hear about samples anymore. And he could cut out that patronizing tone of his. "Don't you understand? My sister *died* from this." How could they just stand there and do *nothing*?

Bill flushed. "Look, we can't just shut businesses down. We can't just pull products from the shelves."

"Then tell me who can," I demanded. "Tell me where I'm supposed to go. Tell me who I'm supposed to talk to."

Bill crossed his arms. Dennis stared at the papers on his desk.

"Right," I said with disgust. "*You're* the people I'm supposed to turn to."

Someone called out in the hall; someone else answered. But in here, there was only silence.

"Let me guess," I said, between clenched teeth. "When you go to collect these samples, you'll be wearing full protective gear."

Dennis looked uneasy.

"Respirators?" I shot at him. "Gloves? A hazmat suit? You say you're waiting for the government to decide whether or not this stuff is dangerous, but you already know."

"Wearing gear is standard," Bill said.

"Sure," I snapped. "Explain *that* to the people in the plant. You'll know who they are. They're the ones in hairnets and latex gloves."

Like Peyton.

I had to get back to Black Bear.

FORTY-SIX

[PEYTON]

SQUIDS ARE LIKE TORPEDOES WITH LEGS AND EYES. *Their tentacles are covered with toothy suckers, and they have a sharp beak for a mouth. The smallest squid is an inch long, the colossal squid over forty feet. No one's actually ever seen a colossal squid alive; we've only found a few carcasses washed up on shore. Scientists guess they must be the legendary sea monsters that terrified fishermen by leaping out of the water in front of their boats and causing them to capsize.*

Squids eat their own kind. They eat anything, period. They change their color to match their surroundings and hang motionless in the water, waiting for their next meal to swim by. If they're threatened, they release a blinding cloud of dark or bioluminescent liquid and escape as it disperses.

Their hunting grounds are the vastest on earth, far larger than all the plains, jungles, and mountains combined. Their brains are enormous and their eyes the most highly developed of all living creatures. Which is strange. Of all the animals in the world, why would one that lives in complete darkness have the best eyesight of all? It makes you think that maybe they're seeing things we don't even know are there.

Eric wasn't waiting for her on the sidewalk, so Peyton texted him. No answer. Maybe he'd slept in or was sick. Leaning against a tree, she watched Mr. Stahlberg drag the trash out to the curb. He waved to her and she waved back. Her dad had forgotten to take out the trash last night, probably wouldn't remember this morning. He'd been quiet, just grunting hello instead of asking her how her day looked.

She walked around to the back of their house, grabbed the handle of the big black can, and rolled it out to the curb.

She texted Eric again.

Still no reply. Even if he'd had his phone confiscated, he'd have found another way to let her know he couldn't walk to school. After waiting another ten minutes, which made it totally too late to walk, she took her mother's car and drove.

She found him by his locker, working the combination. He didn't even look up.

"Where were you? I thought you were sick or something."

"My mom gave me a ride."

"Your mom never gives you a ride."

"She did today."

"How come you didn't text me back last night? What happened at Brenna's party that was so interesting?"

"Nothing."

"Why are you being this way?"

He banged open his locker. "I'm not being any way."

"Right."

"Look, I got into a big fight with my folks last night." He pulled books from his backpack and shoved them inside his locker.

"Okay."

"Not okay. It was about you. They don't want us hanging out anymore."

That was impossible. The Hofseths were like her family. Eric's parents *loved* her. "Be real."

"I am being real. Dad's really pissed about what Dana did."

She stared at him, but Eric refused to meet her gaze. "I can't help what Dana did. I didn't even know about it!"

"I told him that. I even told him your dad kicked her out. He still took away my cellphone. We have to cool it for a while."

"For how long?"

"I don't know."

So Mr. Hofseth hadn't been upset about the mail. He'd been blowing her off. She felt like an idiot, gabbing at him when he only wanted her to shut up and go away. "It's all right," she told Eric. "Dana's moved out. She's gone."

"Yeah." Eric still wasn't looking at her. He was doing everything *but* look at her, staring into his locker like there was something really interesting inside.

"What?" she said.

"Nothing."

She pushed herself between him and his locker, so close she could smell his toothpaste, see the wrinkle in the floppy collar of his shirt, feel the heat coming off his body. "Tell me," she insisted.

He stepped back. Another beat of alarm pulsed through her.

He glanced at the kids milling around. "It's not just Dana he's freaked about."

She was confused. "I didn't do anything."

"I know." He looked miserable, guilty, angry, all at the same time.

Then she got it, suddenly. An icy wash of betrayal. "Eric!" she hissed.

"I had to tell him. My mom saw your dad at the liquor store."

"You weren't supposed to tell *anyone*!"

"It wasn't my fault."

"You are such a *loser.*"

He frowned, slammed his locker. She'd never seen that cold expression on his face. And she didn't care, she was so furious.

"Eric!" Brenna called, hooking her arm through his, acting like she didn't even see Peyton standing there. Acting like she couldn't even tell they were in the middle of a big fight. "You ready?" She pulled him away, Eric not resisting even one little bit. Maybe it wasn't the guy from bio Brenna had been really interested in.

The thought nailed Peyton right in the heart.

The bell rang and the hall emptied, lockers banging and doors closing, until Peyton was the only one there.

People weren't all that different from squid. People ate their own kind, too.

FORTY-SEVEN

[DANA]

JULIE SET THE SLEEPING BABY IN MY ARMS, AND tucked the blanket around the small form, cocooning the infant in sunshine yellow. *She looks just like you did when you were a baby.*

I'm not keeping her.

Dana. Chiding. *You don't mean that.*

Yes, I do.

You're just overwhelmed. That's normal. You'll feel better after you get some sleep.

Don't tell me how I'll feel. She's just going to mess everything up.

You won't be alone. I'll help you every step of the way. You know I will.

Don't. I've already made up my mind.

Time gathered itself like whorls of yarn along a silver knitting needle.

Maybe I could take her, Julie said at last, softly.

So easy. *Tell Frank she's yours. Tell him you wanted to surprise him. You didn't want him to know until you were sure.*

Had I spoken too quickly? Would she see through me? I sneaked a glance. She was looking at the sleeping baby. Tears running down her cheeks.

So it was done.

I'd figured it all out by the time I got to Julie's house. Frank and Peyton would have to leave town. Frank could find a job somewhere else; his skills were transferable. Peyton could start her senior year there, make new friends, make a fresh start. She wouldn't be happy, but she'd understand. She'd have to.

Frank's truck was in the driveway, but Julie's car was gone. The whole week I'd been there, the car hadn't been moved, and I'd gotten used to seeing it there. So who was driving it now?

I hesitated at the front door, then knocked twice, hard, before stepping inside. "Frank? You here?"

He was in the kitchen, glass raised to his lips. "What do you want?"

Five o'clock and he was already digging into the whiskey. Things hadn't gotten better. "I just talked to the people from the EPA. They found nano zinc, Frank. It's in the plant, the water, the ground. It's everywhere."

"Well, good for you. You win."

"It's not about *winning*."

"No? Then, what is it about, Dana?"

"The whole town's poisoned. It's not safe. You and Peyton need to move."

"Quit my job? Sell the house? You bet. I'll get right on that."

"I'm serious, Frank. This is what killed Julie."

Finally, he lowered his glass. "The EPA say that?"

"No. But they will."

"What *did* they say?"

"They have to do more testing. But it's just a matter of time . . ."

"So even though this nano zinc's everywhere, they're not concerned. They're not closing down the plant."

"You can't listen to them."

"You're the one who called them in. Which way is it, Dana? We listen to them, or we don't?"

"I thought they could help."

"You just wanted them to rubber-stamp this crazy notion of yours."

"It's not crazy. They're looking into it. They're worried about it."

"But they're not doing anything."

"It's the government," I snapped. "They're the ones who put lead in paint. Look at asbestos. Thalidomide. They're not going to do anything until more people die. You want Peyton to be one of them?"

"Leave my daughter out of this."

"She's not your daughter."

He started to laugh, then saw the expression on my face. His eyes went blank with confusion. "What are you talking about? Julie tell you that?"

"She's not Julie's, either. She's mine."

"Right. She looks just like Julie."

"And me."

His gaze settled on me, as if he was forced to see me for the very first time.

"That's why Julie and I moved to Hawley that summer. Not so she could be closer to nursing school, but so no one would know I was pregnant."

He set the bottle down.

"You came home for Christmas that year, remember?" I continued. "Of course you'd think Peyton was yours."

"You're lying."

"It was a big surprise, wasn't it, finding out Julie had had a baby? She'd never said a word."

"She said it was because she didn't want to get my hopes up."

"You must have suspected something, but you bought it anyway. Because you *wanted* to believe it."

"Get out."

"The way Peyton holds her spoon with her thumb overlapping? The way she sometimes walks around with just one sock on, sleeps on her stomach with her head in her pillow? That's me, Frank. She's mine."

Red crawled up his cheeks and his eyes went hard. I stumbled back a step as he raised his arm.

"You stay away from her, you interfering bitch! I raised her. She's my daughter—"

The sudden crunch of footsteps outside, the slam of a door. A car was pulling out of the driveway, tires squealing against asphalt.

By the time we reached the door and looked out, all we could see was the car accelerating down the street.

Peyton had heard everything.

FORTY-EIGHT

[PEYTON]

CORAL REEFS ARE BUILT BY LIVING CREATURES called polyps that shape limestone shells all around their soft, vulnerable bodies. They live two to three years, and when they reproduce, they release larvae that settle on the tops of other corals to begin making their own limestone houses. Because they're so tiny, reefs grow only about an inch a year. Scientists estimate that the coral reefs around today are between five and ten thousand years old. Over a million different species of animals and plants live in them. It's the most diverse habitat on earth.

Polyps feed at night by poking their tentacles out to catch plankton. Because these tentacles sting, they also protect the polyps from predators. But it's an inefficient feeding process, not enough to sustain them. It's the microscopic algae inside the polyps, converting sunshine into food, that really keep the polyps alive. Algae require tropical temperatures, a certain level of salinity, ample sunlight, and a current that's not too fast or too sluggish in order to thrive. So when you come down to it, over a million species rely on something so fragile it almost doesn't exist, and so microscopic it's invisible.

. . .

Her mom's lucky charm smacked against the glass. Her books slithered out of her bookbag and thudded to the floor.

Eric's house flew by, hunkered down and smug, like all the houses beside it. Another turn, the road curving up and down and she flew into the air for an instant, a stomach-assaulting moment of pure joy when gravity let go, and then the car of its own accord leaped the curb and crashed to a halt in front of the nursing home where her mom had taken her for countless visits.

Not her mom. She was Dana's daughter.

The entrance doors were closed—someone had once tried to make a run for it. Peyton punched the automatic button and the doors opened slowly like butterfly wings. She strode by the nurse writing at her desk and the old man in his chair, awake today and grinning at her. She'd smack his hand if he reached up toward her. The papers tacked to the bulletin board fluttered as she ran past them. Down the hall past the dining room, where people worked setting up the tables, the steamy smells of overcooked food swarming into the hall.

Her grandma's room was empty. Instead, she sat playing cards with Mrs. Gerkey and two other old ladies in the games room, holding their cards in special little grippers so the cards stayed put and didn't shake to the table.

"Hello, Peyton," Mrs. Gerkey said.

Peyton ignored her. She put her hands on her grandma's thin wrists, the skin papery soft over the bones. "Who's my real dad?"

Her grandma's eyes widened. "I don't think I know you, dear."

"Yes, you do!" She gave her grandma's hands a shake. "I'm Julie's daughter." *Not Julie's daughter.* "Frank's daughter."

Her grandma pursed her lips together, then nodded. "Yes. That's right. Frank's daughter, but not really."

Not really. That was a laugh. "Who *is* my real dad?"

"Dana got herself in trouble. I should have seen it coming."

"Peyton," Mrs. Gerkey said. "None of that matters. You need to calm down."

Calm down? Was the old witch kidding? "It does matter. It matters to me."

"What matters is that Dana did the right thing," Mrs. Gerkey said.

"What do you know about anything?" Peyton snatched back her hands. "She gave me away, like I was garbage. How is *that* the right thing?"

"Don't talk to your grandma that way," Mrs. Gerkey chided.

"I can talk to her any way I want," Peyton shot back. "She's *not* my grandma." She leaned down and spoke the next words into Miriam's startled face. "I never loved you, either."

She should drive to Fargo. It was only an hour away, but what would she do when she got there? The Twin Cities lay hours away and she wasn't really sure how to get there. Eric would have helped, but not now. Hawley? Yuck—that was even smaller than Black Bear. It didn't even have a DQ. There really was only one place.

She swerved off the road and down the long driveway to the plant. The workday was over; there were only a few cars in the parking lot. She skewed into an end space and climbed out, holding her face to the hot sun. Birds cawed nearby; the lake glinted between the trees. She ran for her thinking rock.

She *was* her mom's daughter. Of course she was. They looked just like each other. Didn't they have the same trick of jiggling their right foot when their legs were crossed? Didn't they love the same movies and think kiwi were slimy? When Peyton looked in the mirror, she always saw herself, but with her mother gently shaded in, as if the two of them were together occupying the same space.

She pulled her cigarettes from her bag. Just two left and they were a little bent.

What about her dad? She didn't look like him, but then, she never had. Who was she, if she wasn't his daughter? They hung out together. He'd taught her to fish and ride her bike. When they went camping, the two of them sat out by the campfire after her mom had gone to her sleeping bag, and he told her about the stars in the sky. He'd been the one to approve buying such an expensive aquarium. He'd been the one to look up how to become a marine biologist. They both loved her mom, equally. If that didn't unite them, nothing did. But there was part of him she'd never known, that part that didn't talk about what had happened overseas, the cold scary stranger who emerged whenever he'd been drinking. He was her dad, but he wasn't just like her, not the way her mom had been. He was all Peyton had left. Maybe he really didn't love her, either.

Who did this make her? Joe Connolly's daughter? There was nothing special about him at all, nothing that told her they had anything in common.

Who did this make her mom, the woman who'd lied to Peyton every single day of her entire life? What else had she lied about? Nothing made sense anymore.

She scrabbled through her purse for her lighter, pulled at all the pockets, took out her wallet to look beneath. No luck. She rested her chin on her bent knee and stared out at the lake. So Dana had gotten pregnant. What was the big deal about that? Lots of kids got pregnant. A girl in her class had a three-month-old, and one of the sophomore girls was pregnant, wearing tight shirts that rode up on her belly. What was so horrible about Peyton that made Dana want to give her away? And her mom want to keep it a secret?

She needed her lighter. Jumping down, she made her way around the building toward the parking lot. She couldn't go home again. She could never look her father in the face. She was afraid of what she'd see there. She never wanted to see Dana again. Eric teased into her mind, but she pushed him away. She wasn't Eric's girlfriend anymore, not Julie and Frank's daughter, but someone else. Someone she hadn't figured out.

The side entrance to the plant was ajar. That was weird. Martin always walked around and made sure everything was locked up tight.

Mr. G's secretary smoked. She'd have a lighter or a matchbook in her desk. There were still some people around. She could hear their voices in a nearby room. Machinery thrummed from the other end of the plant, not making noise but making the floor tingle beneath her feet. She hadn't realized that it did so before. What else had she missed or not noticed? Her mother was always telling her to slow down and enjoy the process. Scratch that. *Julie* had always said that.

It was delicious being here, where she had no right being. She ran her fingertips along the wall, recently papered in white and soft gray stripes, the paper bumpy where the gray came in, smoothing out for the white. A metallic scent hung in the air. Maybe one of the machines was running wrong and her dad would be called in to fix it. Nope. Not her dad. Just some guy named Frank.

She found the lighter in the secretary's desk, in one of the compartments of the plastic divider. She thumbed the wheel, holding the lick of flame to the tip of her cigarette. She drew in and the cigarette caught.

The two clownfish were swimming in unison, flipping this way and that, like they were playing a game. Mr. G was right: Charlie was getting along with his new friend, someone who looked just like him, to reflect back his happy self and show him he belonged.

She had a wild thought. The best thought.

All that powder Dana claimed was making people sick. Peyton knew where it was stored. Everyone was so afraid of it, and wouldn't it be something to send it flying all around? She could rig up that fan Ronni used in the packing room, and position it over the opened bin of powder. That would be cool. Then everyone would be equal. She wouldn't be the only rudderless one.

She'd get into the storeroom through the manufacturing room. She knew the code. Fern had tried to be secretive about it, but she was old and her fingers had moved slowly. If anyone had been clever, it had been Peyton, who'd looked away the instant Fern glanced over to see if she'd been watching. Ha.

She turned the corner and saw a bright yellow wire running along the baseboard, like it was leading somewhere. Interesting. She decided to see where it led.

Around the next corner, she saw LT crouching at the end of the corridor. He saw her at the same moment, and scrambled to push himself up. "Peyton?"

LT clasped a reel of yellow wire to his chest. So he'd been the one to string it along the floor. "What are you doing?" she asked him. LT had been fired, hadn't he? So what was he doing here, creeping around after hours?

"Get AWAY! You're not supposed to be here! Get AWAY."

She glanced at the wire by her feet. The most poisonous creatures in the ocean were brightly colored. It was nature's way of warning away other animals, *Bad News. Stay Away.* Here was this glow-in-the-dark neon yellow, the kind that made you automatically pay attention.

LT lurched toward her and the reel dropped, bounced. Now she saw the gray duct tape around his chest, holding a small black box against his sweatshirt. "GET OUT GET OUT GET OUT!"

Yeah, good idea. He was looking real freaky.

"Peyton!"

There was Dana, running toward her, her face twisted in horror.

A loud boom and the world shook.

No one's daughter.

FORTY-NINE

[DANA]

BY THE TIME JULIE ARRIVED HOME, HOURS AFTER she'd told me to expect her, I'd grown crazy with worry. I'd started imagining all sorts of terrible scenarios, fueled by the awful certainty that my sister would be snatched from me at the very time I needed her most. Her car sailing over an embankment. Someone kidnapping her from a parking lot. An angry employee bursting into the office and gunning down everyone in the waiting room.

At last, Julie nudged open the door and dropped her keys on the small table. She looked perfectly fine, wearing the same print blouse and denim skirt she'd left in that morning, her blonde hair falling in soft waves to her shoulders, her cheeks pink from the summer sun. She glanced around the room, at the magazines lying askew on the couch beside me, the glass of ice water sweating condensation on the coffee table, everywhere but at me. *Don't tell me you've been watching TV all day.*

Gently chiding, not a word about why she was so late, but I could tell from the tight way she was controlling her voice that she wasn't the least bit fine. *What did the doctor say?*

350 | CARLA BUCKLEY

There are lots of things you could be doing, Dana. How about learning another language? Or how to cook?

Tell me, I demanded.

She sank into the armchair across from me, its worn cushion scooped and scratchy. It was our least favorite chair in the place, and we used it as a way station for laundry to be folded or library books to be returned, but here my sister was, leaning back against the ugly green fabric as though she did so every day. Her eyes were red-rimmed, her mascara smudged. She'd been crying, but she tried on a smile. *How about knitting?*

So that was it. She'd never be able to have a baby. *Is he sure?*

Pretty sure. She lifted her hair from the nape of her neck and let it fall. *Let's treat ourselves. How about Chinese?*

But...

Don't look like that, Dana. It's not the end of the world. But it *was* the end of the world. I saw it in her eyes. *Frank and I can always adopt.*

You said Frank would never love a child that wasn't his own.

She started to respond, then faltered. She was trying so hard to be brave, and I was making it difficult for her. *I'll have lo mein,* I said, and she smiled.

Just think, she said, reaching for the phone. *Soon I'll have a little niece or nephew to spoil.*

Julie had done everything for me and had asked for nothing in return. I put my hand on my belly and felt the answering kick. Suddenly, I knew what I had to do. But was I strong enough to do it?

Frank and I took separate cars. Even then, we weren't united. Even then, we were on opposite sides.

I rolled through intersections, searching in both directions for Julie's small blue sedan. Thought I saw it in the JCPenney's parking lot, until I spied the Wisconsin license plate. I tried every phone number I could argue out of the operator. When Eric Hofseth answered, he sounded distracted. At the mention of Peyton's name, his voice sharpened.

"I don't know," he told me bleakly, and I believed him.

Sheri sounded worried. "I don't know where she could be, but if she heads this way, I'll let you know. Dana, what's wrong?"

I drove along the lake, turned in to the amusement park, and looked at the mob of people thronging the walkway. Peyton couldn't possibly be there. All that giddy gleefulness would make her sick. She'd look for silence. She'd want to be alone. Where would she find that? I thought I might know.

Sure enough, along the far side of Gerkey's parking lot the car sat at an angle. A few other cars were parked nearby. I didn't recognize any of them.

I banged on the glass doors. A man emerged out of the gloom on the other side, someone I recalled seeing before, though no one I knew. He waved, *We're not open,* and wheeled away. I rapped harder, drawing him back, pressed my hands together in supplication. *Please.*

Shaking his head, he unlocked the door and held it open a few inches. "Read the sign. We're closed."

He'd been one of the workers in the manufacturing area when I'd gone through with the monitor; he'd eyed me the entire time with a dour expression.

"I'm looking for Peyton Kelleher."

"I told you, we're closed."

"Her car's parked right there. She has to be in here somewhere. Just let me look around. I'll only take a minute—"

"No can do. Sorry."

He wasn't sorry. The bastard looked pleased to be shutting the door in my face. I grabbed the handle. "Look. She's upset. She just lost her mom." Twice over. "I'll be quick."

"Frank know you're here?"

"Frank's looking for her, too. Please. It's important." I kept my gaze even on his.

"Okay," he relented, holding open the door. "You got ten minutes." He walked away, toward the manufacturing area, where light spilled through an opened door. People were working, their voices a low mutter.

I headed right, toward the administrative offices.

The hallway was hushed, door after door closed tight. Would Peyton give me a chance to explain? I couldn't just pretend nothing had happened. There'd been enough silence between us. It was time to tell the truth.

I reached a dead end, realized I'd made a wrong turn, and backtracked.

How much did I dare tell Peyton? No one knew the whole story, not even Julie. I'd held tightly on to my secrets all these years, and now they were shriveled reminders of all the ways my life could have been different. I'd refused to think about the past. I'd put my head down and forged forward. But that had been a terrible mistake. In the end, the truth had come out. In the end, I had to accept responsibility.

But how much was truth worth, really? Look how I'd ferreted it out here, and everything had collapsed. Maybe Joe had been right—there might have been a better way.

The administrative suite was dimly lit, the carpeting soft underfoot. The sweet green notes of lilies and roses hung in the air, pleasant. Something tangy and acerbic twined among the floral aromas, something out of place, a smell so familiar it resonated in my very marrow.

Dynamite?

I froze. There, along the baseboard of this handsome office suite, snaked bright yellow detonation cord, heading joyfully and with great purpose around the corner.

Dynamite. I began walking, faster and faster, then I ran. "Peyton!"

Corner after corner, feet pounding, following the yellow cord as it lured me deeper and deeper into the building. The guy who'd let me in stared as I passed. "Get out," I yelled. "Call the fire department."

He backed away, turned and jogged.

"Peyton!"

Another corner and there she was, miraculously whole and unhurt, standing with her back to me. Beyond her was LT, with a black box bristling with wires, duct-taped to his chest.

Space tunneled. Peyton stood miles away, too far.

"PEYTON!"

She wheeled around, her face blank with confusion.

A clap of thunder.

She flew up like a doll.

The floor shook. I stumbled, threw out my hands for balance. The walls collapsed. A wave of gray debris rolled toward me. Instinctively, I threw up my forearm, clenched my eyes shut. Small things rained against me.

Peyton.

White dust coated a topsy-turvy world. The world had gone sickeningly silent.

I clawed at chunks of cement. The ceiling was above me, then it was not. It was gone, revealing a desk on its side, a shattered bulletin board hanging askew, a blinking fluorescent bulb. I fell to my knees, crawled forward. My white-powdered hands reached for things and left behind red smears. I slithered between tented sheets of linoleum. The floor was wet. A tiny black-and-white fish flopped in a dusty patch of linoleum.

Beside it stretched a hand, a slim hand lying beneath it all. *No.* Not again. Not again.

I heaved rocks and boulders. Someone was working beside

me, the flash of hands grasping and lifting. Bit by bit, Peyton's arm was uncovered, her shoulder, her face, pale and bloodless, her beautiful blue eyes unseeing.

I pressed my mouth to Peyton's and blew. I pounded her chest, bent again to blow. My heart and breath and will pouring for all eternity, and then I was jerked away and lifted, kicking, straining to see her as I was carried away, my daughter gone and growing smaller until I could see no more.

FIFTY

———

[PEYTON]

CREATURES IN THE ABYSS SOMETIMES SLITHER OUT *of their homes at night, pulled northward by the rising moon into the middle reaches of the ocean. It's called vertical migration, and they only remain long enough to grab a meal. Well before the sun rises, they turn and make the long journey home, descending through icy black until they've reached the bottom. Why do they do that? Since they've already made the long trek north into warmer waters, why not stick around where there's light and food is plentiful, where they could find a mate and have babies?*

Maybe they're not the least bit lonely down there in the darkness. They probably find it restful living where nothing ever happens. Maybe they find peace in the solitude.

She was thrown up into the air, landed hard into a world gone silent and white.

She hung upside down, things biting into her arms and legs.

Dust clogged her eyes, her mouth, her nose. It was too much trouble to push it out.

Pressure on her chest. The light had changed, gaining texture. A high ringing in her ears, like angels' bells. Somewhere nearby her mother waited. Peyton took a final breath and sailed right into her mother's arms.

FIFTY-ONE

[DANA]

EMERGENCY VEHICLES PULLED IN ONE AFTER AN-
other, sirens wailing, lights cycling blue and red. Police
radios buzzed with staticky, urgent voices. A firefighter, bulky
with gear, gripped my upper arm, dragged me away from the
building.

"Peyton!" I was shouting but could barely hear myself, just
felt the pressure in my lungs from pushing out the frantic words.

The man leaned closer, saying something. I watched his lips
move. *I'll go look.* He patted the air. *Stay.*

I nodded, couldn't stop nodding. He released me.

Frank was there, his face smeared with a paste of cement dust
and water. He grabbed my arms and shook me. He was screaming, too, his mouth wide, his eyes wild. "Where is she?"

I could only shake my head.

"This is all your fault!" He flung me away from him.

Yes. I fell to the ground and buried my face in my arms. Yes,
all of this, from the very beginning, was my fault.

. . .

The hospital doors whooshed open to admit a stretcher. I sprang up, along with so many others, a ripple of motion among the seated crowd, turning to see who had just been rushed in. A doctor pushed into the waiting room, looking for someone. For me? No, he walked over to someone else.

A nurse came over with a rolling cart. Sitting, she snapped on latex gloves and dipped a piece of gauze into a basin of water. "Let's get you cleaned up, huh?" Gently she dabbed at my temple. "Doesn't look like you're going to need stitches." She held my hands in hers, turning them this way and that. Dipping a fresh piece of gauze into the water, she washed the blood from my fingers, patted on some ointment, and unrolled a bandage. "When was your last tetanus shot? Are you allergic to anything?"

"I'm looking for someone," I said. "Peyton Kelleher. Do you know where she is?" I searched the nurse's broad face for a clue, a hint that she knew something she wasn't telling me.

She paused, then resumed wrapping the length of gauze around my palm. "Someone will come out and talk to you." Patting my shoulder, she gathered up her supplies.

Someone called my name, and there was Joe, walking toward me with long strides, his shirt rumpled and his dark blue eyes intent. The relief on his face was so evident that I felt something inside me soften. "Hey," he said. "I've been looking for you." He sat beside me and reached for my hands, hesitating when he saw they were bandaged. "How are you? Are you okay?"

"Joe—I don't know how Peyton is."

A flash of worry in his eyes, swiftly suppressed. "They brought her in?"

"Y-yes."

"It's okay. I'll wait with you. Someone should be out soon."

Another rush of movement as the doors swept open to let in a limping man, leaning heavily on the woman by his side, her arm around his waist.

Joe watched with a frown. "Did you hear they're evacuating Black Bear? The EPA's worried about the release. Something about the warm weather holding everything down and keeping it from blowing away. They've already cordoned off the highways leading into town."

"So quick," I said distantly.

"Dana," he said. "It's been hours. I looked everywhere for you."

An orderly pushed a stretcher past us, IVs dangling from the metal pole, a nurse almost running alongside. The evacuation was beginning.

"Your phone's ringing," Joe said. "Maybe it's Frank."

Yes! I scrabbled inside my purse with my bandaged fingers. Joe took it from me, found my phone, and handed it to me.

"Hello?" I didn't recognize my voice, strangely high-pitched and terse.

"What's the matter? You sound terrible."

Halim. "What is it?"

"I've got marvelous news. Unbelievably miraculous news. Are you sitting down?" When I didn't reply, he went on. "The autopsy came in. The coroner found a bullet in her chest, another one in her throat. She was dead long before they stuck her in Burnside. She was dead long before we blew the building. You can come home, Dana. I've got another project for us, a high-rise in Los Angeles that—"

I closed my phone.

"Anything important?" Joe asked.

I was silent for a moment. "No," I said. "Not anymore."

"Ms. Carlson?" a nurse asked, walking toward us.

Finally.

The nurse held open the swinging door and indicated a curtained room. "The ambulance will be here in five minutes," she told me, then turned and walked to the nurses' station. They were transferring Peyton to Fargo, into the care of a whole fleet of specialists.

I paused outside the room, my hand on the curtain, afraid to pull it open, afraid to keep it closed. Frank came around the corner, talking with a doctor.

"Can I give blood?" Frank was asking. "Even though we're not related?"

The doctor put his hand on Frank's arm and said something in a low voice. Then he strode away, leaving Frank standing alone, shoulders sagging.

I walked up to him and put my arms around him. After a moment, he drew me tight. I could feel him trembling. It didn't matter whom Peyton's real father was. That life-changing winter night seventeen years before, when I'd squabbled with Joe at a party and ended up sleeping with Brian, had blurred from memory. Here was Peyton's true father. Somehow, Julie had been wrong about Frank, or maybe he'd changed. He *could* love a child who wasn't his own, and it was that small misunderstanding long ago that had set everything to follow in motion. I wished Julie were there. I missed her more than ever.

Frank pulled open the curtain and we looked down at Peyton, lying there so still and white, the beeping of the machine beside her the only indication that she was breathing. Her eyes were closed, and she looked impossibly young and fragile. Frank and I stood close, his sleeve touching my shoulder, our shoes inches apart, and I understood.

Maybe Frank did, too. He put his arm around my shoulders and I rested my head on his shoulder. Day by day, we'd knit this family together. It was what Julie had been trying to teach me, all those years ago.

FIFTY-TWO

PEYTON OPENED HER EYES AND SAW HER FISH TANK bubbling away on a plain metal dresser against a faded peach-colored wall. Not her dresser, and certainly not her bedroom wall, so where was she? She lay on her back, propped up in a bed, but not tucked beneath her navy sheets. These sheets were utterly foreign—white and stiff, and smelling faintly of bleach. A machine stood sentinel beside her, blinking red numbers, and a long plastic tube ran up from the back of her hand to a pole. Her arms ached, and her back. Her head pounded. She tried to struggle to a seated position, but something was wrong with her leg. She lifted the sheet and saw the white cast running from her thigh to her heel and firmly anchoring her left leg in place. And was she wearing a *hospital* gown?

Something terrible had happened. She remembered the floor shaking and pieces of wall and ceiling crashing down on her. She was choking, and then her mother suddenly appeared, smiling and holding out her arms. That had *not* been a dream. No one could take that away from her.

She glanced to the window, at the rectangle of blue sky that looked perfectly fine, but must be spinning with billions of tiny dangerous particles.

The murmurs of voices outside in the hall and the door handle turned. Peyton held her breath, hoping to see her father, who would explain everything to her. But it wasn't her dad coming into the room. It was Dana, her slim form slipping quietly through the doorway. Her *mother*. Peyton closed her eyes and lay perfectly still, hoping Dana would go away. The air shifted and she knew Dana stood there, looking down at her.

What did she see? What did she *want*? Peyton was suddenly filled with a yearning so strong that she felt tears collect in her eyes, and desperately hoped Dana wouldn't notice, wouldn't reach out and put her arms around her. Peyton concentrated on breathing slowly and evenly, and after a moment, knew that Dana had moved away.

She opened her eyes the tiniest fraction and saw Dana standing with her back to her, looking down into Peyton's fish tank. Something was wrong there and it took Peyton a moment to figure it out. One tank, not two. Where were the endler babies? Dana reached for the container of fish food on the dresser, and now Peyton saw the tiny flickers of movement inside the tank and realized someone had already dumped the babies in with their parents. Someone had known it was time.

Fish have learned that there's safety in numbers. They hang out together in large groups, mixed species and all, to hide from predators and forage for food. This behavior is called shoaling.

Shoals change shape according to whether fish are fleeing, hunting, or resting. They can be long strings or fat ovals; they move in a gridlike pattern or meander aimlessly. Fish choose their shoals based on the coloring and markings of the other fish, as well as the release of pheromones. They prefer fish of a similar size, the healthier the better. Some fish, such as cod or salmon, shoal for brief periods of time, usually for mating purposes. Other fish, such as anchovy and tuna, shoal their whole lifetimes, and get upset if they're separated even briefly from their shoal mates.

Because it's not all about survival. It's about love, too. The ocean is huge, populated by billions of fish swimming in a hundred million different locations. Fish have long ago lost sight of all their family members, and what are the odds of finding one of them again? Shoals are packed with potential friends. Think of them like college dorms or busy bars. Somewhere, in all those rooms, in all those towns, are the fish that will hang out with you and watch your back, the fish that you can come home to.

And that's all that really matters, isn't it?

ACKNOWLEDGMENTS

Many thanks to Marghi Barone Fauss, who looked across her kitchen counter at me one beautiful May morning, and said, "I know something scary you could write about. . . ."

She was right. The minute I began researching nanotechnology, I learned about the benefits it offers, as well as the threat it poses. The Chinese study upon which this novel is based is real, and it's just the tip of the iceberg. Nanomaterials have already been proven to behave like asbestos in the human body. They're in our blood, the air we breathe, the ground we walk on, and the water we drink. We don't know yet how much we can tolerate before we start showing ill-health effects. Scientists are working hard to figure this out. One scientist, Emma Fauss, PhD, was particularly helpful to me by both discussing her own research and providing a layman's explanation of a very complex technology.

Thank you to Tina Moore, RN, at MeritCare Dialysis Detroit Lakes in Minnesota, for giving me a tour of the dialysis center, and to all the patients at MeritCare who shared their experiences. Thank you to Jill E. Columber of Marion, Ohio, for telling me her inspiring story of living with, and triumphing over, kidney failure.

Thank you to Bill Wymard, marine biologist and owner of Aquarium Adventure, for helping me stock Peyton's and Brian Gerkey's imaginary fish tanks.

I am deeply indebted to my agent, Pam Ahearn, and to my editor, Kate Miciak, who walked snow-blind with me to find this story. I am grateful to others at Random House for their support, including Gina Centrello, Jane von Mehren, Randall Klein, Susan Corcoran, Alison Masciovecchio, and Gianna LaMorte.

Thanks to my sister, Liese Schwarz, for listening to many iterations of this story, to Julie Compton for reading the first draft, and to Chevy Stevens for reading all the drafts that followed. Thank you to the other authors whose friendship sustained me, including Pam Callow, Karen Dionne, Sophie Littlefield, and Brad Parks. A special shout-out to my genius website designer, Madeira James. Finally, I am humbled by, and grateful for, the kindness and generosity of Jacquelyn Mitchard, Lisa Gardner, and Linwood Barclay.

Thank you to my husband, Tim, for inspiring me every day and for being the best person I know. Thank you to our children, Jillian, Jonathon, and Jocelyn, for overcoming having a novelist for a mother, and for the countless ways you have enriched and blessed my life.

INVISIBLE

CARLA BUCKLEY

A Reader's Guide

A CONVERSATION WITH CARLA BUCKLEY

SISTERS

An essay by Carla Buckley

WHEN I WAS YOUNG, I WOULD PESTER MY MOM. SHE had three sisters, I knew, but one she never talked about. I'd met my aunt Jennifer a couple of times, but then the visits abruptly stopped. When would we see her again, I asked my mother. Why couldn't we visit her? My mother was vague in her responses. She's busy, she'd say. Or, we live too far apart. As a family, we had traveled all around the world for my father's work, so I knew that crossing a few hundred miles wasn't really the issue. There was something else there, but whatever it was, my mother wasn't telling me. Deep down, I worried: if she could stop speaking to her beloved sister, could she stop speaking to me?

My mom had grown up during the Depression. She was the oldest of four sisters, and she regaled me with stories of how she once persuaded Jennifer to yell out the window to beg passersby for a chocolate bar, and how she had to sleep under the kitchen table that night as punishment. She told me how she and Jennifer would take turns wearing one pretty dress in a single evening so that they could both go out on dates with soldiers on leave. She watched over her sisters when her father went to jail and her mother worked the night shift. It was a childhood beyond my imagining.

My mother wanted me to be a good sister to my own siblings. *You're all you'll have left after I'm gone,* she warned. But I wasn't sure how to do that. I was troubled by the example she and my aunt set. Would history repeat itself in my own generation? Would there be warning signs, or would alienation strike out of the blue?

I never did see my aunt Jennifer again, and my mother passed away without ever telling me what had come between them. My other aunts wouldn't tell me, either. Whatever it was had to be huge, though. It had to be enormous.

Years later, when I set out to write *Invisible,* I thought about that. What could come between two sisters who had once been so close? My imagination took flight. In writing this story, I would rewrite my own history. I would get to the bottom of the mystery that had haunted me all my life. Who had wronged whom? Had it been my aunt for committing some terrible infraction, or my mother for refusing to forgive her? I understood, or thought I understood, the power of family and the way silence could start out small, then filter down through the generations, taking on weight and substance and power. One way or another, I would work to understand my mother and why she kept her secret to the grave.

It proved difficult for me to come up with something plausible that could keep two sisters, who had once loved one another very much, apart. Everything I tried made no sense. My characters, Dana and Julie, kept pulling back together. They wanted to rely on each other, confide in each other. So was it really possible to excise someone so completely from your life? My mother evidently thought so, or at least, she had tried, but I wondered, *Did her estrangement from her sister gnaw at her, tinge her dreams, and stalk her waking hours? As she watched me and my siblings grow up, did it remind her of all she had lost?*

I remember returning home during my first college break. Everything seemed more intense—the autumn leaves burned with unusual brightness; the hardwood floors gleamed like gold. My mother's homemade vegetable soup had never tasted more delicious. I'd only been away for a few months, but everything was colored with poignancy. I had already taken my first few steps away from home. I was becoming an adult and I would never again view my childhood home in the same, carefree way. Already I was pulling away from my younger siblings. Those complicated feelings, I thought, would be magnified for Dana, who would be coming home after many years of being away.

A homecoming to a large city—where people are always moving in and out—might go unnoticed. But someone returning to a small town, where everyone knows one another, and where loyalties and conflicts run deep, would have the right resonance. I decided to place my fictional small town in northern Minnesota, where I have spent the past twenty summers. In some ways, northern Minnesota feels like home to me; in other ways, it's clear that I'm an outsider. It would be that way for Dana, too.

My first few attempts to reunite Dana and Julie were awkward. They were wary and watchful, and it was hard to believe that they had once been close. Would it have been that way between my mother and her sister, if they had ever met again? Now I began to think about things from my aunt's perspective. What had it felt like to know that she had pushed her sister away? Were her dreams dark and fractured, too? I knew my aunt had made overtures to my mother, attempts at reconciliation that were shot down. At some point, my aunt gave up. Would it be like that for Dana and Julie?

Being capable of maintaining a long silence indicated that

there was a dark side to both Julie and Dana. It would have to color their relationships with other people. Having been away for so long, Dana might find she had nothing in common with the people she had once known so well. She might not be able to rebuild old friendships, or rekindle a lost romance. Too much time might have passed and the differences between them were insurmountable. I wondered, *Could you ever go home again?*

Peyton showed me the world unfiltered, through her clear adolescent eyes. Like me, she would be bewildered by the estrangement between her mother and her aunt; she would wonder why her mother couldn't tell her the truth, and she would resent Dana's absence from her life. I loved the idea of a child who lived in the middle of the country dreaming of becoming a marine biologist. In many ways, Peyton is just like Dana. She, too, keeps the world at arm's length. It was in thinking about this young girl who is overcome by loss but can't talk about it, that I struck on the idea of having her begin her chapters musing on the one thing—the ocean—that she feels most passionate about, thereby revealing herself in the only way she can.

The ocean passages are among my favorite parts of the novel. Other than the occasional trip to the beach, I knew nothing about the sea or the life that inhabits it. During the day, I would write, and at night, I would read everything I could get my hands on about sea urchins, sharks, rays, and clownfish. The ocean is far more vast than I'd envisioned, inhabited by creatures I never knew existed. I was most astounded to learn that fish can behave in very human ways. The more I grew to understand these creatures, the more I grew to understand Peyton. And I saw how the ocean, like families, is much more than what is visible. There are all the undercurrents, the dark secrets that lie hidden beneath the surface. Some are washed ashore and reveal themselves. Others never come to light.

I'm cautious in mothering my own daughters. Talk to one another, I tell them. No one can understand you like your own sister,

I say. I speak from personal experience. There is no one who understands me better than my own sister, no one with the same sense of humor, with the same perspective on the world. I know that, no matter what, my sister will always be there for me. In the end, I'll never know what drove my mother and her sister apart. But my mother had been right: there is no one like your sister. I just wish she had been able to know that for herself.

READING GROUP QUESTIONS
AND TOPICS FOR DISCUSSION

1. Do you believe it is ever justified for a company to put people at risk? When, and how much risk?

2. What lengths would you go to for your sibling? Would you make the same choices Dana and Julie made?

3. Do you think of Peyton as a typical teenager? What makes her unique?

4. A major theme of *Invisible* is the idea of going home again. Has Dana outgrown her hometown? What does that mean to you?

5. If Dana's sister had not died, do you believe she would have made the same crusade against nanochemicals? If she had returned to Black Bear for unrelated reasons, do you think she would have taken up this cause? Why or why not?

6. Is there a company or industry that you would want shut down? Why?

7. On page 280, Eric says to Peyton:
> "Sometimes I feel like I've lost you, which is dumb." He
> reached up and set his baseball cap facing forward

again. "Because how can you lose something you never
really had in the first place?"
Do you believe this is true?

8. Is Brian Gerkey a villain? Why or why not?

9. On pages 293 to 294, Dana narrates:

> A tube of sunscreen poked out of my purse. I'd auto-
> matically started to apply it that morning and caught
> myself just in time. A new tube, an expensive brand
> filled with antioxidants. I couldn't bring myself to
> throw it out. Was the danger in the manufacturing
> process, or in the product itself? Until I knew, I'd hold
> on to it, just in case. It would serve as a reminder for
> all the other things I'd have to be on the watch for.

What would you do if you found that you had to live your life constantly checking products to see if they contain something you
believe harmful? People already do this for other things, like cho-
lesterol, or sodium. How would you manage if every product you
used had to be carefully reviewed?

10. If you knew you would survive, would you willingly donate a
kidney if there were only a chance that the person you were do-
nating it to would survive? If so, what would the chance have to
be before you would agree to do it?

11. How are Dana and Julie alike? How are they different? How
do siblings help shape your worldview and personality?

If you enjoyed *Invisible*, you will be mesmerized

by all of Carla Buckley's powerful novels.

Please read on for sample chapters of

THE THINGS THAT
KEEP US HERE

BY CARLA BUCKLEY

Available now from Orion.

PROLOGUE

I T WAS QUIET COMING HOME FROM THE FUNERAL. Too quiet. Ann wished Peter would say something, but there was just the soft patter of rain and the wipers squeaking back and forth across the windshield. Even the radio was mute, reception having sizzled into static miles before.

As they crossed into Ohio, Ann turned around to see why Maddie hadn't called it, and saw her seven-year-old had fallen asleep, her head tipped back and her lips parted, her book slipped halfway from her grasp. The first hour of their trip had been punctuated by Maddie asking every five minutes, "Mom, what does this spell?" Ann leaned back and teased the opened book from her daughter's fingers, closed it, and put it on the seat beside Maddie. Kate hunched in the opposite corner, a tangle of brown hair falling over her face and obscuring her features, the twin wires of her iPod coiling past her shoulders and into her lap.

Ann turned back around. "The girls are asleep."

Peter nodded.

"Even Kate. I don't know how she can possibly sleep with her music going."

He made no reply.

"Do you know I caught her trying to sneak her iPod into the church? I don't think giving her that was such a great idea." When Peter remained silent, she went on. "It's just one more way for her to tune everyone out."

He shrugged. "She's twelve. That's what twelve-year-olds do."

"I think it's more than that, Peter."

He said nothing, simply glanced into the rearview mirror and flicked on the turn signal, glided the minivan around the slower-moving vehicle in front of them.

It was an old argument, and he wasn't engaging. Still, there was something else lurking beneath his silence. She read it in his narrow focus on the highway and along the tightness of his jaw. "You all right?" Of course he wasn't.

"Just tired. It was a long weekend."

A long, horrible weekend. All those relatives crammed together in that small clapboard house, no air-conditioning, Peter's mother wandering around, plaintively asking everyone where Jerry was. "I'm glad your brother made it."

"Yep."

Not *yes*, or *yeah*. *Yep*. He never talked like that. He was throwing up warning signs, telling her to back off. But fourteen years of marriage made her plow straight through anyway. "Everything okay between you two?"

"Sure."

So he wasn't going to tell her. "Bonni said she saw you and Mike arguing."

He glanced at her. So handsome her breath snagged for a moment—the strong, tanned planes of his face and the beautiful blue-green of his eyes that Kate had inherited. Now he looked drawn and older than his forty years. He returned his attention to the road. She wanted to cup her hand to his cheek, but he was sending out those keep-away signals.

She crossed her arms. "Mike doesn't think it was an accident."

"Mike doesn't know what he's talking about."

"He has a point, though. It *is* strange your father wasn't wearing blaze orange."

"What are you suggesting, Ann? Suicide by hunter? Give me a break."

She should have, but she couldn't let it go. The questions

piled up inside her, three days' worth of strangers whispering, three days of Peter's mother tugging at Ann's sleeve. "Things have gotten so bad with your mom, Peter. I had no idea. This morning, she told Maddie that her parents must be looking for her and that she'd better run along home. You should have seen the hurt look on Maddie's face." Ann shook her head. "It just breaks my heart. We can't leave her like this."

"Bonni will check in on her."

"Checking in's not enough. She needs round-the-clock care."

The rain had stopped. A watery sunshine glinted through the clouds. Peter switched off the wipers. "I don't want to talk about it. Especially with the girls in the car."

"You mean the girls who are sound asleep?"

"Ann."

Maybe she *was* pushing too hard. She leaned her forehead against the window and watched a hawk spin circles high above. "You sure you need to go into the field tomorrow? Maybe one of your students can go in your place."

"I've got no choice. Hunters are nervous enough right now without me sending in some twenty-year-old."

"Because of the bird flu?"

"Exactly."

"Do you think you'll find anything?"

He shifted position. "Probably. But it's not an isolated case that's a problem."

"It's a cluster of cases."

"Right."

The hawk grew smaller and smaller, a smudged dot that eventually disappeared, no doubt to perch on a branch somewhere and watch for prey. "I forgot to tell you, things were so rushed Friday, but that interview came through."

"At Maddie's school?"

She nodded. "I go in next week to meet with the principal. I keep thinking, what if I don't get the job? Then I think, what if I do?"

"You'll be fine."

"I haven't worked in, God, twelve years."

"How hard can it be?"

She flashed him an irritated look, but he was staring straight ahead. "It's not finger painting and Popsicle sticks, Peter."

"I just meant I know you can do it."

"It's theory and history, too. What if I teach above their heads? What if they're bored? What if Maddie hates me being her art teacher?"

"There must be some part of you that's looking forward to it."

Did she want to talk about this? "It's the whole . . . thing. I'm not sure I can do it."

"You mean art in general?"

"Exactly."

He heaved a sigh. She heard the impatience in it. "It's been a long time," he said.

Nine years. An eternity. A blink.

"Maybe you're ready, Ann."

"In other words, I *should* be ready."

He lifted his hands briefly from the steering wheel. *I give up.* "Whatever."

The hills undulated by, the woods fiery red and burnt orange. She caught glimpses of barns and houses set high and solitary. She wondered about the people who lived there, if they were lonely.

"It'd be good for you to go back to work," Peter said. "A fresh start."

She nodded, distracted. They needed the second income, what with two college tuitions coming up. And everything had gotten so frighteningly expensive, especially gas. It was costing as much to fill up the minivan as it was to take everyone out to dinner and the movies.

"Actually." He cleared his throat. "We could both use a fresh start."

She turned to him, worried by the strangeness in his voice. "Okay."

"Not okay, Ann. It hasn't been okay for a long time."

"What does that mean? What are you talking about?" But she knew. This quiet autumn day had suddenly become strange, queered by intensity and the feeling that something terrible was about to happen.

"I think we need some time apart."

She stared at his profile, speechless, feeling her heartbeat accelerate. He was suddenly a stranger to her. The seatbelt slid down her arm, she was skewed so sideways. "You don't mean that."

"I have to."

"I thought we were doing okay. Not good but . . . better." Maybe this weekend had been the last straw. Was it just his father's death? Or had he been thinking about this for a while? How could she not have known? How foolish she'd been, taking things for granted, being her clumsy, pushy self. She'd been too harsh about his father's death. Maybe she should have been kinder, but she'd never really liked the man.

"Dad was sixty-two. Sixty-two." Peter gripped the steering wheel, his knuckles white. "There were so many things he never got to do. So many things he put off. Going to Gettysburg. Seeing the Vietnam Memorial. Finishing that tree house for our girls. I stood there and watched them put his coffin into the ground." He leaned back and let out a breath. "I don't want to be that man. I don't want to live like he did."

She put her hand on his arm, felt the warmth of his skin. "But . . . you're not."

He shook his head. "I'm just like him, living in suspended animation, watching everything go past."

"Is this some kind of midlife crisis?"

He glanced at her. "I wish it were, sweetheart." His eyes were gentle. "Ever since the baby died—"

"Don't," she said, hearing her voice sharpen, and took her hand away. She'd never forget walking into the nursery. Seeing William silent and unmoving in his crib.

"We can't even talk about it."

"This isn't talking about it. This is telling me to get over it." She twisted to look back at the girls, saw that they were still fast asleep. He didn't want to discuss his mother with them sleeping back there, but it was okay to talk about the one thing they struggled every day to get past? She felt a spark of anger at his indifference. "Which is all you've ever done."

"That's not fair. You won't let me in to do anything else. It's like you slammed all the doors shut and threw away the keys."

"I've tried."

"I know you have." There was that horrible kind voice again. "I've tried, too. Don't you think it's time we both stopped trying, and started loving one another the way we used to?"

She stared at him. "But we can't," she said, helpless. "We're not the same people." They couldn't be that man and that woman who fell in love at that insanely crowded party; they couldn't be that naive twosome who thought finding each other was the hard part. She tried again. "We *do* love each other."

"I know."

He sounded so sad. She hated this. Couldn't he understand she was doing the best she could? Couldn't he be happy with the way things were now?

He slowed to take the exit toward Columbus. They passed a cluster of gas stations, then a series of strip malls.

"But Thanksgiving's next week." A stupid thing to say. Who cared about that? She clenched her fists in her lap. It wasn't about Thanksgiving. It was deciding whether to go with his mom's traditional stuffing or her mom's walnut-apple. It was picking out the Christmas tree, loading the dishwasher, and bringing in the mail. It was waking up in the middle of the night, hearing the person breathing next to you. About knowing you weren't alone.

"We both need to move on," he said. "We can't live like this, two people afraid to be real with one another. I love you. I'll always love you." His voice was low but relentless. "I'm just not in love with you anymore."

She didn't want to hear this. She sat back and stared numbly through the glass. This was one of those hideous things that happened to other people. The fabric of her life shredded just like that, all the truths she'd clung to now melted into nothing. Everything she was or thought she was, everything she thought they were, had vanished as though they'd never been.

Another house appeared, tucked among the golden trees by the roadside. Someone was there, crouched and working in a garden. A woman. Ann watched as she straightened, lifted a hand to shade her eyes to watch them shoot past, the four of them entombed in a blue minivan and hurtling toward the unknown.

ONE YEAR LATER

AVIAN INFLUENZA—
SITUATION IN SOUTH KOREA

FIVE MORE PEOPLE HAVE BEEN HOSPITALIZED THIS morning in Seoul with avian influenza. Early tests confirm it as the same strain that killed two people in Singapore earlier this week. Health officials have been unable to determine how and where these people may have contracted the disease. To date, a total of 670 cases of human avian influenza have been confirmed worldwide, resulting in 328 deaths.

World Health Organization
Epidemic and Pandemic Alert and Response

ONE

PETER HEARD THE LOW MUTTER OF A MOTORBOAT somewhere out there in the cold fog. He rolled down his truck window and listened. The sound swelled into a grumble, someone evidently headed in to shore. Already? The sun wasn't even up yet. He fitted his cup into the holder, reached for his tool-box, and climbed out of his truck.

A muffled hiccup as the engine cut off. Water lapped the wooden piles and unsettled the pebbles along the shore. The squeak of fiberglass against rope. Fog rolled back across the water, revealing the frosted grass beneath Peter's boots, a section of pier stretching before him, patches of dark water, the thin, gray sky. Now he could see the motorboat and the two figures working within it.

One of them looked up as Peter approached. Broad face, small mouth, a curl of pale hair beneath a dark cap. The other man turned and revealed himself to be a younger version of the first, possessing the same mouth and squint but with brown hair instead of white. Father and son. They wore heavy brown camouflage jackets, rubber waders, thick gloves with the fingers snipped off. Peter had met so many people these past few weeks that they more or less merged into one wary, jostling group, but he remembered this pair. He'd examined their chocolate Lab, a big, slow-moving dog with white on his muzzle and tail, and a spreading rash across his ribs.

"You again," the son said. He tossed a rope over a pile and tied a knot. "The vet."

More university researcher than veterinarian, but Peter didn't correct him. "Any luck?"

"Not much," the father replied. "Couldn't flush any out."

The son gave the rope a vicious tug. "The ones we did were crappy."

The father rested his hand on the side of the boat and looked at Peter. "I suppose you want to see for yourself."

Peter waited. He had no jurisdiction here. The NSF grant paid for lab work and his graduate student, but that was all. Hunters didn't have to comply with his requests.

The man shrugged. He reached into the center of the boat, lifted out a bundle of feathers, and set it onto the pier. Peter crouched to have a closer look.

Four small ducks, all of them brown-and-cream with a tell-tale blue patch along the wing. The white crescent around the eye revealed three of them to be male. It was uncommon to find blue-winged teal in Ohio in mid-November. Usually by now they'd taken themselves down the Mississippi to South America or across the Great Lakes to the Chesapeake Bay for the winter.

Their presence here was odd, and so was their appearance. Where were the sleek, domed chests? These birds looked deflated, their wings overlarge for their shrunken torsos. He opened his toolbox. "How were they flying?"

"Low and slow." The father looped rope over a second pile and pulled the boat up against the pier. "Like they were drunk. Hardly any challenge."

Teal normally flew fast and erratically. Peter snapped on a pair of gloves, picked up the first teal, and cradled it in his hand.

"Got to be global warming." The son stepped onto the pier and squatted beside Peter.

"Looks poisoned to me." The father was watching Peter. "What do you think?"

"Could be," Peter said.

Botulism would account for the birds' labored flying. Peter

lifted tail feathers to check for signs of diarrhea and found none. He turned to the small tucked head and gently palpated. Here was a worry. Facial edema and, yes, petechial hemorrhage inside the eyelids. He laid the bird down, picked up another male. The edema was more pronounced in this one. He reached for his penlight from the tray of his toolbox. Prying open the duck's bill and tilting back its head, he shone the beam of light down its throat. Blossoms of red against the pale membrane.

"What?" the father said as Peter put the bird down and reached for another.

The eyes of this one were almost swollen shut. Peter couldn't imagine how he'd been able to fly at all. The female showed less swelling about her face, but when Peter checked the inside of one eyelid, he saw bright red. These birds had suffered. He ran a gloved finger along the female's wing. The speckled brown-and-cream feathers were dull, as if they'd lost hope.

"It's either a viral infection or exposure to an environmental contaminant," Peter said. "I'll have to run some tests."

"That's what you're here for, isn't it?" the son said.

True, but he hadn't thought it would be necessary. Naturally, he'd hoped for the opposite. Peter unscrewed a test tube. He peeled the paper back from a sterile swab.

"We can't eat them if they're poisoned," the father said. "Can we?"

"I'm telling you, Dad—"

"You think everything's global warming." The father leaned back and put his hand on the gunwale. "You find anything the other times you been out?"

He was talking to Peter.

"No." Peter dropped the swab into the test tube and twisted on the lid. No one had, not that he knew of. But it was still early days yet. Duck season was just gearing up.

"Poison." Turning, the father spat into the water. "We should've left them where we found them."

"Mind showing me where that was?" Peter said.

Father and son exchanged a glance.

Duck hunters were a unique breed, willing to endure freezing temperatures, sleet, snow, and bitter wind, and secretive as hell about their prime hunting spots. These two were worried he was going to steal their spot, though there was no threat of that. He didn't hunt. Not anymore.

"I need to take water samples." Peter made his voice mild and nonthreatening, the sound of the professor, not the hunter.

The son scowled at the horizon. The rising sun was beginning to thin the fog and cast a general yellow glow over the marsh. The father busied himself in the boat.

"We don't find the cause, the whole season could be like this." Peter indicated the ducks lying on the pier.

A quick glance from the father.

"You try that ointment I recommended?" Peter said. "For Gus?" He hoped he'd remembered the Lab's name.

The son said, "Yeah. His rash is getting better."

Peter nodded. "He should be able to get in the water in another week."

Father and son looked at each other. The father rubbed his chin and then shrugged. "Come on, then. It's a piss-poor spot, anyway."

They motored through the reedy water. Peter sat in the middle, the father at the stern, steering. The son knelt in the prow. Once they were out on open water, the father revved the engine and they bounced across the polished silver surface.

Cold wind buffeted Peter's hair. Spray whipped across his face. The shoreline opened up on both sides, lined by sycamores and red maples blooming gold and crimson and reflected between sky and water. Spangles of sunlight below, bright sky and a wisp of cloud above. Flapping geese lifted themselves from hiding, sounding mournful echoing honks. It was nice to be out here. Uncomplicated.

The son shouted something to his father, stretched out his arm and pointed. The father yelled something unintelligible back.

Peter turned his head and saw a distant dark shape. Another boat trolling these same hunting grounds. The father made a wide loop, watching the other boat as it chopped past, then opened up and headed north.

After a while the engine shifted into a lower gear, and their boat, turning, cut through the waves, rolling in its own wake. The engine slowed even further, thrummed. Around another curve, and there was the duck blind. Wooden poles rose from the water, their tops shrouded with branches, to form an unlikely tree house in the middle of the lake. The two men had taken care constructing it, weaving the branches in a dense mesh, leaving a space high enough to allow them to slide their boat inside.

They slowly circled the structure.

"See?" the son said. "Nothing."

Peter unstoppered a tube and leaned over the side to dip it into the icy water.

"How's it look?" the father said.

"I won't know anything until I get back to the lab." But the tea-colored water appeared clean enough. No scum or creeping algae that would indicate bacterial overgrowth, no white froth or oily bubbles that would suggest a chemical spill. Peter pressed the stopper on top, looked around. It was a peaceful, beautiful morning. Despite it, he felt a growing unease. "Where were the ducks when you found them?"

The son turned around in his seat. "Over there." He pointed to where the shoreline bulged out into the water.

"Waited for two hours," the father said. "And then those four showed."

"Let's take a look," Peter said.

"It's all the same lake," the father said.

"There could be something over there, though, that's not over here."

"Like a dead animal?"

Peter shook his head. "Teal don't feed on carrion, but maybe it's a localized contamination, someone dumping something where they shouldn't." That'd be a welcome sight—a big old rusted barrel sticking out of the water and disrupting the delicate harmony between bird and environment. Even a discarded paint can would do.

The father brought the boat around and sliced through the marshy water.

"Fish look okay," the son said, staring down into the water. "There'd be floaters otherwise, right?"

"Some things can affect one species and do nothing to another," Peter answered. "There are plenty of diseases that are fatal to birds that pass right through fish. And vice versa."

"Where again?" the father said.

"Around there," the son said. "Careful. Water's getting shallow."

The engine dropped to a slow chug. Another tight turn. The engine stuttered, then stopped. All three men stared at the sight before them.

On the clear water, surrounded by golden reeds, bobbed a legion of blue-winged teal, hundreds of them, mottled brown and cream, every one of them silent and turned the wrong way up.

ABOUT THE AUTHOR

CARLA BUCKLEY was born in Washington, D.C. She has worked in a variety of industries, including stints as an assistant press secretary for a U.S. senator, an analyst with the Smithsonian Institution, and a technical writer for a defense contractor. She lives in Columbus, Ohio, with her husband, an environmental scientist, and three children. She is the author of *Invisible* and *The Things That Keep Us Here*, which was nominated for a Thriller Award as a best first novel and the Ohioana Book Award for fiction. She is currently at work on her next novel.

Visit the author's website at www.CarlaBuckley.com.